PRAISE FOR NADINE BRANDES

"A gorgeous fantasy about incredible power just out of reach. Myrthe's and Baastian's stories interweave into a beautiful tale about self-worth, second chances, and mysterious enchantment."

—KATHRYN PURDIE, #1 *NEW YORK TIMES* BESTSELLING
AUTHOR OF *BURNING GLASS* AND *BONE CRIER'S MOON*

"The battle for good and evil gets a unique twist in this imaginative and beautifully written fantasy, with the Wishtress caught in the center of the fight. You'll want a magical wish for yourself when you get the breathtaking finish!"

—SARA B. LARSON, AUTHOR OF *DARK BREAKS*
THE DAWN AND THE *DEFY* TRILOGY

"Breathtaking. Never have I ventured into a more unique and vibrant story world than within the pages of *Wishtress*. It is both fairy tale and literature, modern fable and timeless allegory. Nadine Brandes has crafted the masterpiece of her career. Full of secrets, romance, and magic, *Wishtress* is the book everyone will be wishing never comes to an end!"

—SARA ELLA, AWARD-WINNING AUTHOR OF *THE WONDERLAND*
TRIALS, *CORAL*, AND THE *UNBLEMISHED* TRILOGY

"A touching, remarkable novel. The prose is enchanting and piquant, and paints rich, emotional images."

—ALL ABOUT ROMANCE FOR *ROMANOV*

"Older fans of the animated film *Anastasia* will enjoy this story, as will fans of R. L. LaFevers, Evelyn Skye, and Lucy Worsley's YA novels."

—SCHOOL LIBRARY JOURNAL FOR *ROMANOV*

"If you enjoy re-imagined history, like *The Ring and the Crown* by Melissa de la Cruz, then you'll probably like *Romanov*."

—THE STORY SANCTUARY

"*Romanov* will cast a spell on readers and immerse them in a history anyone would long to be a part of."

—SASHA ALSBERG, #1 *NEW YORK TIMES* BESTSELLING
AUTHOR OF *ZENITH: THE ANDROMA SAGA*

"I am obsessed with this book! *Romanov* is a magical twist on history that will have Anastasia fans wishing for more. I loved every detail Brandes wrote."

—EVELYN SKYE, *NEW YORK TIMES* BESTSELLING AUTHOR OF
THE *CROWN'S GAME* SERIES AND *CIRCLE OF SHADOWS*

"Historical facts, along with captivating characters and quick dialogue, make for an extremely enjoyable novel. A great read for fans of *The Gentleman's Guide to Vice and Virtue, Fawkes* brings new life to the Gunpowder Plot of 1605."

—*SHELF AWARENESS*

"Engrossing historical fantasy."

—*BOOKLIST* FOR *FAWKES*

"A satisfying tale."

—*PUBLISHERS WEEKLY* FOR *FAWKES*

"Allegorical promise and imaginative recasting . . ."

—*KIRKUS* FOR *FAWKES*

"*Fawkes* is the perfect mix of history and magic."

—CYNTHIA HAND, *NEW YORK TIMES* BESTSELLING AUTHOR OF *MY LADY JANE*

"Hold on to your heart as this slow-burning adventure quickly escalates into an explosion of magic, love, and the truth about loyalty."

—MARY WEBER, BESTSELLING AUTHOR OF *TO BEST THE
BOYS* AND THE *STORM SIREN TRILOGY*, FOR *FAWKES*

"*Fawkes* is a must-read for all fantasy fans!"

—LORIE LANGDON, AUTHOR OF *OLIVIA TWIST*

WISHTRESS

ALSO BY NADINE BRANDES

Romanov

Fawkes

Out of Time Series
A Time to Die
A Time to Speak
A Time to Rise

WISHTRESS

NADINE BRANDES

THOMAS NELSON
Since 1798

Published in Nashville, Tennessee, by Thomas Nelson. Thomas Nelson is a registered trademark of HarperCollins Christian Publishing, Inc.

Interior design by Sara Colley

Map by Matthew Covington and Autumn Short

Thomas Nelson titles may be purchased in bulk for educational, business, fundraising, or sales promotional use. For information, please email SpecialMarkets@ThomasNelson.com.

Library of Congress Cataloging-in-Publication Data

Library of Congress Cataloging in Publication Control Number: 2022010764

Printed in the United Kingdom

22 23 24 25 26 CPI 5 4 3 2

FOR MOMMY.

*Only now that I'm a mother do I begin to understand
the depth of your love for your children.
Not one book—not ten books—could
convey my thankfulness for you.
But it's a start.
This one's for you, and for all the sacrifices you made
in the name of love, Jesus, and motherhood.*

CHAPTER 1

MYRTHE

I didn't cry until I was twelve years old.

Mutti and Pappje had caught the pox . . . from me. I'd recovered a fortnight prior and was still weak, unable to fully walk normally again. Oma said the pox ate away some of my bone. That didn't stop me from sitting by their bedsides—in agony—day and night.

"I'm sorry," I whispered.

"Myrthe," my mutti rasped, reaching out a hand so frail the veins popped like scars. I gripped it in my own. Then I grabbed Pappje's limp one. I held the two to my lips. Kissed their knuckles.

"I'm here." How long would they know that? How long would they see and comprehend? Pappje hadn't woken in days. Not even when we half-heartedly celebrated my birthday on the winter solstice last week. Mutti spent most days in feverish delirium. Every time I asked Oma when they'd get better, she responded with a crisp, "They may not."

They grew worse by the day. Oma did what she could for them. Soup. Water. She made me chop and haul firewood into our humble canal cottage despite my limp and the pain shooting up my left leg with every other step.

I didn't complain.

But none of our efforts changed the sickly pallor on my parents' faces.

So I chopped more firewood. I plucked feathers from geese bought from *markt*, and while Oma boiled the meat, I stuffed the feathers into quilt squares and laid them over my parents.

Oma was wrong. *I* got better. So would Mutti and Pappje.

Chills seized Mutti's body as though the three quilts atop her were made of paper. I adjusted them. Again. Pulled my own hat off and settled it over her icy brow.

That's when the burning began in my throat. A fist of fire constricting my air. It moved to my eyes. Was I growing ill? This foreign sensation hurt, but it felt *right*. Like sorrow straining for release.

I bent my head over their clasped hands, listening to Mutti's ragged breathing. This was all my fault. If I'd gotten better sooner, maybe they'd still be well.

"Oh, Mutti . . . I wish you'd never known me." Never birthed me. Never hugged me and caught my illness. "I wish this would *end*."

Get better. Get better. Please *get better.* It had been so different being under Oma's cold care these past several weeks. *Come back to me.*

Mutti's shivering stopped. Pappje's hand became weighted, limper than the riverfish we ate in summer. My thumb swiped over something wet.

I looked at Mutti's and Pappje's hands in mine. Water smeared their knuckles where my face had rested. Wetness covered my cheek too. Tears—things I'd seen on Mutti's face but never felt on my own.

Pappje's hand turned to ice in mine. It suddenly didn't feel like a hand at all. Startled, I dropped it. His arm fell with a slam against the edge of his cot. A chill entered my chest, though I couldn't place why.

Something had changed.

Something unnatural.

"Is he dead?" asked a shaky voice beside me.

I nearly jumped out of my calfskin trousers. Mutti struggled to prop an elbow beneath her. Trembling, she stared at Pappje.

I didn't know which to react to first—her question about Pappje or the fact she was up. Awake. *Talking.*

"Mutti!" I threw myself into her arms, remembering at the last minute to be gentle.

She didn't return the embrace but instead slid out of my arms. Color was already returning to her face. "Mutti?"

She had eyes only for Pappje and scrabbled for his hand, nearly toppling out of her cot from the effort. "Koen. Oh, Koen, don't leave me alone."

"Mutti, I—"

"Give me peace, child," she snapped. I startled away. "I'm not your mother."

I had yet to look at Pappje. I wanted to grasp the joy of Mutti's return. But . . . what did she mean she wasn't my mother?

"Ilse." Oma stepped into the room. If she was surprised to find Mutti awake and recovering, she hardly showed it. "Do you know this child?"

"Wilma!" Mutti reached for Oma. "Your son . . . he is . . . oh, he's *left* us."

"Yes." Oma stared at the scene, held captive by the still-cold body of her own child.

Tears streamed down my face, but I sat. I waited for Mutti to comfort *me*. For her to see me. Why was she so angry at my presence? "Mutti?"

"Get this child away from me!" Mutti collapsed over Pappje's body. "Oh, Koen . . ."

Oma yanked me into her bedroom—the only other room in

our small home. I stumbled to the bed when she released me, sobs tearing from my chest. "Oma, what did she mean?"

"You're crying." She said it like an accusation, then turned her back to me and rummaged in an old trunk.

I sniffed. Not sure I liked crying. The more I did it, the less in control I felt. I was wet everywhere. My eyes, my nose, my face. But more than that, my chest *hurt*. "Why did Mutti say she's not my mother?"

Oma whirled on me with a small bottle clutched in her hand. "Because you removed her memory of you." She sounded . . . triumphant. "I was at the door, listening. You said you wished Ilse had never known you. Your tear struck her hand."

She pressed the bottle against my cheek. I was so confused—so surprised—I didn't think to move. A moment later, Oma held the bottle aloft and a small tear bounced around the bottom of the jar like a trapped guppy, flickering silver and white and magic.

"Finally." She corked the bottle and placed it in her trunk. "You're the Wishtress, Myrthe. Each tear you cry has the power to grant a wish."

Wishtress? I'd heard of her—the most powerful Talented in all of Fairhoven. No, in all of Winterune. Maybe even the world. A Wishtress was born every hundred years or so. Always female. A heroine of the kingdom. That's all I'd ever heard of the Wishtress— all anyone could tell me.

I couldn't be the Wishtress. I was poor. Brittle boned. Distraught. I couldn't even *cry* until today. Then I thought about what Oma said. *"You removed her memory of you."* Because I'd cried and made a wish . . . Mutti couldn't remember me?

Another part of my words—my desperate prayer—teased my memory. *"I wish this would end."* I wished their sickness to end . . . and it did.

"I . . . I killed Pappje?" I gripped my hands in front of me, as though they could keep the broken whisper from reaching Oma's ears.

But she heard. And she nodded. "You used a raw wish. More dangerous than a spark on cotton." She faced me head-on and grabbed my shoulders. I couldn't tear away from her intense gaze. "You're never to use a wish again, Myrthe. Not until you're trained properly. I've studied the ways of the Wishtress my entire life and will teach you in time. Every tear you cry must be bottled. I'll protect them. I will protect *you*. Otherwise you could end up killing others."

My small form seemed to shrink beneath the weight of her words. I was unable to comprehend much other than I killed my own pappje. And I made Mutti forget me.

This was my fault. All of it.

I wanted away from Oma. Away from her knowledge and her icy words. Her lack of feeling and the victorious glint in her eye over this new discovery.

I didn't want to be the Wishtress.

I wanted to be Myrthe, holding my parents' hands again . . . before they'd gone cold. Praying for them. Hoping for them. Caring for them and hugging them.

I fled the bedroom, knocking the doorjamb with my hip in my disjointed attempt at haste. I burst into the main room. It was empty of life. Pappje lay on the cot. Cold. Dead.

Mutti was gone.

The front door hung open on its hinges. Cold night air not yet breathed on by spring gusted into the room and caused the fire to flicker.

I ran toward it. "Mutti? *Mutti!*" I could see nothing in the darkness. No. She couldn't leave me. She wasn't well enough!

I reached for my coat, but Oma stayed my hand. "I'll find her."

"She's my *mutti*!" I had to help. Had to fix this.

"She doesn't remember you. She doesn't want you."

Doesn't want you.

Oma slammed the door behind her, leaving me in our cottage with the body of my dead pappje.

The next morning, we stood over two graves.

She'd found Mutti frozen and lifeless less than a mile from our home. Oma didn't let me see her. Didn't let me kiss either of them goodbye. Instead, she woke me from where I'd curled in the corner by the fireplace. "Come say words over their graves."

I had no words other than, "I'm sorry. I'm so sorry."

I fell to my knees. This was so much worse than when they lay side by side trapped in illness. At least then I had hope. I could tuck myself into their arms and will my love for them to warm their bodies.

Now they lay in the earth, blanketed in darkness. I wanted to be with them, but I didn't want to die. I sniffed hard as the frightening burning built in my throat. There was no stopping it from spilling over in hot tears.

Oma knelt beside me and wrapped an arm around my shoulders, an uncharacteristic show of tenderness. I moved to lean my head on her chest, but something cold and hard met my cheek.

A glass bottle.

"Let it out, child," Oma whispered as the first tear slipped into the vial. "Just keep crying. I'm here."

CHAPTER 2

BASTIAAN

FIVE YEARS LATER

Bastiaan's soul was 107 years old.

His bare feet pressed into the dark soil between rows of blood-red tulips, sending his youthful body forward and leaving behind their signatures of ten toes and young soles. Scattered amid the tulip rows were women of varied ages. One bent over a row of purple buds, a woven basket in one arm and her hand stretched toward a stem. Another rested on her knees, a handkerchief pressed to her brow.

None moved. None breathed. Statues of blood, bone, and frozen breath.

Bastiaan fixed his gaze forward. Ahead, over the hill of carefully tended tulips and beyond the stretch of mature grain stalks ready for harvest, rose a windmill, its wide base pregnant with memories. Its wood-lattice blades paused midrotation.

Home.

He'd been away so long he'd nearly forgotten what that word meant. His fingers itched, begging him for permission to return his surroundings to life, but Bastiaan resisted their call. *Not yet.* He stopped at the front door. It hung open—inviting him back in. He both dreaded and desired what was about to happen.

With a bone-deep breath, he stepped over the threshold.

Sunlight spilled through the open doorway and wide windows, the end of springtime as it had been for the past thirty-two years. Bastiaan took in the equally familiar and foreign space. White stone counters and rough cabinets carved by his own hands before he understood woodwork. A worn and dented table beneath the widest window.

A young boy sat on a tall stool, one foot resting on the lowest rung. His fingers were frozen midtap on the table, his chin resting on the palm of his other hand. His eyes were closed. Anyone might think the boy asleep except for the distinct lack of rise and fall from his chest.

Tears burned Bastiaan's eyes as he gazed upon the lad. A face he'd missed until he'd forgotten the boy's features altogether. As with every return, it felt odd to find this boy, this place, unchanged despite Bastiaan's absence. This time, he'd been gone so long that the Stillness, as he'd come to think of it, had begun to feel more constant than the Aging.

And that's what frightened Bastiaan most.

The itch in his fingers reached an intensity reflective of screaming. He raised his right hand and tugged off his leather glove, finger by finger, until skin and air met like long-separated lovers. A single silver line shone against the tanned pad of his middle finger. The mark of magic—of a Talent.

For years Bastiaan had longed for this moment, yet now that it was upon him, he hesitated. A dim panic threatened his mind. This time the Stillness had changed him. Scarred him. He was far different from the man who'd first entered it. No one would understand. No one could *know*.

He feared the return of the noise. Of the life.

If it's too much for me, I can always reenter the Stillness when the next full moon renews my magic. And with that glimmer of reassurance, he pressed his fingers together and snapped.

The Talent Mark dimmed to grey.

The rhythm hit first—the feeling of time moving once more, the sun inching across the sky, back to the position it held before he'd stopped time. The weight of aging took control of his body again. Bastiaan could never explain how *tangible* time was to him. He *felt* each second pass just as he perceived his own pulse. Each hour dissolved into his skin like moisture, promising to bring wrinkles and weakness and decay.

The sounds struck him next. The whoosh of lungs exhaling, a flutter of bird feathers on the wind. The buzz of a fly and the laughter of the women gardening outside.

Bastiaan squeezed his eyes closed, breathing deeply through the return. When he opened them again, the boy was staring at him. Earth-brown eyes set in a tanned face. Messy black hair ruffled by the breeze floating through the window.

He looked Bastiaan up and down, then slid cautiously off his stool. "Welcome back, sir." He reached for the straps of Bastiaan's pack. Bastiaan flinched but wasn't sure why.

The boy slowed his movements as though approaching a beaten stray. He slid the pack from Bastiaan's shoulders, then set it on the ground next to a set of stairs that spiraled upward in the center of the room. Then the boy withdrew a small leather book from inside his coat. He flipped it open, then dipped a pen nib into a jar of ink on the table. "How long were you gone?"

Bastiaan stared at him.

The boy waited one, two, three breaths. "What's your name?"

"Bastiaan Duur."

The boy made a mark on the page. This moment felt familiar, as though Bastiaan had lived it before.

"What's *my* name?" The boy's pen was poised over the book, ready to mark Bastiaan's answer, as though this question were merely standard and not actually effortful.

But Bastiaan couldn't answer it.

The pause lengthened. The patient cheer slipped from the boy's face as slow confusion took its place, then gradually morphed into horror and then hurt.

Bastiaan broke from his stupor. Something inside him knew that to fail to answer this question would result in damage even his Talent couldn't repair.

The boy opened his mouth, but Bastiaan held up a hand. "Wait."

He clamped his lips shut, hope creeping into his wide eyes. Bastiaan took in his small form, gangly limbs, mussed hair, and chin lifted in an attempt to keep his emotions in check and present himself as a man.

Bastiaan's emotions remembered him before his mind did. Somehow he knew the boy was ten years of age. He knew he loved the boy as a son, even though less than ten years separated them— well, ten years according to the Aging. But if he loved him so deeply, how could he forget his name?

"It's okay, Bastiaan," the lad said in a small voice. "You said this might happen. This is why I ask the questions."

"No," Bastiaan said roughly. "It hasn't happened." Not yet. He closed his eyes and sifted through old memories, pushing himself back to the origin—seeing the boy on the banks of an icy canal, so small Bastiaan almost mistook him for a stump. Fingers black with frostbite yet still holding up a whetstone and flask of oil, saying in a weak voice, "Can I sharpen your skates, sir?"

Bastiaan had stopped, his skates sending a spray of ice shavings along the edge of the canal. "What's your name, boy?"

"I have none," the boy answered through blue lips.

"All things have names."

"What need is there for a name if I've no family?"

"A name is your own. No matter how poor you get, you can never lose it."

"Then give me one."

Bastiaan blinked and returned to the present. The boy still stood in front of him, only in this scene he was taller. No black fingers, no sallow skin. Healthy. Hopeful.

And this time, the boy had a name.

"Runt," Bastiaan said.

Runt's round face broke into a toothy grin. "Welcome home, sir." Then, as though recovered from Bastiaan's appearance and memory lapse, Runt returned to his stool and slapped his small book onto the table. "How long were you in the Stillness?"

"Thirty-two years."

The scribbling stopped. Runt lifted his head slowly and swallowed hard. "Thir . . . thirty-two?"

"Years." Bastiaan released the word as though expelling the weight of two lifetimes. It was supposed to be days. A few weeks at most. But things hadn't gone as planned. Not at the start.

And certainly not at the end.

Fire. Illness. Father.

Bastiaan shook his head. No, that wasn't right. "I'm . . . confused."

"You look it." Runt slid from his stool and disappeared up the spiral stairs. He descended moments later with a leather-bound book in each hand, both much thicker than the one he'd been taking notes in. He slid one toward Bastiaan. "Usually you retrieve these on your own, but . . . I think you need my help."

Bastiaan opened the book and saw two words scratched across the first page in his own handwriting. *The Stillness.*

Runt passed him the dipping pen and inkwell. "Write about the past thirty-two years in this one. Then read through them both."

"What's the other book?" Bastiaan thought he should know.

Runt flipped open the cover on the second journal and Bastiaan read *The Aging*.

"I can't write in these." Bastiaan pushed *The Stillness* journal away from himself. "It would endanger me should anyone find it." He was surprised his old self had even started the habit. Then again, he'd changed a lot in thirty-two years.

"Nah, no one but you can read them or write in them." Runt had adopted the role of mentor—albeit a half-grown one. "You got the journals from a Talented in Gevanstad, remember?"

A rush of warmth toward the boy filled Bastiaan's chest. Right now he needed Runt more than Runt knew. Because returning from thirty-two years in the Stillness—thirty-two years of failure and heartache that weren't supposed to have happened—seemed impossible.

Bastiaan's fingers itched, longing for his time snap to renew. "How long until the full moon?"

"More than a fortnight."

"That's a long wait." Could he handle the Awake that long? He'd have to.

"It'll get easier once you've fully recovered." Runt slid Bastiaan's glove toward him.

Bastiaan held it for a moment, then tugged it on. "Thank you."

He picked up the dipping pen. The ink might as well have been his own blood for all the pain it caused to return to the beginning and write. The goal, the hopes, the hatred he felt for the old man . . . and how drastically everything had changed as the years slid by.

He didn't stop writing when Runt put a plate of stew in front of him, nor when he set a bowl of water at Bastiaan's dirty feet for a soak, nor when the sun set and Runt lit the candles and the women left the tulip fields.

Bastiaan forced himself to remember everything and to write it . . . in order that he might forget.

CHAPTER 3

BASTIAAN

Bastiaan was neither dead nor fully alive.

He'd been so long in the Stillness that he'd forgotten the sounds and feel of daily life. The mere hum of Runt and Mother conversing in the garden startled him his first few days back. Then the memories of what had happened in the Stillness threatened to cripple him.

He kept waiting . . . waiting for the announcement. The news to come.

It didn't come.

Life and time rumbled past, feeling painfully disjointed. When Bastiaan had found himself lingering in bed one morning, dreading the interaction with his own mother, he finally took action and headed to the Fairhoven summer markt on the day it opened—the loudest day.

That was two days ago.

He'd yet to return home. Yet to eat, really. Bastiaan sat in the dirt, barefoot and unshaven, his head back against a wood post that held the edges of a markt tent tight against the early season wind gusts. Eyes closed.

Waiting.

Summertime had hardly tiptoed its way into the breeze—cautious about being swept away by its vicious cousin, Winter. Gossip from the washerwomen floated through the air as smoothly and fine-tuned as the canal ships up and down the Vier. The country of Winterune's notoriously long winters often trampled any evidence of spring. Even the summer breeze through the markt still carried a chill, but the sun sent down splashes of warmth when the drifting clouds allowed its rays through.

"Don't stab me for coming too close." The voice was soft like the approaching colors of the new season.

Bastiaan opened his eyes. A young woman, pale as a shell bleached from the sun, stood before him with a loaf of dark, round bread. Unlike the others who had mistaken him for a beggar, she met his gaze with her own—not with pity but with curiosity. As if she desired to know his story.

She held out the bread. "For you."

"I'm no beggar," he said. "And I certainly wouldn't stab you."

"You've watched passersby since dawn, almost like waiting for an enemy." She delivered this comment with a smile to soften the implications. "Whether beggar or assassin, you've eaten nothing all day."

She'd been watching him? Had she seen the bent of resignation to his spine? The tension from the overwhelming noise and sounds of *life*? "I'll be fine."

"Your mouth is protesting, but I'm certain your stomach is not." She tossed the loaf through the air with an expert flick. It landed square in his lap.

Bastiaan liked this woman. With an incline of his head, he picked up the bread. Still warm. "Thank you."

Someone bolted past them, ramming against the woman's shoulder as he went. She stumbled a few steps and grimaced. By the time she regained her balance, Bastiaan was on his feet scanning the crowd.

"Check your pockets," he told the girl.

She turned toward the crowd as well. "I have no pockets."

Lucky for her. Unlucky for the pickpocket. He finally spotted the thief—a stocky young blond man—still running, yards beyond them already. Since the woman didn't seem concerned about losing a coin purse, Bastiaan didn't give chase.

The woman's brows crashed together, her eyes following the man. "Sven?" She took a few hesitant steps after the perpetrator. "Sven!"

"You know this thief?" Bastiaan asked.

"He's not a thief." She sounded confused. "He knocked into me is all."

Without apology. Practically sent her to the ground.

Sven waved a hand in acknowledgment, but he neither stopped nor turned. "Not now, Myrthe!" Strain edged his voice. Urgency. He shoved through the crowd until he reached the dark, carved, scaffold-like structure that housed the frost bells. He grasped a plank and began to haul himself up.

The girl, Myrthe, gasped. "What's he doing?" She darted through the shoppers, dodging left and right with an uneven gait. Had Sven injured her?

She wasn't fast, but she was efficient. Bastiaan stayed on her heels until they both stood at the base of the tower. "Are you okay?" he asked. "If his impact injured you—"

"I'm fine." She looked away from the tower long enough to give him an appreciative smile. "It's an old injury."

All the more reason Sven should have stopped and checked on her. But Myrthe seemed unbothered by his disinterest. Bastiaan turned his focus to the tower. Sven reached the top in four long stretches, then he got a firm grasp on the cord to the frost bell and pulled.

The deep *clang, clang, clang* sent the markt into a stunned silence. This bell was reserved for winter ice alerts. No one rang it off-season, under severe penalty. It broke the system, caused confusion.

All eyes lifted toward the bells.

Resignation entered Bastiaan's gut. It had finally happened. There was only one other reason to demand attention in such a drastic way.

Sven threw himself against the top railing and bellowed, "The king is dead! King Vämbat is dead! Assassinated! By a Talented."

The trampled earth beneath Bastiaan's bare feet lurched. He pressed a hand against the bell tower until his head—and heart—cleared. They couldn't save him. The king—Bastiaan's king—had died.

The communal shock was broken by shouts. As Sven descended the scaffolding and set foot back on the ground, people swarmed him seeking answers. He lifted his hands. "That's all I know. I came straight from my position at the *schloss*. Heard the news from a militair."

The murmurs grew. A report straight from the schloss—the palace of their country. It held enough clout to stir the whole city.

Once people realized Sven had no further information, they pressed coins into his hands as thanks. Then the theories began, all shopping abandoned.

"Assassinated by a Talented? Now the crown will never let commonfolk travel to the Well of Talents."

"Maybe his heir will be different."

"Not likely. We should strike out for the Well while there's chaos at the schloss."

Even though Bastiaan's glove covered his Talent Mark, he slid his hand into his pocket. If people realized he had a Talent, their growing frenzy would find a new target. Commonfolk had always been hungry for Talents—for an edge over their constant hunger and working to make ends meet. Talents were seen as a strike of gold, better than coming into an inheritance from a rich dead uncle.

A trip to the Well of Talents was always suggested as the easy fix. As though traveling for days to an unmarked Well to then battle four Trials in order to access its magic water was *easy*.

After the Talent talk died, a new question arose again and again as though repetition itself might procure an answer.

"How did the king die?"

"What sort of Talented did this?" This question contained an undertone of awe—as though the Talented who killed the king was fighting for the people. Making a statement.

"Maybe it was a wish," Sven said.

Bastiaan straightened at this bold suggestion. A *wish*? This boy's head had been in the canal too long. The last known Wishtress had died over two hundred seasons ago. He'd spent half of his own life searching for records of the Wishtress Talent. There weren't many.

Myrthe rolled her eyes. "That's quite a speculation." She, at least, seemed grounded.

"I've heard rumor of wishes being sold right here in Fairhoven." Sven's voice rose as his theory picked up speed. "For all we know, this could be the home of the Wishtress herself!"

"Sven, you don't know what you're saying!" Myrthe's voice turned shrill, and she moved to grab his arm. He'd do well to listen to her. If the mob believed what he was saying, they'd tear this markt apart. "There's no proof the next Wishtress is even *alive* yet."

The crowd pressed closer to Sven, ignoring the girl. "They say it was a Talented who killed the king. They must know something."

Bastiaan could bear it no longer. The announcement was his purpose for waiting in the markt. He left the crowd behind, left the limping girl behind, tucking the bread loaf under his arm.

His king was dead. Memories came in waves—of the mentorship, the fathering, the friendship he'd shared with the crown of the land.

And how he, Bastiaan, was the Talented who'd killed him.

CHAPTER 4

MYRTHE

I wish . . .

An unfinished sentence—two little words—that prefaced countless dreams, hopes, and desires. Greed, lust, selfishness. It always started with those two words—words I despised almost as much as I despised the thaw.

Almost.

I sat on the grassy bank of Canal Vier—the main canal of Fairhoven and Winterune's life source. My home rested in a field near one of the four fingers of this mighty canal, my doorstep practically on its banks. It made skating in winter that much easier.

Made it feel like the Vier flowed and froze only for me.

Though it was summer I gripped the laces of my ice skates in one hand and a small glass vial that held a wish in the other. The hand holding the wish trembled.

You stole it, Guilt whispered in my mind.

I made it, I retorted in a mental tug-of-war with my conscience. *It's rightfully mine.* Yet I still shot a glance over my shoulder at our canal house with its carved-wood gables and shutters tied open to let in the fresh air.

I had met Oma's wish quota this week. One wish per week to cover my room and board. When I was younger, it was one wish per day. But then it got harder and harder to make myself cry, so she relented.

She didn't need to know I created one extra. But if she *did* find out I'd kept a wish for myself, all frost would break loose. *"You don't know the rules. You don't know how to use it safely."* She said those words as often as *"Good morning"* and *"Hurry up."*

"So teach me," I whispered to the sky. She had promised once to instruct me in the Wishtress ways. Every age day she allowed me to use a wish for myself. She would write up a contract, we'd discuss the terms, and then the wish would be used. Safely. The right way. *Oma's* way.

I was of age now. Seventeen years. Seventy seasons. Finally. *"At seventy seasons, your wishes are your own,"* Oma would say.

Three months ago marked my season age day—my half birthday. My seventieth season. I woke up expecting fanfare. Freedom.

But Oma said nothing to me other than, *"Snuff that fire in the hearth."*

I'd hoped once summer markt began she'd take me into the wish booth. But three days ago she went to markt Opening Day, expecting me to join her an hour later. She gave me the extra time because of my limp—the one remnant of the pox that served as a constant reminder.

But no word about my Talent.

Oma refused to use a wish to heal me. She said I needed the reminder of the severity of wishes. It worked. I was too afraid to use a wish on myself. What if I ended up causing my own death? Or making the crippling so bad that I couldn't ice-skate? Skating was the one thing that didn't hurt my bones. I could speed along with no resistance, keep up with my peers, taste freedom.

A distant whistle met my ears. I shot to my feet, my pulse

entering a sprint. Through the trees on the other side of the canal came a form I had been both dreading and longing for.

Sven.

I waved and tucked the wish into my pocket. He used a pole to vault himself over the narrow branch of canal, landing lithe and limber on my side. Skin pale as a winter sun, eyes blue like icicles, Sven set down his pole and approached me with a grin. "You gonna kiss me good luck?"

I'd kiss him good anything to feel his lips on mine the way he kissed me in the winter. But summer had come. His kisses weren't the same in summer. Too light. Too quick.

"I have something even better for you." My heart swung to and fro. I wasn't the only one about to take rash action. Since Sven announced King Vämbat's assassination yestermorn, the entire capital of Fairhoven had entered a frenzy. *Militairen* wanting Talented captured. Commonfolk wanting Talents for themselves—willing even to defy the law and make a pilgrimage in search of the Well.

Commonfolk like Sven.

I wasn't about to be left behind. Not now that Oma had failed to keep her promise. I needed help. I couldn't live this life of slavery any longer. "I'm coming with you."

Sven's summer-sun smile dimmed like a sunset. "It's markt season—your oma needs you."

I stood tall. "I'm of age. My life is no longer restricted by the demands of others." Couldn't he see? I could make my own decisions: where to travel, what to pursue . . . who to marry. After all, love was a choice. And I chose Sven.

We chose each other.

"You're a very capable girl, Myrthe, even with . . ." He glanced down at my feet. They were firmly planted in the soil, but I knew he was imagining my limp and the fact I couldn't run. Why couldn't he remember me as I was in winter? On skates? When my legs seemed to work like everyone else's?

"This is no canal skate race. I'm taking the *pilgrimage*. I'm going to find the Well of Talents, once and for all."

"Is Prince Mattias funding your journey?"

Sven let out a hollow laugh. "He relieved me of my position as schloss cartographer."

I reached for him. "Oh, Sven, I'm so sorry." Sven had been so proud when the schloss took him on. It had promised food in his belly, travel, adventure.

He was the first cartographer since the slaughter of Winterune's cartographers fifteen years prior by a wild man. And the destruction of all maps to the Well.

He'd been brave to apply. To pick up the mantle of a lost trade.

"How will you find the Well without a map?"

Firm lines of determination turned his jaw to angles. "I'm not helpless."

"I'll help you." He had no idea how much I could help—how easy I could make this for him. For us.

"Even if I manage to find the Well, I still have to defeat King Vämbat's Trials. I get it, Myrthe. The desire for a Talent is tempting for everyone—especially us commonfolk who aren't allowed to seek one in the first place."

"The crown is *blaming* Talented right now. If you come back with a Talent, what's to stop them from accusing you of the king's murder?"

"It's a risk I'm willing to take—a risk a lot of people are willing to take. A Talent could protect us. Provide for us."

"You don't even know what type of Talent the Well might give you."

"That's the beauty of it. It could be anything! Have you ever heard of a Talent that wasn't appealing?"

I hadn't spent my life dreaming of having a Talent like so many others. But I'd heard of others—Talents to heal, to make bread, to start flame, to grow plants, to perceive truth or hear thoughts.

"I want a Talent, Myrthe. And I'm going to get one. That's worth angering the crown over. But . . . people *die* on this pilgrimage. Almost all of them. I can't . . ." He took a deep breath. "I can't put you at risk like that."

My growing irritation melted. He wasn't refusing me because he thought I'd be a burden. He was trying to protect me. "Sven, I don't want to go so I can acquire a Talent. I want to learn *about* Talents. How they work and how they're supposed to be used."

I skated a dangerous line. Should I tell him? No. Yes. Not yet. I must. I wanted freedom. And I wasn't sure I had the courage to leave without his help. Oma would find me—she'd use a wish and track me down.

I couldn't do this alone. Shouldn't do it alone. I knew what happened the last time I used a raw wish. Pappje died. Mutti died.

I didn't trust myself to manage this Talent alone. Not yet.

"Ah, sweet Myrthe." Sven looked pitying. Almost . . . patronizing. "Your heart is good, but I'll be accompanied by four of my fellows. Strong, smart men. No need to worry yourself." *Or come*, he didn't say.

"Five companions are better than four."

He laughed.

I grew annoyed now. I thought he'd want my company. Instead I was having to *persuade* him.

"You don't need a Talent," he continued. "You're perfect as you—"

"I already have one," I said flatly. "I'm not going for myself. I told you, I'm going to help." Only I no longer felt quite like helping. Or going. Or telling him my secret.

Sven gaped. "What . . . do you mean you already have one?"

"I'm not sure how to make it any clearer. I. Have. A. Talent."

"When did *you* achieve a pilgrimage?" Then, as if realizing what he said, his amusement disappeared. "What are you saying, Myrthe?"

I felt close to tears. This wasn't the freeing reveal I'd envisioned. *I love him,* I told myself. That was supposed to muster up some sort of emotion to strengthen me, but it didn't. It felt more like trying to convince myself of a lie.

But I needed Sven to help get me away from Oma. In exchange I'd help him—us—find the Well. "I never made the pilgrimage. I was born with the Talent."

"No one is born with a Talent," he rebutted in a relieved tone as though calling my bluff. "Not unless you're the—"

"—the Wishtress." My words were a forbidden whisper.

Sven's lips clamped shut. He wasn't smiling now. "You aren't the Wishtress. I would have noticed." Something tainted his voice. A strain of . . . was that jealousy? "You're common."

Why did he see it as a mighty honor for *him* to be common yet seek a Talent, but he sneered at the idea of me being common yet the Wishtress? I plunged my hand into my pocket and withdrew the vial containing the singular wish. "Need proof?" I yanked off the cork.

"You could have bought that," he croaked weakly.

My laugh sounded shrill to my own ears. "You think I could afford a wish?" He shrugged. My eyes burned a warning, starting as a coal and building to a flame until a tear blossomed. No. Not now. How was it so easy to cry in front of him yet I had to burn my own arm with a poker to bring forth a tear for Oma?

Best use this moment to my advantage. I needed Sven to believe me. I needed him to take me with him.

"Fine." I threw the vial to the dirt, letting the liquid wish splash out and soak into the earth, losing its magic. Sven lurched toward the discarded glass—too late. "Then I'll show you."

Everything within me screamed to stop. To stay my hand. To remember what happened last time.

My tear spilled over onto my cheek. Hot then cold, leaving a trail of fire and ice. I scooped it from my cheekbone with the pad of my pointer finger as I'd done a hundred times. But instead of dropping it into a glass vial for Oma . . . I let the tear rest on my skin.

Did I dare?

Sven stared. In that moment I felt no affection toward him and yet at the same time a desperation to prove my worth.

I stretched my hand over the waters of my small branch of Canal Vier, willing my voice to be steady. Water bugs skidded back and forth along the ripples near the bank, oblivious to what was about to come. This would be a simple wish. Nothing more. Besides, I was of age.

"I wish for these waters to turn to ice." *Please work.* I flicked my finger and the tear dropped into the shallows of the canal.

Where I anticipated a *plink* from the droplet reaching the water, the wish hit the smooth shallows with a sky-shattering crack. Sven and I both jumped. A burst of cold, white blue spread from the place of impact like a splash of winter. Thick ice sped across the water, a parched creature lapping up the liquid of the canal and digesting it into a hard, resilient snake.

My forearm twinged under Sven's grip.

The cracking stopped and evening sunlight skipped along the glassy surface of the frozen canal. The very sight of the ice sent my heart sprinting for my skates. Rather than succumb to the urge, I lifted my eyes to Sven's. He stared at the ice, but his jaw worked as though grinding through a hundred meaty thoughts.

I opened my mouth, unsure what I was about to say, but he spoke first in a quiet voice. "Forgive me."

The tightness in my chest eased. "Of course."

"This"—he gestured to the canal—"*you* . . . are amazing. Why didn't you tell me before?"

My arms dropped to my sides. What could I say? That I killed my own parents? That I'd lived in shame my entire life? That the longer I made wishes for Oma, the deeper I desired to escape her?

"Yesterday you accused the Wishtress of murdering the king. How could I know my secret would be safe?"

"*Did* you kill the king?" he asked in a whisper.

My gasp stuck in my throat. How could he ask that?

"It's okay if you did—"

"Of course not!" The peace I thought I'd feel having my secret known had yet to come. Instead my lungs seized as though I'd stepped outdoors at the height of winter. Eyes burned. Tears built.

"I didn't mean to distress you."

I shook my head, embarrassed. "I've . . . I've never told anyone." And Sven's first thought was asking if I killed the king? "I suppose I'm a bit overwhelmed."

"You've never told anyone?"

"Well, Oma's known since I was little." And my cousin, Anouk. But for some reason I didn't want Sven to know that. He'd always admired Anouk and I didn't want to shift the focus to her.

I had already crossed a forbidden line in telling Sven about my Talent. I couldn't tell him about Oma's wish business hidden beneath the tent flaps at markt. "Oma forbade me from telling anyone . . . for my own safety." And for everyone else's safety.

I eyed the pulse in his neck, listened to his rhythmic breathing, waited for his heart to stop or his body to go limp like Pappje's, even though logic told me there was no reason for it to happen. I'd frozen one tiny branch of canal, nothing more.

I willed away the cloying emotions, but not before a tear slipped free. Out of habit I lifted it from my cheek with care. I scrutinized the wish for a moment. I could save it for Oma—use it to fulfill next week's quota. But in an act of defiance I moved to flick it away.

"Wait!" Sven's shout echoed over the darkening canal. "You can't just discard that. It's . . . wasteful!" He scooped up the tossed vial. "Here."

Old anger flared at having my tears valued more than my heart, but I dropped the wish into the bottle and stoppered it. The liquid bounced and danced, held captive by the cork. Sven stared at the tear for a long second, then held the vial out to me.

I tucked it into my pocket. His gaze followed my movements. Of course he was tempted. Who wouldn't be? Yet he did give it back to me. That was . . . noble.

"Now I *really* can't take you with me."

"What?" Even after I told him my secret? "Why?"

"It's a greater risk now that the king is dead. Militairen will be unpredictable. Talented may be rising up. Even if they're not, they'll be hunted until the king's killer is found. The Trials themselves have claimed many lives. How could I lead a woman into that?"

"You're not *leading* me. It's my decision. You can't deny that I'd be invaluable." I'd been waiting for the day to leave. To start living my own life. To discover *why* I'd been born the Wishtress and how to use it without Oma's control. I needed to find the Well of Talents for myself and demand answers from it.

"If anyone else learned of your Talent—"

"They would learn only if you told them." The sky darkened as the sun dipped behind the trees, reflecting my clouding mood.

"Don't you think my companions would wonder where all the wishes were coming from? Or why everything happened so easily? Even if people didn't suspect you, they could suspect me and who knows what they'd do? Blackmail. Torture. Maybe even kill me!"

In truth, I hadn't thought of that. My hopes vanished with the sun. It wasn't a new feeling. I was used to being denied things I wanted.

"Then take this." I pulled the wish from my pocket.

His mouth said, "I can't." But his eyes—and the twitch of his hand—screamed his desire. Oma would flay me for handing over a wish without a strict contract. I of all people knew the damage that could come from a raw wish.

But *I* was the Wishtress. Not Oma. And this was the boy I chose to love. "Take it. And come back to me."

He took it. "Thank you, my love." He kissed me. I clung to him, hoping for some flare of assurance or comfort. But he pulled away too soon and hoisted his pack onto his shoulders.

He called me *"my love."* That must mean he chose me, too, right?

"Be safe," I whispered as he left me standing alone by the canal.

I stayed there long after his departure, body unmoving but mind spinning. I'd told him. Shown him. *Given* him a wish, even. I'd waited for the day I'd be free of my secret. So why did I feel like instead of leaving my cell I'd added another padlock?

I could attribute it to nerves, but something deeper in my mind admitted . . . I regretted telling Sven.

I always told myself that I chose him—I *chose* to love him and I would stick by that. But after today, I saw once and for all that he never chose *me*.

CHAPTER 5

Myrthe

I slept about as well as expected, knowing I broke Oma's sacred rule. I kept waiting for her to burst into my room, demand to know why I told Sven. Why I'd used a raw wish. But she didn't. She shuffled in as usual and went to bed without a hello or good night.

She did, however, remember to grab my bottled wish from the previous morning off the small table.

Come morning, I woke like any other spring Markt Day, pulling on my trousers and a looser blouse that would allow comfort once the heat built. Oma had already left for markt. We never walked together because my limp irritated her. I didn't mind the solitude.

I stepped outside. A glimmer at the base of the escarpment caught my eye as it flickered beneath the midmorning sun. I lifted a hand to shield my eyes. The blinding reflection nearly stilled my pulse as I identified the source. The canal.

The water was still frozen.

Winter's breath. Why hadn't it melted? Had Oma noticed? For the first time I was glad for a sunny day as I hurried to markt. Because as the sun rose, hopefully the ice was melting. Fairhoven's flat countryside made it easier to walk fast. When I was younger, I used to climb the willow trees and felt like I could see every tower, windmill, and ship mast of our capital rising up like a tangible map spread at my feet.

Sharp pain spiked up my left leg and into my lower back with every other step, warning me to slow. To rest. Otherwise I'd be in agony for the next few days. But the farther I walked, the more I worried as I saw the canal frozen on and on and on. At one point I passed a water carriage frozen in place in the center of the canal, abandoned by its owner and patrons.

Winter's breath.

I didn't ease my gait until grass turned to dirt and widened into the markt square. It was busier than usual at this time of day. Louder. A sense of urgent chatter rose into the air thicker than the dust kicked up by booted feet.

I found our booth.

Anouk waved me over as if I wasn't already heading that way. "Did you see Canal Vier?" she asked the moment I moved within earshot. "Frozen like midwinter! The whole thing!"

"I saw." *It was me! It was me!* I glanced around our stacks of wares for Oma. I wanted to say more to Anouk but couldn't risk Oma overhearing. I could tell Anouk anything. The only secret I'd kept from her was how my parents really died. She knew about my Talent. She knew about Oma's oppression. The sale of our wares helped pay for Anouk's living expenses—the one good thing that came from Oma's use of my wishes.

"Today's sun will melt it." I tried to sound casual. Unworried. My hands shook.

"I'm not so sure," Anouk said. "I couldn't even get a block of peat from the fire woman this morning. She was swarmed by people trying to thaw out their boats or get water for washing. People are saying it's a Talented retaliating against Prince Mattias."

"What does the Murder Prince have to do with frozen canals?"

"Don't call him that," Anouk said. She was always seeing the best in people. She refused to believe the rumors about Prince Mattias killing his brothers and now likely his own father. Even though it was *so obvious* he was a backstabber. Now he was to be our king. "This act is likely a Talented spitting in Prince Mattias's face for calling for a census of all Talented."

I gripped her arm. "Anouk, it was me." I had to confess because I didn't know what to do. "Does Oma suspect me? Did she say anything? Has anyone brought up the Wishtress?"

She blinked. *"You?"*

"I used a wish." The confession came out with a groan.

"I thought Oma forbade—"

"She did. Does. But I wanted to tell Sven before he left on the pilgrimage. And I'm finally of age and she hasn't taught me anything. It was foolish, I know!" *Stupid, stupid, stupid.* And then I *gave* a raw wish to Sven. Hopefully he'd be wiser with his wish words than I was. "What do I do?"

"You told *Sven*?" Anouk's sapphire eyes sparkled. "You *were* a rebel yesterday!"

I dragged a hand down my face. I didn't want to get into the Sven details. I still felt sick about telling him, and that wasn't how someone should feel about the person she supposedly loved. "Anouk . . . What do I do?"

"Undo it." She shrugged. "Wish it melted again."

It sounded so simple coming from her mouth, but every day was unpredictable. Yesterday I easily formed tears for Sven. Today . . . I sighed. "I'm a dry husk today."

"Then do it tomorrow." She pulled my hand from my face. "You have to do this, Myrthe. The canals can't stay frozen. Think of the canal rats."

Canal rats, or *crats*, were the abandoned, discarded orphans of the canals. Anouk and I often snuck them food parcels after Markt

Day. Or during. Or before. Or whenever we could. But something in Anouk's word choice pulled me up short. *Canals.*

"I thought I froze the section near our gable house . . ." But I hadn't specified where the ice should stop. Or how long it should last. Or anything.

"There's rumor that even the Handel Sea is frozen as it's connected to the canals. Can you imagine the ships stuck out at sea? Trapped in the ice? You must undo this, Myrthe!"

"Oma was right. I never should have been the Wishtress." I needed to cry—or ask Oma for a wish. Oma herself could use a wish from her stock to undo the canals. If their freezing was truly this detrimental, surely she'd undo it—for her own sake at the very least.

While I was crumbling inside, Anouk seemed far too calm about it all. "The Talent chose *you*, Myrthe. It was no accident."

How did she manage to bat away the worries? The largeness of mistakes? Had she ever made a mistake in her life? It was hard to imagine her weighed down by regrets or navigating them at all. "Don't let Oma hear you say that. She'd be furious."

"Oma's always furious." Anouk unfolded a canvas cloth and draped it over the counter that faced the street. "You've been forced to hide so much of yourself. I'm proud to see you letting some out."

"Girls!" Oma popped up behind us like a squirrel on alert. She smacked my shoulder with her sharp knuckles and gnarled hand. "Get the wares out. With a crowd like this we should sell double."

"Yes, Oma." Always the opportunist. Not a word about the frozen canals. She didn't suspect me, then.

She shoved a crate of oats into Anouk's arms. "Take these to the miller and get them ground."

"Yes, Oma." To me Anouk muttered, "With both you and me of marrying age, you'd think she'd stop treating us like children." She winked and disappeared from the stall.

In the same way my mood soured with the arrival of spring

31

and summer, Oma's took flight, energized by the arrival of markt season—when we made *munten* to see us through winter. Even though with my Talent we shouldn't need to work at all. But Oma refused to use the wishes like that.

She didn't trust using the wishes to create wealth from nothing. There had to be a proper story behind any gains in case militairen came knocking.

How did we make our yearly income? By selling flour and bread at markt. Where did we get the flour for the bread? From a local miller. Oma never told me which one. How did we pay for the flour? From the munten made at markt.

And there was the circle. If more questions were asked, we could play dumb. But the small, in-between things were where we hid the wishes. A wish used for a little extra coin to pay for the grain. A wish used to grind the heads of grain into flour.

I wrestled with this every year. If my tears could grant wishes, why not wish for the people to have food or the income they needed? What would the true harm be if they learned about my Wishtress Talent? I could help them—heal people from the pox, feed the canal rats, or build them warm homes.

But Oma didn't value the same things I did.

Nor did she fear the same things I feared.

Things that kept me captive under my Talent, watching her use my wishes as she deemed best—*sell* my wishes to people she deemed worthy. These were merely a flake of the blizzard of questions that had built up in me. Now that I'd officially reached seventy seasons, I couldn't bear going without answers any longer.

"This is pointless," I said to Anouk when she returned. I lifted a bag of wheat flour onto the counter and shoved a wood scoop into its soft, powdery mouth.

Anouk set a bag of barley flour next to mine. "We have this conversation every year. Just *ask* her."

"She ignored my age day."

"She'll explain it all to you, I'm sure, in time."

"In whose time? Hers? When she's on her deathbed? When my wishes have all dried up?" Anouk had far more faith in Oma than I did. I'd spent the last five and a half years waiting—hoping—for Oma to teach me to use my wishes. Teach me to write up the contracts she penned. Teach me how to be *safe* with these wishes. She knew so much about them, but she wouldn't tell me how she knew or how she learned. I was at her mercy. And if she ever learned that I was the cause behind the frozen canal, she'd keep me filling wish quotas to the end of my days.

I turned my back on the shoppers and dropped my voice. "This Markt Day was supposed to be different." I stacked fat rounds of bread in a basket while Oma prepared for the secret wealthy vendors inside the back tent.

Preparing *my* wishes to sell.

Despite my irritation, I was nervous to ask her. Oma was a spitfire, but she was also practical. Surely she would understand my inquiry. She had to, because I had already broken the rules. I'd used a wish—a *raw* wish. For Sven. Part of me feared Sven might reveal that to Oma.

I had to get to her first.

I eyed the tent behind us and sucked in a deep breath. Better now before I lost my nerve. I placed the last loaf in the basket and brushed off my hands, but the patter of bare feet on dusty earth gave me pause. Or rather an excuse to stay at the front of the booth.

This was the one part of summer that lifted my spirits.

The children came straight to my booth, ignoring shouts of "Canal rats!" from other vendors. The vendor irritation wasn't unfounded. Children who lived off canal water and homes of tree bark scraps were expert pickpockets and sly thieves. In the rush of Markt Day, a vendor could do little to fend off their deft fingers.

33

But they never stole from our booth—and if they did, I wouldn't care. Anouk and I passed them handfuls of button rolls, taking turns keeping watch for Oma. She'd caught us a few times before and rapped our skulls. The swarm of children descended on the free bread like a crow on a carcass, one grimy hand pawing the contents of the basket and the other yanking a fellow's hair to keep him back.

One little boy darted away from the stall, rolls stuffed up his sleeves and down the front of his shirt. Anouk grabbed his upper arm before he got too far.

"Leave him be, Anouk." I laughed.

The boy fought for a moment, but Anouk didn't try to take the rolls away. She knelt and said something in a low voice I couldn't make out. The boy shook his head and tugged away. Anouk rushed through another few sentences. He shook his head again and she let him go.

"What was that?"

Anouk's lips tightened. It took a moment before she responded, and even then it was a dismissal. "Just asking about the frozen canals and if they were okay."

I didn't press her. She had a tender place in her heart toward the canal rats—she had instigated our visiting what dwellings we could find in the harsher seasons to bring blankets, logs, and flints. I instigated the free bread. But I always dreamed of using wishes to better their lives, to stop frostbite, to give them warm homes.

I'd once joked that Anouk should get married and raise all the canal rats as her own, but my cousin had brusquely replied, "I will never marry."

Cheeks, fists, and pockets bulging, the canal rats managed all manner of mumbled thanks and then were gone. I smiled in spite of myself.

"Spoiling the canal rats keeps them from seeking proper work or provision for themselves," someone said from my left.

"How in winter's name is *feeding* a child spoiling them?" Anouk snapped.

The man before us wore tailored trousers with golden buttons along the hips. Tall but not gangly, and a mere handful of years our senior. He certainly wasn't here to purchase bread.

"I meant no offense." He held up uncalloused hands in apology, but his shaven face showed no regret, only caution. He feared being denied what he came to buy.

"Why bother yourself over a few button rolls when you're not even here for bread?" I wanted to deal with him and be done with his face.

He dropped his voice. "I was told to see you for"—he licked his lips—"for a . . . a wish?"

I didn't miss the appraising flick of his skeptical gaze, taking in my simple clothes—scuffed trousers, a billowy shirt with sleeves rolled up to my elbows. Common clothing. So he thought me too lowly to deal in wishes? "I can't help you."

"It's for a good cause."

They always said that. "I said I can't help you." I was sorely tempted to leave it at that, but Oma would have my backside—or worse, my skates—if I turned away one of *these* customers. "You have to inquire inside the tent." I jerked my head to the four-walled tent behind me and then turned to the small line of new customers queuing up for bread.

He sniffed at the dismissal but seemed to swallow his pride and marched into the tent. It took twenty minutes before he swaggered back out again with a smirk. I felt ill. What had he desired enough to purchase a wish?

I slammed a wooden lid back over the flour barrel. "Enough is enough. I'm talking to Oma."

Anouk's eyebrows shot up, but then she grinned. "It's about time."

I rolled my eyes, yanked off my apron, and strode back to the tent. As I swept aside the flap to enter, Oma barreled out. We collided and Oma regained her feet with a snort and a stamp like a territorial boar. "Get in here, girl."

Any bold words I had planned to deliver disintegrated on my tongue. "Yes, Oma?"

"When you bring the next customer, you'll stay too."

I couldn't believe my ears. "Truly?"

Oma didn't bother to respond. She turned to her table of papers and bottles, the glow of candlelight illuminating the bottle of ink.

The joy that struck me was almost painful. At last Oma saw me as my own person, knowing my own mind and capable of using my Talent with discretion. Yet almost immediately a pang of guilt hit. I'd told Sven about my Wishtress Talent yesterday—the one order I was not to have broken. I didn't deserve her trust.

"Tend the stalls then," Oma barked, waving a hand without looking at me.

I spun from the tent and rushed back out to the front of the booth, breathing hard. Ears abuzz, I hardly recognized Anouk's voice until she shouted in my face. "Was it that terrible?"

I snapped out of my reverie. "Huh?"

"Confronting Oma, how did it go?"

Oh. "I . . . forgot."

"What? You were gone hardly a minute."

I grabbed Anouk's hands. "She's going to teach me!" I squealed. Then, as though at risk of undoing Oma's declaration, my voice dropped to a disbelieving whisper. "She's finally going to teach me to control my Talent."

"Winter's breath." Anouk searched the sacks of flour and grain as though she might find her thoughts buried beneath a scoop or price card. "When?"

"With the next customer." I turned my eyes to the crowd, willing someone to come and purchase a wish. Why couldn't Oma have told me *before* the snarky man? We encountered the most customers the first week of markt—customers who had been waiting all through winter to finally seek out the Wishtress. But sometimes we went weeks without a wish seeker.

I couldn't bear to wait weeks.

So I kept busy. I measured flour, wrapped loaves of bread, weighed grain. And morning turned to afternoon. I scanned the skies out of habit, reading them for a whisper of snow before I remembered the budding branches, warm breeze, and barefooted canal rats.

My gaze dropped to accept a man's coin as he hefted a bag of flour from my stall. He moved aside and the next customer stumbled into the counter with a ragged gasp.

The woman, tall and skeletal, was draped in shredded black-and-purple cloths that might have been a dress once. She bent over the counter as though to hold herself up. Wild eyes darted in sunken sockets, and long ribbons of crusted brownish-red scrapes interrupted thick smears of mud on her face where she'd seemingly dragged her nails down her skin.

A madwoman.

"Please," she gasped, settling her rolling eyes on me. "A wish. I heard . . ."

I stumbled back, ensuring Anouk was safe at the other stall. "I can't help you. Take what bread or flour you need."

The woman shot out a hand and wrapped spindly fingers around my wrist. "Please." She took several deep breaths as though to compose herself. With visible effort she straightened, closed her eyes, and tried again. "I . . . I heard there might be someone here who could help."

Perhaps it was the woman's agony etched in the creases of her face, her trembling lips, or maybe the fact that she was so different from the pompous man who had purchased a wish in the morn, but my heart went out to her.

"Come." I took her trembling hand and led her toward the tent.

This was what I wanted to do as Wishtress—help those in distress, not sell wishes to cocky customers with deep pockets.

I held the tent flap open for the broken woman. "What's your name?"

"Co-Coralythe," the woman croaked, ducking into the tent.

Oma looked up from the table of scrolls and candles in the center of the tent. Prior to today, this would be when I stepped out and allowed her to get to business. This time, I stayed.

She stared at Coralythe. Though less than half the woman's height, Oma merely seemed annoyed. Coralythe didn't seem like the deep-pocket type. I doubted she could afford a wish if she couldn't even afford decent clothing.

"Sit." Oma slapped a hand on the back of a wooden chair near the table.

Coralythe took a deep breath, then obeyed. With each inhale she seemed to gather strength and composure.

I stepped deeper into the tent, nerves gripped in my fists. Where was I supposed to stand? Was Oma going to instruct me? Was I supposed to ask Coralythe questions?

"What is it you want?" Oma asked.

"I heard . . . wishes," Coralythe breathed.

"Where did you hear that?" I asked. Oma shot me a silencing glare. I clamped my lips shut, but the question was already asked. Had Sven told this woman?

"A wealthy man. This morning. He didn't say anything outright, but I made some assumptions."

Oma muttered a curse. "I should have used a stronger bind on that one."

Bind? What was a bind? I forced a deep breath. *Don't worry.*

You'll learn. Oma would teach me—she promised. This was the first step.

I was in the tent. During a transaction. For the first time.

Oma remained before the ragged woman, arms folded and a stare hard as iron. Waiting.

This was all the opening Coralythe needed. "I beg of you, have mercy. My boys." Her voice broke. "My two sons were"— she wrapped a piece of her shredded sleeve around her knuckles, tightening and loosening and tightening again—"murdered," she managed, though it seemed to cost her every ounce of energy. Then she screamed an unearthly shriek. "Killed with no cause! Mere *boys*!"

I flinched. Oma didn't even twitch. "Wishes cannot bring back the dead."

Coralythe's head swayed from side to side and she closed her eyes. "I know this. I wish only to find their murderer. To ask . . . *why*. Why they killed my boys."

"For revenge?" Oma lifted an eyebrow. How she maintained such stoicism when faced with raw emotion, I couldn't guess.

"Of course I wish revenge upon them! If they would murder my children—neither one older than twelve springs—what other children might they target? This killer was a Talented." Coralythe slammed a palm on the table. "It could be the same person who murdered the king!"

"If that's the case," Oma said, "it's not up to you to deliver justice."

"Is it up to you to deny me?" Coralythe must've realized she wouldn't win this standoff against Oma. "I want to find the one who murdered my children."

Oma gave a single curt nod. "I empathize with you. But wishes are no small fee."

Trembling, Coralythe withdrew a leather bag from within her

torn gown. The clink of coins was the lone sound in the tent as she placed it on the table. "It's not much . . ."

"It's not enough."

"Oma," I whispered, but Oma cut me off with the swipe of a hand.

"I . . . I also have this." Coralythe placed a tangled necklace beside the bag. "The chain is gold . . ." But Oma was already shaking her head. Coralythe's trembling increased. "Please. Have mercy."

"This is not about mercy. It is about the cost of a wish."

I felt sick. The wish cost Oma *nothing*. It was a tear from *my* emotions. This was all a facade—an act to make wishes seem rarer than they were. And where did that munten even go? We didn't need it, not at the cost of this woman's sanity over the brutal murder of her two sons.

"Myrthe will see you out." Oma gestured toward the tent flap, but Coralythe gripped the sides of her chair to cement herself in place. Tears left trails down the mud on her face.

"Wait. *Please.*" Her eyes, wide and unsure, darted between the two of us before eyeing the doorway. "I can offer one last thing."

Oma lifted an eyebrow.

"A . . . a curse on your enemies."

Oma let out a cry. "You have a Bane?"

I went cold inside. Banes were gained from the Nightwell—the antithesis of the Well of Talents. Banes were rumored to only ever cause harm. But how would she get a Bane? All the maps to the two Wells had been destroyed over a decade ago.

Apparently Coralythe had found it. And her Bane let her curse someone. Was that why she wanted the wish? To curse her sons' murderer?

"I've not used my power in years." Coralythe tried to backtrack. "Not since before my sons were born. If you don't want a curse, I can give you—any of you—a Bane instead. A power of your own!"

A twofold power? How was that possible?

"A curse and a Bane are the same thing in my mind," Oma said.

"But they're not. One will harm you, but the other can benefit you. I'm offering you a gift!"

"You entered the waters of the Nightwell." Oma boarded up her heart and sympathy like shutters slammed closed against a snowstorm. "That's an abomination—a danger to our lands."

"I don't use my Bane, I say! I was *birthed* in the Nightwell waters. I never searched them out. My mother forced the Bane upon me as a babe. It was not my choice!"

My heart lurched in empathy. Like my Wishtress Talent, she had been born with it. It had been no choice of mine either. What if I had been like Coralythe and born with a Bane instead of a Talent? How much more would I suffer shame and confusion?

"You offer a curse as payment for a wish—as though the exchange is equal."

I could bear it no more. I stepped forward. "Keep your curse and keep your jewelry. Your coins are enough."

Oma moved into my line of sight. "Stop this nonsense."

"I have a vote in this matter just as you. She's a mother whose heart has been torn by cruel fate. If we can't give a wish to her, who are the wishes for?"

"They are not gifts," Oma snapped. "They are merchandise."

My face settled into stone. Merchandise. That was how Oma saw me. With all her goodwill of providing bread and grain for the people, she still saw her own granddaughter as nothing more than an object to be used and sold. "If you don't give her a wish, I will find a way."

Oma's eyes widened. She recognized my threat. Good. Coralythe fell to her knees at my feet. "Thank you. Oh, *thank you.*"

"You're being rash, child." Oma's clipped words came through taut lips.

"The singular reason we're denying her a wish is because of poor payment. You call rash what I call compassionate. Charge the next purchaser double if you must. If they're anything like the man who left here this morning, it shouldn't be too difficult."

Oma clucked her tongue and unrolled a blank piece of parchment. "Be it on your own head."

Coralythe clung to my ankles until I finally knelt and guided the woman back to her feet. "May you find peace for your sons' deaths."

The contract took several minutes of Oma discussing restrictions and terms. I stood as near as I dared, but much of their exchange was lost on me. Wishes were tricky to control—wording had to be specific and guided, and there were several rules to the wishes that Oma had learned over the years. I had spent hours trying to eavesdrop and jot down any notes, but I'd come away with very little. Once Coralythe left, I would ask for an explanation of the contract.

At last Oma finished the final line and held it out to Coralythe to read. "When you're ready to use the wish, you must speak these exact words." Oma gestured to the paper. "Otherwise the wish will diffuse once it's released from the bottle and shall not work. The wish will reveal a path leading you to the person who took the lives of your children. Once you've touched that person, the path will disappear and the wish will be deemed complete."

Coralythe finished reading the paper and nodded firmly. Her strength seemed to return with each word. She signed the bottom and Oma took a small bottle from her pocket.

A single liquid wish bounced around inside, ready to be given freedom and a purpose . . . not unlike myself.

Oma popped out the cork and poured the drop onto the contract parchment. It landed in the center, leaving a dark spot of wet. The spot spread toward the edges, growing far beyond what a regular drop of water could. Once it filled the entire page with its liquid stain, it retreated back to the center. Oma held the vial beneath the spot and the wish dropped back into its glass cage.

It was no longer translucent and dancing with spunk but instead a stormy dark grey, sitting at the bottom of the vial, biding its time until Coralythe released it, bound under contract.

Oma scooped up Coralythe's meager coinage and thrust the bottle and contract at her. "Take them and go."

Coralythe stood, stuffing the new treasures into a pouch in the folds of her dress. Her glare swept over Oma and shifted to grateful appreciation when it landed on me. Then she was gone.

I expelled a long breath.

Oma rounded on me and sent bony knuckles to the top of my skull. "Foolish child! There is an order to selling wishes that involves far more precision than you seem to have room for in that shallow head of yours."

Filled with the conviction of having stood for something just, I didn't cower. "If it were truly such an important matter, you wouldn't have bent to my will."

"I gave you a chance to step into the role of your birth, and you squandered a wish because of your own swayed emotions."

"Squandered?" I laughed humorlessly. "I *made* that wish—"

Oma slapped me. Not for the first time.

"I had every right to gift it as I deemed fit."

Oma gathered up the other loose scrolls and stuffed them in a sack. "You don't have the wisdom to make these decisions yet."

"How can I when you haven't taught me!"

"I'm not about to start now."

"You can't deny me! I'm of age." How dare Oma go back on her word? "You act as though *you* are the Wishtress and have never intended to let me use *my* Talent the way it was meant to be used!"

"This wasn't how it was meant—"

"I'll never know how it was meant to be used because I've been nothing more than a cooped hen to you, giving you wishes instead of eggs. Waiting to be either slaughtered or freed."

Oma breathed deeply through her nose. When she spoke again, her withered voice cut like jagged lumber saw blades. "I was wrong to include you."

"I never should have been excluded from wish transactions since the day you started them." Last word. I *needed* the last word in this.

"Don't think you'll be included again." Oma marched across the tent to leave, but my anger settled into a hot loathing, and my next sentence came out in a dangerous hiss.

"Don't think I'll *ever* make another wish for you to sell."

Instead of being shocked like I expected, Oma cackled. "As if you could control your childish emotions long enough to stop them!" Then she was gone.

It took me a long moment to gather my anger and stuff it into the pocket of my heart firmly enough to exit the tent. Anouk met me on the other side, eyes wide and breathing fast.

"I heard it all," she whispered. "We had no customers so . . . so I stood here. I'm so proud of you, Myrthe."

My throat burned, but I swallowed it down. If I cried now, I'd prove Oma right. "Was I wrong, Anouk? To help that hurting woman?"

Anouk took my hand. "*You* are the Wishtress. I've always believed you would see things in a way unique to you and your Talent. You showed compassion. And that is never wrong."

The burning grew hotter and I took several deep breaths. I wanted to be comforted by her words—I wanted to take credit for compassion, but deeper in my heart I knew it wasn't compassion that drove me to give Coralythe a wish but something far less honorable. A word I didn't want to voice, but I knew carried the truth within its letters.

Defiance.

CHAPTER 6

MYRTHE

The cold, empty house embraced me with icy arms. Dim moonlight filtered through the windows as I hung up my coat beside my ice skates. The evenings still bit sharply enough to warrant a coat, even at the entrance of summer.

Which meant the canal had less chance of melting.

I'd checked on my walk back, and it was no less frozen than when I'd first used the wish. Anouk was right—the only way to melt it would be with another wish. But my heart felt locked away in a prison of stone. So distant from emotions that producing a tear seemed almost laughable.

I built a small fire in the hearth to tame the brisk night. As the flames licked the logs, crawling between cracks in the bark and sending sounds and woodsy smells that made me long for winter, I couldn't stop thinking about Coralythe. Little was known about those who submerged in the Nightwell except that they received a Bane—a power in competition with Talents. Rumored to be more weapon than gift.

Talents were supposedly for serving the people and the kingdom. Those with Talents were expected to swear fealty and loyalty to the king. But people with Banes had loyalty to no one but themselves. Or so the tales claimed.

Rumors had a way of painting the Nightwell in a dark light . . . but tempting and alluring as well.

Its location had once been common knowledge until a ruler of old ordered it blotted off the maps. Then the maps of Fairhoven were destroyed by a madman.

That didn't stop people from searching. King Vämbat set up the Trials, making the Well of Talents so difficult to approach that many people, out of pure desperation, turned to the Nightwell instead. At least, this was what Oma had told me. And her words always came from a place of agenda.

I had never met a Talented or a Baned before. Coralythe seemed to recoil from the idea of her ability to curse. She said her Bane had been forced upon her as a child. What mother would *do* that?

Were Coralythe's boys murdered by someone she'd cursed? Now that time had passed and emotions had settled, I wished I'd asked more questions. I didn't like that Oma and I had argued. More than argued—fallen out. I might have given up my chance to finally learn about my own Talent and how to use it properly. I regretted some of my words, but I didn't regret standing up to Oma's passivity toward Coralythe's plight.

Or the fact that Oma viewed me as merchandise.

I had grown up with a bottle to my cheek more often than an arm around my shoulders when I cried. I didn't know this was abnormal until Anouk—the one person who comforted instead of used me. It was the brightest day of my life when she entered it five years ago. I'd told her almost immediately that I was the Wishtress, and instead of using me like Oma warned she would, Anouk helped me work through all the questions that seemed to have no answers.

The Wishtress was the only Talented *born* with a Talent. All others had to drink from the Well. Why was I given this Talent?

Why was I chosen? I wanted to use my Talent right. I wanted to swear fealty to my country and see how I could make life better—for canal rats, for women like Coralythe, for bighearted people like Anouk.

Well, maybe not fealty to the Murder Prince.

I needed to go to the source for answers. The Well of Talents.

Sven wouldn't take me. Oma definitely would not take me. Perhaps it was time to travel there on my own.

I pushed myself up from the floor and glanced outside. The moon still hung low—Oma would not be back from town for another turn of the hour. With resolution I marched across the living space to her room.

I halted on the threshold. I'd never been in Oma's room before. Never been permitted.

Today was a day of eliminating nevers.

I pushed the door open. I surveyed the room. A tidy bed in a carved frame. A single nightstand with a half-burned candle and a pile of used matches. On the floor against the wall with a window were stacks of books and papers. Halfway to them to write her a note, I spied a carved trunk tucked beneath the foot of the bed and secured with a thick padlock.

The last time I'd seen her open it was the day my Talent revealed itself. The day I killed my parents.

No key rested on the nightstand, nor in the drawer. I ran my hands along the smooth sheets and pillowcases. Nothing. There weren't many places to search. Knowing Oma, she probably kept the key on her person.

What was I doing?

I paused but couldn't seem to turn away from the trunk. I knelt beside it. Why did I want to see inside so badly? With all these papers and Oma's contract writing, perhaps she'd hidden her notes and instructions about the Wishtress power. They could be right here, beneath this lid.

I stared at the trunk. The lock. Though I'd not found the key, there was another way to open it. The same way I could thaw the canal ice.

I closed my eyes and let my mind jump back to Oma's comment about *merchandise*. It burned my heart. Then I thought of Sven and how uneasy I felt after telling him about my gift. How I didn't feel valued by him even after revealing the most hidden part of myself. That stung.

But no tear formed.

I shut my eyes tighter and willed up the feelings of being used, of losing Mutti and Pappje, of how captive I always felt when summertime came. Still nothing. I was too angry to cry. So I did the next best thing.

I grabbed the fireplace poker and smashed it against the trunk until the lock lay on the ground in pieces. Since I'd broken the rules by freezing the canal, it seemed I now had no care and no self-control to keep them again. What was the point? I'd already rebelled.

I eased open the lid.

The first item lay flat and enticing—a book. A single word appeared on the black cover, painted in gold ink.

WISHTRESS

I snatched it and cracked it open. The pages cracked and groaned like ancient voices pleading to return to their slumber. Some pages clung to the spine by mere threads. But page after page revealed handwritten notes like journal entries, several in different penmanship.

I skimmed some of the larger-print headers on different pages and found what looked like instructions for different aspects of the Wishtress Talent. *How to store unused wishes. Ungrantable wishes. Using wishes on oneself.* And on and on.

This was it. An entire *manual* about . . . me. My Talent.

Everything Oma knew she must have learned from here. She could have taught me years ago! Could have handed me this book when my Talent first showed itself. But she hadn't. She'd hoarded it for herself.

I tucked the book down my shirt and took in the rest of the trunk's contents.

Vials and vials of glass. Tens. Hundreds. And in each vial hopped a shining, silvery wish. Unbound. Unused. Straight from my lashes to Oma's stockpile. I didn't need to think of old painful memories now. The tears came freely. I let them fall to the wood beneath my knees and dissipate without being stored or used.

"Oma doesn't even *need* me." She had enough wishes to fund her markt booth and provide a comfortable living until the end of her days. I carefully sifted through the vials. The trunk was filled nearly to the brim with wishes. My tears. My *sorrow* that Oma sold for munten.

I recoiled from the bottles as though burned.

But the heat didn't stop. It twisted around my chest like an anaconda, and before I considered my actions, I grabbed a handful and threw the vials against the wall, watching the glass shatter and the wishes perish. Again and again and again.

Only once the trunk was empty and the wall spattered did I take a breath and pause my fury. Blood smeared the palms of my hands and my trousers. I must have crushed a vial in my fist at some point.

Then I noticed light flickering off my hands, the exterior of the trunk, the floor. A shining golden light similar to but different from the bottled wishes. It was too golden to be from the fire. I looked for the source. A thin, glowing string wound around my ankle.

I knelt. My fingers passed right through it. The string was made of light. I felt nothing around my ankle, but no matter how I moved, the light string acted like a regular cord tied around me.

It led out of Oma's door. *Winter's breath*. Oma had used a wish to place a guard on the chest against theft. Of course she had! How long had the light string been around my ankle?

Confused panic inflamed my bones. Oma would be home any moment and I'd be caught. There would be no recovering from this. The day seemed destined to shatter what fragile threads remained of our relationship.

I couldn't bring myself to feel sad about it.

Shuffling came from the entrance of the house. I left the trunk open and stood tall, bracing for Oma's entrance. I had *made* these wishes. They belonged to me. It was time I stood up for my own Talent and worth.

The front door creaked open. I didn't hear it shut. No voices. Tiptoeing. Maybe Oma thought I was asleep. No. She must see the cord of light by now and was following it.

I lifted my chin. "I'm in here."

The face that emerged from the shadows and into the doorway stood two heads above Oma's height. The lithe woman clothed in purple held a dagger in each white-knuckled fist.

Coralythe.

She looked nothing like she had in the markt tent today. No longer withered, ragged, and broken. Instead, she stretched so tall her wild hair almost brushed the beams in the ceiling. Spine straight, face clean, and muscles taut with determination.

She was here to take a life.

Her wide eyes fixed on my ankle—on the string of light. A frown broke her murderous face. "Why are *you* here?"

"I . . . This is my home. Coralythe. What . . . what do you want?" She must have learned I was the Wishtress and not Oma. Was she going to force me to give her more wishes?

Coralythe struck out with a dagger. I flinched too late, but she didn't cut me. Instead, she smacked the back of her hand against my cheek. The moment our skin connected, the string of light around my ankle disappeared.

"You?" Coralythe breathed.

Then I understood. Coralythe's wish had led her *here*. She thought . . .

"*You* killed my sons?"

I held up my hands. "Of course not!" I grappled for some explanation—something to make sense of all this. How could the wish lead Coralythe *here* when it was specifically contracted to lead her to her children's murderer? "There must have been a mistake with the contract."

Did Oma miswrite it? To punish me somehow? To sabotage me?

Coralythe's voice sank into an unearthly cold. "The contract can't be wrong. I read every word."

"Why would I sell you a wish that would implicate me?" I couldn't bring myself to be afraid of her, not under the buzz of confusion. "I don't even know how your boys died."

"Ice," Coralythe hissed, her gaze unfocused and turned to a memory. "Last night they were swimming in the canal and then it froze." Pain pinched the corners of her eyes. "Trapped beneath its surface. Suffocating. I was . . . helpless."

I stilled. Horror overtook me. No. My time with Sven . . . the wish . . .

Coralythe's expression hardened. "It *was* you. I see the understanding in your face. You didn't even *know*!"

I stumbled back and my heel kicked the chest of broken glass and wish water. Coralythe noticed the contents and somehow, in her rage and wildness, pieced together scraps of information at an impossible speed. "*You're* the Wishtress. You wished that canal frozen! For what? For fun?"

Mute, I could only shake my head.

"How many people were killed because of that wish? My boys. Canal rats. Washerwomen. Sailors. Because of your precious *Talent*." Coralythe spat on the floor. "King Vāmbat was right to block off that Well from the foolish and ignorant."

"I-I'm . . ." What could I say? What could I do? "I-I didn't mean to." Meaningless words. I'd killed *children*. To prove my worth to Sven.

Oma was right. I didn't deserve this Talent. I had no right to hand out wishes or use them for my own desires.

The daggers dropped from Coralythe's fists and clanked on the floor. I might have thought she was relenting, but the thunder in her gaze said otherwise. Thick purple clouds rolled across the whites of her eyes. Lightning sparked across her exposed skin. She lifted her hands toward me.

"You despicable child. I curse you. I curse you with all the curses I've not spent."

I couldn't move, still in shock from the revelation of what I'd done.

"At the drop of your next tear, you're cursed to die. Let your emotions never have release. Let your heart feel eternal torture, robbed of relief. May you become as cold as the ice with which you snuffed out life."

Fire pierced my eyes and my vision went blinding white, then storm purple. A scream tore from my throat. The pain of a thousand summer suns mixed with the claws of frostbite cut through my skin. My Wishtress Talent writhed inside me like an animal thrashing against a throttling grip. I felt it suffocating, gasping for breath. Wholly separate from my own body and yet inseparable. Then the Talent went limp.

Something hard struck the side of my head.

Shattering glass. Rain. Fire.

Black.

CHAPTER 7

BASTIAAN

"The king is dead!" Runt raced out of the windmill to meet Bastiaan.

"I heard." Bastiaan wiped his feet clean with a rag after dipping them in the bowl of water by the door. The weight of regret and sorrow pressed him deeper into the ground.

"We learned of it yesterday from the crats." Word always spread among the canal rats first. And Runt, having been a crat once, was Bastiaan's top informant. "And the canals are frozen! Did you hear that? Don't worry, our creek's still okay. Diantha said it's because it's not connected to the canals."

Runt took the soiled cloth from Bastiaan.

"You don't need to do—"

"There's cheese on the table." Runt pushed him farther inside with his free hand.

Though Runt was a mere ten years of age, he acted as both loyal serving boy and stubborn parent. Bastiaan hung up his travel bag and pulled out what was left of the bread he'd received from Myrthe, shoved it into Runt's hands. "You and Mother eat. I need . . ."

He couldn't finish the sentence. He stumbled up the spiral

staircase, memory after memory pounding in his brain. The king teaching him how to use a sword. Telling him the history of Fairhoven as they traveled. Arguing good-naturedly over their differing opinions on the Well. Teaching him how to overcome his fear of water and swim.

"Bastiaan!" Runt's holler was a dim echo. "Wait! There's a summons!"

Bastiaan burst upward through the door into his study and collapsed on his bed, pressing the palms of his hands against his temples as though that would silence the memories. The guilt.

The king's voice spoke through the memories. *"How long will you keep me here, Bastiaan?"*

"As long as it takes for you to change your mind."

"Until I die, then?"

Bastiaan had laughed. *"I certainly hope not."*

"Stop," he whispered to his empty room. "Please . . . stop . . . stop . . . stop." It wasn't supposed to go that far. They weren't supposed to be in the Stillness that long. It was only supposed to take a conversation. Show the king his perspective. Make him understand.

But King Vämbat wouldn't bend. *"The commonfolk can't handle Talents. They're not educated enough. They'd misuse them."*

"I am common! The Well chose to give me a Talent, yet you still resist that."

"You're proof that commonfolk shouldn't have Talents. You kidnapped me, after all."

"Why is the decision up to you? Let the Well decide. It's capable of giving or denying Talents."

Bastiaan's vision went black against the pressure from his fists. "Stop . . . stop . . . *stop* . . ." His plea turned to a shout until it drowned out all other speech or thought. "STOP!"

Bastiaan emerged from the darkness a fortnight later. The full moon had come and gone, renewing his time snap. He couldn't even look at his Talent Mark. *I will never use a snap again.* Though that was a lie.

"I've never seen you so endangered," Mother said during breakfast on his first morn with them.

"Endangered? From whom?" Had schloss militairen sought him out while he was . . . whatever he was? A captive of his mind's darkness?

"From yourself, Bastiaan." Her somber tone was all that kept him from laughing. "Whatever happened in the Stillness, you need to reconcile with your Talent, with the Well, and with your heart."

She and Runt had endured his moody returns many a time. They recognized the intensity of this one and had kindly given him time. Bastiaan wanted to recover faster, but he also needed to respect the toll his Talent took on his mind in order to move forward with his duties to the kingdom and to the Well of Talents.

Mother knew something terrible had happened in the Stillness. But what made it ache all the more was that something beautiful had happened too. "I can never tell you."

"You can always tell me. To share your story is a choice. Don't underestimate the healing that can come from daring not to suffer alone."

"I'm better now." Bastiaan snagged a knife for the fresh loaf of bread and round of cheese on the table. "Fetch Runt, please."

He was lying and she knew it. But Bastiaan had learned better than anyone else that time blunted pain. He needed to start forgetting. Ignoring. *Healing* was too laughable a word.

Mother sighed, then walked out the door to do as he asked.

He placed a jug of water on the table before seating himself. The breeze delivered birdsong and earth scents alike through the open window. Beyond the rhythmic passing of each windmill blade stretched row after row of raised soil. Woven baskets on their hips, women chatted with each other as they plucked weed sprouts with careful fingers so as not to uproot the newborn grain stalks.

Mother strolled among the rows with a bag of canal water, testing the dirt's dryness. Bastiaan had repeatedly told her she need not work, but her reply was always the same. "I worked alongside these women in captivity. You rescued us and I am now blessed to work alongside them in freedom."

She reached Runt in the field and they spoke briefly. She gestured toward the windmill, spotted Bastiaan through the window, and smiled.

He waved, but his stomach recoiled. She always looked so pleased—so proud—when she saw him. But she didn't know what he'd done. How would she look at him if she knew? He wanted to tell her about the king—about how conflicted he felt over the king's death. His regrets and how they were too late. Bastiaan didn't have the strength to grieve alone.

So he wouldn't.

He would let the people of Fairhoven do the grieving, and he would move on. Find a new plan.

"You missed the census!" Runt exclaimed from the doorway. "We had to go to the schloss and everything. It was gargantuan! And I think I saw the Murder Prince through a window!"

Bastiaan's mood lightened at Runt's enthusiasm. "That's amazing." There had been a census?

Mother entered at the tail end of Runt's story. "You need to report to the schloss."

"I'd hoped to meet with the prince anyway."

Mother sat at the table and slid a piece of parchment toward him. "Runt, fetch him some ink."

It was on the table in front of him with a quill and blotter within seconds. Then Runt climbed onto a stool and eyed the cheese. Bastiaan wrote a letter to the prince's *generaal*, requesting an audience with Prince Mattias as soon as possible. It wasn't likely to happen. Bastiaan was no one to the prince. But maybe the census report would grant him an opening. He made sure to include that he was a Talented.

He signed and sealed it, then slid the letter across the table to Runt's left. "Deliver this to the schloss for me?"

Runt brightened at the prospect of a job—something he alone could do to help—and snatched the letter from the table. "Yes, sir!"

He moved to bolt out the door, but Bastiaan caught him by the back of his shirt. "Eat first, wild one. And call me by my name. I may be older, but my value to this world is equal to yours."

Runt plopped into his seat. "Okay, Bastiaan."

Mother brushed the dirt from the knees of her trousers, washed her hands, and then they broke the bread into three portions.

"To King Vämbat's death!" Runt tore a chunk off his wedge of cheese.

Bastiaan nearly choked on his own. "That is not a thing to celebrate."

Both Runt and Mother raised their eyebrows. "Isn't it what we've been waiting for?" Runt asked. "Because he refused to allow commoners to access the Well. You've been"—he shifted uncomfortably—"you've been ranting about it for ages."

For Runt, that was mere weeks ago. For Bastiaan it was a foreign former life. Before he knew the king. Before he and King Vämbat had spent thirty-two years trapped outside of time together.

He forced himself to recall the reason behind kidnapping the king. "His death doesn't open up the Well to commoners. Thus, I've requested an audience with the prince, urging him to unravel an entire system of Talent restrictions."

Runt opened his mouth. Closed it. Then busied himself with his cheese, face pinched in thought. Bastiaan had a suspicion of what Runt wanted to ask, but he wasn't ready to answer it. Though he'd not be able to avoid the difficult decisions for long.

"How is the prince handling the situation with Canal Vier?" Two weeks Bastiaan had been out of commission and still the Vier was frozen.

Mother sliced her own cheese thin and set it over a slice of bread. "It's messy. People are panicking now that they have such little access to water. Even the Handel Sea is frozen. No merchant deliveries or ships arriving or leaving port. Public travel has halted except those who are willing to skate. He's trying to route some of the mountain rivers into the canals, but many fear that will only freeze the rivers. We've already had people dipping into our own creek here."

"Any trouble yet?"

She shook her head. "But it's coming. No water. No trade. No crops. The people grow frantic. I do not envy the prince. Losing his father one day, an attack on his country the next."

Bastiaan didn't allow his thoughts to travel the canal of compassion for the prince. That would lead to guilt—*he* had brought this sudden family loss upon the prince's shoulders. And yet he expected the prince to trust him? To take his counsel?

Then there was the Vier.

What sort of Talented had frozen the canal? Or perhaps it was someone with a Bane. But the bigger question was *why*? It happened the day after King Vämbat's death, yet Bastiaan could pinpoint no correlation. Unless someone thought they could skate their way to the Well of Talents. But so few people knew the location since the maps were destroyed.

The generaal sent a reply to Bastiaan's inquiry the next day. His mother delivered it to him while he was out in the fields, getting his hands dirty for no other reason than to bury his unrest in the steady soil. After the typical formalities and greetings, the letter came down to one sentence. *The crown prince is accepting no audiences at this time. Please present yourself for census accounting.*

Bastiaan fisted the letter. He was no peasant seeking to plead for lower taxes or to settle a domestic dispute. He'd been a Talented in service to the king. And after a time—a lifetime—he'd become a friend. But he couldn't very well tell Prince Mattias that King Vämbat bid Bastiaan to become an advisor. He had no proof.

He liked to think that Mattias was currently mourning his father's death. Like Bastiaan was. Though as heir to the throne, Mattias was also likely trying to solve the riddle of the frozen canal and growing suspicious of the Talented.

Bastiaan must not push his request. Until Mattias would receive him, Bastiaan would continue to gather as much information as possible.

Runt galloped over, always observant and curious. "Is that a letter from the king?"

"His generaal. The king isn't accepting visitors."

"How long will you wait before you send him another letter?" Runt asked.

"It depends on what's happened over the past couple weeks. While I was indisposed." He turned to Runt for a report.

"A bunch of commoners traveled to the Well." Runt scooped up a clod of dirt and broke it open, searching for worms. "We've only heard about deaths. No successes yet." Runt's discomfort from the day earlier resurfaced. He tossed the wormless soil back to the ground, disappointed. "It seems like a good time to go to the Well ourselves."

Bastiaan rubbed his scruffy jaw. He was in desperate need of a shave.

Runt plowed on. "I'm two years past the age of manifestation and I've studied your books so faithfully. I'm sure a Talent will awaken in me."

Despite his hesitance Bastiaan felt a fierce burst of pride toward Runt. This boy—found starving and beaten so long ago—had logic and determination beyond many an adult in Fairhoven. He wouldn't insult the boy's intelligence with a brush-off answer.

"It's a tenuous time for the kingdom, Runt. Prince Mattias is about to make a lot of decisions, and I must be here to advise him the moment he'll see me. To pursue the Well of Talents as a commoner is still breaking the law. Doing such a thing during the monarchy's weakness would be seen as rebellion. It could sway Mattias to maintain restrictions on the Well."

Runt nodded, but his next words revealed how desperately he desired a Talent despite Bastiaan's explanation. "You could use your time snap. Then no one need know we went. Nothing would change except I would have a Talent that could help repay you for all you've done for me. Maybe I'll even get a Talent that lets me thaw the canals. I could save the kingdom!"

Bastiaan pulled Runt close and met his gaze. Firm. Fierce. "You're my one constant friend, Runt. There's no repayment between you and me."

Runt's eyes swam and he choked out his next words. "I just want to be like you."

"And yet I desperately need you to be like *you*."

Runt's chin quivered, but he lifted it high and gave a nod.

"You know my time snap doesn't allow me to take someone through the Trials." Not unless that person already had a Talent.

"Then take me *to* the Trials! I can defeat them—I know I can! And then I'll *earn* my Talent."

"You shouldn't *need* to earn your Talent." Bastiaan ran a hand through his hair. That was the whole point behind trying to eliminate the Trials. They were made by a king—by a *man*—as though the Well itself couldn't discern between worthy and unworthy. Talents were a gift from the Well . . . and the Trials made it seem as though they could be earned.

"The Trials are deadly, Runt. I can't take that risk yet. But hear this vow: I *will* take you at your next age day. Whether the laws are lifted or not."

Runt gave a little wobble that might have been a bow. "Thank you, Bastiaan." It made Bastiaan feel rotten.

The boy left the fields, passing Mother, who stood two rows down with her arms crossed. Judging by the comfort in her position and her lips pursed to one side, she'd been there awhile—long enough to hear the entire conversation at least.

She peered after Runt to ensure he was out of earshot. "You told him the same thing last year, you know."

Bastiaan pulled up short. "I did?"

For Mother and Runt, that promise was spoken one year past. But Bastiaan had forgotten. That didn't sit well with him. He wanted his words to be as reliable as the count of the sun—to stand upon a trustworthy character.

"I thought you of all people would understand why I'm not taking him."

"I know the Trials enticed your father to abandon his family and ultimately claimed his life. But that was his choice. *You* are trying to make Runt's choice for him."

"He's just a boy!"

"But you are not his father."

"I'm the closest thing he has to one." Or maybe a brother. Sometimes he wasn't sure exactly what he and Runt were other than united by something far deeper than blood.

Mother crossed the row separating them and blocked the glare of the sun. "You're afraid, Bastiaan. It's so clear."

Of the Trials. He hated how exposed he felt with his fear vocalized. After everything he'd been through, he shouldn't fear anything. But the Trials had always remained an unknown threat—a threat he'd seen defeat man after man, wealthy and peasant alike.

"I can't lose Runt. Not after . . . not after everything." That was no excuse. That didn't give him permission to try to control Runt—to use the boy's loyalty against him. "I'm going to convince Prince Mattias to remove the Trials. *Then* I'll take Runt."

Mother laid a hand on his cheek. "This last visit to the Stillness took something out of you. Before you left—weeks ago for me—you were filled with life. Zest. Hope for a better future and recognized convictions. You've returned to us so . . . tired. So unsure."

She saw him—much more than he saw himself. Her observation reminded him of another. Of the king.

"Things didn't go as planned."

"They rarely do," she said. "Despite the Talents, we don't dictate the moves of this world. We can only learn to balance and skim along the crest of the waves. You're still awakening, Bastiaan. And once you've recovered you'll rediscover who you've now become."

The rumors came with the sprout of the year's first head of grain. A young man—a commoner—had found the Well. Survived the Trials. Eluded the prince's militairen and returned to Fairhoven with a Talent. Masses swarmed him in the center of the markt, begging to know how he'd done it—how he'd found it and survived.

Bastiaan and Runt stood among the crowd, gathering what news they could. The head of messy blond hair belonged to the same man who'd announced the king's death. The bread girl—Myrthe—had run after him.

Sven, was it?

He stood on a dusty crate speaking to the people in a voice that invited both rebellion and trouble.

"Just because we're common doesn't mean we don't have rights! The Well existed before the kings and it chose to give me a Talent! I'm proof that the Well accepts commoners even though our old and new king alike do not!"

"How did you find it without a map?" someone shouted.

"I was *meant* to find it . . . so I could bring others to it."

This incited murmurs and shouts that drowned out any clarity. Almost chaos but not quite. Sven was handing the people hope after a summer of need, loss, and desperation. It was so enticing even Bastiaan was intrigued.

"Can your Talent thaw Canal Vier?" another voice managed to ask above the ruckus.

"Alas, no, but I have faith that someone who joins me—who follows me to the Well—will receive a Talent that can." Sven searched the crowd as though he'd be able to spot the lucky one by sight alone.

Someone bumped Bastiaan from behind. His hand went to his pockets to check for his coin purse and weaponry. Still there. It'd be easy to empty someone's pockets in a crowd like this. He was jostled a second time and noticed the source.

Schloss militairen wove through the crowd, swords at their belts. Purposeful but not forceful. Bastiaan could warn Sven. Instead, he waited to see what the man would do.

"Why allow Prince Mattias to lead us when he doesn't even *value* us?" Sven said.

The militairen reached the inner circle. Sven spotted them and pointed a defiant finger. "You have no authority over me! By the laws of Winterune and our capital, Fairhoven, Prince Mattias has no authority over the people *or* their pilgrimages until he is crowned king."

The militairen held up their palms in a calming gesture,

seemingly amused by Sven's vehemence. "We come as escorts. The prince desires an audience with you."

Sven stilled atop his crate. "This . . . is a request then?"

"Indeed," the taller of the two militairen affirmed.

"Then you can tell the Murder Prince thank you but no. I will not see him." Many in the crowd gasped. Some cheered. "He's not yet my king. He's not my friend. And until he agrees to allow commoners access to the Well of Talents, he is my enemy!"

The militairen's faces turned to stone. Diplomatic, Sven was not. But he was effective. He'd delivered the same message to Prince Mattias that Bastiaan had hoped to, except Sven's defiant words would likely result in Mattias's anger. Whereas Bastiaan hoped to discuss the matter with logic and respect.

The Well had always been a topic of sensitivity to both the king and his subjects. No one fully understood the magic its waters held or who that magic belonged to. All maps displaying its location had been burned during a madman's slaughter of Fairhoven's cartographers. Bastiaan had spent many years searching for and studying the Well extensively. One thing had always been clear—Talents were meant to serve others. To serve the king in order to help *him* serve the people.

Many kings before Vämbat had viewed the Well as one of their tools—to use against or for the people. The commonfolk started resisting. And now they were finally at the crux of what was about to become an all-out war. After the freezing of Canal Vier, what did they have to lose?

The militairen murmured between themselves and the crowd stilled, anticipating their response. Then a young woman—not Myrthe—tugged Sven down from the crate. She was all sharp angles and dark coal eyes. Fierce and warrior-like. She whispered in Sven's ear. He glanced at the militairen, then nodded to her, and they slipped away. A few spectators noticed a minute too late and searched the sea of heads for him.

Bastiaan had not taken his eyes off the stocky blond man. "Runt . . ."

"I'm on it." Runt slipped into the thickness of the onlookers. He'd follow Sven, learn where he was hiding out, and return with far more information than Bastiaan could ask for. He always did.

Meanwhile, Bastiaan's gaze turned to the departing militairen. Their report would not bode well with the prince, and Bastiaan expected a swift reaction. What that reaction would entail, however, he could not guess.

He wrote another letter to the generaal all the same.

Marriage. That was not the response Bastiaan expected, but Prince Mattias chose a bride from among the people of Fairhoven, wed her, and was then crowned the new king within two weeks. What Bastiaan found most interesting was that Mattias chose a commoner. A young woman with little to no family history or status.

It gave Bastiaan hope. Maybe this was a sign that King Mattias would care for and consider the commonfolk.

Sven could no longer claim allegiance to no king. His resistance would now be seen as rebellion. But maybe his fire had died down after the marriage.

Runt returned after the coronation.

Bastiaan had grown antsy for news. And though Mattias had a private coronation with the country's elite in attendance, Runt had turned snoop and observed nearly the whole thing from an alcove in the schloss. This was after he'd already dogged Sven for a week like the thorough eavesdropper he was.

Bastiaan plucked a dead leaf from Runt's shaggy head. "You need a haircut, young friend."

"And a bath." Runt plunked himself down, cross-legged, against the inner wall of the windmill.

"If you're the one suggesting it, your reek must truly be great."

"The greatest." Runt pretended to waft fumes toward Bastiaan.

Bastiaan threw one of their empty water pails at him. "Don't bring that greatness into our home. Come on."

"It's cold outside!"

"Hardly. Summer's barely yawning and it's going to get colder as autumn comes. Do it now and I'll let you burn an extra log on the evening fire." It was nice to feel a changing season, though Bastiaan hardly noticed the passing of summer during his recovery from the Stillness.

Runt rolled his eyes. "What bribery."

Laughing, they headed out the door and across the grain fields to the tiny river of snowmelt used for irrigation and water supply. Its waters had waned as people redirected their own channels from nearer the source. Bastiaan didn't blame them, but if they kept at it, he'd end up with no water and have to put up a fight. "Okay, divulge. What did you discover?"

"Loads!" Runt practically skipped in his pride. "Sven can see the future!"

Bastiaan's pace slowed. "Truly?" That was a powerful Talent indeed, one he'd never encountered in his studies. A new Knowledge Talent—he'd have to write it down in his research book. There were three classifications of Talents—ones that affected the body, such as a Healer; Talents that had an external effect, such as his own time-stopping skill; and then Talents of Knowledge or Mind, such as seeing the future. The lone exception was the Wishtress, who could be any or all of these with a single wish.

It was hard to collect information about the Talents since

there were so few of them and the location of the Well had been hidden.

"Do you know the breadth of Sven's Talent? How far into the future he can see? Does the Talent have limits?"

"He saw a lot of what was to come—he already knew about the prince's marriage and the coronation that would follow. He claims King Mattias is still going to refuse commoners access to the Well, but Sven didn't give details. He said the canals would be thawed by this time next year!"

That didn't sound like seeing the future. That sounded like educated political guesswork. "Interesting. How did you discover his Talent?"

Runt slid his bare feet into the lazy water and clumps of dirt floated away. "Listening at windows, of course. He stayed in a cottage for a couple days, but then militairen came for him and he's been living in the forest ever since."

"You didn't see him use it?"

"How could I see him use it? It's not like he had to snap like you do. At one point his face went all slack and dumb looking. So maybe that was him seeing the future. Or maybe he just looks like that sometimes."

"Probably the latter," Bastiaan joked. Runt snorted. "Does anyone else know about his Talent?"

"Lots of people. I think maybe the girl he was with told someone. Commoners have been joining him in the forest. Woodsfolk."

More strategy. There was no better way to amass a loyal following than to hint toward a powerful Talent and offer promises of hope. A Talent would ensure Sven's leadership. But what was Sven rebelling against? King Mattias had yet to take any action as sovereign. Was Sven's sole motivation to take people to the Well?

Bastiaan dunked his bucket into the creek water. "Can you locate this spot in the forest?"

"Of course." Runt lifted his chin, offended. "I can get you there by sundown."

"Tomorrow." Bastiaan hauled out the filled bucket and proceeded to fill Runt's. "You still need that bath. And a good meal. We need to pack accordingly in case we're in the forest several days."

Runt took his filled bucket from Bastiaan, determined to use every measly string of muscle in his gangly limbs. Bastiaan matched Runt's labored stride, but when he lifted his gaze, it landed on his mother hurrying toward him, a parchment in hand.

"You've had a message," she said upon reaching them. "From the schloss."

Bastiaan tore the seal open. The time had come at last. King Mattias had granted him an audience. "Well, Runt, change of plans. Let's go see this new king for ourselves."

Runt heaved the bucket into the crook of his elbow with a great sigh. "I'd better bathe twice then."

CHAPTER 8

CORALYTHE

The last time Coralythe had worn such a nice dress was on her wedding day. When she married an unfaithful beast. Now she wore one to meet the Murder King, though her plan had not included being dragged before him by his militairen.

In fact, her original plan had never involved losing her sons, begging for a wish, cursing the Wishtress, or coming to the schloss in hopes of a new life. And new power.

"Let me at least walk upright." She tugged against the hold of one militair. "I'm not going to run." She needed her dignity.

The man's grip tightened around both her and the hilt of his sword. She rolled her eyes. She could curse him within seconds but didn't. The mere knowledge that she *could* gave her a measure of peace.

The militair shoved open a heavy double door and yanked her inside a study far smaller than an audience chamber. A single window lit the space, allowing in a hint of the fading sunset, so her eyes took a moment to adjust. Then she saw him. A mere reach away.

The Murder King.

The man who could—if he'd hear her out—give her some semblance of a future. He stood over a table of parchments while another man spoke with him. Both cut off their conversation upon her entrance. King Mattias frowned when his iron-grey eyes alighted on her, then turned to the militair on her left. "Explain."

"She arrived with a 'gift,' but we believe it's an assassination attempt."

"What?" she sputtered. They'd told her the water seemed an odd gift. No one mentioned thinking she was here to kill the king. "Your *Majesteit*, I would *never*—"

"Are you a Talented?" King Mattias demanded.

She straightened as a rod of indignation shot through her. "I am not. And I never will be."

"Who are you and what's your gift?"

She could, at least, appreciate that he was talking to her and not the militairen. They seemed to remain in the room more out of curiosity than allegiance to their king. She made sure to use that. "My name is Coralythe Avond. I am loyal to the king—to you."

A militair cleared his throat to cover a snicker. King Mattias's jaw clenched. "I'll take it from here."

The militairen left with nothing more than petulant irritation. No bows. No salutes. A generaal and the council member remained. "You'd best get to your point."

Very well. "Long have the Talented turned on the crown they were supposed to be serving—turned on you. They enact their own agendas. And so I present you with a gift that was long ago taken from the crown when it should have been *given* to the king."

She pulled a stoppered flask on a neck chain from beneath her dress. "This is but a splash of the gift I've brought to the schloss. Water . . . from the Nightwell."

The generaal and council member recoiled. But Mattias's eyebrows went up. "That's forbidden." He took the flask from her. "The Nightwell was dammed up long before my father's birth." He lifted his eyes to her. "Are you saying you have a Bane?"

To confess could be the death of her. But it would also reveal her loyalty—at least the appearance of it. She was truly devoted to no one but herself. "I do."

"Witch!" The generaal drew his sword and stepped between King Mattias and Coralythe.

She held her ground. "I broke no law."

"You traveled to the Nightwell," King Mattias pointed out. "That was forbidden centuries ago."

"By ancient and dead kings, Your Majesteit."

"I gather you know its location then?"

She bowed her head. "Yes." He was not silencing her like his generaal wanted to. He was listening. Asking questions. He was *curious*. He would keep listening, so she would keep offering up information. "My late mother birthed me in the waters of the Nightwell. I'm its messenger. I know the heart of the Nightwell more deeply than any scholar."

"You speak of it as though it's a person."

"It's more than water, Your Majesteit." She inclined her head. "It gave me a Bane as well as the ability to pass a Bane on to another once per season." At last he looked intrigued. So . . . the young king was tempted by Banes. She'd hoped as much. "But I have not used that gift—not without the command or permission of my king."

King Mattias smirked, not wholly seduced by her smooth words. "Why bring this to me? Why expose yourself—and your lawbreaking—to your king?"

She bowed her head. "Because I want to serve you the way the Talented were meant to—my Bane is yours. My barrels of Nightwell water are yours. All my knowledge is yours—for the betterment of your reign and your kingdom. You deserve faithful subjects and power. I have the ability to give you both."

She had practiced those words during the long wagon ride back from the Nightwell, after bending and breaking her back loading the water into wide barrels to deliver here to the king. Six wide barrels pregnant with mystery, their exteriors as common as their contents were rare.

She needed this chance—to change not only her future but the future of all those with Banes. And to defeat the Talented once and for all. If he accepted her . . . it would be the start of a new life. And a new power. One where folks wouldn't wrinkle their noses in disgust or thrust her out of their circles when they learned what she was.

She had to hope such a future could exist.

"We shall see." He placed a hand on his councilman's shoulder. "Have the barrels of Nightwell water delivered to my chambers." The councilman bowed and left.

Then King Mattias turned to Coralythe. "I appreciate your sentiment and your gift. I don't fully believe in your loyalty. You have your own agenda. No person is truly selfless."

"I do not claim to be selfless, Your Majesteit. Of course I desire good for myself. But I, too, lost my loved ones to a Talented. My two sons were murdered. Long have I been shunned simply because of my birth." A shame she had no control over—like Mattias being born as the third son.

She met his eyes and saw understanding. Not kindness, but at least an acknowledgment of their similarities. "I don't believe you are my enemy, Coralythe."

She released a pent-up breath.

"Nor do I believe you are my ally. Time will reveal your true motives." He gave a small nod. "Thank you for your gift."

She'd done it. He'd accepted. She hadn't even had to play all her cards—she could tell him about the identity of the Wishtress later when it would serve her best. If the girl was still alive. "It is my honor."

King Mattias indulged her with a smile, then turned to his generaal. "Throw this woman in the dungeons."

CHAPTER 9

MYRTHE

First came the sounds. Softer than the kiss of a snowflake on a frosy cheek. Gentle shuffles, the breath of a breeze, a rustle of leaves, bird chatter, pouring water. Sounds of life.

Next came the disorientation.

I drifted up toward consciousness, fragments of knowledge gathering at the edges of my mind, leaving scrambled memories trying to catch up.

I am asleep.

I am waking up.

I am Myrthe.

"Here we go," someone said from overhead.

Something was wrong. My emotions felt it first—an offness, like when snow on the mountainside shifted underfoot. One's body could feel the warning before the mind processed the danger.

More sounds poured in: leaves skittering across earth, rattled breathing, the pop of a fire. Dim light flickered from the other side of my eyelids. My emotions recoiled from a punch of pain—a recollection of fear. And suddenly I didn't want to wake. I scrabbled for the comfort of darkness. Oblivion. Then . . .

"It's time to wake, child. Open your eyes."

One did not disobey Oma's command.

Against my will, my body shed the sluggishness of slumber. My senses awoke—nose inhaling the crisp chill of autumn and woodsmoke. The world called, coaxed. I could not deny it.

My eyes opened.

Branches and twigs wove like a tapestry overhead with large gaps letting in bursts of sunlight that made it through the waving foliage. My eyes ached. Burned. I blinked several times and reached up a hand to rub them. My fist weighed as much as a river stone, and I barely got it to my face, the resistance of thick coat fabric along my arm feeling more like stone than cloth.

"Myrthe." Oma sounded cautious. "What are you remembering?"

Remembering? Terror, guilt, and despair tugged at me again.

"Look at me, child."

I blinked away the blur, but the confusion remained. I turned my head and found her form framed by a triangle slice of light—a doorway of sorts into this bird's nest cocooning me.

"We are . . . outside?" My voice grated like a dull skate blade. I cleared my throat.

"In a crude shelter, yes." Oma stepped into my line of sight, easing the strain of my neck. She was short enough not to need to stoop beneath the tangle of boughs, but a few stray nubs caught bits of her white hair. She didn't seem to notice. Or maybe she didn't care. "Can you sit up?"

Fear rattled from behind its cell door inside my chest. I ignored it. Once I unlocked that door and faced the memories, I couldn't go back.

I managed to get an elbow beneath me. Oma didn't move to help—this was all on me. It gave me a surge of defiant energy. But the pain in my body originated mostly from stiffness. It didn't feel like it had when I recovered from the pox—as though someone had drained my body of its muscle and bone and replaced them with fire oak and coals.

The most pain shot from my groin and legs, bones grating against one another. They always hurt after I'd slept for a long while, though not quite to *this* extent. "Was I sick? How long have I been asleep?"

Oma dragged a narrow stump over from the doorway and plopped herself on it with a slight wobble beneath her broad backside. "A full season. It's midautumn."

I shook my head. "A *season*?" I felt my body, took in my appearance. Autumn blended into winter in our country, hardly lasting a couple weeks before snow came. "How is that possible? What happened?"

"I hired a Talented healer. She made a draught to keep you asleep until . . ." She pursed her lips as though deciding against giving me information. "What do you remember, child?"

Knowing I could ignore the memories no longer, I focused inward but I couldn't unlock the cell door. I searched my mind but couldn't find the key. "I . . . I can't remember."

"Then it's working." Oma's decision to remain cryptic chafed at my nerves.

"What's working?" I snapped. "What have you done to me? Tell me what's going on."

Oma fixed me with a gaze of steel. "Coralythe."

That single name threw open the door restraining the memories. Regret hit first. Coralythe's sons: dead. Me: guilty. The frozen canal. Coralythe finding me. Blaming me. Hunting me.

My breaths came fast. Faster. I'd murdered. Again. *Children.* With my Talent.

Gasping.

After all the years of regret and grief over my parents, I'd done it all over. After all of Oma's warnings, I'd *done it again*.

Something inside me was screaming. Screaming. Screaming. Coralythe had come to kill me, but she didn't. Why? Why would she let me live with this?

I clutched my head in my hands. What had I done?

"Myrthe." Oma's bark lifted my head.

"She cursed me." My voice broke, and the burning moved from my chest to my throat to my eyes.

Oma slapped a wet cloth over my nose and mouth. Instinctively I jerked away, but whatever herbs were soaked into the cloth did their job. I fell back against the pillows into darkness's embrace.

My next awakening happened faster. I sat up before my eyes were fully open. A headache blossomed behind my eyes. I groaned and lifted a hand to my head. Oma sat in the same seat as before.

"You drugged me!" I accused.

"I had to. What do you remember about Coralythe's curse?" Oma's practical presentation of the question—as if we were discussing arithmetic—helped settle my emotions. I needed to understand. I needed to remember.

"She cursed my Talent." Thinking of my Wishtress gift and all the bitterness that had built during Oma's control of it tensed my sore muscles. "I'm to die by my next tear."

"That's what I heard too."

"You were there?"

"I entered the house when Coralythe was cursing you," Oma said. "I heard her but didn't reach you in time to stop her."

Not that it would have mattered. I deserved the curse. I deserved death for what I'd done. I dropped my face into my hands, but Oma rapped her knuckles on my skull. "None of that now."

"Ouch!"

"You mustn't cry."

I released a scornful laugh. "Oh, now I mustn't? The moment I turned twelve you demanded I let the tears out. To let you collect them. To let you keep them in a trunk like a treasure-hoarding dragon."

"If you cry, you'll perish."

"Then that's *my* choice!" Silence dropped upon the small shelter and hung like a fog.

"Your life was given to you." Oma's grey eyes sparked with orange fire. "A gift. And just because it's yours doesn't give you the right to end it."

I knew where she was going with this. She wanted my Talent back. She wanted wishes again. This had nothing to do with my "gift of life." Oma had never been moved by death—not my pappje's, not my mutti's, not Coralythe's sons'. The only reason she cared about mine was because I was a *commodity*.

I took a long breath. "Why aren't we home?"

"The gable house burned to the ground."

"What?"

She held my gaze, showing more emotion over *this* than over death itself. "After you were cursed, Coralythe fled and I assume she must have gone to the king because hardly two months later, militairen set fire to our home. Anouk had gotten wind of the order and sent warning in time for me to get you out and into hiding here."

Our home, gone. "Why does the king want to kill me?"

"There are likely many reasons. Perhaps he thinks you killed King Vämbat. But he also needs a wish to thaw Canal Vier."

"The canal is still frozen?" Even after the curse? After all this time?

"Whoever froze it is an enemy of Fairhoven. They are trying to destroy us. No summer crop grew because no one could water their fields. People have fled to other cities built around rivers because they need water. All trade has stopped. Food and supplies have grown scarce. The schloss itself is importing water, but it's hardly enough to sustain them. I'd have used a wish to undo it, but Coralythe destroyed my stash."

Oma said this almost as a question. I didn't meet her gaze. *I* had destroyed the wishes in a petty tantrum.

She threw something on my lap. I flinched, expecting a fist to follow, but when it didn't I glanced at the item. The black cover with gold script. The book about the Wishtress—the one I'd stolen from her trunk.

"You need to get your Talent back. So I'm giving you what you always wanted."

"A book," I said, voice wooden. "You think I've always wanted a book? All I ever wanted from you, Oma, was kept promises."

I wanted her to teach me what she said she'd teach me. She spent so many years caulking the crevices of my brain with fear, I always hoped she'd be just as thorough in providing me instruction. But now . . . I'm certain she never meant to teach me anything. All that talk of "when you're of age" was nonsense.

Perhaps she knew I'd gain a mind of my own—that rebellion would strike and I wouldn't stay compliant forever.

She didn't count on a curse.

"I kept the promises that mattered." She nodded toward the book. "Where do you think I got such a thing?"

I didn't want to hear her excuses. She could have wished this book into existence for all I cared.

"I knew the last Wishtress. I, a mere girl, helped my mother tend her as she was dying. The Wishtress used her final wish to pass on the Talent to my blood. *My* blood." She pounded a fist to her chest. "She entrusted me with that book that had only ever been in the hands of the current Wishtress. She told me I was of the right heart. The Talent should have been mine. But her final wish was a raw wish. No time to draw up a contract and specify details. It took a path of its own. It didn't connect to my blood. It didn't even connect to the blood of my own son. But finally *you* were born and there was my Talent."

I listened to her share a secret that had formed her into the coldhearted oma she'd become. Through the shock and emotions her story roused in me, I couldn't help but see the irony. She'd spent her life being loyal to the Wishtress she served as a girl. And then she betrayed and used and suppressed the next Wishtress. Me. Because she saw my Talent as belonging to her. So she'd set aside any sort of kindness or motherliness to control me. Perhaps that was why the Talent skipped her and went to someone else.

The worst thing for Oma would be if I no longer had wishes to give her.

She felt the loss of my Talent more than I did. I had a sudden desire to be away from Oma. Forever. Even if that meant death. "You can't stop me from crying, Oma. You've trained me too well to let the tears come." Even with the book about the Wishtress, I didn't have the ability to keep my emotions in check for the rest of my life!

"It's your duty. As Wishtress. You must find a cure."

I was already shaking my head. "There's nothing in this life for me. There never was."

"Not even your own mother? Mutti?"

Oma had never spoken of my parents after their deaths—not out of reverence but because she never seemed to care enough. "My mutti is dead."

"She's alive. Your wish removed her memories of you, but she never died. And if you ever want to find her, you *must* find a cure to your curse."

CHAPTER 10

MYRTHE

Oma had played her last card.

And it worked.

Mutti was alive? Not only had Oma lied to me—to the point of digging a false grave—but she'd robbed me of a potential life with my own mother.

Mutti was alive. I couldn't leave that stone unturned. I couldn't let my life end without answers. All this time Mutti had been living life unaware she had a daughter.

"Where is she?" I growled.

Oma shrugged. "I haven't seen her since the day she left. I gave her a cloak, food, and pointed her to the road."

"Your own daughter?"

"Daughter by marriage. She's not blood."

I wished *I* wasn't blood. But Oma's confession did what she'd been counting on. It planted a spark of desire . . . desire to live. To find Mutti, even if she didn't remember me. She was still a chance at love—love Oma never gave.

And Mutti deserved to know she had a daughter.

I suddenly craved safety. Friendship. Someone I could trust and talk to and process with. "Where's Anouk?"

"Much has happened since your curse."

Fear choked me. "Is she okay?"

"Anouk is queen."

"What?" I sputtered. "But . . . how?"

"Fairhoven law states that Prince Mattias could not take his father's place as king until he wed, so he chose Anouk."

"Why would he choose her? How did he even know she existed?" It sounded like a fable. Anouk had told me repeatedly that she would never marry.

"He sent out militairen to inquire of the people, then twenty eligible women were brought to his palace and he chose Anouk."

It was no secret that all who met Anouk adored her. But why would she even go? Anouk had never desired riches or royalty. Had the prince forced her? She was common! So much did not add up.

"You should be thankful. Had she not become queen, she wouldn't have been able to warn us of the militairen attack on our gable house. You'd likely be dead."

"What a horror," I said dryly. But then I thought about Anouk being trapped in the schloss with the Murder Prince-become-King. "Does Anouk know what happened to me?"

"She knows you were attacked, but she doesn't know about the curse. No one does." Oma knocked a spider off the branch above her head, perhaps in an attempt to act nonchalant about her next question. "Why *did* Coralythe curse you, Myrthe?"

Oma still didn't know I'd frozen the Vier or that I'd killed Coralythe's sons. What a relief. But the familiar weight of secrecy settled upon my shoulders again. Would I never be able to live free of its lock and key? I wasn't about to hand Oma more leverage, so I let the silence stretch on.

"After all I've done for you, you won't tell me?"

I snorted. "What have you done?"

"I used every last coin of mine to keep you alive these past few months—"

"You drugged me."

"I've given you a home—"

"That you made me pay rent for with wishes."

"I've raised you—"

"Because you lied about my mother's death."

Oma cursed and stomped out of the shelter. Good riddance. But at her absence the burn of tears threatened. My inner walls crumbled at the safety that accompanied solitude.

Anouk was queen and didn't know how to find me. Mutti was alive but didn't know who I was. And I was cursed to die the next time I allowed myself to *feel* something.

I gulped my tea. It burned my throat. Even after I swallowed, the burning continued from the overload of information and my turbulent feelings. I didn't want to talk anymore. I didn't want to assess my next move or accept the repercussions of my predicament. My breathing quickened and I barely managed to abandon my tea on the bedside table. I fumbled for the herb cloth and slapped it to my own nose.

As I breathed in the new scent of sleep, I clung to one thought. I had to break this curse. It was the only way to atone. Then maybe, just maybe, I could die without a suffocating weight of guilt.

CHAPTER 11

BASTIAAN

 King Mattias wore his throne like a cloak of carved stone and gold.

Bastiaan stood on the gleaming marble floor at the king's feet, his own inverted reflection bloated with secrets. The new queen stood in the shadows behind the king, long dark hair and regal stance. Runt stayed flush with the entry wall, the proper place for a servant. His bowed head and subservient stance made him practically invisible to the eyes of the elite, but his ears were alert and seeking. Gathering information to share with Bastiaan upon their exit.

"Who exactly were you to my father?" King Mattias asked.

Bastiaan's reply would set the tone for this audience. There were too many paths toward failure. He must weigh and measure every word. Every breath. He needed Mattias to trust him—to see him as one with great knowledge who could benefit him. Train him. Teach him.

Who was Bastiaan to the former king? At the beginning he was a distant servant. Then a dear friend and son. At the end . . . murderer.

"I started out as a private messenger for him. Before he died . . . I served as confidant and advisor."

King Mattias remained as still and firm as the throne upon which he sat. "Can you prove this?"

Bastiaan bowed. "I have only my words and character as proof."

King Mattias's only response was a rhythmic tap of his fingers on the arm of his throne. Waiting. "You're a commoner."

"I am. But I believe all people are equal."

King Mattias's fingers stopped tapping. "That's easy to say when you're living on the lowest rung. Of course you want to be seen as equal. Yet you have a Talent, *commoner*. Why should I not throw you straight into prison?"

Bastiaan had prepared for this. His story about receiving his Talent was one he never had to embellish or twist. It was his proudest moment. "My mother and I were servants to a dye merchant in Gevanstad since my birth. While my mother worked with cloths, I was given to the merchant's son as a manservant. His son, Dehaan, decided to make the pilgrimage to the Well. I was to accompany him."

"What age were you?"

"Fourteen. After getting through the Trials, we reached the Well and he drank, then spent the day praying. Nothing happened. He drank again and prayed some more, first demanding a Talent, then pleading for one. Still nothing happened, so he told me to pray with him. For him. I did so . . . and to my great surprise I received a Talent."

"Yet you hadn't drunk of the water?"

"No, Majesteit. I'd not been allowed."

"Did you tell this tale to my father?"

"Yes, Majesteit." A hundred times over again.

"And did he consider your advice? About allowing commoners to access the Well?"

A bittersweet memory twisted Bastiaan's lips. "It took a long time, but by the end he started to see my point of view." Once it was too late. Once he was too old. Once Bastiaan realized he couldn't undo what he'd started.

"By the end?" King Mattias leaned forward, elbows propped on the wide throne arms. "When did you last speak with him?"

Bastiaan had allowed himself to grow too conversational. "Four days before his death."

"Tell me, did you understand my father's stance on the Well of Talents?"

Bastiaan understood more than Mattias would ever know. He knew so many details about King Vämbat's beliefs, it felt nearly impossible to condense them into a few sentences' explanation. But Bastiaan was an old friend of the impossible.

"He believed that those who desired Talents should be tested and tried to the utmost as they pursued the Well to prove their worth. Hence the Trials." And now for the part Bastiaan hated. "He also believed commoners were not educated enough to use their Talents properly."

The irony was not lost on Bastiaan. As a commoner he'd used his Talent *against* the king to force him to listen to reason. And it resulted in Vämbat's death. Thus proving his concerns valid.

King Mattias nodded, a subtle change in his features betraying his agreement with his father's ways. "How would *you* see the Well handled?"

It had finally come to it. Bastiaan unearthed every seed of strength and confidence rooting in the soil of his soul. King Mattias was already skeptical. Bastiaan's words needed to be delivered in a firm yet humble explanation if he wished for Mattias to consider them.

"I would see the Trials dismantled. Allow the people to pursue a Talent at their will. Let the Well be the judge of their worth. It is capable of denying Talents to those who shouldn't have them."

King Mattias's face darkened like a field beneath a roll of storm clouds. "And yet it seemingly gives Talents to those who would murder our king and freeze the Vier."

Bastiaan's mouth went dry. "I think even those who received Talents under the crown's restrictions still possess the freedom of will to make poor choices."

"'Poor choices' . . . Such a simple way of summarizing my father's brutal murder." Mockery seasoned Mattias's words. "So you would open the Well for all men. Why? What role do you believe the Talented play in our kingdom? I've witnessed nothing more than a selfish thirst for power."

"Talents exist to serve mankind and the crown. They are meant to improve our way of life, like any craft or skill. They exist in all people for a reason."

"Though not *truly* in all people."

"I disagree, Majesteit. Just as I believe every soul has both light and darkness, so a person has a propensity for a Talent or a Bane, depending on which Well they drink from."

At the word *Bane*, shrewd curiosity stole over King Mattias's face. He'd heard the word before—maybe even recently.

Yet he didn't ask Bastiaan about it. Instead, he continued their conversation as though no shift had taken place. "What if one should drink from the Well of Talents and come away still empty? Like your former master, Dehaan? Are you saying they have nothing more than a propensity for darkness? For a Bane?"

The question was more personal than curious. Bastiaan chose his words carefully. "If someone drinks from the Well of Talents and comes away empty . . . I believe the Talent is not yet ready to be awoken."

"But you think it will awaken eventually?"

"I hope that's the case."

"Did this happen with your master?"

"I wouldn't know. I stopped working for him after our pilgrimage." Bastiaan's Talent had been his path to freedom, for both himself and his mother. And the other women slaving away in that man's cellar dyeing cloths until their hands were raw and cracked.

King Mattias inquired no further but spent a good while observing Bastiaan. Bastiaan offered no additional information and willed his posture and mannerisms to reflect trustworthiness.

"You must become my son's advisor. His most trusted. It's the only way to save the kingdom." King Vämbat's last words to Bastiaan throbbed like a heightened pulse in his veins. He couldn't fail. But Mattias didn't seem interested in another advisor. Or anyone's advice for that matter.

"I know who you are, Bastiaan Duur. I know you've gathered great knowledge about the Well of Talents. Many bring me your name, claiming you're a seasoned scholar."

Bastiaan held his ground. Renown could either work for him or ruin him. "I've always seen it as my duty to collect information to help serve our kingdom."

"I have a job for you." Mattias lifted a rolled piece of parchment from the small table beside his throne. He handed it to a militair who strode toward Bastiaan. "I want you to find me the Wishtress."

Bastiaan's mind reeled. The Wishtress was the one Talent he knew the least about. There were no books on her. The most he'd discovered were a few letters of theories during one of his forays into the Stillness.

A woman born with a Talent—having never even *visited* the Well. And it was the most coveted Talent in the world. No one was even sure when she existed. According to the meager texts he'd read, the Wishtress might come immediately after the previous Wishtress or a hundred years later.

Of all the things King Mattias could have asked him to do, this was the nearest to impossible. "I . . ."

"She resides in Fairhoven—or at least she did at the start of summer. I thought I'd found her, but . . ." King Mattias's lips tightened until they turned white. "We need her to thaw the Vier."

The queen shifted her stance ever so slightly. Mattias nodded to the piece of paper. "That is a sketch provided for us by a new . . . ally." He snickered. Bastiaan tried not to read into the repeated undertones that flavored Mattias's statements. "Find her and deliver her to me. And perhaps I will see your desires for the Well of Talents granted."

Perhaps. Not the most promising word.

"My desire is to serve my king." Bastiaan bowed and accepted the parchment from the militair. If this was how he could keep his promise to Vämbat, he'd do it.

King Mattias maintained a stoic expression. He leaned back in his throne and the deep scrutiny faded. "I meet with my council in three days. I'd like you to attend. You are not a voting member, but your perspective is one I'm curious to hear."

Although Bastiaan had hoped for this response, he still registered disbelief at receiving it. His spirit lifted and a burden melted from his shoulders. He'd done the right thing with King Vämbat. Bastiaan would prove his worth. He would show this young king the lengths he would go to for the people of Fairhoven and all of Winterune.

Behind King Mattias the queen summoned a militair and whispered in his ear. A moment later, that militair strode to where Runt stood against the wall and said something to the boy. Runt shook his head and pointed to Bastiaan. The militair put a hand on his sword hilt and spoke again. Runt edged away with another shake of his head.

Bastiaan was so distracted by this exchange he almost missed King Mattias's dismissal. "You may take your leave."

He bowed. "Majesteit." Then he hurried toward the militair who gripped Runt's forearm. Another person took Bastiaan's place before the king, bringing a petition or request.

Bastiaan reached Runt and the militair at the same time as the queen. "May I be of assistance?"

Runt stopped struggling. "He's trying to take me away, Bastiaan!"

Queen Anouk laid a hand on the militair's shoulder. The moment he realized the hand belonged to his queen, the militair released Runt.

"I requested a private word with the boy," she said in a voice as soft as lamb fleece. She made eye contact with Runt—as though they were equals. He lifted his chin in defiance. She smiled. "It was a request, young sir. You may refuse."

Runt was not yet mollified. "As I told your oaf of a militair, I must ask my master's permission first."

Queen Anouk lifted her fair gaze to Bastiaan. "One cannot purchase such depth of loyalty. You must be a noble master."

"That he is," Runt answered before Bastiaan could unearth a response.

"He and I are equals," Bastiaan said. "We have an equally noble queen, Runt. Your decision is your own."

Runt sighed and turned to her. "What do ya want?"

She took him aside and they conversed in private for several minutes. Bastiaan didn't bother trying to eavesdrop. Runt would relay the entire conversation upon their departure.

A militair interrupted to deliver a folded note to the queen. She concluded her discussion with Runt and thanked him, but while Runt made his way back to Bastiaan, Queen Anouk opened her letter. Her eyes skimmed the page faster and faster and she paled, then hurried from the throne room.

She seemed to hold as many mysteries as Bastiaan did.

Bastiaan and Runt waited the appropriate half bell until court was at a pause, then made their way toward the exit of the schloss.

Bastiaan didn't even have to prompt him before Runt spoke up. "She's trying to find some canal rat kid named Cairden. Said he'd be about six years old. The boy probably froze to death the first week he was abandoned. Told her I'd keep an ear to the ice, though."

"Did she say why she was seeking him?"

"Something about the bread booth at markt and wanting to get food to him and the other crats. I recognize her from there, you know. They gave us free bread. Any crat would be willing to help her. I'll spread the name around at least."

"You're a good lad."

"I do it for the reward that's bound to come."

Bastiaan stepped out from the shadows of the schloss and into sunlight. Only then did he unroll the parchment Mattias had given him. At the top was a scribbled address, not far from the schloss and on the banks of a main channel of Canal Vier.

Underneath was a sketch of a face. The supposed Wishtress. Smooth lines, soft eyes . . . Bastiaan almost dropped the parchment. He'd seen that face before.

It belonged to the girl who'd given him bread.

CHAPTER 12

MYRTHE

How could the most powerful Talented in Fairhoven break a curse that was trying to kill her? So far Oma's *Wishtress* book held nothing about curses. But it had a lot of details about how to write a proper contract. How to store tears. How to force out a wish in a moment of need—I'd mastered that.

The Wishtress didn't cry until between the ages of twelve and fourteen.

A Wishtress's tear could be bottled for up to seventy years before it lost its power to grant a wish, as long as it was corked securely.

Details on how to use a wish and how not to use a wish that didn't matter to me anymore. I had one wish left, and if I released it, I would die.

It took me hours to decipher the different handwritings in the book, which infuriated me because I wanted to read through its entirety as soon as possible, but some scribblings seemed to be in other languages. One page in particular had several notes that other Wishtresses had apparently taken offense to. At least two other writers had left notes in the margins in my own language.

This is disputed and has never been proven.

And, *This is heresy against the Well of Talents.*

They made me want to translate this page all the more. Anouk was the only person I knew who'd studied a language other than that of Fairhoven. She wasn't fluent by any means, but she'd been able to hold an entire conversation with a foreign canal rat once.

She was my lone option at this point.

I buckled my leather satchel to the band around my waist and peeked inside the smaller pouch to ensure it housed a bottle of sleep herbs and a strip of cloth. I tucked the *Wishtress* journal into the satchel, then I tied the laces of my most prized possession—my skates with their wooden guards strapped over the blades—into a metal loop.

Oma returned from gathering berries to find me in the entrance of our small twig hut. "Where are you going?"

"I'm leaving."

"To break the curse?"

"I haven't decided yet." I would have left without a goodbye, but I had to ask one last time to make sure she wasn't holding back any final information. "Can you tell me anything else about my mother?"

"She's likely dead by now."

I let out a disgusted noise and shoved off the tree trunk. "I give up. There is no light in you, Oma. My entire life I kept hoping for a glimmer, but you bring only shadow and hopelessness."

She threw her bundle of sticks to the ground beside the fire. "Not to the people who buy my wishes."

My wishes. She still saw them as her own. "They don't see light. They see greed and opportunity. You and your power-lusting customers are one and the same." I walked out of the small camp.

"Stop this nonsense, Myrthe."

I didn't stop. Not when I heard her following me. Not when her demands turned to shouting as her voice grew more distant.

Not even when she begged me to think of the danger I was putting myself in. Then cursed my stubbornness to all eternity.

I never looked back. She couldn't keep up, even with my limp more pronounced than ever from the stiffness of months in bed. The goodbye was easier than I thought it would be. Perhaps because she'd taught me through example how to turn my heart to stone.

I headed toward the schloss. To the home of the Murder King. Possibly to my death.

But at least it was *forward*.

It was a choice all my own—one that might lead to more mistakes, more regrets, more guilt. But I'd carried plenty of that already. I could handle more if I needed to.

A bluster of autumn wind whispered of approaching winter and swirled among my loose hair strands and around my ears. Soothing me. Promising the familiar. If all else failed, I'd always have winter.

The bone-on-bone pain settled in my left leg joints, and lifting my foot over a branch, a log, even a lump of dirt sent a sharp stab through my groin. I let myself grimace. I let myself groan. I let myself drag my foot—all things I wouldn't do around others. The silent forest was more home than Oma's gable house or hut, more accepting than Sven. It was safety, where I could be myself without fear of judgment.

Two full bells passed before I reached a branch of Canal Vier—still frozen solid as though it were midwinter and not the start of autumn. As a seasoned *schaatser* I could tell the ice went deep. Almost to the very canal bed. Hardly a trickle of water survived beneath the thick frozen surface. Beautiful . . . but deadly. A smattering of trees lining the canal were brittle and brown. Their parched, dead leaves waved stiffly like one final plea for rescue. There hadn't been enough rain through the summer to make up for the irrigation from the canals.

I sat down and pulled on my skates, warring within myself between ignoring the pain I'd caused to my city and owning up to it. It had been a mistake, like the wish I'd used on Pappje and Mutti. Like what happened to Coralythe's sons.

How many mistakes was one allowed before they had to atone?

Who was the one doling out the grace? Who delivered the judgment? I wasn't sure I wanted the answer yet. That's why I needed to talk to Anouk.

My skates hugged my feet with a promise of strength and speed. I set aside my regret and guilt and stepped onto the ice with an exhale. This, at least, was one good thing that came from my raw wish.

Skating.

I hissed a breath through my teeth at the picture of two boys trapped beneath the glassy surface. Freezing to death. Suffocating. I couldn't breathe. Couldn't shut my eyes against the scene. A chilled, hollow feeling replaced my midsection. How had I come to this?

The snap of a branch beneath a shove of wind drew my eyes upward. *Go. Just go.* Like I did at the start of a race, I burst forward determined to leave any thoughts or emotions far behind.

The *schck-schck-schck* of my blades on the ice picked up a rhythm as I found my stride, as pain fled my body and fluid motion took over. Autumn leaves skittered along the ice, joining me in my dance. I didn't know my exact location, but I understood the makeup of the canals, and it didn't take me long to find the main snake. I followed it toward Fairhoven, where it would eventually cut through the heart of the city toward the schloss.

Fairhoven looked so different from what I'd left behind two months ago.

Dead streets and brittle trees. No one skating. No one out walking. No fall markt of autumn produce and bakes.

My skate toe caught on something and I sprawled forward,

cracking my knees and elbows against the ice. Only once I skidded to a stop did I see the state of the canal. Ice had been hacked away from the bank, leaving treacherous caverns and gaps—one such crack being the culprit that caught my skate.

People were desperate for water.

I did this.

The canal was unskateable, so I marched along the bank on my skate guards. No people. No canal rats. The canals were their life source—where the crats got their water, where they built their homes, where they offered services to those boating or schaatsing.

But now they couldn't live here because they had no water.

Where had they gone? I thought of the many dirty faces swarming our bread booth, and my traitorous imagination immediately drew up a scene of them dead in the forest, frozen in the canal water, starving or thirsting to death in city alleyways.

And what about my mother? Was Mutti even in Fairhoven? Had the frozen canal affected her?

I should have gone around the city. No. I needed to see what I'd done. And I needed to fix this. I stumbled back onto the ice, my determination to get to the schloss renewed.

As I set blade to ice, my eye caught on a paper nailed to a notice tree on the bank. The wind flapped the corners. I glided over and smoothed them flat.

My face stared back at me.

A sketch done by a deft hand and thorough description. The cheekbones were a little wider than mine and my eyes seemed cruel, but it was clearly me. Words adorned the top of the paper.

Wanted: Myrthe Valling

Guilty of freezing the canals, possible assassin of the king

Reward: 1,000 silver munten or Well water

Last seen in Fairhoven markt

The schloss offered *Well* water as a reward?

I glanced around, suddenly fearful of hidden eyes piecing together who I was with this poster they'd likely seen hundreds of times while I slept in a birdcage in the forest. If it was posted here, it was posted other places.

And if people were angry about the frozen canal, they likely had my face memorized as a target for their hatred. The wind changed its whistle and I thought I heard a noise, caught the brush of cloth on bark somewhere behind me.

I felt watched.

I tore the paper from the tree and skated out of there as fast as I could. The idea of marching right up to the schloss now seemed even more foolish. Oma's warnings ricocheted in my memory.

I thought of the times I'd ignored her. Despite her cruelty and control, she had wisdom. I didn't heed her when I used a raw wish. Perhaps I should learn my lesson. But her warnings were from a heart of self-preservation and desire to keep me under her thumb.

I needed to free myself from her voice.

So I prayed for my own wisdom. For my own wit. To whatever power created Talents and decided that I, of all people, should be this century's Wishtress . . . I asked it for grace. Almost angrily. It owed me that.

I skated onward.

CHAPTER 13

ꟿYRTHE

A militair dragged me into the schloss.

I didn't know if this was by Anouk's order or because he recognized me. I'd pulled my scarf over my chin and mouth, tucked my hair up into a hat, and smeared a little charcoal over half my face after writing Anouk a note on a leaf of blank paper from the *Wishtress* journal.

I didn't think the militair would deliver it to her.

I didn't think he'd come back.

I *did* expect to be dragged into the schloss at some point.

The wool-white entrance stretched mere feet before us—a wide sweep of stairs flowing out of an entryway the size of my childhood cottage, like the train of a royal gown. Sky-blue roofing capped the white walls, like winter painted on a building.

The militair took me toward a small entrance off the corner. He didn't have his sword out. That was something. And he was alone. I tried to match his stride, but my limp wouldn't allow it. I stumbled and he slowed. "Are you injured?"

I didn't see myself that way, but neither was I as healthy or capable as the average citizen. Unless I was on skates. "Yes. From having the pox as a child."

He slowed even more. Courtesy of this sort implied I was, perhaps, a guest and not a prisoner. "We're not far."

With a deep breath and fists ready to beat back any unwelcome emotions, I entered the schloss for the first time to see my cousin. My best friend. My queen.

Queen.

I could think of no one better to be queen of Winterune, but I could also think of no one less inclined. What had happened to Anouk to make her marry the Murder Prince? And how did that change our relationship?

I wasn't so naïve to think our friendship would be the same as it was the last time we'd seen each other at markt. Yet I was hopeful. I wanted to tell her everything. About Oma, about Mutti being alive, about the *Wishtress* journal, about Coralythe and the curse.

But telling her of the curse would include telling her of the death of Coralythe's sons. I deserved to be imprisoned. Tried. Executed. Could I expect Anouk—as a new queen—to keep a secret like that? Additionally, to tell of the curse would be to reveal Coralythe as having a Bane. Mattias the Murder King would send for her, question her . . . maybe even imprison her.

I couldn't do that to Coralythe because I didn't blame her. I deserved the curse.

"Myrthe!"

We'd hardly passed through a doorway into a glass-domed room of potted dirt and wilting plants when Anouk rushed to my side. The militair stopped immediately, bowed, and backed from the room. He closed the door behind him, where I assumed he'd be standing guard . . . and possibly listening in.

Anouk wore an intricately layered silver floor-length gown

and her dark hair hung in loose curls around her face. I almost didn't recognize her, but a burst of relief sent me into her arms. The embrace was normal, familiar, and as comforting as ever.

We broke apart after a long moment. Then Anouk led me to a stone bench near the back of the room, so close to the glass it was as though we were outside except without the cold or the breeze. This space might have been a beautiful topiary once, but I assumed the dry dirt and wilted seedlings were results of the water shortage. My foolish wish.

I didn't look at them again.

A fire crackled in a stone fireplace that rose alone in the middle of a multipaned glass wall. That was where the summerlike heat came from. A small luncheon awaited us on porcelain and silver dishes beside the bench with more items of cutlery than I'd ever seen.

"It was the only place I could think of where we wouldn't be overheard," Anouk said.

"It's very pretty." My voice sounded hollow. Why? Because this setting was so different from any place Anouk and I had ever occupied before—not merely the location, but the situation. Where did I start? What did I say?

"I tried to contact you so many times after they set fire to Oma's gable house." Anouk took both my hands in hers. "But there was no way to find you. Oma left no word, which was safest for you. But . . . I feared for you. Myrthe, are you well?"

"As well as could be hoped."

"You shouldn't have come here. It's so dangerous. I would have met you somewhere—anywhere. You're *wanted*."

"I saw." Anouk's own husband had issued the order. I hardly understood her decisions since I was cursed. It felt like I faced a stranger. I needed to understand. "Oma told me of your marriage to the Murder King."

I reached for the food, for no other reason than to occupy my hands. Anouk sprinkled an autumn spice blend atop a soft cheese spread over a piece of toast. "Don't call him that."

I almost laughed—I'd always called him that. Anouk still defended him? "So . . . he's innocent then?"

Murderous Mattias—the Murder Prince now turned Murder King—had been third in line for the crown. Then his eldest brother mysteriously disappeared and showed up dead a year later. His second brother died in a hunting "accident." His own mother—the queen!—died giving birth to Mattias. And then mere months ago his father went to sleep healthy and was pronounced dead in the morning.

Mattias took the crown.

He had no respect among the people nor likely his own militairen, and it was no wonder.

Anouk returned her toast to the plate without taking a second bite. Her hand trembled and she swallowed twice before facing me with a grim exhale. "He married me because he thought I was the Wishtress. He thought I was *you*."

My own toast tumbled to my lap. "Me?"

"The day you ran after Sven in the markt, militairen scouted out our booth. Someone had tipped them off that Oma was dealing in wishes. You weren't there. For some reason they concluded that *I* was the Wishtress."

King Mattias wanted a wish. More than that, he wanted to *own* the Wishtress . . . as his wife. Where he could use me as often as he desired. An endless supply of wishes. "Does he know you're not . . . that I'm . . . ?"

"He knows now." Anouk touched her cheek almost unconsciously. "For a while he thought I was simply trying to protect my secret. But then he found a Talented who could read other people's Talents. The man confirmed I had none."

"And he . . . kept you here?"

"I'm his wife. The new queen, Wishtress or not. There are still advantages to that. He married a commoner to gain the trust of his people and his council. An alliance of sorts with his own kingdom. It's a wise move to start rebuilding trust."

Yet he was still searching for the Wishtress. "Why does he want a wish?"

"I can only guess, but there are several reasons that make sense. I think he wants to find his father's murderer to prove to the people he's innocent. A wish would make that easy."

The same way Coralythe used a wish that led her to her sons' murderer. To me. Of course Anouk would think King Mattias wanted to clear his name—she was always inclined to think the best about people. I was not.

"I also think Mattias wants to destroy the Well of Talents," Anouk added.

My napkin froze halfway to my mouth. "Destroy it? Why?" The Well was the lifeblood of Winterune. They said its water had magicked the canals and that was why our produce and harvests were so lush. Why weaken his own country?

"Because of King Vämbat's murder." Anouk's voice dropped to a near whisper. "The morning of his death, he was found in bed aged and burned as though all his life had been drawn out of his body by fire. He was so changed in appearance that his militairen thought him an imposter at first. But as he lay dying, he managed a single word. 'Talent . . .'"

"What do you think he was trying to tell them?"

"That a Talented killed him. Everyone thought it was someone with a Bane."

I frowned and nibbled at my toast. "That's a lot to assume given he said that singular word."

Anouk shrugged. "Perhaps, but Mattias already didn't trust the

101

Talented. You need to hide, Myrthe. Not even a half bell ago, the king charged a Talented to find you. To hunt you down. He even has a sketch of your likeness."

My appetite dried up. The king was after *me*. "How did he get that sketch of my face? How did he find out where I lived?" Surely Anouk didn't . . .

"He said it was a new ally."

Would Oma have betrayed me? Surely not. But now a *Talented* was hunting me? I hardly dared voice my other suspicion. "Could it have been Sven?"

Only as I asked the question did I realize I didn't even know what had happened to him. I hadn't even wondered. He'd been out of my mind as much as my curse had been at the forefront. "Where *is* Sven? Did he return?"

"He returned a month ago. He found it, Myrthe. He found the Well and came back with a Talent. But at a high cost. All his companions perished."

Poor Sven. He'd known the dangers setting out, but I knew the pang of loss all too well.

"He's in rebellion against the king now. Amassing a following in the forest. I don't believe he would have betrayed you."

Rebellion against the king. Sven had always hated the royal authority, hence his pilgrimage the very day after King Vämbat died. Which reminded me of how I'd told him about my Talent, of how I realized he didn't choose to love me the same way I'd chosen to love him. The thought didn't sting like it used to.

If nothing else, it made me feel freer in this new expedition of survival. I needed to break this curse—to find Mutti. To thaw the canal. But most importantly to *survive*. To be truly free.

I pulled the *Wishtress* book from my satchel. "I took this from Oma. She knew the last Wishtress before me."

I cracked open the book and passed it to Anouk. "There's a

page written in a different language and I wondered if you could translate it."

Anouk laughed softly under her breath. "I know a portion of the Verstad language, and it's been a long time since I studied it." She scanned the page all the same, brows pinched in concentration. She pointed to one word. "This means *Well*. Like the Well of Talents. And here is another word—*cleanse*." She read on, muttering the words she recognized. *"Water will teach. Talent."*

"What about the parts with the notes from other Wishtresses?" Where others claimed heresy against the Well and that certain statements had not been proven.

Anouk's gaze skipped down. "The only words I recognize are *tear*, *Well*, and *Talent*." She scanned the rest of the page. "I think that's all I have for you. But I can send a militair to search the schloss library for a translation volume or perhaps ask a Verstad scholar to read it."

"I wouldn't trust sharing this with anyone else just yet."

She nodded. It was enough to get started. *Well. Water will teach. Talent. Cleanse.* If nothing else, it led me to believe I needed to go to the Well of Talents. I'd suspected as much, but now I knew. I had a vision for my future.

Anouk thumbed the rest of the pages. "Is there a map to the Well of Talents?"

I shook my head. "No. I've turned every page." Though I'd yet to read them all. "And there's no map in the schloss?"

"Not that I've seen or heard since that commoner burned them all when we were children."

"I'd hoped the king might have one."

"I've never seen it."

I knew one person who'd made it to the Well. I needed to find Sven. "Thank you for your help, Anouk."

"Of course." She fidgeted with the lacy cuff of her sleeve.

Nervous about my leaving, perhaps? I couldn't imagine how lonely it must be to live in the schloss with no family, married to a murderous tyrant. How could I leave her here like this?

I took Anouk's hand. "Do you . . . like being married to Mattias? Is he kind?" I couldn't imagine so, but perhaps I could channel my inner Anouk and try to think generous thoughts toward him.

Anouk gave a half smile. "He's kind enough as a husband. Admittedly I hardly ever see him. I'm content with that. But he's a very paranoid king."

"How can you say he's kind when he *forced* you to marry him?" So much for being like Anouk. "You should leave the schloss. Come with me."

She shook her head. "I wasn't forced."

"But you swore you'd never marry."

"I changed my mind."

"Why?" Clearly not because she was swept off her skates by the prince's courtship. Did she *want* this life?

Anouk pulled a loose thread and a portion of lace fell from her cuff. She startled as she realized what she'd done. "I hoped being queen would provide me with certain resources that would allow me to . . . well, to do things that my regular life didn't."

Her vagueness piqued my curiosity. Anouk had never been evasive with me before. We didn't keep secrets from each other . . . until now, apparently. We were both hiding things.

"Oma used a wish on me." Her hands fell limp in her lap. "Years ago."

I stared, aghast. "Oma did *what*?"

"She took me in after my father's death." Anouk's voice turned cold. "Without explanation, she pulled a wish from her locked trunk and said, 'Anouk Valling shall never ask Myrthe for a wish.' Then she splashed it on my face."

No contract. Oma used a raw wish just as she'd commanded me again and again never to do. She was no better than Coralythe.

"I've spent years thinking about those words—the wish she used almost like a curse. And I finally saw a way out. I am no longer Anouk Valling. I am now Anouk Vorst."

Dread pooled in my stomach. I sensed what was coming and a hollow panic dammed up my words. All this time—all the years of our friendship—I thought Anouk hadn't asked me for a wish because she didn't want to be like Oma. Because she loved me more than my Talent.

Instead, she'd been biding her time.

"Myrthe, I wouldn't ask unless it was my last possible option." Anouk's voice descended into a vulnerable whisper.

I felt sick. Betrayed by my closest heart-friend.

"Do you understand what I'm saying?"

"You need a wish." She wanted a wish so badly she'd allowed herself to marry a *murderer* so she could finally ask me.

Anouk expelled a long, shaky breath. "Just one. For me and me alone. Not for Mattias."

I stared at the carpet. The idea of giving any sort of response felt as difficult as creating snow on a midsummer's day. *This* was why she was so happy to see me. Why she'd tried to find Oma after our gable house burned to the ground.

"It doesn't have to be immediate." Wariness turned Anouk's voice wobbly. "Take what time you nee—"

"How generous of you." My words were winter. Frozen canals and frosted skate blades.

Shocked silence was the only reply. Anouk never expected refusal. As well she shouldn't, because for years I *would* have handed her a wish—ten wishes, even—without thought.

But now she'd shown her true colors.

"I'd pay, of course." Something in Anouk's tone hardened. "Handsomely."

"I can't give you one, Anouk." For a moment I was glad I was cursed. Glad I had no choice but to refuse her.

"I could command you, you know." Her threat was hollow, and we both knew it.

"It wouldn't make a difference."

Anouk sighed. "I won't force you, Myrthe. But . . . won't you reconsider?"

"I told you I can't." My statement came out sharper than I intended, partly because the burning in my chest was making its way to my eyes and the only way I knew to fight it was with inner ice.

"I don't ask you to cry!" Anouk burst out. "Don't you have a single tear saved somewhere? Hasn't Oma demanded a restock by now?" She lifted glassy eyes to mine and must have seen the resolve in my face, because she threw herself to her knees and gripped my hands in her own. "I beg of you, Myrthe. Please . . . please grant me a wish."

This was too much for my shattered heart. I shot to my feet, tearing my hands from Anouk's. "Why do you need one?"

I regretted the question the moment it passed my lips. Anouk's answer wouldn't change my inability to help, and asking for a reason implied that I denied her simply because I wasn't convinced she deserved one.

Anouk's pleading died. "If my request alone is not enough to convince you of my need, I doubt my story will be either." She rose from her knees, breathing hard. "It's time for you to leave."

Anouk strode across the room, dashing any remnant of tears from her face, and pulled a golden cord resting along the wall. "You awoke a different person. I hardly even recognize you."

"You don't recognize *me*?" My laugh was sharp. "Your entire friendship has been a *lie*."

The militair who'd escorted me here strode in, hand on his sword hilt.

"Remove this woman from the schloss." Anouk turned her back on me. "She's not to visit me again."

I hedged away from the militair, but he wasn't the hesitating type. He yanked me toward the doors, no longer gentle or obliging. As he dragged me past dead tulip stalks and tumbling frostvine, I wondered for a moment if this exit—this rift in our friendship—was worth it.

The militair had me through the door before I reached a conclusion. I could see Anouk's ramrod-straight spine. I'd never told her about my curse. I hadn't even told her my mutti was alive. This entire visit was falling to pieces.

"Anouk!" I screamed. Anger. Desperation. Betrayal. Hopelessness.

The door swung closed. The militair tightened his grip and quickened his pace. I could put up very little fight as the increased movement sent knife blades into my joints. The anger I'd felt toward Anouk sloughed away, and instead I felt a surge of despair. Pressure rose in my chest.

I couldn't get out of the schloss fast enough. I strained against the militair—forward this time. He marched faster.

Anouk's words rang in my mind. How she called me "this woman," how she begged me on her knees.

I should have told her. Should have told her everything. I should have tried to understand.

Brisk autumn air hit my face. The militair thrust me onto the cobblestones. I barely kept my feet, stumbling to a halt beside another man presumably waiting for a carriage or horse. The militair set up post in the doorway, blocking reentry.

I suppose I should have been thankful he wasn't dragging me in front of the king. Hadn't recognized me, perhaps.

I fumbled with my satchel, biting my lip against the tears. They were coming. Death loomed. I sniffed hard.

"Are you well?" a voice said from my left.

A tanned young man rubbed his gloved hands together against the wind, a crumpled paper lodged in his armpit. My brief look was enough for him to see my face—to see my fight.

He paled. "You?" He reached for me.

I flinched away, my fingers finally closing around the small cloth. "I . . . must go." I barely croaked the words out. If anything, speaking increased the rise of deathly fire in my eyes.

"Miss!"

I stumbled away, running at a broken gallop toward the gates— away from the schloss. Away from my one dearest friend whom I'd failed and who had failed me. A sob tore from my throat and I splashed sleep herbs on the cloth. As I passed the gates, I clamped the cloth over my mouth and nose, throwing myself into the hedge-row off the road.

Darkness struck me before the earth had a chance.

CHAPTER 14

BASTIAAN

"I wouldn't touch her, sir. She looks dead." Runt nudged the woman's foot with the toe of his shoe.

"Her name is Myrthe." Bastiaan knelt and gently turned her head so she wasn't breathing in the dirt. This freed her fist, which clutched a damp piece of cloth. He caught a whiff of heady herbs. *Sleep* herbs. She did this to herself. Why?

"You know her?" Runt stopped nudging her.

"She gave me bread once." *She saw me.* "We've hardly spoken."

And she was supposedly the Wishtress. Right here in the most vulnerable position she could be. He could gather her up and deliver her to the king within a matter of minutes. Prove his loyalty. Gain Mattias's trust.

"Well, now you have to rescue her."

Bastiaan looked up, amused. "From what?"

"From whatever made her flee the schloss. If she's not dead, then it's up to us to take care of her." Runt must not have seen the sketch; otherwise he'd demand they turn her in.

"My, what a swift change of heart you've had." A militair had thrown her out of the schloss. Why? Clearly King Mattias had not known she was visiting.

Bastiaan took in her gentle features not quite at peace in her unconscious state. Then he saw it—a single shining white eyelash. Not age-white. *Magic*-white. Delicate and nearly hidden among its dark counterparts.

Her Talent Mark.

Wishtress or not, she *was* a Talented. That made her kin.

But his king had commanded him to deliver the Wishtress to the schloss. The opportunity to complete that task was here . . . in his very hands.

Yet it wouldn't be that easy.

King Mattias would thank him—possibly reward him—and then move on. He would not be compelled to make Bastiaan an advisor, let alone take his advice. Bastiaan was loyal to Mattias, yes. But he was also loyal to King Vämbat, may he rest in peace. And Vämbat had asked him to be his son's advisor.

That was Bastiaan's first task.

He needed more than a loyal act to complete that mission. He couldn't risk turning in the wrong person. He needed to make sure Myrthe *was* the Wishtress before he claimed a victory for the king.

Besides, she'd given him a good turn during a dark time. The least he could do was return the favor. For today, at least.

"Get the horses." He lifted her from the ground. Runt fetched the horses and they mounted. It took some finagling to get Myrthe situated in front of him.

"Where are you going to take her?" Runt asked.

"Windmill Cottage." He could take her into town to a healer. But selfishly he wanted to be with her when she woke. He wanted to hear her story.

"You're taking her to *our* house? But what if she's not right in the head? She did this to herself!"

110

"I'd like to know why." He clucked his stallion, Sterk, into motion. "Windmill Cottage is a place of refuge and always will be."

"Yeah, yeah." Runt rolled his eyes. "Don't expect me to share my room."

"I wouldn't dream of calling your stinky bog of a sleeping space a place of refuge."

CHAPTER 15

MYRTHE

For the second time since being drugged, I woke in a dwelling not my own. It was an odd room—hexagonal with a single spiral staircase disappearing into both the ceiling and the floor. A rhythmic creak of wood drew my attention to the lattice window in time to see a giant webbed blade sweep through the air. I was in a windmill.

My mind scrambled to bridge the time gap from the schloss to here, but only an herb-soaked fog stood out. I'd survived the emotional wreckage of my visit with Anouk. With the memory came the pang of loss again. How had Anouk worded it? *"I finally saw a way out."* A way out of Oma's wish so she would be free to ask me for one.

Why? Why did she need a wish so badly? If only she'd told me.

Another windmill blade passed the window and I pulled myself back to the present. Someone must have found me in the shrubbery. But who? I wasn't in chains, so it likely wasn't a militair.

The room was packed full with stacks of books, timepieces, ropes, maps . . .

Maps.

I hurried to the pile of rolled and folded parchments, catching glimpses of forests and rivers and webbed sketches of the canals. Could there be a map to the Well of Talents in here? I'd hardly unfolded a single one when tousled black hair popped into view through the floor. I snatched my hands away from my snooping.

I barely caught sight of a young boy's face before he disappeared back down the stairs with a holler. "She's awake!"

"*Runt.*" A low female voice. "That's not something one shouts to an entire house. You'll embarrass the lady." The boy mumbled something. "I'll go up," the woman said.

"Let me," a man interrupted.

Not about to be a caged creature awaiting the spectators, I scrambled from the window and made it halfway down the spiral stairs to meet my host. An ascending body blocked my way. A barefoot young man's body.

He pulled up short and we stood at an impasse for one startled moment before he backpedaled. He knocked his hip against the railing in his haste, mumbling words like, "Apologies . . . foolish of me . . ."

I recognized his face, though from where I couldn't recall. It stirred a pleasant feeling in my chest. Hopefully that meant these people hadn't captured me for the reward on my head.

The stairs deposited me into an open eating room of sorts— one part stove and one part pantry and one part seating. The boy, the man, and the woman stood in a bunch near the window, each side-eyeing the other until the woman stepped forward.

"Welcome to Windmill Cottage. Please have a seat." She wore wool trousers with mud-stained knees and a cloth to hold her hair back. A working woman. It made me feel better about the mud stains on my own calfskin trousers. I sat at the table.

The boy—Runt?—slipped onto a stool in the shadows across the room, nearly disappearing from sight and notice. The young man leaned against the stair railing, but the woman sat across from me.

"My name is Diantha, and this is my son, Bastiaan."

She was his *mother*? I sometimes forgot that grown people could have parents. Mine were dead—well, I'd thought they were. Anouk's were dead. That this man still had a mother—envy blossomed in me.

"He found you outside the schloss walls," Diantha went on. "How are you feeling after some rest?"

He found me. What had *that* looked like? "One typically finds mushrooms or berries, not people." I attempted a humored smile. "It must have been quite a shock."

"Far better than mushrooms or berries, I assure you," Bastiaan said.

He was the man who had been waiting outside the entrance of the schloss. But that wasn't the first time I'd seen his face. It had happened before that. His eyes were silver like a sharpened skate blade. "I believe we met somewhere else."

"At the markt." His low voice fell soft upon the room like fresh snow dust. "You gave me bread."

I tried to wrangle the memory. "Nowhere else?" I hadn't been to markt since before Coralythe. But I felt as though I'd seen his face more than once. In a dream, maybe.

He frowned. "You don't remember?"

"I gave bread to a lot of people." Though none quite so handsome.

He grinned but also seemed a little disappointed. "It was the day we learned the king . . . that King Vämbat died."

Sven ringing the frost bells. Me shoving through the crowd after him. People whispering about the Wishtress being the assassin. I'd been speaking to a man who sat forlorn in the dirt. He seemed so lonely and hungry. I wanted to warm him—both spirit and belly.

He'd taken the bread and shown me kindness. But the entire encounter was overshadowed by Sven's news about the king's murder.

Sven. I needed to get to him. "Thank you for your hospitality. I'd best be going."

Bastiaan pushed off the railing. "Are you well enough? Perhaps you should stay and rest another day."

Diantha eyed him with an amused quirk of her lips. If they didn't think I was recovered enough to travel, I must have given them quite the scare. "I'm well."

"I can see you to your home then," he said. "Is it in Fairhoven?"

"There's no home to see me to." I didn't know where to start with that. "I'm in search of a . . . a friend."

"Sven Hebzucht." Bastiaan seemed a little shocked when the name crossed his lips, but not as shocked as I was.

My former calm snapped to suspicion. "How do you know Sven?" Moreover, how did he know I knew Sven? Did he know I was the Wishtress? Maybe he was working for the king. Or perhaps Anouk hired him to coax a wish from me.

No. Anouk wouldn't do that. Would she? I no longer knew my cousin.

"Don't be alarmed—"

"Why were you at the schloss?" I demanded.

He paused for a single pass of the windmill blade. "I merely remember you and Sven interacting at the markt when he rang the frost bells. I've been keeping up on his new, ah, pursuits."

"That was a full season ago. How could you recall such a brief interaction between us after so long a time?"

"For you, giving bread to strangers is so frequent the events blend together. For me . . . it was a gift much needed but unlooked for. Those are the moments that brand one's memory."

It was foreign to imagine leaving a positive impact on someone after all the horrible revelations I'd awoken to. Perhaps I could use this to my advantage. "Do you know where Sven is?"

"I do."

So Bastiaan might be an ally. He might be trustworthy. At the very least, I could ask Sven about him.

"In that case, may I hire you as a guide?" What other choice did I have? Fate had handed me this gift. I'd best not waste it.

"I don't need coin."

"So you won't take me?" I placed my small purse on the kitchen table. It didn't contain many coins. Was this how Coralythe felt when trying to bargain for a wish? Destitute but desperate?

Bastiaan stared at the coin purse for a long time but didn't seem to be thinking about the munten. After a moment's thought, he took a deep breath. "I'll take you."

We were ready within an hour. Bastiaan refused to touch the coin purse, so I tucked it in my pack to give him later. If he was doing this for free, there had to be a reason. Possibly sinister. Or perhaps just stubborn gallantry.

The boy named Runt prepared three horses. Even though Bastiaan was my escort, Runt was our guide.

"We'll be there before dark." The boy hauled himself atop the tallest of the three steeds.

I lifted myself into the saddle of the mare designated for me—Diantha's own horse. I had ridden twice before in my life but enough to know that the oft-ridden horses were accustomed to being willing followers and less likely to bolt. I preferred the risk over riding in Bastiaan's arms again . . . unconscious.

He drew my gaze a bit too easily with his gentle voice and demeanor. Best keep my distance. What would Sven think if I arrived astride the same horse as another man?

Bastiaan exited the windmill in low conversation with Diantha. He carried a shoulder pack, which he slung over the rump of his coal-black stallion.

Despite the crisp air, the fields around Windmill Cottage were sprinkled with groups of women workers. They chattered together, finding joy in their work. Some rested; others beat away the chaff from the harvested stalks or hauled buckets of water from the small stream that wasn't connected to the frozen canal.

Warmth filled me as I scanned the fields, though I wasn't sure why. Perhaps it was their comfort and joy in their work here or the fact Windmill Cottage was home to so many. One woman caught my gaze. The smile slid off her face and she nudged her thin companion who sat in the dirt sawing at a thick root with slow, weak movements. The thin woman straightened and looked my way, but I dropped my gaze and turned my head so they could no longer see my face.

What a fool I was. A sketch of my likeness had been posted in Fairhoven. These women had probably seen it. They knew I was wanted. There was the smallest chance that Bastiaan did not yet know. We needed to get away from Windmill Cottage.

Now.

"I'm ready." I tried not to let tension paint my words.

Bastiaan mounted and nodded to Runt. Out of the corner of my eye, I caught the two women making their way toward us. Runt squeezed his heels enough to set his horse into a slow walk. Mine and Bastiaan's followed.

One woman lifted a hand. "Wait!"

I slammed my heels into the flanks of Diantha's mare. I let a scream loose—hoping the sound would propel the horse forward. It worked. She bolted and I clenched the reins in white-knuckled fists.

No matter how hard I pulled at the reins, I couldn't seem to get my weight back in the center of the saddle. I slipped back and back until my head slammed against the mare's rump and I abandoned the reins altogether.

Another slam of body on horseflesh and then I was airborne.

My body struck another. A surprised cry. Then *slam*. Ground. Limbs. Tumbling. Once I skidded to a stop, I pushed myself up, brushing dust from my face. The mare stood mere feet away, nibbling grass as though nothing had happened. Bastiaan's stallion danced around her.

I spotted Bastiaan behind me, a body length away. He pushed himself up with a groan. "So much for catching you."

He tried to catch me? At the very least, he softened my fall. I tried not to picture him tumbling off his stallion in a messy dive, only to miss and crash into the earth. I snorted, then covered it with a cough.

"Weather and woods," he breathed, offering a hand. "Are you alright?"

I allowed him to pull me to my feet and gripped him a moment longer than necessary to make sure my aching hip and leg would hold me. I glanced back. Windmill Cottage was a speck in the distance. I relaxed.

I nodded and rolled my neck. "Thank you. I'm not accustomed to riding."

"The mare is not one to spook. I don't know what happened."

I looked into his face, which might have been a mistake because it was very close. And the concern in his eyes was enough to make me confess my guilt right there. "She must have sensed my tension. And I might have urged her onward a little too . . . hard."

Why couldn't I catch my breath?

"We should continue on foot."

"No!" I cleared my throat as Runt caught up on his own horse. "No. That will be . . . I'd like to try riding again." I wouldn't be able to manage such a long walk, even if Bastiaan and Runt checked their own paces.

Besides, my pride wouldn't allow it.

"Then why don't you ride with me for now? Sterk can easily carry two." He gave a small whistle and Sterk clopped over to us.

That would be far worse, only because it sounded so appealing. "Thank you, but I'll manage."

I clambered back onto the mare, who seemed just as calm as before I bruised her with my heels. Bastiaan hoisted me into the saddle. I patted her neck and took the reins, trying to relax into the rhythm of her gait.

"Comfortable?" he asked, climbing back on Sterk.

"I usually entrust my body and balance to two skate blades, not an animal with a mind of its own."

He gave a surprised grin. "You're a schaatser?"

I floundered a moment between joy and sorrow at remembering my skate-racing days. "I was. Do you race?"

"I've not done so for a very, very long time." He nodded toward the boy. "But that's how I met Runt. He used to sharpen blades as a canal rat."

"And now he's your servant?"

"Bodyguard, actually." Bastiaan winked.

I smiled in spite of myself. He had a way of inviting me to forget the weight of my curse and the sting of Anouk's rejection and the nerves of seeing Sven again.

Sven now had a Talent. Would he be willing to share the location of the Well with me? After everything that had happened today, it grew hard to cling to optimism.

"So what's your story?" Bastiaan asked. "What you're willing to tell of it, at least."

I stiffened and the mare quirked her ears. I couldn't blame Bastiaan for asking—he'd found me drugged in a hedgerow after all.

He must think me mad.

Part of me wanted to divulge my story. See him recoil at the ugly truths. My guilt. At least then I would be *known*. Hiding my past was exhausting, and when facing a stranger it was tempting to find relief. But I couldn't let myself. Even now, Oma's lifelong warnings of staying silent, keeping information about my Talent invisible, guided me. Especially now that the king was hunting me.

Secrets were lonely things.

"There's not much to say. I worked the bread stall at markt and then our business went under. So I'm in search of a new life." Or *life* in general. Because death hovered too close for comfort.

"How do you know Sven?" His casual tone masked the layers beneath the question.

"Oh." Did I even know Sven anymore? "He and I are . . ." I stopped before saying, "in love." Were we ever? "I loved him," I finally concluded, but the declaration sounded awkward in past tense. "I've not seen him in months."

Bastiaan glanced sidelong at me.

"I've been . . . ill." The more I skirted his questions, the more unstable I sounded. For some reason I wanted Bastiaan to approve of me. I cleared my throat. "I'm recovered now, though."

"I'm sure Sven will be glad to see you so healthy." Bastiaan thought I looked healthy? "What do you know of his current pursuits?"

I knew next to nothing other than Sven alone had survived the Trials, had come home with a Talent, and was now involved in some militant group of woodsfolk. Could I share these things with Bastiaan? He knew where Sven lived. Did that make him part of Sven's group?

"This will be a very long ride if we can't manage a casual conversation," Bastiaan said.

"This is casual?" I joked feebly.

"It's hardly a quarter day's ride," Runt hollered from ahead. "No matter how awkward your conversation attempts, they can't last that long."

I giggled.

"That lad scares me with his ears sometimes." Bastiaan turned in his saddle. "In the name of avoiding a dreary ride, let's keep talking. I . . . need practice."

Practice talking? "Sven always wanted a Talent."

"And what about you? Have you always wanted a Talent?"

"No," I said flatly. "I've never wanted one."

"How could you not want a Talent?" This time Runt spoke.

"They're not always the good things people present them to be. People can misuse them. I don't want that responsibility."

I could feel Bastiaan's gaze on me but didn't meet it, afraid he'd see more to my statement than I intended. "Besides, I'm common."

"So is Sven," Bastiaan said in a low voice.

"Yes. He alone survived of his companions." And that was with my wish to help him. "I'm very proud of him."

"Yet he never presented himself in service to the crown. Instead, he used the chaos of King Vämbat's death to his advantage and is turning others against the new king."

"If that tenacity helped him get through the Trials, why shouldn't he use the advantages given him?" Why did I feel the need to present Sven in a good light? His reputation was not my responsibility. "Or do you think the Well is for the wealthy?"

Bastiaan's stallion huffed as though expressing its own opinion about the matter. "Back when the way was known, the wealthy got through the Trials because they paid someone else to defeat them. Commoners, at least, try to defeat the Trials on their own . . . but they end up dying. The system is faulty. The whole purpose of the pilgrimage is to reach the Well with a heart and mind ready to receive. It's about self-searching. Humility. It's to better oneself in order to use the Talent for the betterment of the country."

I felt robbed. I'd never traveled to the Well, never taken a pilgrimage of self-searching to prepare myself for a Talent. Yet I had one. The most powerful one. How could I have been expected to use such a rare Talent of wish-making with the appropriate wisdom when it was simply *handed* to me at birth?

"You seem to know quite a lot about the Well," I muttered.

"I've studied it my entire life."

My ears perked up. I was traveling with some impassioned Well fanatic. That could explain the maps in his windmill. "Have you ever been there? Do you know the way?" I tried to soften the desperate questions with a compliment. "You must know a lot about Talents."

"I learn all I can." His statement hung in the air, leaving me wanting. I didn't miss that he ignored my question about how to get to the Well.

"What do you know about the Wishtress?" was on the tip of my tongue, but I couldn't seem to ask it. It seemed too brash. Too soon. "So Talents are for serving the king?"

"He's the head of the kingdom, so in many ways . . . yes."

If I followed Bastiaan's line of thinking, he'd likely have me turn myself in to Murderous Mattias and be used as the schloss's personal wish maker. It would be no different from being Oma's source of income. "No wonder you disapprove of Sven."

"To take advantage of people's fear, of a kingdom's chaos, solely to gain a Talent is the wrong intention altogether." Bastiaan's statement pierced the silence like the sharp tip of an icicle.

"Sven must have done something right despite your disapproval. The Well gave him a Talent, after all."

"His actions caused King Mattias to grow more hostile toward commoners."

"The king *married* a commoner."

"That action is its own mystery."

And I knew the answer—he married Anouk because he thought she was the Wishtress, not in some attempt to unite the kingdom's classes.

"You can't blame Sven for the Murder King's actions." My firm statement sent a nearby bird into flight. The fierce flutter of its wings sent a warning. I was getting too defensive. This argument was leading me into the dangerous waters of my curse. *Get control. Rein it in.*

I couldn't compromise myself—my life—with care for others.

I needed to focus on myself in order to survive. A lonely path, but it was my only choice.

"Your Sven has amassed a disgruntled following. He's a threat."

"He's a champion for commoners."

"That's what *I'm* trying to—" Bastiaan's fist gripped the reins as though to suffocate the sentence he allowed to slip out. "Listen. He's going about it all wrong. Sven is stoking the fire for war, not dousing it. His focus is all about the Well, when what the people really need right now—what the kingdom needs—is for Canal Vier and the Handel Sea to be thawed. His focus is off—"

"Stop," I demanded.

He clamped his mouth shut.

I took one deep breath and pictured frostbite turning my heart cracked and white. I let it spread over the heat of emotions until it cooled into something hard and heavy. My next words emerged glacial. "I'm not interested in your opinion of Sven or if he's stealing your glory by helping the commoners."

"That's not what I—"

"I. Said. *Stop.*" It was unkind of me not to allow him to defend himself. But I had to stay in one piece long enough to get to the Well. If that meant insulting the man who'd pulled me out of the bushes, opened his home to me, and volunteered to guide me, so be it.

Besides, I'd paid him—or at least tried to. I owed him nothing more.

From ahead, Runt gave a low whistle and averted his gaze, trying to act as though he hadn't heard our exchange. I couldn't let myself care.

The horses plodded along, their hoofbeats a drum of sound between Bastiaan and me. Finally, when I thought he'd succumbed to my request of silence, he said, "You're quite a different girl from the one I met at markt."

Stay cold. Don't crack. "Yes. Yes, I am."

The evening turned a pale orange beneath the drowsy sunset sky by the time we reached the forest. If Oma knew I was riding under a dark canopy of leaves with a canal rat and a strange man cloaked in secrets, she'd have my hide. But a wildness had gripped me since leaving the schloss. A disregard for my own safety, my own life even.

"Almost there." Runt broke the long silence that had taken over our ride the past hour.

Bastiaan and I were about to go our separate ways. I shouldn't allow our parting to be so tense. He had helped me, after all. Significantly. Maybe I could ease into a casual conversation. Sprinkle some dusting sugar over the crusted mogul that was our current state. "So . . . you live in a windmill?"

He eyed me, fully aware of what I was trying to do. I gave a weak shrug, and he indulged me. "My mother and I restored and converted part of it into living quarters. The other part is for grinding grain, which we then sell to the villagers and the schloss. The bread you sell—rather, that you give away—is likely made from our grain."

No, it was made from wishes Oma used to create our own flour to sell. Did she know that her actions were taking away a part of Bastiaan's livelihood? "Your farmers. I saw all women."

"Strong, capable women who escaped oppressive employment. The land is for them. They dwell on it, farm it, sell its produce, and keep the profits. My mother is one such woman. I'm simply the man who tends the windmill."

I sensed far more to the story existed. How did Bastiaan find these women? What compelled him to turn over such a large piece of land to their keeping? He was hardly older than me, yet had accomplished so much. I was the Wishtress, and what had I done?

Allowed my wishes to be sold to the wealthy elite . . . and then misused for personal gain, which ended in murder.

"And how do you know where Sven is since you're not one of his supporters?" I shouldn't reenter these waters, but the question had been niggling in the back of my mind.

"Heard him speak in the markt. Runt gathered his location. It's one of Runt's many gifts—not being seen yet hearing and remembering everything."

"Is it a Talent?" Could children gain Talents? I hadn't cried until I was twelve, so I'd assumed Talents manifested at that age. Runt seemed to be somewhere around ten.

Ahead, Runt's shoulders tensed and he inclined his head ever so slightly. Listening.

"Runt . . . er . . . Runt doesn't have a Talent. Not from the Well. Not yet at least."

Not yet. So did Bastiaan plan to visit the Well someday? With Runt? He spoke as if it was accessible. As if he knew the location.

"How old does one have to be for a Talent?"

"Talents come at all ages."

He said it so certainly. "Where do you get your Well knowledge from?"

"Books. Interviews. Travel." He shrugged. "I've collected it piece by piece, year by year. There's so much more I still desire to learn. So many mysterious Talents that have such little research."

I felt his eyes on me, the same way I'd felt watched in deserted Fairhoven.

Did he suspect what I was?

"Halt!" Two men stepped into our path, bows drawn and arrows nocked.

My horse tossed her neck. Before I even tugged on the reins, Runt had leaped from the back of his steed and sprinted into the woods.

One man spun after him, taking aim. Bastiaan twitched. The

man's arrowhead dropped to the ground, severed cleanly from its shaft. He lowered his bow, startled.

Runt was nowhere to be seen. Only then did I realize the second guard's arrow no longer bore a tip either. He hadn't noticed yet and continued to aim his blunt stick at us.

I glanced at Bastiaan. What sort of man was I with?

"Gentlemen." Bastiaan sat relaxed in his saddle. "How can we help you?"

"No talking!" The one nearest us—bald and stocky—lifted the bow and only then saw the missing head. Bastiaan's lip twitched. The man dropped the broken arrow and nocked a new one. He jerked his chin toward me. "Down. Now."

Bounty hunters. These must be the men the king sent after me.

Bastiaan's amusement vanished. "No."

I scrambled from my saddle. "What do you want?"

"Quiet." Then, to his companion, the bowman said, "Gag her, Luuk."

"Now *that's* not going to happen, gents." Bastiaan stood in his stirrups. Two silver discs with wicked-sharp edges glinted between his fingers. "Your arrowheads were a warning."

"There are two of us and one of you," the bald one said in a shrill voice.

Bastiaan flicked his wrists, almost lazily. The discs struck the narrow wood of each man's bow, centimeters above their clenched fists, and stuck there. Bastiaan had two new discs in his hands before I could blink. "One for each of you," he said. "And I *never* miss."

The bald man lowered his bow. "I'm not willing to die for these orders," he muttered. His mate, Luuk, followed suit.

"What orders?" They weren't dressed like militairen. Maybe they weren't from the king.

Neither man spoke.

"Tell me!" I demanded. Bastiaan lifted the two deadly discs and raised his eyebrows.

"Sven told us to intercept you . . . and not to let you speak. So"—the man called Luuk scuffed his boot in the leaves—"will you come?"

Sven gave orders about *me*. "Okay—"

"Absolutely not." Incredulous, Bastiaan looked at me.

"This was my entire purpose," I said in an undertone.

"Ah yes, to travel bound and gagged at the point of an arrow into the arms of your true love."

"He's not . . ." Ugh, what did it matter? I didn't understand Sven's order any more than Bastiaan did, but I needed to see Sven. I addressed the two men. "Hand over your bows and then I'll follow you to Sven." I passed my reins to Bastiaan. "Thank Diantha for lending me her horse. And thank you for accompanying me here."

"You think I'm going to leave you in the hands of these ruffians?" He dismounted.

Bastiaan didn't owe me anything—he shouldn't follow me into trouble. But I couldn't deny that his company in this situation brought me ease.

The bowmen did as I demanded and headed farther into the forest. I waited for Bastiaan to collect his four thrown discs before following. "What happened to Runt? And what about his horse?"

"He's likely following us. Master of stealth, that lad. His horse will find its way back to the windmill."

"I'm glad to hear it." I fell silent, my thoughts gliding elsewhere. Somehow Sven had known I was coming. What bothered me most were the details in his order—that the men were to gag me. Silence me. Would they have shot me had I resisted?

Was *Sven* trying to collect the reward from the king? He wasn't that callous, was he?

I waited for the stab of hurt like when Anouk had banished me from the schloss. Waited for the hearth coals of betrayal to burn my throat, my eyes. Instead a tight anger pressed against my ribs, and I let it.

We marched through a dell, across a mossy sward, and ended up in a small camp made of canvas tent dwellings and even a little stone cottage. The low chatter of people joined the song of dusk creatures. How long had this group been here?

Several people sat around a small fire, warming their hands against the chill that arrived with the sunset. They looked up as we strode into their midst. Conversations stilled. Fingers fiddled with various weapons. One man shot to his feet.

Sven. Tall, blond, sunbeam skin. Familiar, yet unfamiliar. His youthful face held a new frost to its angles and scruff coated his jaw. His eyes met mine and then flickered to the bald man who'd threatened Bastiaan and me.

"The man was armed. What could we do?" The bald man shrugged.

"Thanks, Archer." Sven strode forward and wrapped me in a tight embrace. I didn't soften. "You're safe," he whispered. He sounded genuine.

"No thanks to your friends. They'd have shot us."

He steered me away from the others. The only thing that followed us was Bastiaan's gaze. All light friendliness had gone from him, replaced by the stalwart defender he'd become when facing the bowmen.

"Who's he?" Sven asked once we were in a private section of woods.

I stepped back, surprised. "You don't know him? I thought he was one of your followers."

"I've never seen him before."

"Well, he knew where your camp was. I met him this morning, and he acted as my guide here."

"You brought him into my camp?"

My heart was tempted to quail at Sven's anger, but emotions had to become my past . . . in order to give me a future.

I redirected my feelings into outrage. "He brought himself here. I followed. There was no other way for me to find you. You left no word."

"That's because I wasn't settled—"

"Furthermore, if you want to be precise, *you* brought him here. At least, your armed friends did." My breathing doubled by the time I finished.

Sven stood silent for a long moment, taking me in. "You've changed, Myrthe." His voice held admiration, but all I could hear was Bastiaan's similar comment that certainly wasn't a compliment. *"You're quite a different girl from the one I met at markt."*

"A lot has happened in the past several months . . . to both of us." Should I tell him of the curse?

"Very true." He led me farther from camp where not even Bastiaan's keen gaze could follow. "Have you come to join the cause?"

"I don't even know what that cause *is*. And as much as I'd like to be part of it with you, I'm here for hel—"

"I'm not simply part of it. I'm its leader. Oh, Myrthe, what a tale I have to tell you!" His blue eyes lit with the flame of memory, and my heart was tempted to warm itself at his hearth.

I lowered myself onto the mossy trunk of a fallen tree. "Then tell me everything." Sven felt the most loved when he felt heard. I'd learned this early on. And if he felt heard, perhaps he would hear me when I asked if he could tell me how to find the Well.

What if he refused to tell me? What would I do then? Could I attempt the pilgrimage alone?

"The Well was everything you could imagine. I wouldn't have gotten there without the help of your wish." He took my hands in his. "You saved my life, Myrthe."

"You would have come home victorious either way," I encouraged. "How did you even know how to get there?"

He glanced toward the fellows we'd left. Their chatter was distant and indecipherable. Far enough away for secrets. I leaned forward, giving Sven my full attention. *Tell me. Tell me.*

"Family knowledge." He put more space between us. I had the feeling he'd been about to tell me something else. Something more.

I needed to know what that *more* was. "You are able to keep it all in your head like that?" I tried to make my voice sound awed, admiring.

He swelled. "Most of it."

Wide-eyed and enraptured, I asked in a breathless tone, "But what if you forget the way?"

"Don't you worry, Myrthe. I know better than to rely on my memory."

That he thought I was truly concerned almost made me laugh. All it took was a decently placed compliment and he was eating from the palm of my hand. I wouldn't have noticed this before the curse—I was softer then.

"Family knowledge," he'd said. But he'd been raised by his grandfather who died several years ago. I needed more. "Will you tell me how to get there?"

"You haven't even asked about my Talent." He pretend-pouted like a petulant child.

So focused on finding out how to get to the Well, I'd forgotten about his Talent. Forgotten he was like me. Maybe he'd understand, to an extent, my loneliness. My struggles. Maybe I could use that as a point of unity between us . . . and I could ask about the Well again after a little time passed.

"Tell me about it," I said, though it cost me a slice of will to step back from the prior topic.

130

"I can see the future."

I gasped. "You can? How far ahead?" Could he see my future? Right now? Could he read what my true motives were for being here? I suddenly felt vulnerable, a feeling I was learning to hate.

"I'm still figuring it out. I see snippets here and there. The Talent is very limited. I have visions, but they don't always involve me. I can choose what I see only some of the time. It also seems limited to a day or two in the future." He stopped to catch his breath, then grinned apologetically. "I haven't talked to anyone else about the details. They're not . . . well, they're not like us."

Us. For this brief moment, he *saw* me. Would that still be the case if he knew my Talent was broken?

Something cold inside me whispered he wouldn't. Sven was finally choosing me in return after I chose to love him. But I'd rejected that choice the moment I woke up cursed.

I didn't think I could rectify that.

I didn't want to.

"That's how I knew you were coming. Where my men could find you in the forest."

Any warmth of welcome iced over. "You wanted to have me *gagged.*" As I recalled the frightening scenario, my anger returned. "And forced by arrow tip."

"The arrows were for the man with you. I didn't know who he was or if he'd kidnapped you because of what you are."

Again, claiming to protect me. But his men had pointed their arrows at me as much as at Bastiaan. "And the gagging?"

"I didn't want you to be forced to tell the men about your Talent. I trust them with bows and arrows but not with my Myrthe. I couldn't risk them taking advantage of you."

Sven had never been this protective of me. I would have liked to think his pilgrimage had changed him, but it was more likely my newly revealed Wishtress status.

"So what's your cause? Why have all these people joined you?"

He scratched at the stubble on his chin. It made him look older. Fiercer. "We started with a petition to King Mattias, asking him to remove the Talent restriction for commoners."

"And?"

"Still waiting."

"Did you ask Anouk to help? Surely the king will consider her voice."

He scoffed. "She's his *wife*, not his confidant or counselor. Her voice is for singing him sonnets and soothing babies now."

I gaped. Sven had always admired Anouk—often to the point that I wondered if he'd rather be with her than with me. His opinion had taken quite a turn now that she'd married.

I couldn't see anyone from his camp through the trees. "Did you say other Talented live here?"

"A few. Most are hopeful to gain Talents someday. And then there are some with . . . special powers."

The way he said those last two words sent chills along my arms. "Banes?"

His mouth opened in a pleasantly surprised smile. "You know about Banes?"

"I've recently encountered someone with one. You're comfortable having these people in your camp?"

"There's nothing wrong with them!"

"Banes destroy. They cause *harm*." I pictured Coralythe's transformation once she started speaking her curse upon me. Powerful. Terrifying.

"Banes are a helpful tool against the king. Those with Banes are more warrior-like than the Talented."

I still had a lot to learn about Banes and Talents. I hadn't even been to the Well yet, so I bit back any further argument with Sven.

He knew things I didn't. He knew *the future*. "What happens if King Mattias rejects your petition?"

"I lead these people to the Well . . . and we destroy the Trials."

He was going to the Well. One way or another, I'd get there. At the very least I could stay in his camp until they traveled to the Well—either in rebellion against King Mattias or under the freedom of new laws I doubted the king would agree to.

There was no telling how long any of this would take. I wasn't sure I could last that long. "You really think you can destroy the Trials?"

Sven lowered himself to his knees and took my cold hands in his warm ones. "I have much hope, now that you're here."

"I'm just one more person . . ." My voice faded as his meaning sank in. I went stiff as an ice shard.

He kissed my palms. "You never told me if your wishes had a limit. Is it every tear or only certain ones?"

I yanked my hands away.

"Myrthe, surely you must see how important our cause is. Are you not for it?"

"You want wishes from me." Like Oma.

"Of course I do! For the people! To allow everyone to seek a Talent. To deny them that opportunity is to be in league with the Murder King. Don't you see, Myrthe? You would be the people's savior. I wonder if that is your purpose—why you were chosen as the Wishtress in the first place."

"Chosen?" I scoffed. "By whom?"

"By the Well. The power inside the Well. I don't think you're Wishtress merely by happenstance."

"You speak as though the king has already denied your petition."

"We're preparing for the worst."

"Sven, I can't—"

He pressed his lips to mine, silencing my protest. On a different day I would have sunk into his arms and clung to the brief affection. My heart would've danced in thrilled intoxication. I used to crave Sven's kisses.

But the intoxication didn't come. Instead I was irritated. *"I can't make wishes anymore"* was what I'd been about to say. I wasn't sure I had the strength to try again.

I pushed him away. He hardly seemed to notice.

"Think about it. It's a big decision, and I know it'd be a great sacrifice for you—"

"Wishes are complicated. Oma hasn't taught me how to use them properly yet." Why was I speaking as though I still had wishes to give? "You saw what happened to the canal."

"I know! Unbelievable power! It's crippled the king and turned more people to our cause. You've already joined us, supported us, *enabled* us. I ask for one more step. One more gift." He lifted my chin. "I have faith in you, Myrthe. I love you."

How ironic that when I was at my worst, my coldest, when I felt the most distant from him, that's when he chose to tell me he loved me for the first time.

But he didn't see me. He saw only my Talent. And his desire for a wish made him lie to my face. If he could truly see the future, maybe he'd see that I didn't trust him. I didn't choose him anymore.

I doubted that made a difference.

I couldn't wait around for his timing. I needed to get to the Well. Alone. Which meant somehow I needed to convince him into giving up the location of the Well.

Asking hadn't worked.

Maybe blackmail would.

CHAPTER 16

Imbeciles. Bastiaan resisted the urge to kick a boulder. His foot thanked him.

Sven's petition to allow commoners access to the Well would aggravate King Mattias. People were losing their homes and livelihoods because of the frozen canal, and Sven was feeding them a meal of misguided hope. *"If you follow me, I'll get you a Talent, and all your problems will be fixed."*

He was using tragedy as a tool.

Bastiaan never should have delivered Myrthe to him. He should have taken her to the king. Or, at the very least, demanded that she fix the canals. Yet if she hadn't thawed them in all this time, perhaps she *couldn't* fix them. She didn't strike him as the type of person to leave them frozen by will.

When Bastiaan first entered Sven's camp, he hadn't been sure about Myrthe being the Wishtress. She hid it well. But then he listened in on part of her conversation with Sven.

And he heard enough.

She was the Wishtress, and it was because of *her* that Sven had made it to the Well. But hauling her to the schloss was a different matter altogether. If she wasn't able to thaw the canals—or *chose* not to—that would land her in the schloss dungeon.

He wanted to understand.

The one upside was that he'd be attending the king's next council meeting. At the very least he could make himself heard and hopefully learn if Mattias had any other plans for the canal.

"Are you sure you want to stay here?" he asked Myrthe for the third time. He'd escorted her to keep her within sight, but he didn't like the idea of leaving her with Sven.

"I'm sure." Her gaze flicked to where Sven sat near the fire, his eyes burning with thoughts hotter than the coals. "I've nowhere else to go."

She spoke this last sentence in barely more than a whisper. Did she mean to say it aloud?

"Come back to Windmill Cottage. You'll be provided for there."

She shook her head and he let it go. Though he still stood by his dislike of Sven, he was willing to give the man a chance for Myrthe's sake. She had secrets—a Talent she wouldn't speak of, no home to return to, and a boy she said she once loved but seemed uncomfortable around now. Whatever other secrets she held seemed to torture her.

He knew how a Talent could be both gift and torment.

"Thank you, Bastiaan. Truly." She sent a resigned smile his way. "But I know my next course of action."

"Very well." If he'd learned anything from thirty-two years in the Stillness with the late king, it was patience. If he truly wanted to serve the king, he would handle Myrthe's Wishtress Talent delicately. And that meant he needed her to feel safe with him.

He swung himself into his saddle. He needed time to think, and he knew where to find her. "The mare stays with you. Hobble her near the stream and she can graze."

"That's not necessary." She fingered her skates as though they were an adequate replacement for a horse. But if he left the mare with her, she'd have to stay with it. His own stallion, Sterk, could always find the mare—so much so that Bastiaan often wondered if horses could have Talents. He attributed it to the canal water the horses drank. He'd always suspected a small vein of Well water resided in the canals.

The mare also offered a reliable escape if Myrthe needed to get away from Sven. Bastiaan wanted her to have something faster than skates and far faster than her limp. He nodded toward Sven. "Be careful with that one." Then he left.

He wanted her to feel like he was letting her go, giving her freedom and space. That he didn't suspect who she was.

That he wasn't a threat.

All lies.

Bastiaan stopped a half bell toll from camp, where he made his own meager camp. Runt would likely find him within the hour. He'd spent more of his lifetime sleeping outdoors than in. It was second nature to gather firewood, tuck his bedroll against a tree trunk, and allow the sounds of the woods to direct his thoughts.

Tonight they were about Myrthe . . . and the good of the kingdom. But to give Myrthe to King Mattias was to give him unlimited wishes. And the king wanted to prove himself, wanted more loyalty from his militairen—and had big plans he wasn't sharing.

Bastiaan would learn more at the council meeting.

He took the drawing of Myrthe out of his pocket. It wasn't an exact likeness. In fact, he wasn't sure a stranger would connect the picture with her. Who had described her to the king's artist? Someone knew Myrthe was the Wishtress but couldn't lead the king to her. Interesting.

Runt strode into camp carrying an armload of kindling. His horse plodded in behind him.

"Hey, Runt."

Runt dropped the kindling, removed his horse's bridle, and then hobbled it near Bastiaan's. "She was pretty fiery. Think she's the Wishtress?"

Talent Mark. Never visited the Well. Matched the drawing. "I think she is." Though he still didn't know how she *made* a wish. What were the limitations? Could she make one per month like Bastiaan's time snaps? Did she have to snap her fingers or prick her thumb to grant a wish?

"Well, I've thought it through. We can use the drugs from her pack—the ones she used on herself for whatever wild reason. Make her sleep. Deliver her to the schloss."

That had crossed Bastiaan's mind. "That would be the easiest way . . ."

"But"—Runt plucked a long thin piece of kindling from the pile and poked the meager fire Bastiaan had started—"why not get a wish for ourselves first?"

Bastiaan raised an eyebrow. Perhaps the boy *was* able to read minds. He hadn't brought it up to Runt for fear of stoking his thirst for Talents.

Apparently he'd already been stoked.

"We could use it to destroy the Trials, or to change Mattias's mind about the Well, or to transport us to the Well."

"I'm sure there are rules and limitations to her wishes."

"If one wish doesn't work, then we take another one."

"Take?"

Runt gave a sheepish grin. "Or ask her for one." He looked at Bastiaan. "Yeah, probably ask."

"You know what I always tell you."

"Yeah, yeah. Treat others with respect. Better than ourselves. On and on and on."

No matter how often he talked to Runt about treating others

with respect, Runt was almost always willing to take a shortcut when he wanted something. Someday it would bite the boy something fierce, and he would learn a hard lesson.

"That's right," Bastiaan said. "Respect. Kindness."

"Except for with the Wishtress, right? Because we have to turn her in."

The blood flow in Bastiaan's veins paused. "Well . . ."

Weather and woods, he was a hypocrite. Of the worst kind. Here he was considering turning in Myrthe with the hope that it would endear King Mattias to him. A selfish move, not obedient. But he was no henchman. To deliver one of his Talented kin to a king who deeply mistrusted the Talented would be like murdering Myrthe. Or at least murdering her free will. She'd become one of the king's pawns. "No."

"No?" Runt repeated.

"We're not turning her in." Bastiaan carefully folded the likeness of her along the existing creases. "She's one of us."

This could very well destroy what little headway he'd made with King Mattias. But if he couldn't hold to his morals as a Talented, then how could he hope to advise a king or fight for the rights of Talented?

"Us?"

"Yes, *us,* little parrot. A Talented."

"But I'm not a Talented," Runt moped.

"Not yet." He put the drawing back in his pocket. "We're finally going to change that."

"How?"

The fire popped as it met a piece of damp wood, sending sparks into the darkening sky. "After the council meeting . . . we're going to ask Myrthe for a wish."

CHAPTER 17

BASTIAAN

Only a fool went weaponless into a wolf's den.

"Name and business?" the schloss militair asked.

"Bastiaan Duur." *A fool.* "Here upon invitation from the king for a council meeting."

"Leave your weapons."

"I have none." Bastiaan had already left his weapons with his horse a mile from the schloss. He didn't want to insult the king, and if a serious predicament arose, he had this month's time snap.

An escort met him and Runt at the entrance and led them to the council room.

"Your manservant will remain out here." The escort gestured to the hallway where a line of other servants stood, backs to the wall, dutifully awaiting the return of their masters.

"You hear that, Bastiaan?" Runt muttered. "You get to stay in the hall."

Bastiaan swallowed his smile and almost pinched the boy. Runt was not his servant, but they often let the assumption stand when it benefited them. Runt gave a sarcastic bow, then took his place with the other servants. The escort checked Bastiaan for weapons before allowing him to enter.

The small room housed one long table in the shape of a horse-shoe with a high-backed throne chair at the top of the curve. A few people milled about, all men except one: a lone woman among the king's advisors was draped in flowing shades of purple. Bone-white skin with black hair cascading down her back. She engaged in no mingling nor conversation. Was she as new as he or just so mysterious looking that no one dared approach her?

She stepped to the table and sat to the left of the king.

Mattias finished greeting the other attendees and then approached Bastiaan with a young man at his side. "Welcome to my council, Bastiaan Duur. This is Baron Hartmut, my personal advisor and scholar regarding Talents and Banes."

"Ah, a man who shares my passions." Minus the Banes. Bastiaan extended his hand.

Hartmut smirked indulgently and took the proffered hand. "Why the glove?"

"It covers my Talent Mark and keeps me from using it accidentally."

Hartmut gave a nod. "The king mentioned you were a Talented. I appreciate that you don't hide it. When did you make the pilgrimage?"

"Many years ago." His Talent Mark burned with a calling to snap, to stop time. Surprised by the sudden urge, he forced the temptation away.

"It can't have been *that* many years ago. You're no older than two score."

Technically it was five years, but to Bastiaan it was two lifetimes ago. "I suppose when one fills each day with life, it makes time multiply." Bastiaan adjusted his glove. "It feels long ago to me."

"Well said." Hartmut ran a hand through his light hair and

Bastiaan caught the Talent Mark on his temple. He suspected that was Hartmut's intention.

"Any news regarding the Wishtress?" King Mattias asked as Baron Hartmut took his seat to the right of the king's chair.

Bastiaan bowed. "I've learned of her whereabouts."

"And where might that be?"

"With the woodsfolk rebels." Since Mattias was already trying to locate the rebels, this changed very little for him . . . except perhaps incentive.

The meeting bell rang.

"I'm disappointed you haven't made more progress." King Mattias moved to his place. Bastiaan waited until all seats were filled and took the last one. "Shall we begin?"

The chattering quieted and faces turned to the young king, some amused, some prepared to listen. How many council sessions had Mattias led thus far? It didn't seem like all the members took him seriously yet.

"I've learned more during these first several weeks as king than I have my entire life as prince. Some of that has come from your advising." Several members turned smug, but Mattias hadn't necessarily said it as a positive thing. "Most has come from those willing to risk their reputations and lives to bring me knowledge. To strengthen my hand as king."

Bastiaan gathered from the frowns that this hadn't come from council members.

"Of the ten of you here, four have Talents."

Aside from Bastiaan and Hartmut, who else had a Talent? And what were those Talents? Two men swelled a bit, the smugness remaining on their faces.

"My father never trusted the Talented," Mattias went on. "Not even those on his own council." Clothes shifted like the ruffling of feathers. "He once told me, 'If you leave them be, they will leave you be. They're like spiders. Let them spin their webs and catch their flies, but in their own corners of the world.'"

Bastiaan had heard those exact words from King Vämbat's mouth at the beginning. And he'd heard them retracted at the end.

Mattias's face hardened to granite. "Yet a spider dared to scuttle out of its corner and murder him."

No. It wasn't like that.

"My father was wrong. The Talented don't keep to their corners or webs. They're among us." Tense silence robbed the room of its air. "That's why we had a census—not to number the people of our great capital, but to keep track of the Talented."

Bastiaan folded his fingers so tightly that a knuckle cracked. He hadn't shared the details of his Talent with Mattias yet.

"Few of you know that a Talented saved my life when I was a boy. My eldest brother, Prince Dedrick, feared I would steal the crown, so he had me abducted to be sent across the sea to Timberfell. A Talented rescued me and saw me returned safely to the schloss. When I asked this man why he saved me, he said . . ." Mattias clapped a hand on Baron Hartmut's shoulder. "Do you remember, Hartmut?"

Hartmut responded in a low voice. "I said it is the duty of a Talented to serve the king. That's why we exist."

"Indeed you did." Mattias turned his gaze to Bastiaan. "Do you agree, Bastiaan?"

Taken aback by the sudden address, Bastiaan answered before he could censor his own bluntness. "I agree that it's the duty of a Talented to serve the king, just as it is the king's duty to serve the people. One cannot find balance without the other."

"Candidly spoken. Balance. This is why I must bring order to the madness my father's system left behind. And so I've visited the Nightwell."

Bastiaan's throat went dry. Several men blustered nonsense

while a handful of others paled and remained silent. This . . . this was not what he'd expected from the new king.

One of the men, Duke of something, managed to find his voice. "That is . . . that's punishable by death!"

Mattias's mouth twisted. "Ironic, isn't it? That it would be punishable by death, and yet the past five kings of Winterune have all visited it, immersed themselves in it, and returned home with a Bane."

"Are you saying King Vämbat had a Bane?" In all his time with the former king, Bastiaan had neither heard of nor seen evidence of a Bane in him. Vämbat was against the Nightwell as fiercely as he was against commoners receiving Talents.

"Indeed I am. But he didn't use it, nor did he share the location of the Nightwell with me. Had fate not intervened, the secret of the Nightwell would have been lost with the death of my father."

Unless, of course, Bastiaan knew the location of the Nightwell. Which he did.

"That would have been a relief!" the duke said. "What are you saying, Mattias?"

Mattias waved a hand with a sigh. "I'm saying that the Well of Talents has failed us. It is nearly unfindable and it gives Talents to those who misuse them—assassins, rebels, enemies of the country."

Bastiaan struggled to defend the Well in his mind. It was true that the few with Talents were hurting the kingdom, hurting others. But that was because the kings had restricted access to the Well. It was because there were fewer Talented, and they were not allowed to serve the kingdom without risk of execution.

Right?

"The Well gives and denies Talents to whomever it chooses. *It* is acting as king and I will stand for it no longer." King Mattias met Bastiaan's gaze and held it. As if the next words were spoken only for him. "I'm ordering the Well of Talents to be filled."

Shocked silence stole all voices. At last one advisor managed to choke out the question on Bastiaan's mind. "Filled?"

Mattias leaned back in his chair. "We'll gather several barrels of the Talent water for the schloss coffers. Those who desire a Talent must come to me. No one need die by the Trials—that should please the little band of rebels currently dwelling in the forest—and no more unknown Talented will run around murdering kings."

"Are you sure this is the time for such drastic action?" the duke asked. "People are starving, winter is coming, there were no crops because of the frozen canal, and we received no trade. We can't even *find* the Well!"

"Bringing the Well to the schloss will allow many more people to receive Talents. As we monitor those Talents, we will hopefully find one that can thaw the Vier. Do you have a different solution, Duke?"

The duke balked. "What about those of us who've been waiting patiently for our turn to drink of its water? Will we be given access?"

"You can submit a formal request to your king," Mattias said almost lazily, then turned to Hartmut, who whispered something to him. No one else seemed to find their voice. Not even Bastiaan.

He hated and feared the Trials, but they at least were neutral. To have King Mattias as the deciding factor between receiving Well water or not—it changed everything.

"My militairen will take action within a fortnight," Mattias said.

Another advisor stood and lifted his hands in calm. "You've undergone a lot of strain these past few months, Majesteit. Losing your father, assuming the role of king, taking a bride, attempting your own pilgrimage to the Well . . . Should we not consider other options before stoppering up a Well that has served our kingdom and people for centuries?"

King Mattias had visited the Well? Cryptic clues clicked into place. No wonder Mattias seemed bitter toward Talents. Bastiaan had seen this type of bitterness before. Mattias had been denied a Talent like Bastiaan's former master, Dehaan, had been.

"A king is always under strain," King Mattias said. "This is no rash decision on my part. But fret not, Duke. I have a gift for you. For all of you. Come." He stood from his chair so swiftly, Hartmut reached out a hand to keep it from toppling.

Then King Mattias left the council room, the woman and Hartmut trailing him. Bastiaan hurried after them, not about to miss a thing. The scraping of chairs and disgruntled mutters followed.

They passed the line of servants, and Runt didn't even glance at him. An expert spy, that boy. Though the widening of his eyes showed his confusion. Bastiaan offered a small shrug without eye contact.

They descended into the belly of the schloss. Down great corridors and wide staircases and then narrow hallways and dark stone stairwells. The duke puffed to keep up. King Mattias didn't slow.

Two militairen joined the procession. It gave the appearance of nonthreat, but Bastiaan wished he had his weapons all the same. At least he had a time snap. He tugged his gloves off and stuffed them in his belt, just in case.

Hartmut whispered to the king. Bastiaan couldn't shake the feeling that somehow Hartmut knew his thoughts. But in all Bastiaan's studies, he'd never come across a Talent that allowed someone to read minds.

Hartmut's Talent Mark was at his temple, so his ability was likely something mental, like Sven's ability to see the future, though Bastiaan had yet to locate Sven's Talent Mark.

"Through here." They were in corridors of stone and the air smelled damp and old. The muttering of water lapped at Bastiaan's ear. King Mattias walked through a wide stone archway into an open room where a web of light reflected off a pool of water in the center of the room onto the walls and ceiling, illuminated by lit sconces.

Though no current existed, the water churned and moved on its own. The hairs along Bastiaan's arms stood up. This water was magic. But not the magic he was accustomed to.

"Water from the Nightwell," King Mattias pronounced. "A gift brought to me by a most loyal subject."

"What have you done?" the duke said. The other council members stared at the water with something akin to desire. "You expect us to acquire a *Bane*? Banes are destructive. Those with a Bane should be stamped out!"

The woman in purple tensed. Mattias placed a hand briefly over hers. "What you call destructive I call . . . different. I've found a cure for our land. Isn't it obvious? The wealthy want a Talent. The commoners want a Talent. Even my militairen want Talents. We all crave power, but Talents are too wild. Too dangerous if they are not loyal to the king. The Wishtress herself has been trading wishes behind our backs for years, unwilling to serve the people or the crown."

Behind him, Hartmut gave a firm nod. Bastiaan felt more and more uneasy. The king knew Bastiaan had a Talent, yet he spoke against the Talented.

Bastiaan was in danger.

Two militairen filled the exit arch. That wasn't coincidence. If things went wrong, he'd have to use his time snap to get out. Until then, he needed to risk what tenuous position he had to gain as much information as possible.

"So what are you suggesting?" the duke demanded, though Bastiaan suspected the answer.

"We give the people Banes. And you're to be the first."

A few council members released sounds of awe.

"How do you know it's safe?" one man asked. "We have texts on the Talents, but I know of none on Banes."

Bastiaan knew of at least two texts on the Banes, but they weren't very thorough. He'd tracked them down during one of his times in the Stillness and read them through multiple times.

"Because *I* have a Bane. As your king I would not ask you to do something I wouldn't do myself. You'll have to trust your king."

Trust your king. Receive a Bane. Or else.

The militairen at the entryway rested their hands on their hilts now.

"So what of the Talented already in your land? Those already loyal to you?" Bastiaan didn't agree with King Mattias's course of action, but he agreed with Hartmut's assessment of Talents.

"I'm glad you asked." King Mattias's grin was as sharp as a fresh-sprung blade of grass. He held a hand toward Bastiaan. "Come here by me so all can see."

Bastiaan should have kept his mouth shut. He walked along the edge of the pool until he stood at King Mattias's side, facing the other council members.

"Reveal your Talent Mark."

Bastiaan obeyed and held his right hand aloft. A single thread of silver encircled the skin between his first and second knuckle.

"Tell them what your Talent is." Mattias's tone held a hint of testing. Bastiaan had never submitted himself for the census. His Talent had remained private. To reveal his Talent could bring suspicion upon himself regarding Vämbat's death.

So he lied. "Immediate transportation to a location of my choosing or, more importantly, the king's choosing."

"Aren't I a lucky king?" The sarcasm hung before Bastiaan like a pendulum of poison. King Mattias gestured to Hartmut, who brushed his hair away from his temple to reveal a constellation of silver dots. "The baron has a rare and magnificent Talent of being able to discern another's Talent through mere touch."

Bastiaan's mouth turned as dry as heat-scorched earth. He'd shaken Hartmut's hand, but he'd had his glove on. Yet his Talent Mark had burned.

Hartmut knew exactly what Bastiaan's Talent was.

And he'd told King Mattias.

"Those who are truthful and swear fealty to me will be monitored and given commands to test their loyalty. But the deceivers must be dealt with, yes? We cannot reward twisted hearts with more power." It was as though Mattias spoke to Bastiaan alone.

"Let me introduce Lady Coralythe." The woman at his left stepped forward. Bastiaan moved to return to his spot among the council members, but Mattias gripped his shoulder. "Stay." Then to the room he continued, "Lady Coralythe brought me this gift of Nightwell water. It has proved very worthwhile."

He pulled back his sleeve. Deep purple vapor rose from his skin like a sleepy mist. "Purple . . . like royalty. The Nightwell acknowledged my status as king and it gifted me two Banes. Coralythe, tell them what the first Bane is."

She inhaled through her thin nostrils and seemed to swell with strength. "It binds all those with Banes to King Mattias—both their loyalty and their lives."

This time, no questions came forth. Bastiaan couldn't manage even a swallow.

"Go on," the king commanded.

Her lips pursed for the briefest moment. "I have a Bane. The king can command me and I cannot"—she cleared her throat—"I *will* not disobey him. Should I betray him . . . I would perish."

She tried to word this delivery as something powerful. Something to be admired about King Mattias. But even Bastiaan caught the tremulous note of fear in her voice. Almost as one, the council members backed away from the Bane water.

Mattias laughed. "Are you so afraid to obey your king? You all claim to be loyal to me. What difference does my Bane make to you if you're already so obedient?"

A trap of tongue. To resist a Bane would be to declare disloyalty. To get one would be to hand over one's free will to the Murder King. Did Mattias's Bane have limitations? It sounded like he needed to speak commands to a person directly in order to compel them to obey.

This woman—Coralythe—had brought King Mattias the Nightwell, and now she was bound to him. The rest of the council was about to experience the same fate.

Bastiaan eyed the pool. Its waters shivered under his gaze. What would happen if he submerged himself? What would happen to his Talent? He had suspicions. Theories. In truth he didn't want to find out.

"My second Bane is a bit more . . . unique." Mattias seemed to grow in power the longer he talked.

"As I floated beneath the surface of the Nightwell water, I asked it for a second Bane. It granted my request, and instead of telling you about it, I thought I'd offer a display. It's what we do to those who misuse their Talent. To the man who claims to have a Talent of transportation but is *actually* able to stop time for everyone but himself." He gripped Bastiaan's wrist.

Weather and woods, Bastiaan was found out. He couldn't fix this. If he snapped while King Mattias was touching him, the king would enter the Stillness too. Not ideal, but Bastiaan would do it if necessary.

King Mattias lifted Bastiaan's marked hand for all to see. "When such deception happens, I will take action against the liar. This man here has a Talent to control time. According to Hartmut,

Bastiaan does not age when he stops time, but anyone who joins him in his stopped world *does* age. When my father showed up in his bed, burned nearly to death, he was old. Weathered. Decrepit."

Bastiaan's ears rang. He'd thought he'd been so careful, but King Mattias was too shrewd.

"I have reason to suspect Bastiaan Duur used his Talent to murder my father, King Vämbat." He turned to Bastiaan. "Do you deny it?"

Nothing else to do. Bastiaan sucked in a deep breath and snapped his fingers, summoning the Stillness.

Noise remained. Nothing changed. Mattias's fingers tightened around his wrist. Bastiaan double-checked that his glove was off, and that was when he saw the Nightwell vapors from King Mattias's Bane. They'd wrapped around his hand and the silver string around Bastiaan's finger flickered like a candle in the breeze.

He felt suddenly empty. "What . . . what have you done?"

Mattias released him. "You tried to deceive me, Bastiaan Duur. So I've taken away your Talent."

CHAPTER 18

No. No one could take away a Talent. It was a gift from the Well. It was *his*.

King Mattias jerked his head at the militairen. "Dungeon."

Hands rough as a windstorm. Armor clanking like thunder. Bastiaan was swept from the room before he could push a single protest through his numb lips.

He was a fool. He should have been able to read Mattias better, but spending thirty-two years away from people had taken its toll. He'd returned to the moving world more unaware than when he'd left it.

King Mattias's voice followed him out, moving on now that Fairhoven's spider had been caught. "So you see, gentlemen, why we cannot allow Talents. Particularly to commoners. Now who wants to enter the Nightwell water fir—"

The door slammed shut. Since his infiltration of King Mattias's council had failed, there was no time to waste. No reason to comply.

Bastiaan cracked his elbow into the shorter militair's nose. The militair cried out and Bastiaan wrenched himself free, dropped into a roll, then stood and sprinted up the corridor back the way they'd come. He reached the line of dutiful servants within a minute. "Time to go, Runt!"

The boy was not among the servants. He had likely heard the commotion and tucked himself into a spy nook. Bastiaan flew down the hallways and into the entryway, boots sliding along the polished marble.

"Bastiaan!" A cluster of militairen held Runt bound between them.

Bastiaan skidded to a halt and reached for his throwing discs only to come up empty. Blast. They were with his horse.

"You have to use one!" Runt hollered.

A time snap. Runt reached out his hand. In any other circumstance, Bastiaan would have used that moon's time snap to freeze all the world and then pull Runt into the Stillness. But today his Talent was dead. He felt it.

"I can't," he croaked.

Runt's face registered confusion, then hurt. The militairen pursuing Bastiaan caught up. His skills with throwing weapons and archery were unmatchable, but he had little to no chance of victory in physical combat, despite the training from King Vämbat. That left only one option—the one he loathed the most.

"I'm coming back for you, Runt!" He feigned a sprint toward the door. Militairen moved to intercept and he redirected toward the window. He heard the click of an arrow locking into a crossbow. *Three . . . two . . . one . . .* He ducked. The window shattered from the released arrow. "I'll be getting that promise!"

The wish. He hoped Runt pieced it together—he'd be with Myrthe. Getting a wish. Until he could rescue Runt.

He leaped over the sill, bursting through the crumbling lattice and glass shards. At a whistle his stallion abandoned the stables and intercepted him. Within moments he was galloping away from the schloss, leaving behind a weeping boy.

CHAPTER 19

MYRTHE

I scanned the camp for Sven before sneaking to the firepit with an armload of kindling. This truly was ridiculous. I shouldn't feel *guilty* for gathering firewood.

I set it down, then stacked it quickly. Large pieces in one pile, smaller sticks in another.

"I thought I told you to stop that." Sven strode from his tent to my side.

Winter's breath. "I want to be useful."

"You know how you can be useful . . . and this isn't it."

Give him a wish. Give him ten wishes. Become *his* wish business. "I can't yet." I cringed. *Yet.* I'd started speaking as though I *planned* to give him a wish. That wasn't the message I wanted to send at all, but I couldn't find any other way to deter him.

If I told him I couldn't create a wish, he'd be angry and then he'd never tell me the location of the Well.

"You did it so easily by the canal that day."

The day I wished I could undo. "Some days it's easier."

"Why don't you get some rest?" He took the sticks from my hands. "Let *me* take care of *you*."

154

The past two nights he'd given me a sleeping pallet and plenty of food and asked if I'd thought about his request. He'd been kind. Sweet. Caring. All the things I used to long for.

All for a wish.

In return I'd asked him—twice more—about directions to the Well. The last time I brought it up, he seemed suspicious so I stopped. And I'd spent the past several hours honing my blackmail.

It would include lying. I didn't like that, but what other choice did I have?

Every scenario started with, *If you don't tell me how to get to the Well, I'll use a wish to . . .*

To what? He had no family to threaten. I wasn't sure what he cared about other than his own status.

. . . *to make you ugly.*

. . . *to make you forget your own story, like I did to Mutti.*

. . . *to force you into servitude under the king.*

The more I crafted my threat, the more I realized I didn't know Sven. I didn't know what he cared about, not deep enough to ensure my threat would result in him caving. Then there was the fact I couldn't follow through on any of my threats in the first place.

Not only that, but I didn't want to *lie*. It would all come down to the wording.

I'd hoped I would have gotten his cooperation by now and been long gone. But I was still here. Still letting Sven think I was staying for him. I tucked the secret of my curse away. At the very least I was safer and more protected here than in Fairhoven with my likeness posted on trees and boards in the markt.

"I don't need rest." I sat back on my heels, watching Sven toss the handful of sticks into one of the piles without even sorting them.

"Myrthe, I want you in my inner circle." His whisper met my ear like a tender kiss. I resisted the urge to lean away.

Heart: *Why now? Why not when I was willing to be yours?*

Mouth: "I'd like that."

How cruel that to keep my heart beating I had to silence it.

"What exactly does your inner circle involve?" Maybe people in his inner circle knew how to get to the Well. Maybe this was progress.

"Come to the meeting tonight. You'll see. We're the ones with the fire of conviction."

I didn't have a fire of conviction for Sven's vision. What if they did succeed and destroyed the Trials? More people would have Talents.

More people would make mistakes like I did.

More boys would die in frozen canals.

The dirt-muffled clopping of hooves met my ears. I spun. Had the mare gotten loose?

Bastiaan and his horse, powerful as thunder, approached through the trees. Foreign relief loosened the skate laces constricting my ribs. Surprise followed. How had my comfort shifted to being unsure around Sven and reassured by the appearance of Bastiaan the stranger?

He dismounted and acknowledged me with a pained nod that hid the story of whatever had happened since I last saw him.

His first words were directed at Sven. "I have news from the schloss, direct from the king's private council. Gather those you wish to hear it."

A brief battle of emotions swept over Sven's face: irritation, insult, curiosity. It passed with a clench of his jaw and he nodded. Then his gaze lost focus and he frowned. "You need help. That boy . . . He's imprisoned in the schloss."

I gasped. "Runt?"

Bastiaan grimaced. "How can you know that?"

"My Talent," Sven answered simply, then said to me: "They chased Bastiaan and got his servant instead."

"He's not my servant," Bastiaan growled.

"Bastiaan can tell us everything once we're gathered," I said. "For now, let me fetch some stew."

The pot over the coals needed but a single stir to release the heat. I ladled it into a crudely carved bowl someone lent to me yesterday and handed it to Bastiaan. He accepted it with a deeper gratitude in his eyes than he managed to express with his mouth.

Sven continued eyeing Bastiaan—for what reason, I couldn't tell. Bastiaan sipped some broth. "That was your vision for today? Runt's capture?"

"So it would seem. Not very useful."

"No other information about him?"

"Just the scene of you escaping through a window while mili-tairen dragged the boy to the dungeons . . . screaming."

Bastiaan looked like he wanted to drown in his bowl of stew. He managed another sip, but the effort to swallow the broth seemed as difficult as swallowing a river stone.

Maybe he needed a distraction, because Bastiaan asked in a forced-casual voice, "Where's your Talent Mark?"

He'd addressed Sven, but I frowned. "What's a Talent Mark?"

"Surely you . . ." Bastiaan glanced between me and Sven, who appeared equally as quizzical. His gaze rested on me for a pro-longed moment. "It's a silvery white marking that shows you have a Talent. I'd assume it's near your temple or your eyes. Another man at the council had a Knowledge Talent."

"Oh." Sven shrugged. "I guess I haven't found my Talent Mark yet."

"Didn't it burn when you received your Talent?"

Sven laughed off the question. "You can't believe everything you read about the Well of Talents."

"This isn't book knowledge—"

"We should gather for the meeting." Sven crossed his arms, reminding Bastiaan who the leader of the rebellion was.

"Of course." Bastiaan lifted the bowl back to his lips. I clamped my own shut. I wanted to know more. Talent Mark? Nothing on me ever burned when I made wishes. Was that because I was born with a Talent instead of obtaining one by drinking from the Well?

Bastiaan knew so much about Talents. The more I was around him, the more I was tempted to ask him about the Wishtress Talent. For now I squeezed his hand. "I'm sure we'll be able to retrieve Runt."

Sven noticed my hand on Bastiaan's and I withdrew it, cheeks aflame. My own reaction turned my embarrassment into anger. I had no reason to be ashamed of offering comfort to Bastiaan. I wasn't Sven's.

"Hurry up then." Sven marched back toward the main hub of camp.

"Thank you, Myrthe." Bastiaan removed the saddle from his horse. This time his packs bulged as though he planned to be in the woods awhile. He rested his head against the horse's flank for a moment. "My past has caught up with me and Runt is paying for it."

I returned my hand to Bastiaan's arm. I didn't know how to comfort without touch. I certainly didn't have words for his pain. Although . . . maybe I did. To an extent. "I know what it is to regret one's past."

He looked up, a brief sheen of hope in his eyes. Hope for understanding. "I'd undo it if I could."

"Me too," I whispered.

Something connected us in that moment—something that transcended arguments, differences, and the unknown. We both had regrets. And somehow we'd found each other almost as though someone beyond us knew we needed each other for this time.

I wanted to know his story. I wanted to share my own story. But for now, the silent shared ache beneath the tangled forest branches was salve enough.

"The mare is doing well." I gestured toward the stream where the mare had spent three calm days grazing. It had become my companion and listening ears as I shared my secrets and fears, for there was no one else to listen.

"I'll put Sterk with her." We headed that way together. Bastiaan didn't need my help, but I was tired of the emotional dance that took place with every conversation between Sven and me.

"What news did I miss?" Bastiaan led his horse by the reins toward the river at a comfortable pace.

"It's been rather uneventful." The people following Sven spent most of the day foraging, butchering kills, carving necessary items, and stonecutting arrowheads. Sven wouldn't tell me anything. Hopefully that would change at the meeting tonight. With his *inner circle*.

We reached the mare. "How often does Sven have a vision?"

"Once a day." I rubbed the nose of his horse as he removed the bridle. The stallion shook me off, not quite as affectionate as the mare. "Though he doesn't always share their contents." I often wondered how much Sven knew about other things. Secret things. Even about me.

Bastiaan opened his mouth, then closed it. Did he have the same uneasy feeling about Sven's vision? I wrestled with guilt over my suspicion. Wasn't that exactly what I had feared as the Wishtress? That if people—if Sven—knew what I was, they would fear me, hate me, use me, suspect me?

That's what Oma had raised me to believe.

That's what Oma *did*.

I couldn't afford to invite guilt to the hearth of my heart. I had to let the heart embers die out. Turn cold. Ice over so I didn't feel the things that would stir up emotions. I needed to approach my Wishtress Talent with indifference. Shut off the temptation to let others' needs sway me. So I needed answers. Knowledge. About myself. And Bastiaan was the only person I knew who had that.

I took a breath to steel myself. "You know so much about Talents . . ." *Tell him you're the Wishtress. Tell him now.* I took another breath—

"That's because I have one." The blunt way in which Bastiaan said this held resignation. Bitterness, even.

I stared, my sprinting thoughts crashing into a snow berm. Bastiaan had made the pilgrimage? Survived it? As a commoner?

He had a Talent! He was like *me!* "Why . . . why would you tell me?" I'd lived seventeen years chained to the code of secrecy. I'd assumed most other Talented did too.

"Because the whole kingdom is about to know." He wrapped his saddle and tack in an earth-toned blanket, then tucked the lot of it inside a tree hollow. "I wanted to tell someone of my own volition—as a friend, not as a strategic informant."

"Are we friends then?" I joked.

"I suppose if we have to be. I can endure it." His joke seemed pained, weighed down by whatever happened to Runt.

"So you've been to the Well?" What if Bastiaan could take me there? I wouldn't have to threaten Sven. Was there anything I could offer Bastiaan that would compel him to do so? He never accepted my coin, I had no wish, and our "friendship" certainly wasn't enough reason. If only I'd stowed away some of Oma's wish stash instead of smashing them!

"A long time ago."

"Do you remember how to get there?" My heart pounded. "Maybe you could tell—"

"Oy! Bastiaan!" Sven hollered from across the way. "We're ready."

Bastiaan stared at me. "We'd best go." Though we'd been interrupted, he'd heard my request, I was sure of it.

And he chose not to acknowledge it.

CHAPTER 20

ꙮMYRTHEꙮ

Acorns coated the forest floor like nature's cobblestones, hollowed out by wintering squirrels and ready for a coating of snow. As the last of the acorns fell, they hit rocks and branches in their descent, sending sharp cracks of sound through the forest, mimicking the snap of sinister footsteps.

Sven's inner circle met around a night fire. I wasn't sure what I'd expected—a table strewn with maps and plans beneath the canvas of a private tent? A group of bearded men ready to give counsel? Whatever it was, I hadn't expected it to be so . . . informal.

Two other people were present. A woman and man. "This is Hadewyck—" Sven started.

"Hedy." The woman lifted her chin in greeting. Aside from the fire glow on her skin, she exuded no warmth.

"Are you a Talented?" I asked outright.

Hedy lifted an eyebrow. "No." There had to be more to her answer. If she was in Sven's inner circle, she must have some special skill. Sven didn't surround himself with anyone average.

"Hedy likes to play devil's advocate." Sven sounded proud.

"Someone has to." She spit in the fire.

The man beside her had hair as red as lit coals and was nearly a head shorter than Sven. He raised a hand in greeting. "I'm Kees, the water to the ale in these two." He jerked a thumb at Sven and Hedy, who grinned. "And Hedy's big brother. So don't believe her when she says she can best me."

Had Sven always known Hedy and Kees? He'd never mentioned them to me, yet they seemed so bonded.

"I am a Talented," Kees continued. "We met Sven on our return from the Well—he saved our lives, actually. How could we not join the cause?"

Interesting that Kees and Hedy visited the Well of Talents together, yet Hedy didn't have a Talent and Kees did. Did he intentionally withhold the nature of his Talent, or was that an oversight? I didn't ask. Sven might not wish for it to be revealed to Bastiaan, who was joining the inner circle only to share his news.

"Bastiaan comes to us for help." Sven resumed his tone of leadership. "He claims to have news from the schloss."

Bastiaan wasted no time. "My friend, a boy of ten, was taken prisoner by King Mattias. He's being held as leverage. The king is hoping to capture me."

"Who are you, then?" Kees asked.

"A Talented. I used to advise King Vämbat in matters of the Well and attempted to do the same for King Mattias."

"So you're a king's lackey." Hedy snorted. "Why would we help you?"

"He's not a lackey," I snapped. "Didn't you hear him? He's *wanted* by the crown . . . like you lot."

Sven's eyebrows shot up. I'd never opposed Sven or anyone he supported.

It felt wrong. It felt *good*.

Bastiaan gave Hedy a small bow. "You'd do better to ask questions before assuming conclusions."

"Then why does the king want to capture you?" she shot back.

We'd hardly begun the meeting. Surely Hedy and the others could muster enough maturity to converse with respect.

"He believes I assassinated his father, King Vämbat . . . hence the capture of Runt. Leverage."

"And did you?" Hedy demanded at the same time Kees asked, "How do you propose we get your boy out?" Kees glanced at Sven as he finished with, "That's the matter at hand, is it not?"

Sven gave a single nod, watching Bastiaan. I had so many questions for him. *Did* he kill King Vämbat? The kindness he'd shown me would tempt me to believe it impossible, yet I remembered his skill with his throwing weapons. He was a man unshakable. If he wanted something, barriers shrank from him. I imagined even the Trials quaked before him when he took his pilgrimage.

"According to Sven's vision, Runt is likely being kept in the dungeon." Bastiaan's voice grew tight. "Do you have anyone on the inside? At the schloss?"

Sven shook his head. "No one we trust to be loyal to our cause."

I kept my peace, but my mind whirred. Sven didn't even consider Anouk. He saw her status as King Mattias's wife as useless and degrading. Was that his view of marriage or just of Anouk's choice to marry the king?

"That dungeon is impenetrable," Kees said. "Short of storming the schloss itself or contacting a Talented with powers that could aid us, there's no answer I see. Not even if all the militairen were unarmed." Whatever his Talent was, he didn't consider it something useful in rescue.

"I can't endanger the Talented in our camp for a lone man's dilemma separate from our cause," Sven said.

"What about those with Banes?" I asked. He kept talking about the Talents and Talented but wasn't owning up to the fact that he claimed to accept and even *approved* of Banes.

Bastiaan looked sharply at me. "Banes? What's this?"

Sven waved it off, but Hedy smiled darkly. "Let's keep to the matter at hand: We can't help you."

"Runt's predicament is not wholly detached from your cause," Bastiaan argued. "He knows your location. The king's dungeon master may very well be trying to pry that information from him as we speak."

"Then we'll move camp." The way Sven said this implied their conversation was over. No compassion. It made me sick.

Didn't he realize that if they saved Runt and helped Bastiaan they would have two loyal followers with great insight, connections, and a *Talent*? They hadn't even asked after Bastiaan's Talent! They were disregarding him before even knowing him. Sven was trying to rid himself of Bastiaan—that much was clear.

I could no longer sit in silence. "Sven. Will you really leave Runt in the dungeon? Possibly to die?"

"We've no way of rescuing him. It isn't worth the risk." He leveled a stare at me. "It's not like I have a wish in my pocket."

The breath left my throat. The neutrality with which he said these words—able to deliver a jab with such ease—disgusted me. His patience was wearing thin. He seemed to be a different person around Bastiaan.

Bastiaan's gaze flickered between Sven and me. Seeing. Reading. Waiting . . . for what? Sven to explain his asinine comment? Or did Bastiaan already suspect?

"So what's the news from the schloss?" Hedy challenged, as though she expected Bastiaan to withhold it now that he knew they wouldn't help Runt.

I officially disliked her.

"The king is going to stop up the Well within a fortnight." A blunt axe blade to the thigh would have been less of a blow.

I leaped to my feet as though to run to the Well that very moment. "So soon?" My outcry was lost amid the others'.

Kees's protestations rose the loudest. "He doesn't have the authority to do that. The Well of Talents doesn't belong to Fairhoven."

"Yet he's doing it," Bastiaan said flatly.

Sven seemed unconcerned. "He can't." That silenced us. "He can't stop up the Well because he can't get to it. There are no maps in the schloss."

"He's the king." Bastiaan sounded pitying. "He has resources we commoners can't fathom."

"I'm not common of *mind*," Sven retorted. "This is no desperate assumption. There's one map left intact and the king doesn't have it."

"Do *you*?" I asked. It was almost like he *wanted* one of us to ask.

"My grandfather is the commoner who burned the maps of Winterune."

My mouth went dry. "Your . . . grandfather was the madman?"

Sven cut me off with a sweep of his hand. "Not mad. He was *betrayed*. As a young man he was servant to a militair charged with getting water from the Well to bring back to the king and his nobles. The militair died in the Trials, but my grandfather completed the task. He risked his own life to bring water back to the schloss alone. He never drank any for himself, out of loyalty to the king." He said the word *loyalty* with a sneer.

"He was common and he knew the laws. But when he handed the water over to King Vämbat, he asked for a sip—a single sip. King Vämbat laughed in his face."

"And your grandfather turned on him," Bastiaan filled in grimly.

"As well he should! His own king spat on his loyalty and sacrifice! So he destroyed all the cartographers and maps of the Well of

Talents . . . except one. Eventually he traveled to the Well and got a Talent for himself." Sven's grandfather had died several years ago; otherwise I might have suspected *he* killed the king.

"His actions showed the king he was not worthy of a Talent," Bastiaan said. "Talents are for the service of the crown! Your grandfather murdered good men for his own damaged pride."

Sven pounded a fist into his thigh. "This is not about your righteous opinions, Duur."

Sven only ever told me he was raised by his grandfather until a militair ran him through for no reason. Yet he was a murderer. *He* was the reason Winterune had lost a part of its history.

He was the reason I couldn't get to the Well on my own.

Now Sven all but admitted to having the only map in existence.

"King Mattias has been to the Well once," Bastiaan said. "Whether he has a map or not, he knows the way."

Hedy seemed to be the only one not sickened by Sven's story. "Then we must get to the Well first."

"And do what?" Kees asked in a somber voice. "Die defending it from his thousands of militairen?"

Numb, I sank back onto my block of wood. This ruined everything. If the king stopped up the Well, I'd never learn what the water could do for me . . . or for my curse.

And I couldn't ask Bastiaan to take me to the Well now that he had Runt to rescue.

I was stuck with Sven and his constant badgering for a wish.

"We wouldn't get that far anyway." Kees's low rumble ushered a calm breath into the rising panic. "There are still the Trials. I'm not willing to go through them again."

Everyone went silent at this last comment—the men especially. The ones with Talents. The only ones to have defeated the Trials. Yet I saw no ease of victory, just fear. "We're going to destroy the Trials anyway," Sven muttered.

"What's the point?" Hedy shrieked. "Then we have a standoff against the king at the Well?"

"We can take stores of the Well's water for ourselves." Sven's eyes lit up as new thoughts sprang like sparks of the fire. "And then *we* could stopper the Well. The king would have no control. He'd have to succumb to *our* demands. We would be the ones with power."

That would make Sven as guilty as the king. Couldn't he see?

Hedy's hysteria transformed to a face of wild wonder. Kees nodded in contemplation. "We still haven't solved the issue of the Trials. I can't go through them again. Besides, how would we get barrels of water back without detection?"

"I have resources." Sven gave me a pointed look. Meaning me . . . and my wish.

He let the implications linger, then pointed at Bastiaan with a half-burned twig. "What's your Talent? Could it help us?"

Bastiaan's eyes turned sharp. "My Talent has been silenced." He tugged the glove off his right hand to reveal a deep-purple ring marked into his thumb like ink.

It seemed a big moment for Bastiaan, but no one gave much reaction. I had never seen a Talent Mark before, but I could wager a guess it wasn't supposed to look rotten like that. My wishes used to glow the brightest silver when bottled.

"The king has a Bane," Bastiaan said grimly. "Two, actually."

I gasped, but I was the only one. Bastiaan, at least, seemed to consider Banes dangerous. Why didn't Sven?

"Mattias's very touch destroys a Talent." Bastiaan sounded defeated. "And he has a Talented on his council—Baron Hartmut—who can identify someone's Talent. That's why Mattias held a census shortly after his father's death. He now knows who has a Talent and what that Talent is."

Kees paled. Sven shrugged. "I didn't attend the census call."

No surprise. "You said he has *two* Banes?" A combination of fear and awe painted his face. "How did he manage that?"

"The woman with him said it was because the Nightwell recognized his sovereignty."

Hedy cocked her head. "Mattias has a *woman* on his council?"

"She brought him water from the Nightwell. Which means she knows how to get there . . . so now the king does too."

"What does his second Bane do?" Kees choked.

Bastiaan faced Hedy when he answered. "It controls anyone else who has a Bane—makes them loyal to him."

For once the warrior woman went silent. Cowed. My suspicions were confirmed: Hedy must have a Bane.

"Winter's breath . . ." Kees gulped.

Winter's breath, indeed. That much control in one man—one man with a paranoid loathing for Talented *and* an unquenchable thirst for power. It would be the end of Fairhoven.

"I believe his Bane is limited to vocal commands, though." Bastiaan's words did nothing to ease Hedy's tense posture. "You'd have to be in his presence. It's a theory, but I believe I'm right."

"How can such a power exist?" Sven thundered. "This is tyranny!" For once, his smooth words fled him. He grabbed Hedy by the shoulders. "You'll be okay. We'll defeat him. You will *not* be his!"

"The Well has the power to undo your Bane," Bastiaan offered. Hedy glowered at him.

"Get the camp ready," Sven growled to Kees. "We're leaving by sunset tomorrow."

His protectiveness over Hedy spoke volumes. Strangely, it relieved me. It further proved that his affection for me was false. Shallow.

But the part that stood out to me most was Bastiaan's last

statement. If the Well of Talents could undo a Bane, surely it could undo a curse. I just needed to get to it. Now that I finally knew who had a map . . .

All that remained was for me to steal it.

CHAPTER 21

MYRTHE

I should abandon Bastiaan. If I wanted to strengthen my heart against the invasion of emotions, I should flee this temptation of empathy toward him, toward Runt. Sven had a map. I didn't have to ask for Bastiaan's help—I didn't have to keep him away from rescuing Runt.

I'd been handed a flake of hope, and it felt intoxicating—like the fall of winter's first snow. I wanted to share it before it melted. I had to share it . . . because I alone could help Runt.

I found Bastiaan with the horses, picking pebbles from their hooves with a bent metal tool. "Looks like it's my turn."

He glanced up, then held the hoof pick aloft. "I just finished. But don't fret. Let them graze another day and you'll have plenty to clean. Sterk here seems to attract every pebble to be found." He patted his stallion's rump. "If I'd known you liked doing it, I'd have saved it for you. Spare my back an ache."

Even now, with all help refused him, Bastiaan turned my increasingly chilly heart warm. How did he maintain joy when he'd lost something so dear to him? Anyone could see the pain turning the agonized lines of his face into scars. He looked desperate.

Helpless, even. Where had his confidence gone? He truly must have exhausted every avenue of thought.

I stepped into the glade and leaned against a tree. "That's not quite what I meant." I didn't want to admit I had no idea a horse's hooves needed cleaning, let alone how to clean them.

"Oh?" Bastiaan pocketed the hoof pick and turned Sterk loose to graze on the tough stems of autumn's weeds.

"I'm sorry you lost your Talent. That was cruel of the king."

Bastiaan's hand fisted. "Even more reason he must be stopped. Filling up the Well of Talents and robbing people of their Talents . . ."

I couldn't help fearing for my cousin. Did Anouk know about any of this? Did she *support* it? "Bastiaan . . . there's something you don't know about me."

"I'd guess there are many things I don't know about you." He twitched a smile to show he was joking, but his body stilled the same way it had when we encountered Sven's archers. Tense. Waiting. Maybe even hopeful?

Deep breath. "Queen Anouk is my cousin." Cousin. Sister. Dearest friend.

His eyebrows shot up. Whatever he thought I would share, clearly that wasn't it. "You're royalty?" An appreciative wonder filled his gaze. "But you live so simply."

"I'm common." I never minded being common. As the Wishtress I was beyond royalty, but I'd never viewed myself as such. "Anouk started out common as well. But she and I are no longer on good terms. We had a misunderstanding on the day you found me, actually."

"I'm so sorry." He'd seen me at my worst. Distraught. Fleeing from pain. Drugging myself to avoid *feeling*.

I pushed onward to avoid sinking into the much-craved empathy. "I'm writing her a letter and I want . . . I want to mention Runt. She's always had a soft spot for children, especially those from the canals."

His shoulders fell. "A letter."

"Yes." I hoped he didn't ask why I was willing to help, because my answer would be far too personal. *I feel comfortable with you, so I want to help you.* I couldn't risk getting personal.

"There's . . . nothing else?"

Writing to the queen—aligning myself with the king's potential assassin—wasn't enough? "If I had something more, I'd give it."

He nodded and let out a breath, resting his forehead on Sterk's back for a moment. There seemed to be more on his mind, more behind his previous question. He'd expected something more from me but wouldn't say what. A sick twist in my gut discerned the truth.

"You know about my Talent," I said in a voice almost as soft as the cloud of frosty air that emerged from my lips and hung in the space between us. Fragile. Temporary.

"You're the Wishtress." The way he said it, he'd known for a while.

I stood my ground, sent up the ice walls around my heart. I'd let myself be too soft with him. A spear of anger stuck in my sternum. "What gave it away? All the wishes I've been granting?"

"I'm not after you." He stayed calm. It allowed me to take a few breaths, to try to see him and not my fear.

He pulled a piece of paper from his pocket. I unfolded it to see my likeness. A drawing of *me*. With the location of my old home—the place I'd been cursed—scrawled across the top. "Where did you get this?"

"From the king's very hand."

Bastiaan had been hunting me. All that feigned kindness—taking me in at Windmill Cottage, guiding me to Sven, protecting me, befriending me . . . He'd been working for the king the whole time.

Was any of his story true?

"Is Runt even in the dungeon?" I folded up the paper and tried to act unfazed. I waited for the boy to reveal himself from the tree shadows.

"Yes, he is." Bastiaan tucked the paper back in his pocket. "And I'm deeply thankful for your offer to write the queen for help."

"Yet you'd rather have a wish." I wanted him to admit it. To reveal that was the whole reason he plucked me out of the hedgerow by the schloss.

"If you had the ability to give one so easily, then obviously that would make things simpler. But you haven't offered one. I trust you have a reason. I've not spent much time with you, Myrthe, but it's been enough to glimpse your heart."

My anger receded long enough to allow in other considerations. He had an order to capture me in his pocket. He'd known I was the Wishtress this whole time yet never asked about it. Never asked for a wish. Never pressured me. He even left me at Sven's camp—let me go on my way—without bringing it up.

Even in this conversation I was the one to reveal my Talent.

I didn't know what to do with this . . . courtesy. This obvious show of respect for who I was as a person. My defenses dropped.

I stepped closer to him, though I wasn't sure why. To show I was hearing him? Maybe because this was the safest I'd ever felt—in the presence of a man sent to hunt me. A man who knew my secret and didn't see it as a tool.

He received my closeness with a mixture of sadness and understanding—like he knew the struggles that came with hiding a Talent. He lifted his hand to my face and I sucked in a breath, tensing for his touch—*ready* for his touch.

His finger brushed my eyelashes ever so softly, then traced the path of my eyebrow. "Right here," he said gently. "Your Talent Mark. It's a single eyelash. White as snow with flickers of silver."

"Oh." The only word my pounding heart would allow to escape. I had a Talent Mark? I had a Talent Mark!

Bastiaan—a man who had once been a stranger and was now something so tenuously welcoming—had noticed this small detail about me in less than a handful of days knowing me.

No one else ever saw it. Because no one else ever saw *me*.

His hand returned to his side, but neither of us stepped back. I wanted to give him a wish right then. Ten wishes. A hundred. My breathing hitched as memory of my curse speared my mind. I took an abrupt step backward as the comfort fled.

This acceptance he offered was based off a half-knowing. While it gave me a moment of peace, reality brought me sharply back to the half-frozen forest.

He didn't know what I'd done to my own parents or Coralythe's sons.

I cleared my throat. "I'd best write that letter to Anouk."

"Thank you, Myrthe."

I moved to walk away, but his hand found mine and tugged me back. My lungs seized. Logic told me to put more space between us, but my heart demanded I stay perfectly still so as not to risk our skin separating.

"I've heard you. I want you to know that." He held my gaze, his expression intense and determined. "I know you're trying to get to the Well."

My mouth snapped shut. *Winter's breath*, how much else had he noticed about me and my motives? Did he want me to explain? I couldn't. I couldn't tell him of my darkness—it would break me. Especially in this moment. "I can't tell you why."

"I don't need to know why. I don't have a map, but I know the way." His hand tightened around mine, almost protectively. Promising. "When Runt is safe again, I'll take you to the Well myself."

CHAPTER 22

CORALYTHE

The boy hung from the chains like a soiled, torn garment. Coralythe could not take her eyes off him, even as the dungeon master—Kravin—chained her beside the boy. Even as she spit blood from a mouth that, mere hours ago, had been guiding the young new king as a parent would a blindfolded child.

The boy lifted his head with a grimace at the noise of chains clanking against Coralythe's bony wrists. His toes hardly brushed the dungeon floor.

"We'll see which one of you rots first," Kravin said with a dark chuckle. Then he departed, leaving behind the creaks of metal on stone and *drip drip* of wastewater in the gutter along the wall.

The dungeon stank. Her senses would adapt eventually. After all, she'd been here before. For much longer than she planned to be here this time. Mattias promised it'd be no more than a few days.

He had faith she could complete her task.

Since she had a Bane—and he was able to command her—she didn't really have a choice. Already the oh-too-recent memories of torn flesh, ridicule, and bone-splitting cold returned full force. She wanted out. She needed out.

But she couldn't do it alone.

The boy eyed her through tired lids and attempted a smile. To comfort her? "Welcome to my home," he joked. "Sorry my man-servant treated you so harshly. I'll dismiss him."

Despite the darkness of the humor, she chuckled. He and her younger son would have gotten along. "What atrocity could a boy your age commit to land you in here? You must be pretty important."

The boy swallowed several times before he spoke. "I can do plenty."

Defiant even after two days of imprisonment. "What's your name?"

"Runt."

Hardly a real name. A canal rat, then. "I'm Coralythe."

"What atrocity does a lady have to commit to be chained up beside such an important prisoner like me?"

She laughed softly. She liked this boy. "You remind me of my youngest son. He was killed. Brutally. He was probably your age— eleven years old. I'm here because I want to avenge his death."

"That's not really an answer."

"You don't talk like a boy of eleven—"

"That's because I'm ten."

"You're smart." And eloquent. What had the man Bastiaan taught this child?

"You still haven't answered me."

This time Coralythe threw back her head and laughed—a foreign sound in such a dismal place. It strained her shoulder muscles, but she couldn't stop herself. If she shared her story with this boy, he would see the depth. He would read between the lines because of his intelligence.

It would be refreshing to talk to someone who could *see* her.

"I came to the schloss several months ago to present myself to the new king. I have powers—kind of like a Talent. I offered them to King Mattias. In doing so I found we shared a common goal."

"You sound like Bastiaan. He says Talents are for serving the king and the people."

And that was why Bastiaan was being hunted and Coralythe still had a chance to be at the king's right hand. "Mattias was paranoid and had me thrown in here. For a month. I was tormented and tested but didn't bend. I knew he'd see my value eventually, and he did. He released me and allowed me to join his private council."

"Why are you back in the dungeon then?"

"The others on his council don't trust me, not even after he showed them something that would change their lives—change this kingdom. So he sent me back here either to test my loyalty or to appease the stiff-necked men on his council."

Runt snorted. "That's not very nice after you promised to serve him."

"He has his reasons." Even if she didn't like them. He'd promised her a great role in the destruction of the Talents. She had to trust he'd follow through.

"What . . . sort of powers do you have?" Something deeper than curiosity instigated Runt's question. He'd stilled as though nervous she wouldn't answer.

Her laugh was brittle. "Nothing you'd want."

He shook his head, seeming confused. "But Talents are to help people. They're good."

"As I said, it's not quite a Talent. Have you heard of the Nightwell?" The name burned her tongue as it did when she first spoke of it to King Mattias. She wasn't yet used to speaking openly about it.

Runt shook his head.

"Good." She didn't want to take him there. The dungeon was dark enough. "Why are *you* here?" She already knew the answer—she'd seen Bastiaan Duur's flight from the schloss after the council meeting. Heard King Mattias send his militairen after his servant. But she wanted to hear Runt's point of view.

"I'm here until my master retrieves me." Runt's words were more hollow than his emaciated chest cavity.

"Does he know you're here?" She twisted her left wrist in the shackle, trying to relieve the pinch already creating a welt on her skin.

"He . . . left me." The statement was almost a question, as though he couldn't believe his own words.

"Intentionally?"

Runt didn't respond. Didn't move. The burn of protectiveness rose in Coralythe, followed swiftly by a sharp sting of grief. No. She'd moved past this—redirected the pain into a forge of revenge. She must remember her new goals. New role. New life that she would achieve no matter who stood in her way.

But would it cause that much harm to allow her heart to care for the boy? He had no one else but the master who'd abandoned him. She knew what it was like to be abandoned.

"I've been left before. By someone I thought loved me. I learned that I could manage on my own."

Runt looked over at her. "He'll come back."

"My husband has been gone five years now." A blessed but cruel day when he finally abandoned her—showed his true colors.

"I meant . . . Bastiaan. He'll come back for me."

"You don't sound convinced."

"He will!" Tears dropped from his eyes. "You don't know him! And when he comes for me, I'll ask him to free you too."

Part of her hoped Bastiaan would return for the boy. But everyone eventually had to live through betrayal. Disappointment. It was the cruel way of the world. And it was Runt's turn to learn. He'd be stronger for it. Someday.

"Bastiaan must have kept many promises to earn such loyalty." She watched him out of the corner of her eye. His head hung. Lower. Lower. Until he shook it ever so slightly.

"Tears already?" Kravin reentered the room, and Coralythe cursed him to the depths of the murkiest bog. Though not a *true* curse like she'd given the Wishtress. She could do that only once per death of a loved one. Since both of her sons had died, she had one curse left.

Her future relied on using this curse strategically.

"You've hardly been in here two days and you look ready to give up the ghost." Kravin chuckled as he poked Runt in the ribs with the butt of a short, corded whip. "Shall we break you today?"

Runt's small body trembled.

"Wait another day, Kravin," Coralythe said. "Runt and I have only just met."

Kravin's backhand was swift and sharp. Practiced. Her head snapped to the side and her vision swam.

Mattias had told her to get answers from the boy. But he didn't seem to have told Kravin anything. The dungeon master saw her as another piece of meat to fillet. Nothing more.

"Leave her alone!" Runt hollered, fighting his chains to claw at Kravin.

Kravin laughed, inches out of reach. "Maybe I'll give *her* your medicine today."

Too young to understand negotiating, Runt growled like a cornered cub and Coralythe wanted to throttle Kravin with his own whip.

She lifted her chin. "Someday you'll die of your own medicine."

She hadn't forgotten the last time she was his victim, before she managed to bargain her way out by giving King Mattias information about the Wishtress.

Kravin got in Runt's face and whispered, "What do you think, boy? Want to hear her scream?"

"No," Runt croaked, parched and desperate. Too desperate.

Kravin grinned. "Down here, *no* means *yes*." He rounded Coralythe so he faced her back, then shook out the whip.

Coralythe squeezed her eyes shut and swore to herself she would not scream. But it mattered not. Runt did enough screaming for the both of them.

CHAPTER 23

MYRTHE

I haven't forgiven you." Anouk alighted from her snowy steed onto the frosted sward.

I sprang to my feet from my spot beside the frozen canal waters. "I didn't think you'd come."

I'd daringly ridden into Fairhoven to have a boy deliver my message yesterday evening after talking with Bastiaan. I still hadn't dismounted the cloud of hope it sent me on. But I sobered quickly when Anouk responded less than two hours later.

She'd agreed to meet at sunrise.

"I came for the glade mostly." Anouk stepped into the spot where we'd spent most of our youth. A secret place off a small side canal where we'd confessed all manner of secrets, dreams, and confidences. If the canopy of branches could speak, our very souls would be laid bare to the listener.

For a moment Anouk's features softened with memories, and despite her elegant riding gown, she looked every bit the cousin who used to race me on the ice and cry with me over Oma's harshness. Then her gaze found mine and the young queen returned. "A militair and one of my attendants are within screaming distance."

My heart crumpled beneath the weight of what we'd lost. "Do you believe me such a threat to you?"

"I'm not sure yet." Anouk still stood at her horse's side. "What is it you want?"

"To tell you a story," I whispered, daring a step closer. My emotions rippled on the surface, but part of me didn't mind the idea of losing control and ending my life in my favorite place with the person dearest to me.

"I already know about the boy in the dungeon."

I shook my head. "A different story." I would get to Runt's predicament in a moment. But I couldn't let the bitterness that had begun between us grow into something permanent. She'd wanted a wish from me my entire life. Perhaps my talk with Bastiaan last night allowed my heart to soften.

He'd said that he hadn't asked me for a wish because he knew I'd give one if I could. I wanted to show Anouk the same courtesy. If she was asking me for a wish, it was because there was no other option for her. I wanted to understand, but first I needed to help *her* understand.

"I'm cursed." No reason to deliver the information gently. It wasn't gentle news. "The day I fell ill was because a woman with a Bane cursed me to . . . to die by my next wish. But"—I dropped to my knees and took Anouk's soft hand—"if you ask it of me, I'll give it to you."

Anouk's expression was one of shock, then grief. "Myrthe . . . what?"

"I'm cursed! Ruined. I can't make a wish unless I choose to die."

"That's why Oma kept you asleep so long? To keep you from crying until she could come up with a plan?" Anouk joined me in the grass. "Oh, cousin . . . Why didn't you tell me?"

My chest tightened. "Shame." I was so tempted to leave it at the curse. To let Anouk believe I was unjustly attacked, but the pressure of guilt pushed from the inside. I needed someone to know. To see how despicable I was.

"I murdered two boys. Her sons." I said the words so softly they almost dissolved into the damp soil unnoticed.

Anouk sat silent, letting me speak.

I told her everything. How I froze the canal to prove my Talent to Sven. How that resulted in the boys' deaths. How I'd given Sven my last wish for his journey to the Well. How the curse came not even a full day later.

"I was wrong to refuse you a wish with no explanation. I should have been forthright with you of all people."

"Oh, Myrthe, you have no need to apologize! What happened with those boys swimming, it was an acciden—"

"No!" I shoved away. "Don't give me grace!" Already the burn of tears threatened my composure. "Don't *excuse* this." I reached for the ice inside. Called for winter until the beating of my heart slowed from the cold.

My next words came out stiffer than the metal of the frost bells. "I killed children with my Talent. Death should have been my sentence." Death would have been easier. "And that's not all. I killed my parents."

Anouk gave a sharp inhale. There it was—the judgment. The disgust. That had to be what she was thinking.

"My Talent manifested when I was twelve. Mutti and Pappje were sick because of *me*. I came home with the pox and infected them both. I'd never cried before and we didn't know what I was. I was so afraid they were going to die. I wished they'd never known me. I wished for their illnesses to end. And my very first tears granted those wishes. Pappje never woke. Oma told me Mutti died too, but that was another one of her lies."

I was breathing too fast, remembering too much, burning, burning, burning, but I plunged on. "When I woke from my curse,

Oma revealed that Mutti didn't die from the pox. She's alive some-where, ignorant to the fact that I exist. That I'm hers." I squeezed my eyes closed.

"Stop!" Anouk commanded. "Don't you dare cry." She said this through her own cracked voice.

I opened my eyes, dizzy, but forced ice into my heart. *Don't feel.* Instead . . . anger. Oma did this. Oma robbed me of a relationship with my mother. She used me. Coralythe ruined my chances of mak-ing my own—or anyone else's—life better, after I'd given her a wish!

"Good. Keep going, Myrthe."

I laughed hollowly. "Keep turning to ice?"

"If that's what it takes. You need to stay alive."

Several deep breaths later, I was composed. My story told.

I looked into Anouk's eyes and saw anger in them for the first time. "How *dare* Oma? And who is this mysterious woman who's able to curse you and go her merry way? Revenge isn't justice! She needs to reckon for her actions."

"She was grieving. She didn't strike me as one who went around cursing others. Besides, it doesn't matter. Her sons are dead now. My own wish led her to me." My Talent had turned against me, as though it knew I'd never used it for good. "Coralythe had every right to curse me."

"Coralythe?" Anouk's eyes searched the air before her, as though seeing invisible threads and connecting them with the needle of her vision. "She lives in the schloss! She's on Mattias's advisory council."

Coralythe worked for the king? This must be the council mem-ber Bastiaan mentioned. "Does Mattias know she has a Bane?"

"Are you sure it's a Bane, Myrthe? Not a Talent?"

I gestured to myself. "Cursed! To die! Talents don't do that." At least I didn't think they did. "Coralythe told me herself it was a Bane when she first asked for a wish in the tent at markt."

"Why would she reveal something like that?"

"She was distraught. She didn't seem to care *what* she revealed as long as she got a wish." Which I'd handed right over. It was hard to recall the compassion I'd felt for the woman after everything that had transpired since then.

"That's how Mattias sketched your likeness and knew where you lived. Coralythe gave him that information." Anouk went silent, deep in thought.

I wanted to fix this. To help, not add burdens to my cousin. "Please . . . let me help you. Whatever you needed the wish for, I'll give it."

"No, Myrthe. That's what you do—you help people to your detriment. You let yourself help Oma and it led you to forced servitude. You helped Coralythe and it resulted in a curse. You even used wishes to help Sven with his pilgrimage. And now you're willing to die to help me when you don't even know what I need."

"So compassion is my downfall." I thought of Bastiaan and giving him bread. That, at least, had resulted in something beautiful.

"No, it's your strength. But other people use it to take you down. I will not be one of those people."

"Then I'll help in other ways." I had a few guesses as to why Anouk needed the wish, most of which revolved around her marriage to King Mattias. But Anouk spoke about it as though it was to solve a problem she'd had long before that.

Anouk released a great sigh. "It's my turn to tell you a story. I fear it's just as grim."

Winter's breath, was she cursed too?

"You remember my father." She sounded resigned.

"Yes." I swallowed. "He died . . . four years ago?" I never brought it up because Anouk never spoke of it. Even though he'd been my uncle—Oma's other son.

When he passed away, Anouk wept no tear. If anything, she

became a more joyful person. I'd interacted with my uncle a handful of times, and he'd always been pleasant. He liked to talk business and profit with Oma.

Like mother, like son.

Every time he visited meant Oma would leave me alone. It gave Anouk and me glorious hours together outside.

"We were poor once." Anouk grimaced and held her stomach. "Before we moved to Fairhoven. Hard to believe, I know. Father had debts. And when they became too much, he . . . well, he sold me."

My mouth went dry.

"To men." As if that clarification were necessary. "Only a few times at first, begging my forgiveness and promising it was the only way for us to eliminate those debts. But a few times turned into several a week and . . . he made good munten. I . . . I should have left. Moved. Told someone. *Something.*"

Her hands gripped her skirt. "Then we moved here. Men paid more here, so he didn't have to bring in as many. A couple months after the move, I got pregnant."

I remembered Anouk's arrival. I was ten, Anouk fourteen. A cousin had been a much-needed gift of friendship. But a few months into our new acquaintance, Anouk had stopped visiting. Stopped responding to letters. I assumed she decided I wasn't worth friendship.

Instead . . . she'd been hiding a pregnancy.

"I had a son." Her eyes shone. "I named him Cairden. He'd be six years old now. I begged Father to let me keep him. He said yes, but he didn't mean it."

How could a father be so cruel? Suddenly my struggles with Oma seemed so trivial.

"I woke one morning and Cairden was gone. Father had left him in the canals. I told him I'd never attend to one of his customers again until he took me to the canal. He gave in. Footprints were everywhere in the surrounding snow. Someone found him. Saved him. I thank the Well every day for whoever rescued my baby from freezing to death. But I've been searching for him ever since."

"Oh, Anouk." The silence that filled the glade spoke more comfort than any words could. We both felt the same weight of helplessness in each other's plights.

"That's why I married Mattias." Anouk's voice grew the quietest it had been yet. "I . . . I'm pretty sure he's the father."

"What?" I sputtered. "The *king* hired a . . ." I almost said prostitute, but that wasn't what Anouk was. Anouk was a victim. Yet also a warrior.

"This was years ago. I was practically a child! And he was a rebellious prince flirting with the ways of the world. He had two older brothers at the time. Being king wasn't on his mind."

Until his brothers died. From accidents. And all of Fairhoven speculated his involvement. It wasn't the first time royalty slaughtered each other for status. "You married him." I couldn't imagine it. "You married . . . your abuser."

"I was nothing more than a commodity. And he was . . ." She shrugged. "Well, he was the gentlest."

"That's no excuse!"

"It's sick, isn't it? That I would do this?" She pressed a wad of her dress against her mouth. Squeezed her eyes tight, then composed herself with a deep breath. "He doesn't know. He didn't recognize me. You alone know, Myrthe."

I'd run out of words. What could I say to comfort Anouk? To understand her choices? "You have my vowed silence."

She took a deep breath and the trees seemed to inhale along with her. "It was the only way. The *only* way for me to access every means possible to find Cairden. I've been able to send militairen to investigate. I've inquired after Talented. I've interviewed and searched and hired and done everything I can think of. And finally I was able to ask for a wish."

"It's why you always questioned the canal rats at markt." So many small things clicked into place. Anouk had turned to me as her very last hope.

If only Oma hadn't used a wish to silence Anouk from asking for my help. If only I had stashed a few wishes of my own. If only I'd given Anouk a wish without her asking! I'd given Sven a wish and not Anouk. I was utterly disgusted with myself.

If I'd never gotten myself cursed, I could help Anouk. Help Runt. Help Bastiaan. Find Mutti. My determination solidified more firmly than ever. "I'm going to the Well of Talents . . . to break the curse."

"That will work?"

I picked pieces of ice from between the dead blades of grass. "Each Wishtress has written her story in that book. Of the ones I've managed to read, they all end up traveling to the Well at one point or another. I think I'm supposed to go there."

But there was nothing about breaking curses in those pages. I hoped I could be the one to write that entry.

"How will you get there?"

"Bastiaan said he'll take me . . . after Runt is safe."

"Well . . . this brings us back to the original reason for your letter." Anouk fingered the hem of her dress splayed around her as though she was still unused to the finery. "I'm afraid I can do little about your friend Runt. He's the one connection Mattias has to his father's murderer."

"But we don't know that Bastiaan murdered King Vämbat. He could very well be innocent!" In all honesty I'd completely forgotten Bastiaan was suspected of murder. How could someone so kind have done something so heinous? Then again, he'd taken an order from King Mattias to hunt me down and turn me in.

Anouk opened her mouth, closed it, then released a sympathetic sigh. "Oh, Myrthe. Do you have feelings for this man? Bastiaan?"

"Feelings?" I let out a hysterical laugh. "I can't allow myself to have feelings about *anything*." That statement felt like a lie I was trying to convince myself of.

Anouk saw right through it, but her face showed pity. "He's likely a murderer."

So am I. "We don't know that."

"I'll ask Mattias to be kind to the boy, but how can I ask him to abandon the quest of bringing his father's killer to justice?"

"Isn't Mattias himself a murderer?" I challenged.

Her mouth quirked up. "Call me foolish, but I don't believe he is. He told me what happened to his brothers—and their deaths were not at his hand. There was no audience when he told me. No reason for him to lie."

"I hope for your own happiness that he told you the truth."

We rose from the grass, leaving two indents like those of two resting does. I didn't want to leave, didn't want to return to Bastiaan empty-handed. But there was no more to say. "For the first time in our lives, you and I are on opposite sides, Anouk."

She embraced me and kissed my forehead. "We may be on opposite sides, but that doesn't mean we're enemies."

CHAPTER 24

CORALYTHE

"Fingers or toes?" The dungeon keeper had returned.

Coralythe peered at him through tired, swollen eyes. She wasn't supposed to fear him. Not this time.

But he wasn't talking to her.

Runt wouldn't even spare the man a glance. This seemed to irritate Kravin because his face turned blotchy. He poked Runt's dirty toes with a rusty metal pair of curved scissors. "Maybe I'll take a couple of each, eh? Before I even ask you for the location of your master."

"Go ahead," Runt croaked with forced bravado. "I'm ready."

"Oh no." Kravin grinned. "I'll give you some time to *really* think about it. To think about how it will feel to have your pinkie toe chopped off. It's not a quick job, you know. The bone—"

"Enough." Coralythe could not abide this man's slimy voice or lust for violence. "Give him his time, would you?"

With a leer Kravin walked out.

"This is why I wanted a Talent," Runt said, not much louder than the drips of water from the walls. "So I could protect myself.

And others. Escape. Bastiaan said he'd always protect me. His Talent lets him do that. But this last time . . ."

"He hasn't come for you," Coralythe murmured. "Perhaps something happened to him. Maybe it's keeping him from coming."

This forced hope didn't seem to have crossed Runt's mind. His master was too indestructible, but at her comment he lifted his head and stared, eyes round as coins. "That must be it. Maybe he needs *my* help! And I'm stuck here!" He writhed against the chains, which dug into his young skin all the more, sending a string of blood down his arm to his elbow.

She wanted so badly to let that hope carry him free. To save a young boy who reminded her of her sons. But was it worth using her Bane? The very thought of using it created a draw inside her, a distant, deep voice urging her to use it. She'd spent half her lifetime resisting that voice—per the demands of her husband—yet ever since she gave in and cursed the Wishtress, she'd been set free.

Resisting the voice was no longer a desire. "I . . . may be able to help."

"With your Talent?"

"It's not a Talent, Runt. It's called a Bane."

"From the . . . Nightwell?"

She bowed her head and let herself wander back down the path of history she had so long ignored. "The Nightwell is a lake near the Well of Talents. Should you choose to submerge yourself in its waters, you'll reemerge with what is called a Bane—a great power."

"Like the Well of Talents!"

"No," she snapped. "The Well of Talents gives out Talents recklessly. Then people with Talents murder children and kings alike." She forced herself to take a calming breath. "The Well of Talents is a tiny spring, and its power is nothing compared to the Nightwell's."

"You've been to it?" Runt asked, awed. "The Well of Talents?"

Why couldn't he see she was talking about something greater? He was too caught up in wonder at the Well of Talents, like those decrepit advisors on Mattias's council. "Focus, Runt."

Never mind that she hadn't been to the Well of Talents. The Nightwell had told her plenty about it. "I was birthed in the waters of the Nightwell. And I was gifted a Bane that allowed me to curse someone or give them a Bane."

"Curse?"

"Not a pleasant word, is it?" She gave a wry smile. "It's a complicated gift."

"I've always wanted a Talent. Bastiaan told me again and again he'd take me to the Well of Talents. He must not know about the Nightwell."

"You'd be surprised at how many people *do* know about the Nightwell, but they keep it secret. More people have Banes than Talents in Fairhoven." A door slammed out of view and Coralythe's attention snapped back to her purpose. "Enough history, Runt. I can give you a Bane. It might be able to save you, but I won't know what type of Bane can be woven until I start to give it. Do you want it?"

"You can do that . . . even if I don't swim in the water?"

She was an ambassador of the Nightwell. She *was* the water. "Yes."

"It's not the same thing as a curse?"

"No, that's a different power."

"But what about you?" he cried.

"It doesn't work on me." Not that she wanted another Bane anyway. She had felt like an outcast in her life long enough. Now, at least, the king was revealing how Banes were superior to Talents. She was no longer less than. Eventually, everyone would have a Bane whether they wanted it or not.

"My very own Talent," he breathed, hope shining fully on his face for the first time.

Fine. Let him think it was a Talent. As long as it saved him, she cared not about his ignorance. She caught a few notes of Kravin's raucous singing in the distance. He was likely gathering his torture tools.

She closed her eyes and dove into the dark waters of her mind. The Nightwell power rose swiftly to meet her, ready to be used once again. She lost herself to it, sifting through the curses and Banes it offered. *Something to defeat another. Something that will not harm the boy. Something that will defend him and be a weapon.*

She found the streams of color, of power, and wove them together. They had a mind of their own and spun foreign strands into the Bane. Thick purple smoke burst from her palms and encompassed Runt's small body, swirling and pressing against his skin. He bucked against it.

"Don't fight it," she said.

The mist absorbed into his small body and his eyes snapped open—black, then purple, then their normal brown again. The flood in her mind subsided, leaving her gasping for air.

"I feel it," he whispered. "There's . . . a voice."

"What's it telling you? It will explain your Bane."

He looked at Coralythe in horror. "What . . . what is this?"

"What's it telling you?" she demanded again. Kravin's whistle drew closer. "Quick!"

He shook his head, fearful. "I'm . . . my . . ." He choked on a sob. "My blood is . . . poison. It will kill whoever touches it." He raised hollow eyes to hers. "How is that power?"

Deadly blood. Just as it gave him life while in his veins, if another person touched even a droplet, they would die. It was one of her better Banes. "It's a defense!"

"I don't think I want it."

"It feels foreign and frightening right now, but you'll be one with it. You'll see." She remembered all too well the pain of fighting her Bane as a young girl. Relief came once she accepted it—let it fully in and used the curses or Banes on those who deserved them.

"Did you decide, boy?" Kravin called from around the corner, his heavy clomps bringing him nearer.

"It can get you back to Bastiaan," Coralythe hissed. "You can defend yourself, as you desired. Focus on that."

"It didn't give me a weapon. It made *me* into one." He sounded on the verge of tears. "This isn't like Bastiaan's Talent. I can't turn it off." He leaned away from the trickle of blood that had half dried along his bare arm.

"You have to be strong, Runt. Like Bastiaan." Invoking Bastiaan's name seemed to be the most effective way to impact him.

Kravin walked in with a grin more sickly than decaying fruit. "I've decided on fingers."

Runt curled his hands into fists. "Leave me alone."

Kravin snapped the bone scissors open and closed in response. "Ready to tell me where your master is?" Silence hung in the tense air, shackled alongside Runt. "Fingers it is, then."

"No!" Runt thrashed as Kravin approached. "Don't touch me!"

The dungeon master unlocked the shackles around his wrists and let Runt crumple to the floor. The boy scrambled away, which excited Kravin further. "I'm always up for a good fight. And I *always* win." He advanced.

"Stop! I'll kill you!" It wasn't a threat but a panicked warning.

Kravin laughed and grabbed Runt's wrist and pulled until it gave a small *pop* and the boy yelled, then stopped fighting.

"Good," Kravin crooned. "I want you to watch. It's an art, really."

Runt stared not at the bone scissors but at the smear of blood that led from his own arm to Kravin's hand. Coralythe could hardly breathe. Kravin gave his wrist a shake, as though relieving a hand cramp. Then a sharp inhale followed. His eyes bulged, blinked once, and went dead as a snuffed candle.

He slumped to the side and Runt wriggled his wrist free. "I warned him," he gasped.

"Yes, you did." She felt a surge of pride.

"I told him to stop."

"Men like that don't stop. Not for anything." Coralythe stared at Kravin's bulbous body, relieved and exhilarated by its lack of movement. "Now go. Find Bastiaan and help him."

"I'm getting you free first—"

"There's no time!" The clank of militairen making their rounds preceded raised voices. "Militairen are coming!" If they walked past this cell, they would see Kravin's body and Runt with one arm free.

The boy fumbled with Kravin's belt, digging for the keys. He yanked the leather cord several times before the attached ring came loose. He got his shackle unlocked by the second try and then scrambled over to Coralythe's.

"You need to leave, Runt." It wasn't that she didn't want to be free, but she knew the punishment Runt would undergo if they found him escaping.

"You saved me. I'm not leaving without you."

She tried to nudge him toward the door with her knee. "Foolish boy!"

"Stubborn too." He dodged her attempts and tried the first key, careful to use his nonbleeding hand.

"Kravin?" a militair hollered. No concern tainted his voice. It sounded like he had a message for the dungeon master. Rotten timing.

Runt worked faster, moving on to the next key and then the next. Until he went through them all and none worked. "I . . . I must have gone through them too fast."

Coralythe shook her head. "Go, Runt."

He started over with the first key. She could strangle him!

The militair's footsteps sounded mere yards away. A voice murmured. More than one. Runt moved on to the second key for the second time. The lock clicked. He shoved the key ring into Coralythe's hand, then spun toward the doorway as two militairen peered in.

Runt stepped on top of Kravin's dead body and planted his fists on his hips. "That's right! I killed your dungeon master and my blood will kill you, too, if you get in my way!"

The militairen hardly had a moment to process the scene or Runt's words before the boy bolted through the doorway, inches from their hands, and up the stairs toward the exit.

"Oy!" One militair gave chase. Runt cackled like a wildling and then Coralythe heard him no more.

She picked at the lock to her other wrist, hoping the key worked for both. The militair who had remained behind turned his attention to her. "Still working at that, even with me right here in the doorway?"

"It's worth a shot." She shrugged but didn't lower the key. So close.

He walked into the room and nudged Kravin's dead body. "Kravin taken down by a canal rat. That wasn't expected." He turned to Coralythe and took the key ring from her hand. "I think the kid thought we'd follow him, leaving you to escape."

"You'd have been wise to do so."

He fit the correct key into the shackle, turned it, and released her hand. Her legs accepted her full weight for the first time in two days and barely kept her upright. She braced herself against the sticky, stained wall, then rubbed her raw wrists.

"Well done, Coralythe," the militair said. "King Mattias will be pleased."

CHAPTER 25

฿ASTIAAN

Bastiaan was unused to being cornered.

He examined his Talent Mark . . . for the tenth time that day. Depending on the amount of sunlight splashing through the branches, the purple mist appeared lighter. But then he'd look again and it was as dark as ever.

"I'm sorry Anouk could not offer more help." Myrthe stepped from behind the mare.

He hadn't even noticed he'd wandered to the horse grazing spot—a spot where he knew Myrthe would be, especially after he received her note about Queen Anouk's response that morning.

"It's not her problem to solve, nor yours." When Myrthe first offered to write the queen, he'd been annoyed. She hadn't offered a wish. But there must be a reason. Perhaps she had a limited supply. Or maybe her ability to create a wish hadn't renewed since she last used one.

When she confessed her Talent to him willingly, he saw kindness. When he'd taken her hand, touched her face, she'd become so soft—like he'd gotten a peek past her invisible armor.

"What are you going to do?" Her fingers combed through the mare's mane, undoing the tangles as though she could undo his predicament.

"Go after him." No hesitation. "I'll go to the schloss. Give Mattias what he seeks."

"Turn yourself in?" she asked, aghast. "How long do you think he'd keep you there?"

"I don't expect a trial will last very long." Because he was guilty. He'd admit to it if that would save Runt. The only reason he'd taken King Vämbat into the Stillness was to convince him to give the people equal access to the Well of Talents.

He wanted to tell her—wanted to release the secret and breathe in the freedom of owning his guilt instead of being admired by the woman before him. *Ask me. Ask me if I killed him.*

"What about . . . ?" The question hung between them like an unfinished song. She spun to the mare and attacked the tangles with renewed vigor, as if wishing she could retract her half question.

Or maybe wishing she had finished it.

He knew the rest. *What about going to the Well?*

He didn't know why she needed to get there. But he was letting her down. "I'll answer whatever question you ask of me, Myrthe . . . for whatever reason."

She pivoted. "What was your Talent?"

Was. The word pierced sharper than a hornet's sting, carrying the weight of finality. He was no longer a Talented.

He took off his glove, revealing once again the dark purple mark. The reminder of his Talent calling to be used. "It doesn't matter now."

So if it didn't matter, why wouldn't he tell her? The words stuck in his throat. "I used to be able to . . ." It pained him too much. The answer led to too many memories. Regrets.

She laid a hand on his arm, startling him out of the reverie. "You miss it." Why did she sound surprised?

He nodded, taking comfort from her touch. "My Talent was a gift unexpectedly given to me by the Well. Now it's been stripped away." A punishment he deserved. How, after a full lifetime spent studying the Talents, did he not see his trajectory toward failure?

"Do you not feel the least bit free?" she asked.

The question so caught him by surprise he barked a laugh. "Free?"

"You no longer have to hold that secret. You're no longer in danger as a Talented or sought out by those who would use you."

She didn't seem to be talking about him anymore. Was that why she was so stubborn against using her Wishtress Talent? Because people—Sven, maybe?—had used her for it? The very idea of wanting to be free of his Talent was foreign to Bastiaan. He cherished it, protected it fiercely. Maybe a little too fiercely.

Because of it, Runt was in the schloss dungeons.

"I'm sorry I can't help you get to the Well." He'd hoped to free Runt and then spend the next several days traveling with Myrthe—the three of them. Getting to know her, talking to her, learning about her Talent. Learning about her heart.

"I'm sorry I can't give you a wish." She said *can't*. As though something were blocking her. But her Talent Mark shone perfectly, filled with magic. Ready to give a wish. He had so many questions.

Something—the potential for something sweet and blossoming—had been broken between them. And it didn't matter . . . because he was leaving and she was staying.

He'd failed Runt.

He'd failed his country.

He'd failed Vämbat.

But this wouldn't be the end. For a moment he allowed himself to dream of a hopeful ending to all this—somehow he'd get

Runt free and gain King Mattias's trust. He'd gain Myrthe's trust and she'd give him a wish, which he would use to become a schloss advisor. He'd help make the Well accessible to all. He'd destroy the Nightwell. Myrthe would thaw the Vier. There would be no more rebels in the forest, no more fear of the Talented, and no more paranoia running the kingdom.

While it felt backhanded to imagine Myrthe in such a way, she was the Wishtress—this was part of her *purpose*. He hoped she'd start seeing it that way in time to make a difference.

In another lifetime he could have helped her with that.

Someone hollered from the central camp area. Myrthe inclined her head. "That sounds like Sven."

Bastiaan should leave. Let Myrthe and those following Sven go ahead with their plans. He should have already headed for the schloss, but it felt like giving up.

"Where's Bastiaan?" Sven's shout tumbled down the hill.

Bastiaan strode toward the sound, Myrthe hot on his heels, until Sven came into view. The other people in camp scrambled to douse fires and gather belongings. Bastiaan lifted an arm to catch Sven's attention. "What's going—?"

"Your boy's leading schloss militairen here." Sven stumbled to a halt inches from Bastiaan's face. "He betrayed us!"

Bastiaan pulled up short. "Runt would never betray you."

"Then how do you explain what I saw?"

"Maybe your visions aren't always correct." Bastiaan tried to calm his defensiveness. Sven was this camp's leader. He was right to be concerned. "Tell me what you saw."

"He's in the plains. Not far from here. He entered and then exited my vision. A few moments later I saw a militair."

"Only one? A scout then." Judging by Sven's vision, Runt was unaware of the militair. Which was saying something because the boy could practically hear the whisper of shadows. How did he not know he was being followed? If Runt knew, he never would have come to the forest.

But how did he get out of the schloss dungeon?

Bastiaan bolted back down the hill toward Sterk.

"I hope you're buying us some time to get out of here!" Sven yelled after him.

At one point Bastiaan could have done that . . . literally. "Best not rely on me to save your skin," he called back. The only skin he was interested in saving was Runt's.

"Well then, don't bother coming back!"

Myrthe gasped. "Sven!"

"What? He doesn't even have his Talent anymore. He's no more use to us than a woodcutter now."

If Myrthe responded, Bastiaan didn't hear it. He was already through the trees and at the grazing glade. He reached Sterk, tore the hobbles from the horse's ankles, grabbed his bow and quiver, and threw them over his shoulder.

Myrthe burst into the glade just after he'd saddled Sterk. "Where are you going?"

"To head them off." He mounted. "Hopefully I can take down the scout and get to Runt." He almost choked on the words "take down the scout." After their conversation, the regret of murder hung dark in his mind.

But this was different. Defense. Battle.

He tapped his heels. Sterk lunged forward and was in a gallop before another word made it to his ears.

It took a quarter bell to reach the edge of the forest. He traversed inside the tree line. Without knowing the timing of Sven's visions, he figured Runt could be anywhere. Maybe he was still out on the plains—

Hoofbeats sounded from behind. Bastiaan spun, an arrow nocked before his eyes made sense of the approacher. Myrthe pulled the mare to a stop and lifted her hands. Her ivory hair hung wild about her like a mane. To have followed him at such a speed . . . and her being an inexperienced rider . . .

Bastiaan dropped his arrow point swifter than the plummet of a spring hawk. "Myrthe."

"You shouldn't be protecting the camp alone. That's Sven's job. I care for Runt too." Her chin lifted in determination that spoke volumes of secrets beneath the statement. "Besides, the mare still belongs to you even though she clearly likes me better."

She had no weapon. Only one thing she'd brought with her could help.

Bastiaan's fear melted. He had the Wishtress helping him. Everything suddenly felt right. Unstoppable. *Possible.* "Thank y—"

"There he is!" Her gaze had slid beyond him to the plains.

Bastiaan leaned low over his horse and peered out into the plains. A speck of a boy with almost no shadow beneath the noon sun ambled toward the tree line. Bastiaan couldn't see a scout. Either he was really good at tracking, or he was farther behind Runt than Bastiaan thought. Which would be ideal because he and Runt could lose the scout easily once on horseback.

Bastiaan was about to slide from his horse when he saw it—a sway of the stiff tan grasses that went against the direction of the wind. The flicker of a form. Here, then gone, blending with the grasses as though his skin changed color.

A scout with a Concealing Talent. And far closer than he ought to be.

Bastiaan gave a low three-note whistle. Runt's head snapped his direction and the boy broke into a jog. The schloss scout must have had the ears of a fox because he abandoned his cover and burst from the grasses, giving chase.

"Runt!" Bastiaan kicked Sterk into motion.

Runt threw a glance over his shoulder, then started sprinting. He spied Bastiaan and distress filled his expression.

"No!" His voice was no louder than the brief chirp of a cricket trampled beneath the powerful thunder of Sterk's hooves. "They're coming for *you*!"

The scout unslung a crossbow and let loose an arrow. It flew so close to Bastiaan's ear that the hiss of foiled death left behind the echo of a curse. Bastiaan was too far to use his throwing discs, so he nocked his own arrow and released it just as the scout swerved. Bastiaan had a second arrow nocked before he even registered the miss.

So did the scout. He stopped. Aimed. But this time it wasn't at Bastiaan.

"Runt!" A strangled warning. Bastiaan released his arrow and it thunked into the scout's chest . . . a blink too late.

The scout had shot first.

Runt toppled into the grass, an arrow in his back.

CHAPTER 26

BASTIAAN

Time stopped, but not because Bastiaan willed it. The twitter of birds and buzz of insects—the very wind—turned mute. His own breath was squeezed from his body.

The grass around where Runt fell swayed from the gust of his collapse.

A scream startled him back into the world of sound. Of life . . . except life was being drained out of Runt into the soil. Myrthe rode the mare toward them, her determined gaze on Runt.

Bastiaan's body moved of its own accord, leaping from Sterk's back, bow clenched beneath white knuckles. He landed mere feet from Runt.

The boy had managed to roll onto his side, his small face twisted. Weeping.

Alive.

Blood soaked the soil beneath him like red rain. He needed aid. And fast. Bastiaan moved to scoop Runt into his arms.

"No!" Runt writhed away like a frightened stray, then cried out.

Bastiaan recoiled, afraid he'd somehow hurt him. "I'm helping you." Perhaps Runt didn't understand. "I have to get you to Mother. To Diantha."

"That's too far away," Myrthe whispered from over his shoulder.

"Don't . . . touch me!" Runt screamed, scrambling to put distance between them. Did he . . . fear Bastiaan?

Bastiaan leaned away with his hands up in an attempt to reassure the boy. As Runt's panic escalated, Bastiaan's calm thickened. "Let me help you." He'd gather Runt by force in the next few seconds no matter what the boy said, but it'd be better if he didn't have to worry about Runt further injuring himself through hysterics.

"I'm bleeding," Runt sobbed.

"I know, Runt. I know." Bastiaan shed his coat and bunched it up to stopper the wound around the arrow shaft.

"It's poison! Poison!" Runt shrieked. "My blood will kill you! Like Kravin! It's what they want!" He coughed. It sounded wet.

Bastiaan tried to make sense of Runt's babblings. Poison? "I don't understand." They were wasting time.

"She . . . gave me a cursed Talent." Something had happened to Runt in the schloss. "You'll die, Bastiaan."

Cursed Talent? *She.* The woman from King Mattias's council. Coralythe. She'd done something to Runt to make him think his blood would poison Bastiaan. But people couldn't *give* Talents.

"Coralythe gave him a Bane," Myrthe breathed.

"You know of her?" Bastiaan's mind spun. King Mattias had hinted that she could give Banes, but Bastiaan thought it was because she brought Nightwell water to the king, not because of her own power.

The scout shot Runt, not Bastiaan. He must have counted on Runt's blood doing the job. The Bane must be real. "I . . . we . . . won't touch your blood, Runt. I'll be very careful. I promise."

This mollified the boy, though he still wept.

Myrthe stepped into Bastiaan's line of sight. The fear on her face ran deeper than the fear drumming in his chest. She trembled and knelt beside Runt, careful to avoid his blood.

She seemed on the verge of tears.

"He's going to be okay," Bastiaan said, both for her and for Runt. And for himself.

Myrthe blinked fiercely and swayed. "Are you sure? He won't . . . die?"

Runt shuddered, possibly against the same question.

Bastiaan had no idea, but he knew the power of hope could heal even greater than that of a Talented. "Of course he won't die." He refused to speak within Runt's hearing about the chances of death. Refused to think about it. "The arrow is in a good place."

Except it wasn't.

"Now give us a wish!" he wanted to shout. His hands trembled. He didn't know what to do first—cut away clothing? Stopper the wound? Change Runt's position?

Runt's breathing leveled out. Myrthe's features turned controlled and practical. "Very well." She seemed to fight some internal battle and came out of it with a flash of relief. "There's a healer in Sven's camp."

She wouldn't look at Runt. Wouldn't look at Bastiaan. She seemed almost disinterested in Runt's pain.

"What about . . . ?" Bastiaan jerked his head toward her. *Your Talent,* he mouthed.

"If you think he's going to be okay, you don't need my help." She had the gall to sound bothered. As though Bastiaan were trying to inconvenience her. Earlier she had said she *couldn't* give a wish. But now it sounded like she simply didn't *want* to. She seemed to shrug it off like one would an easy decision between fish or fowl for dinner.

She kept her wish to herself.

Now, of all times.

His vision flashed red. Of all the selfish— "Get out of here!" Why had she even come? To watch the action? Report to Sven?

She recoiled. "I'm sorry . . ."

He gave a bark of a laugh. "Tell that to Runt."

"You said—"

"I'm taking him to my mother."

"But that's so far . . ."

"It's the only place that can help." His words were as stiff as the winter-chilled leather on his saddle. Mother had trained and studied all there was to know about healing beyond having a Talent of that sort. She knew Runt. She had the tools and necessities.

And frankly, after Sven refused to rescue Runt and Myrthe refused to help him with a wish, Bastiaan wasn't about to entrust the dying boy into the hands of a frantic camp and disinterested leader.

He needed to get away from these people.

He pulled his gloves onto both hands, then leaned over Runt and snapped the arrow from the shaft. Runt let out a brief shout. Bastiaan left the head and stub in to act as a dam against bleeding out. Then he used the blanket from his pack to wrap Runt carefully without moving the stub.

Runt shuddered and finally lost consciousness.

Bastiaan lifted the boy from the ground. Myrthe moved to help him get Runt onto Sterk's back, but Bastiaan jerked away from her touch. "Get away from me."

She snatched her hand back. A flare of hurt filled her eyes. Then cold resignation.

He mounted and managed to settle Runt in front of him. "Wake up, Runt." No response. Not even a shift in his breathing.

Bastiaan was running out of time . . . a problem he'd never faced before. It was a three-bell ride to the windmill at a leisurely pace. He intended to make it in less than half that. Myrthe held out the mare's reins. He grabbed them, then slapped the mare's rump and she took off.

He wasn't about to leave the mare with Myrthe.

He couldn't stand to see her face. Her Talent Mark shone against the sun and he hated it—hated *her*. She valued her own wishes more than Runt's life. She was worse than Sven. Worse than Hedy's bloodlust. She never deserved a Talent in the first place.

"Bastiaan . . ." Her desperate whisper angered him further.

Without a single word of farewell, he gave Sterk a swift command and the stallion burst forward, carrying Bastiaan both toward and away from hell.

If he ever came back—if he ever saw Myrthe again—it would be to do what he should have done in the first place: turn her over to the king and let him have what wishes he could force from her.

CHAPTER 27

Myrthe

I had almost given up my last wish. My last *breath*.

I'd been caught up in Runt's pain. In Bastiaan's distress. In the cruelty of the scout's attack. And before logic or self-preservation could lift its voice, I'd found myself at Runt's side. I'd wanted nothing more in that moment than to use my final wish to give life.

Just like Anouk had warned me. My greatest weakness was others. It felt wrong that it could be a weakness—it tried to destroy me again and again.

When Bastiaan assured me Runt would live, I returned to a state of clarity. Tore my gaze away from Runt's trembling, helpless form. Retreated into the ice cavern in my chest.

As I stood by Runt's frail body, I got a taste of what I *could* have done as the Wishtress. How I could have spent the first seventeen years of my life had Oma not interfered and dictated my worth. Saving others in the direst moments. Offering rescue when hope was bleeding out. But I'd had to deny myself that fulfillment and deny Runt that relief. All to keep my lungs expanding and contracting with purposeless oxygen.

That was how quickly it could happen. Death.

This reaction to Runt's shooting proved how little of a handle I had over my emotions. I needed to try harder, to care less. Disengage.

And Bastiaan . . . Bastiaan left.

He left.

No hope of seeing him again. No opportunity to tell him the truth—to bring relief to the tight agony in my chest over the fact that he must think me a selfish monster. I didn't blame him. But watching him leave felt so personal. As though I was bidding a final farewell to a friend I was meant to know so much better than I did.

I dreaded returning to Sven.

I could already hear his reprimand for riding off. *Winter's breath*, the idea of continuing to dance around his desire for a wish while "supporting" his status as leader was exhausting. If he'd sent a few bowmen—even the rude bald one—they could have stopped the scout. Runt need never have been shot. But I couldn't say these things.

Because Sven was now my last hope.

It was a long walk back to camp. The thorns in my bones sheared my body with every step. By the end I could hardly take a step without clinging to a tree branch or trunk for support.

I hardly recognized camp. Fires doused. Tents collapsed and packed up. Weapons no longer in piles, but in sheaths and quivers and pockets of the gathering crowd.

I found Sven conversing in low tones with Hedy while Kees rolled up the last tent. I could let them finish their conversation . . .

. . . or not.

"The scout is dead." I planted myself at Sven's side, cutting him off midword. I had a difficult time keeping disdain out of my voice.

But why be polite when kindness made me soft and anger made me hard? Hard meant alive. "You should have been there, Sven."

He turned away from Hedy and faced me. "Been where?"

"With Bastiaan . . . heading off that scout and protecting these people."

He hardly blinked. "Why was I needed? *You* went with him."

Hedy pursed her lips and moved to help Kees tie the canvas together, but I could see the strain in her muscles as she tried to listen in.

"I'm not the leader of this rebellion," I hissed.

"But you"—he spotted Hedy and lowered his voice—"you are unstoppable." A compliment delivered on a cold stone platter. He wasn't proud of me. He was annoyed that I'd gone after Bastiaan. Did he think I used a wish to kill the scout?

The assumptions he made about my Talent told me exactly how he thought Talents should be used . . . and what he might do if I gave him another wish. Somehow I knew that even if I *could* grant his request, he wouldn't stop with one.

"So where's your hero?" he asked.

"I have no hero." Not Bastiaan, not Sven. "But if you're talking about Bastiaan, he took Runt back to Fairhoven city for a healer. The boy was shot and may die."

"Why didn't *you* save the kid?" A challenge. Again.

I needed to ease up. I could argue with Sven *after* I had a copy of his map. I swallowed my retort and laid a hand gently on his arm. "Wishes are not that simple. And I never told Bastiaan I'm the Wishtress." The sweetness in my voice twisted my stomach like arsenic and honey. It wasn't a lie—Bastiaan had figured it out on his own. But my words had the necessary effect.

Sven relaxed. "You have no idea how happy that makes me." His thick whisper sent hot breath against my cheek. I promptly put more distance between us.

211

A few yards away, Hedy eyed us, her neck flushed. People had gone from stuffing their packs to milling around, waiting for Sven. "We're leaving to go to the Well."

"I know." And I was counting on him consulting his map.

"It's going to be a rough journey on foot."

I frowned. "Don't you have a horse?"

"I'm not thinking about myself."

As though summoned by his implications, the discomfort in my hip and groin flared for a moment. I was so used to living with it that I didn't view it as an obstacle unless I had to, whereas it always seemed to be one of the first things Sven saw or thought about me. With a start I realized Bastiaan had only inquired about it once. After I told him it was from the pox, he'd let it be.

Was that because it didn't bother him? Or because he was embarrassed to talk to me about it?

"I'll be fine, Sven."

"You'll slow us down."

I raised an eyebrow. "What are you getting at?" Surely he wasn't implying I stay behind. That didn't align with his constant demand for a wish. Maybe he wondered why I hadn't healed myself.

Oma had refused to let me use a wish on my ailment because she said people would suspect me far less of being the Wishtress if I looked frail. She was so good at running every excuse through the sieve of fear.

How was I so blind for so long?

And now that I was thinking for myself, I couldn't use a wish on my bones even if I wanted to. I wasn't sure I wanted to. It felt like erasing part of my story. Part of my strength.

"The people already suspect you're something special. Some even recognize you from the posters. I can't always protect you." He gestured to the now-flattened camp. "These people are relying on me. And I'm . . . well, I'm relying on you."

Ah, there it was. He wanted the wish. Now. He wanted it to be like last time—me handing him a wish in a vial and kissing him good luck.

Well, this wasn't last time.

That was a different Myrthe.

"I can't give you a wish." Finally. I'd said it. Now to wait . . . for the anger. For the rejection.

A vein pulsed in Sven's temple. "Can't? Or won't?"

"Can't." I banished any remorse into a black barrel at the bottom of my chest. "You want to know why I was sick? It was because of the wish I showed you, Sven. The one that froze the canal." My words came out sharper. Hard like armor. Or were they weapons?

Get to the part about the curse. Get it over with.

Sven took a sharp breath, as if to deliver a verbal blow, but he clamped his lips shut. Exhaled through his nose, eyes closed. "Okay. You don't have to explain any more." He scuffed his shoe against the dead leaves on the forest floor. "But I have a confession."

"What is it?"

He cocked his head to the side and ducked to meet my eyes. "I had a vision. Several days back, actually . . . and it showed you giving me a wish."

Hope soared in me. "Really?" Did this mean I would break the curse?

"We were out among nature, surrounded by trees not unlike these." He tucked a strand of hair behind my ear. "This vision told me something: You've already made the choice in your heart. Give me a wish. Help these people."

I took in the flattened camp. I wanted to help them in so many ways—give them back their water source, give them a better king, give them safe places to live . . .

It wasn't a want; it was a *need.* I needed to live. I needed to be the Wishtress I was meant to be. And I wanted to earn a place in that book—to write my story of victory and service to the people. To pass on a legacy of hope and healing.

But the longer I looked at the people, the more I caught their sideways glances. Their suspicion as I talked to their leader—as he constantly sought me out and opened his tent for my comfort. The idea of traveling on foot for who knew how long with these strangers, limping my way, brought on a new feeling of vulnerability.

"They don't trust me," I said.

"But *I* trust you. And they trust me." He followed my gaze and resolve turned his jaw firm. "I can change this."

Sven led me by the hand into the gathered crowd and climbed a boulder before the people. Like domestic fish drawn to a sprinkle of bread crumbs, they drifted toward him, ready to consume his words. He lifted both hands and that was all it took for them to quiet.

"Today we head for the Well. It's time for action." The people cheered. I was silent among them, too busy trying to figure out what had spurred this action. This speech. *"I can change this,"* he'd said. What did he mean?

"The king wants to steal the Well from us, but we're going to take it for ourselves!"

More cheers.

I folded my arms. Was he going to provide them with any content, or would this be a motivational marching speech?

"We'll be traveling quickly to beat the king's militairen. We're heading north. The cold is coming. If there's anything we common-folk have as an advantage over the king and his ilk, it's our durability in harsh weather and our knowledge of the ice. With any luck we'll be at the Trials by full moon."

I was no stranger to cold, but I'd never slept in it before. I spent the days skating, but always returned to a warm home with a crackling fire and soup in a pot.

"Today we leave behind our hideout and head for the Trials—to defeat and destroy them once and for all!" This brought the loudest cheer of all. But the roar of approval subsided into an expectant silence. They were waiting for more. An explanation.

I leaned forward with the unspoken question from the masses. *How?*

"Not only do I have intricate knowledge of the Trials, but the Well has given us a great gift." Sven made no mention of the fact that Hedy and Kees knew the Trials too. All glory for himself. "A supporter beyond what we ever could have hoped—beyond even the power of the king. A wish!"

A communal gasp, mine included. Oh no. He wouldn't be so brazen—

"The Wishtress has joined our cause. She has brought her wishes for our service, for our hope, for our victory!"

There were no cheers now. Just shock brought on by the lone word *Wishtress.*

Sven swept his arms out, directing the attention my way. "My beloved Myrthe!"

CHAPTER 28

MYRTHE

How. Dare. He.

The eyes of the crowd swung as one. Fixated on me. I was exposed. Laid bare. Sven had revealed my secret. He had painted the target so fixedly on me that I now had no choice but to cling to his side for protection among these people.

Mouths gaped. Eyes stared. I could almost see their thoughts spinning with the possibilities of having the Wishtress among them. Hedy, however, looked downright murderous.

I hated Sven in that moment. I gave no wave, no nod, no acknowledgment. I would not meet anyone's gaze except his. His eyes shone with pride and never wavered. He wasn't proud of me—he was proud of finding me. Claiming me.

Lying to his followers that I'd committed a wish—*all* my wishes—to them and their cause.

Sven might trust his woodsfolk, but I certainly didn't. By nightfall I'd be facing threats, bribes, begging, and maybe even kidnapping from those who wanted a wish.

I had seen what this knowledge did to a person—to Oma, to Sven, even to Bastiaan in his deepest moment of need with Runt.

Sven had stolen what little freedom I still had.

I didn't hear another word of his speech. I doubted anyone else did either. He must have commanded something about traveling because the people moved as a flowing river to follow him, parting around me like I was a boulder. Out of respect for Sven. For now.

But they stared as they passed.

My eyes fixed on the forest floor, and I didn't move until someone near my ear said, "For you, Wishtress."

Kees was at my side, leading a horse with a blanket over its back and wearing a roughly made bridle.

"Don't call me that." Just because he now knew my Talent did not mean I'd lost my name.

"Need help mounting?"

"I'd rather walk."

"Sven requests that you ride with him. If not at his side, at least at the front of the crowd. For your safety."

I would have liked to tell Sven where he could stick his request. "The reason I'm unsafe is because he told everyone who I am," I snapped.

Kees wove his fingers together and held them out like a step for me. "It gave the people hope. And hope can fill the empty belly for far longer than any meal can."

Not if the hope itself was empty too. I plopped my booted foot in his hands, and he hoisted me up. This horse was bonier than Diantha's mare. I clucked it forward until we were not far behind Sven. He acknowledged me with a wave, but I kept my distance. For both our sakes.

I fumed the entire ride—so much I could hardly track our path other than we were moving north. I felt their eyes. Heard their whispers. Bent under their speculations and hopes and desires. When we stopped for water at a stream, I almost didn't dismount. I didn't want to be among the people.

They watched me too closely.

But I needed to refill my water pouch, so I slid off the mare's back with a deep ache that forced me to ensure my footing and let my muscles loosen before daring a step. When I finally approached the stream, the people parted. Like I had the pox. Or a curse. But they left behind the residue of their longing.

To know. To touch. To ask.

I hurried back to my horse, but the hairs on the back of my neck prickled. A man stood a foot away, holding out a piece of dried meat in a bowl of bark. "Thank you, Wishtress. Thank you for coming with us."

Dumbfounded, I allowed this strange man to place the meat in my palm. He left, but then a young woman came twisting mittens in her hands. "It's such a comfort to know the Wishtress is one of us—a commoner. It's like the Well is on our side."

Then a line formed, as though permission had been granted to approach me. One after the other, people grew bolder and bolder.

"My son has the pox. Please heal him."

"I lost my ferry business when the canal froze. Can you free me from the debt?"

"Why not give each of us a wish to use once we get to the Well? That's why you're here, isn't it?"

The closer they got, the less I received gentle thanks like the first two people. I saw need that I wanted to meet. But I also saw dangerous desire.

Oma's face on a dozen commoners.

No one called me Myrthe. I was "Wishtress" now. A new identity wholly detached from my person. I tried to mount, but a hand pulled me back to the earth. I shoved it off, panic building in my throat.

"Let's go!" Sven's shout silenced and stilled the crowd. They scattered like children caught sneaking sugar from a baker's box.

Sven sounded firm. Maybe even angry, but then I saw his face. Pride. Pleasure. He devoured the attention as though it were due him. In a way it was. The people saw him as the one who secured the loyalty of the Wishtress.

I could vomit.

Kees offered me a foot up on the mare again. I ignored him. I ignored everyone. I clambered atop the mare and nudged her forward. Sven said nothing to me and I preferred it that way. He saw their fawning as a good thing. Their threats, even. He thought my fear would keep me clinging to his side.

I couldn't wait to prove him wrong.

When we made camp that night, it was with bows strung and arrows within arm's reach. Sven relied on his foresight to keep the group hidden from the king's militairen, but if they knew the details of his Talent, I doubt they'd sleep with daggers sheathed.

The group was small enough to set up in a clearing but large enough that we had scouts patrol the perimeter. I saw Luuk and Archer set out for the first shift. Fires were allowed at dusk and dawn. Once the darkness of night fell, people laid out beds of coal beneath rock slabs to sleep on warm stones.

Only Sven had a tent, and it was the size of a small cabin. It set him apart from the rest—made him both a target and an idol. After a few woodsfolk pounded the last peg and unrolled the final animal skin, I made my move.

I wasn't tired. Wasn't hungry for anything other than action. I swept into the empty tent as though it'd been assembled for me alone. Sven wasn't in it yet, but his belongings were.

I tore into them.

I dumped everything out onto the closest animal fur. Unrolled every shirt and cloth. Unsheathed every weapon—two daggers and a spare bowstring. I even dug through the wad of beeswax inside the small tree bark jar used for protecting his clothes and boots against the wet. I shoved a hand into each of his skates and even searched inside the grooves of his skate guards.

No map.

Nothing.

There wasn't much else in the tent, but I turned over every blanket, glanced under every rug, even felt among the seams of his pillow—he had a *pillow*!—and came up empty. A small table rested in the center of the room.

I slid my hands along the corners and edges. Scrambled under the thing and examined every crook and crack and corner. Still no map. I was tempted to kick the piece once I got back to my feet.

The tent was a pigsty. Ransacked to completion.

I left it that way.

And I waited.

An hour later, Sven finally swaggered in. He smelled of ale, but by the way he stopped short at the sight of his plundered tent, it hadn't gone to his head yet. His face registered shock, then anger. "Myrthe, what—"

"Tell me how to get to the Well." I stood with arms folded, chin high, and all my belongings secured to my body.

His eyes scanned his scattered possessions again. "*That's* what you're looking for?"

"Show it to me." I was strangely calm. I had nothing to lose. No reason to stay. No reason to mollify Sven any longer. I needed to get to the Well. For myself. For Fairhoven. I would not be Sven's tool, no matter how much protection or fawning he promised.

"Sorry, Myrthe." He tapped his temple with a finger. "It's all up here."

I expected this could be an answer, so I tossed my *Wishtress* book onto the table between us and flipped to a blank page marked by a length of hard charcoal I'd found in his pack. "Draw it for me."

"No."

I expected this too. "Then you leave me no choice." I withdrew a glass vial from my belt pouch. Inside sat a droplet of water. For all Sven knew, it could be a wish. "If you don't give me directions to the Well, then I'll use my next wish to strip you of your Talent."

Sven paled. I didn't wait. I popped the cork off the bottle.

"Stop!" He took two strides forward.

I took two steps back. "Those are my terms, Sven. You have one minute to give me what I want."

"You're being ridiculous!"

I shrugged and lifted the vial. "Forty seconds."

"After all I've done for you?" he thundered.

"Like making me the target of the camp?"

"I was giving them *hope*."

I rolled my eyes. "Ten seconds." I wasn't about to waste my energy arguing *that* point. I tilted the bottle on its side, almost believing myself that it was a wish. "I wish . . ."

"Winter's breath, Myrthe, *stop!*" The pitch of his plea stayed my hand. He riffled in a hidden line of cloth strapped against his chest beneath his coat and shirt, then tossed a stained and folded piece of parchment on the table between us. "There."

I strode forward and unfolded the parchment. It was larger than I expected and far more detailed. For a moment I was tempted to lose myself in its flowing curves of mountain ranges and the spiderweb map of canals I'd only ever studied with the path of my skates. I scanned until I saw the Well of Talents.

North. Tucked away in a lone mountain peak. The canals stretched almost the entire way there. I wouldn't need to walk—I could *skate*.

I folded up the map and shoved it into my own shirt, followed by the *Wishtress* journal.

"Hey, you can't take that."

I walked to the tent door, giving him a wide berth. "You said it's all locked away in your head. You were a royal cartographer for a time. By your own words and actions, you don't need the map anymore."

"You're abandoning us?" He was doing it again. If Anouk hadn't pointed out my weakness for helping others beyond my own safety, maybe I wouldn't have noticed. But Sven had seen it and used it against me.

"I'm saving everyone the only way I know how." I didn't elaborate—that was all the explanation he deserved. If all went well, I'd get to the Well before any sort of war or skirmish broke out between Sven's followers and Mattias's militairen. I'd break the curse. I'd *live* and I'd fix everything.

"Does my love for you mean nothing?"

"You and I have very different definitions of love, Sven." While I couldn't claim to know if I'd ever truly loved him, I'd at least tried. Maybe he tried, too, but nothing between us ever reached heart level. Now that I was cursed, I couldn't allow myself to go heart level with anyone or anything. I was safer that way.

I walked through the tent flaps but made it barely two steps before fingers grabbed my upper arm with a grip of fire. "You're *not* leaving," Sven growled in my ear, more wolf than man.

I tried to tug away from him, but his grip tightened. "That hurts!" I exclaimed, not bothering to keep my voice low. A few people sat up from their beds of warmed stones.

"Get in the tent, Wishtress." I'd never seen him like this. Gritted teeth and anger so black a moonless night would have cowered from him.

"No." I tried to sound strong, but my refusal came as a mere breath.

People rose from their beds now, drawing closer. Curious. Hungry.

Sven tried to steer me back to the tent, but I dug my heels in. It sent a shard of pain up my left leg, which crumpled. Sven was going to force me. And he'd win. He had an entire loyal following who would help him, if only to keep the wishes in their possession.

Wishes.

I lifted the little glass vial so it caught a glimmer of moonlight. "Do you know what this is?" I hollered to those watching. I didn't tell them it wasn't a wish. I didn't tell them it *was*. I let their own imaginations take them to their own conclusions.

Sharp inhales. Murmurs. Panic dilating Sven's pupils.

"It's free for the taking!" I threw it into the black woods. The people stood stock-still for a long-held breath, then surged after the little bottle.

Sven released me with a shove and dove into the crowd. "Everyone back! Back! That wish is for the cause!"

His use of the word *wish* incensed them further. Someone screamed.

I turned and ran—or tried to. My legs wouldn't cooperate— liquid from nerves, sharp agony from the pox. The most I could manage was a frenzied half skip. I clambered atop the mare Sven had lent me. The bare bones of her spine hurt almost more than my attempts at speed, but at least she could get me out of camp.

No reins. No saddle. I gave her a kick and she popped into a trot. Into the shadows. I could still hear the people's screams, yelling, and Sven's angry, frantic shouts rising above them all.

But on I rode until I reached the frozen canal. A schaatser ready to skate the greatest race.

A thief ready to find the Well.

A murderer with a heart of stone.

I was Myrthe. I was the Wishtress. However ugly that looked, at least I was free.

CHAPTER 29

ʙASTIAAN

A dead fish held more color in its cheeks than Runt.

On the second sunrise since Bastiaan brought him home, winter had begun to prowl the skies, bringing thin sunlight and cutting cold at night.

The windmill smelled of herbs and blood. A pot of water boiled on the stove, refilled every couple hours by Bastiaan to keep his hands busy while Mother meticulously tended, rebandaged, and cleaned Runt's wound without touching his blood.

When Bastiaan wasn't refilling the water pot, he prayed. Even with King Mattias's damning touch on his Talent, Bastiaan could still sense the Talent's presence like he could when in the Stillness. When he had first traveled to the Well in the Stillness, he drank the water to see what might happen. The cool liquid had relieved his parched heart with a single swallow, and he never again felt thirst in his soul like that.

That difference—that satiated thirst—remained, even if his Talent didn't. And to that inner spring Bastiaan prayed. Pleaded. Promised to do anything within his power if it would somehow revive Runt.

He'd spent the past two days on edge, watching the boy and watching the window, ready to fight should the king send militairen to the windmill.

The schloss would be foolish to think it had succeeded in killing Bastiaan. The scout never returned—that should be alert enough. King Mattias was no fool. He wouldn't be satisfied without a dead or shackled body. He'd released Runt to show his power. His control. His cunning.

But schloss militairen hadn't come. This increased Bastiaan's tension.

King Mattias knew Bastiaan had killed his father. He now saw Bastiaan as an enemy of the worst kind. The only way he could have rectified the relationship was through a wish. Now even that opportunity was lost.

"You've been moping for two days." Mother stood in the doorway. "And don't tell me it's because of Runt's injury."

"I don't need a heart-to-heart," he growled, grabbing books from a messy pile on the ground. If nothing else, they busied his hands.

"How about a head-to-head? Tell me what's on your mind."

He slammed three books on top of another stack. "I don't *need* to."

"*I* need you to," she barked.

He looked up. Her arms were folded and both shoulders brushed the frame of the narrow doorway. She seemed as though she wouldn't move from that spot or let him pass until he acquiesced.

"You don't like to talk. You don't open up. I understand that about you, Bastiaan. But I also understand it's a *choice*. And when something is eating you from the inside, the way to rid yourself of it is to get it out. I'm your mother. Despite not having a Talent, I have wisdom. You'd be a fool not to seek it."

Sometimes she reminded him of King Vämbat. A force to be

reckoned with. A leader firm and stalwart. If women had been allowed to rule Winterune, she'd have made a brilliant queen. Of course, she'd refuse the position, which made her all the more brilliant.

But that didn't make him want to talk. Still, she *was* his mother, and despite the lifetimes he'd lived, he still sometimes felt like a new man sprouting from the soil of youth.

"This is about Myrthe," she said.

"She's the Wishtress." His stomach twisted with the information. Again. "But she hoards her wishes. She wouldn't even use one to save Runt." He waited for Mother's face to mirror his own horror and fury.

It wasn't there.

Her lips quirked to one side. "Did you ask her why?"

"Why what?"

"Why she wouldn't give a wish for Runt?"

"It was obvious! She heard me say you could help him and then she changed. She separated herself from the situation. Detached. Like she was hardly even human." So different from the girl he'd met at markt. The girl he'd wanted to kiss in the forest. The girl he'd wanted to know better.

How far had he fallen to be taken in by someone like Myrthe?

"Bastiaan! You know nothing about her."

"I know enough."

Mother strode into his room and yanked the books from his hands. "Look at me."

He barely managed to keep back an eye roll.

"You don't even know how her Talent *works*. Do you know how many wishes she can create at a time?"

"No," he griped.

"Do you know what the cost might be of creating a wish?"

Sigh. "No."

"The reason you feel betrayed is because you built your knowledge of Myrthe based on assumptions."

"I *do* know her." He knew enough.

Mother shook her head. "What would your attitude toward her be if you hadn't known she was the Wishtress—if you thought she was a regular girl?"

He wasn't about to play this game. "That doesn't matter. She's *not* some simple Talentless girl."

"You would have treated her differently. But suddenly, when you learned she had a Talent, you started expecting things from her. You did exactly what you hate. You've always bemoaned how people want to use Talents for their own purposes. What is it you always tell me? The Talents are for the purpose of the kingdom—the will of the water. That's why they're given. You don't know what purpose the Well gave to Myrthe. For all you know, you could have been hindering her."

"Mother . . ."

"Do you hear me?"

She was relentless! And the worst part was . . . she made sense.

"When you first met her in the markt, did you want a wish from her?"

"Of course not. I didn't know she was the Wishtress." Ugh. He was driving her point home. She had the decency to merely lift her eyebrows instead of claim victory.

"When you first wanted a wish, what was it for?"

"To take Runt to the Well. But I didn't ask for it. I didn't rely on one—"

"And then?"

He saw where this was going and his stomach churned. "Then I wanted to use it to cure my muted Talent . . . and then I wanted a wish to heal Runt. And now I want one to use on King Mattias so he'll trust me." He dropped his head into his hands. "I'm such a hypocrite."

He'd lectured *kings* about the purposes of Talents. And even though he saw the wishes as serving a greater purpose, he'd also started to see Myrthe as something other than a person. He saw her as a *resource*.

Mother patted his shoulder. "It's not over yet. She's still out in that forest. You'd be amazed at what a humble apology can accomplish."

"I can't leave Runt."

"Runt is with me now. He'll do nothing but sleep until you return. With the fire under your saddle, it shouldn't take you more than a few bell tolls."

He mounted Sterk within the hour. Flew across the fields. Through the trees. Thinking of Myrthe and how he'd left her with a young man in power who wanted a wish from her.

He would get her out of that forest, ask forgiveness, and take her to the Well. And maybe—*maybe*—she'd trust him enough to tell him about her Talent. But that wasn't his goal. Not this time.

This time he wasn't seeking more knowledge. He was seeking to be more human. For the first time he thought King Vämbat would truly be proud of him.

CHAPTER 30

The camp was gone.

Hardly a charred log or footprint. The area had been so cleared out that Bastiaan thought at first he was in the wrong location. But then he found the hollow tree on the canal bank where he and Myrthe had talked.

They'd left.

He'd lost her. For now. Sven was heading to the Well, but that didn't guarantee Myrthe would be with him. Sven knew Myrthe was the Wishtress. What might he do to get wishes from her?

With a heavy feeling of missed chances, Bastiaan turned back toward home.

Mother was standing in the doorway when he arrived. She surveyed his face and gave him a sad smile. "There will be other opportunities."

He stabled Sterk and then knocked the mud from his boots on the cottage threshold. "How's Runt?"

"Awake and asking for you."

"Awake?" Bastiaan scrambled to kick off his boots altogether, flung his cloak on the corner of the door, and hurried inside.

Runt lay on a cot beside the cooking hearth. Slow blinks and hollow eyes. He looked so . . . cold despite being weighed down by countless blankets.

"Bastiaan, I'm sorry," he croaked.

"None of that now." Bastiaan pulled up a three-legged stool and plopped himself beside Runt so the boy wouldn't need to lift his head to see him. "How are you feeling?"

"Wretched. You should send me away."

"Send you away? That's akin to cutting off my own left arm. There's nothing you could do to warrant that punishment anyway. Nothing."

"But I betrayed you."

Bastiaan had thought maybe Runt wouldn't want to speak of his time at the schloss. He'd been willing to give his friend plenty of time to rest before asking any questions. "You're incapable of betrayal."

"I led them to the forest—"

"On accident."

"I should have known! I doubled back and checked my tracks. I did everything I normally do. I was *certain* no one was following me. Otherwise I wouldn't have gone back to the camp."

"I think the scout had a Talent." Runt had spent his entire life being invisible and listening. For him to make a slip like that, it must have been Talent or Bane related.

"Really?"

"Yes. See? You did nothing wrong."

"I . . . but I didn't trust you."

Ah, so it was a matter of the heart. Runt felt like he'd betrayed their friendship somehow. "That's okay. I've . . . I've taken advantage of your trust in many ways." Like with the Well of Talents. He should have taken Runt long ago. Given him a chance at the Trials, even if it claimed his life—that was Runt's choice.

"I started to think you'd never take me to get a Talent. And she said she could help. We were alone in there and had to save each other. It was the only way to escape. She said Banes are like Talents."

"Banes are nothing like Talents." Bastiaan tried to deliver the statement gently—he tried to withhold saying it altogether, but it went against his nature to allow such a comparison. Banes were shortcuts. People who sought out a Bane didn't have the patience or appreciation for a Talent. They sought power with little thought of serving the people with it. They were driven by selfishness.

Bastiaan knew this because he'd once considered getting one. Before he had a Talent, when he wanted to free himself and Mother from the merchant.

"I think Coralythe was in the dungeon because of her Bane." Runt's voice took on a gentle tone. He'd befriended this woman—Coralythe. A servant of the king and of the Nightwell.

How had she gone from being on the council one moment to being in the dungeon the next? One answer made sense. "Did Coralythe escape too?"

"I undid her shackles and led the militairen away from her. I'm sure she escaped."

Bastiaan closed his eyes. The entire situation in the dungeon had been a setup. When he opened his eyes again, Runt was staring at him. "You know who she is, I can tell."

"Coralythe. Yes." He didn't want to tell Runt she was a plant by the crown. It would crush him. But he'd kept enough from Runt. Too much. He owed him openness, even if it pained them both. "She's on King Mattias's council. Runt, she . . . she's loyal to the king."

Runt's small face fought Bastiaan's words. He shook his head. "No. They *tortured* her, Bastiaan." His voice broke. "She helped me escape—"

"So you could lead the scout to me."

"No! I never told her where I was going."

Bastiaan hated this growing argument. "Where else would you go?"

"You don't know her," Runt accused, his voice rising.

"She was in the council meeting the day you were captured."

"I was captured because *you* left me!" Runt screamed, tears squeezing from the corners of his eyes.

Bastiaan reeled, struck. He'd meant to address this matter much sooner. Instead he'd gotten caught up in a senseless argument.

"Runt." Mother slipped into the room and gave Bastiaan a warning look.

He couldn't leave until he'd explained. "I'm so sorry, Runt. I did everything I could—"

"You could have used a snap. But you never do. You save them for everyone except me."

Bastiaan pulled off his glove and extended his hand for Runt's inspection. Ever so gently, he snapped his fingers in front of Runt's face. Nothing happened and his vain hopes plummeted. "My Talent is gone."

"What?" Runt asked, aghast.

"King Mattias has a Bane and he used it to silence my Talent. That's why I couldn't save you."

Runt stared at the marred Talent Mark and grief twisted his face. He'd never hidden his admiration for Bastiaan's Talent. It belonged to Runt almost as much as it did to Bastiaan. Runt helped keep Bastiaan grounded after his times in the Stillness. He kept records and studied the Talent and asked questions to better assist Bastiaan whenever he did use it. He'd entered the Stillness with Bastiaan several times, trusting he would start time again and return Runt to regular life.

"I really wanted one." Runt turned tortured eyes to Bastiaan. "A Talent. More than anything. I wanted to be like you."

Bastiaan shook his head, the haunted feeling in his chest growing. "And yet I would be a much better man if I were more like *you*, Runt."

Runt frowned, as though waiting for Bastiaan to laugh off his statement as a joke. But Bastiaan didn't laugh. He held Runt's gaze until the boy's confusion turned to wonder. "You aren't . . . ashamed of me?"

"How could I be?"

"I . . . cheated. I took a Bane instead."

Bastiaan sighed. He knew the hollow feeling of choosing his own way instead of the *right* way. The aftermath was always a cold torment. "I've cheated too, Runt, in many ways in my life. But you can *always* return to the right path. It will never turn you away."

"Can this be undone?" Runt fingered the edge of his bandage.

Bastiaan had spent his life studying the Well of Talents, not Banes or curses. But he knew enough. There were a few records in history of people accepting both Bane and Talent. Each record he'd found or read resulted in an internal battle between the two until one won out.

It wasn't pretty.

But it was hope.

Not only was Runt a danger to others, but his own life and loyalty were compromised. King Mattias need only command Runt to tell him everything he knew about Bastiaan, and Runt would be forced to comply.

Perhaps that was why they'd let Runt go.

"I read long ago of one thing that might help. It's no guarantee. A lot will fall upon your strength of will."

"I'll do it. Anything." The desperation on Runt's face was enough to convince Bastiaan to try.

"Runt, it's time I made good on my promise. I'm taking you to the Well of Talents."

CHAPTER 31

Myrthe

The first snowfall of the year brought a blue midnight. I was used to watching the snow come through a windowpane. Now it swirled around me like a tossed cloak of stars. Cold but also filled with promise of freezing canals and the winter culture of Fairhoven I so craved.

I loved how it reflected the moon at night and made everything brighter. A defiance against the darkness. It allowed me to travel longer. Later. Which was good because it kept me moving, sweating, warm against the air that had become cruel and needled as the temperature plummeted. Every time I pinched my lips against the knives in my inhale, I reminded myself that the cold was also delaying Sven from finding or following me.

The second night after I fled his camp, I left the horse on the banks of Canal Vier and skated north toward the Well of Talents. He'd likely learned by now the wish was fake. Or maybe the entire camp had slaughtered each other over the little glass vial.

I prayed not.

If that *had* happened, I prayed I never learned about it. I couldn't handle that guilt.

I sat on the edge of the canal at dawn, debating whether to catch a few hours of sleep or get in another leg of skating. According to Sven's map, which lay over my lap like a blanket, I'd be taking a smaller branch off the Vier northwest, which led to an even smaller canal, and then I'd continue on foot from there.

A distant *schck!* of blade on ice jolted me upright. I paused my breathing, my movements.

Schck! Schck!

Winter's breath, they'd caught up.

I scrambled to fold up Sven's map and tighten my skate laces. No, never mind the laces. I burst out on the ice and away from my pursuers with renewed energy—fear numbing me to any pain in my legs.

Over the cut of my own blades I heard a shout. My heart leaped into my throat and I skated even faster, though my muscles trembled from strain, cold, and lack of proper food the past two days.

I glanced over my shoulder and thought I saw a form skating.

That was the last time I looked behind me. It only slowed me. I could veer off the canal and hide in the trees, but due to the recent snowfall, my tracks would be clear to anyone with a sharp eye. If they'd followed me this far, I had little chance of losing them that way.

I could only outskate them.

I didn't stop for hours. Not when the snow picked up. Not when my skate lace snapped against my ankles and the movement of foot in skate created blisters. Not when my left leg screamed for mercy. Not until my heart slowed could I allow my skates to do the same.

I skated until I reached the small offshoot canal marked on Sven's map. Something about sliding onto a narrow canal over-grown with brambles and bushes and hanging tree limbs brought a semblance of safety.

I managed a handful of minutes skating along the fingerling canal before I finally crashed into a snow berm and sank into the powder that fell over me like a blanket. I could only hope—nay, pray—that I'd gotten far enough. My body could push no farther. My will, at this point, tucked itself away into a quilt of surrender.

There, in the snow, I let sleep win.

I'd pushed myself so hard. It would have to be enough to outdo my pursuer.

I woke to the snap of brambles.

Darkness.

Labored breathing interrupting the silent night. Someone clawing toward me. Though I'd hardly been moving, I stilled. Caught my breath in my throat and minimized it to nothing more than a brief exhale.

They were so close. I tried to become one with the snow. One with the silence. One with the darkness.

A flint struck stone. A spark flared to life, catching the wick of a candle in a trembling hand mere feet from me. The person tilted the candle toward the ice, searching for my tracks?

The light illuminated my face.

My hunter gasped. I leaped from the snow, throwing a handful of the powder toward where I thought their face was. I crashed to the ice but scrambled to my skates almost immediately. I took two strides, then was yanked back.

They'd caught my blade. I tugged, felt a little give, but not enough to get free. I shrieked, shoving my skate blade back and forth, hoping to cut the hand of whoever held it.

"Myrthe! *Myrthe!* Please." A sob.

I stopped my thrashing, stunned to hear my name. I spun onto my back to get a better kick. The voice was female but not one I recognized. The candle illuminated a small form, but it sank to the ice, releasing my blade. I shoved away—out of arm's reach. Ready to bolt.

"Look at me," she rasped. "Please." She held the candle up next to her face—so close it almost caught on her pale, ratted hair. But she held it firm.

Shadows covered half her face, but I still saw the angles. Saw the familiar cheekbones that looked as sickly as the last time I'd seen them.

I lifted a trembling gloved hand to my mouth, not daring to believe my eyes. "Mutti?"

CHAPTER 32

MYRTHE

You know me." Mutti wiped hair from her face and lowered the candle.

That was an understatement. I'd had her face painted upon my memory with the watercolor of guilt. Since Oma told me Mutti was alive, the pain and longing had resurfaced—tugging me forward toward the Well. To banish my curse, to use a wish, to find her.

Yet here she was.

She had found *me*.

My flapping heart calmed. I couldn't bring myself to think of Mutti as a threat. "You've been following me?"

"For days."

I wanted to launch myself into her arms—return to the body of my twelve-year-old self and be embraced by my mother. But too many questions filled the space between us. I didn't understand and I couldn't let down my guard. Not yet.

"How do you know who I am?" Was she after me because I was the Wishtress?

"My first memory of you is you as a young girl—eleven or

twelve. My husband, Koen, was dead on a cot beside me. I remembered him. I remembered his mother—Wilma—and her home. But I didn't know you. Yet you called me *Mutti*."

I wanted to explain, to beg forgiveness, but I bit my tongue.

"I was afraid. Lost. I fled the house but didn't make it far. I was so weak. Wilma came after me and urged me to leave. She said she couldn't take me back in. I had no choice since my husband was dead. I found a place of employment with a merchant. Many other women worked for him as well, and he took advantage of us—not paying us enough wages, charging us penalties for every mistake or miststep. We could never pay him back what we owed or make enough to get free of him."

She placed the candle on the ice between us. The sky lightened a touch, signaling early morning. Enough that I could now see more of her face. She stared at mine with equal intensity. She looked the same to me, but I was five years older than when she last saw me.

"I couldn't stop thinking about you—how you'd called me your mother. It felt like I'd lost something—some part of my life. Some part of my heart was incomplete, and it kept bringing me back to you. Somehow, Myrthe, I started to know—deeper than logic or even memory—that you were my daughter. I knew I needed to find you."

She coughed and it rattled in her chest, bringing back a shock of memories from when she had the pox. I passed her my water pouch. She took a long drink. When she returned it to me, I busied myself packing handfuls of snow into its mouth and then tucking the cold pouch against my body to warm it enough to melt the water.

"The young son of one of the other women ended up receiving a Talent from the Well and rescued all of us women. He took us to a new home that could be all our own. A windmill with lands to tend and freshly built housing beside a stream." She tilted her head. "Bastiaan Duur."

I jolted at his name. "Bastiaan?"

She nodded. "I was working the fields the day you showed up at the windmill. I'd seen your face sketch posted in the Fairhoven markt a week prior, and that was the first time I learned your name. Myrthe. I saw you astride Diantha's horse. You met my eye for a moment but seemed afraid. I could hardly believe it was you. Then you bolted away from Windmill Cottage."

"I didn't recognize you!" *Winter's breath,* I'd been so consumed with my fear of being hunted as the Wishtress, it blinded me to seeing my own *mother.* Right there. So close. Instead I'd run from her. "I thought maybe the women in the field recognized me from the king's poster and wanted to claim the reward."

She shook her head with a wan smile.

"You've been following me this whole time?"

"I left the fields that very minute, pausing only to grab food. In hindsight I should have waited until Bastiaan's return—asked for his help. But I didn't know when he would return. I couldn't wait. All I knew was that I saw my daughter. And I needed to get to you."

Her daughter. Me. Myrthe. Not the Wishtress. Not a commodity. She didn't have memory of our life together, but she knew me. A single memory of me calling her Mutti was enough to remind her heart that she loved me.

Not even my wishes could erase her love for me.

A tide built in my chest, swelling until it pushed a sob out of my throat. "Oh, Mutti."

I scrambled for my sleep herbs with numb fingers and a raw, vulnerable heart. The fire burned in my throat. I barely managed to croak out, "I'll explain when I wake." I pressed the soaked cloth against my nose and mouth. My vision went dark.

When my eyes fluttered open, dawn was fully upon us. Mutti

had a small fire going on the bank and had slid me as near to it as she could.

Mutti. Still here. Could this be real? I pushed myself to a sitting position.

"It's so nice to see your full face beneath the sun and not from a piece of paper or memory," she said.

"Likewise." Except her face looked even sicklier now that it was fully illuminated. I made my way over to the fire and held my hands out to warm them.

The air felt formal between us, even though I now knew her story. Maybe that was a result of my own heart hardening. Or maybe we were an awkward pair, separated for years, only just reuniting to piece together broken memories.

"Why the sleep herbs?"

"I'm cursed." The words came so easily from my lips in her presence. Somehow I knew it wouldn't bother her. I told her everything. Starting from now and moving my way back. Bastiaan, Sven, the map, Coralythe and her sons, Oma, the *Wishtress* journal, all the way back to her first memory of me. How those were my first tears—my first ever wishes. The fateful words I wished I could take back.

"I killed Pappje."

Mutti shook her head. "That's not how I see it." She made a snowball in her lap, then sucked some water from it. I offered her my canteen, but she shook her head again. "You wished for our illnesses to end. You didn't wish for us to die. What you did was stop the suffering—you sped up time. Koen's end was death. He was not meant to recover. My end was healing."

I'd never thought about it like that. Could it be true?

"Don't carry that guilt, Myrthe."

"But your memories . . . I erased them!" I thought of all the different stories we could have lived. If Mutti had stayed with Oma and me, she'd have taken care of me—she would have been a shield between Oma and me. Maybe even helped me decipher the ins and outs of being the Wishtress.

"It was an accident, Myrthe. But you can only carry that shame for so long; otherwise it will destroy you."

"How do I release it?"

"You give it up. You give it to the Well water inside you. It created your Talent; it is helping write your story. Let it write healing into it."

"So it wrote in my mistakes too?"

"No, *you* did. Living life with a Talent is sharing a pen with the Well. You both get to write your story, but the longer you live, the more you'll learn to surrender your ink."

I'd never heard the Well spoken of like that, except maybe by Bastiaan. As though it was more than water with magic. "Do you have a Talent?"

"No. I learned a lot from Bastiaan. He taught many of us about the Well. We may not have Talents, but that doesn't mean we can't understand its power." She peered up at me over her slowly melting snowball. "Do you know how Bastiaan got his Talent?"

I shook my head.

She smiled. "You should ask him someday. I think you'll find it enlightening."

Bastiaan. Bastiaan had saved my mother and didn't even know it. What I had broken, he had mended . . . and then fate brought us together. I wish I knew how he was, how Runt was.

"Bastiaan is angry with me." I scraped ice from the tip of my skate lace.

"He'll move past that. Bastiaan has strong emotions, but he has a stronger heart. It doesn't take him long to find the truth through the muck of his feelings. Give him another chance."

"If there is another chance." When would I see him again? "He doesn't know about my curse."

"That secret is yours to keep or to tell. It should not be the reason people accept or reject you."

I couldn't believe she was here, right in front of me, sharing wisdom and love and words and life. My own mother. I wanted to say so much, to spill my soul on the snow and be fully hers. Her daughter through and through. My desires and hopes for family culminated in this moment. I felt my mistakes sliding from my shoulders the longer we spoke.

Urgency, panic, loneliness, my iced-over heart all turned to shadows in my mind. In their place came the freedom of unadulterated companionship. "Will you come to the Well with me?"

"Of course," Mutti said, but she sounded sad. What was she leaving behind to be with me? To stay with me? I didn't blame her for wanting to return to Windmill Cottage and the family and safety she had there. But it was such a long journey back. And I wasn't sure I could continue forward without her.

I'd only just found her.

We laced our skates and shared a late breakfast. She didn't eat much but declared herself ready to go as soon as I packed away the last of my dried meat.

The skating was slow, almost leisurely. No more fleeing. Even with a slower pace, Mutti struggled to keep up, so I slowed even more. I tried not to think of the chase I put her through and the toll it must have taken on her already-thin body. She didn't seem to hold it against me.

I told her about the time I used to race on skates. I explained my limp from the pox and how skating was the only freedom from that pain. She pointed out her favorite type of shadows through the trees, and we even held hands for a time. I couldn't get enough of her presence, her voice, her face, her words of wisdom. Her love.

It was everything I remembered about her but more.

All my life, she'd been searching for me. Wanting me. For *me*.

Now that I'd experienced this mother's love for her daughter, it compelled me further to break this curse and give Anouk a wish to find her son. So he could know what it was like to be truly and deeply and infinitely loved.

We stopped early because of the cold and built a fire. The very flames seemed to shiver against the air, hiding themselves beneath the logs and making half-hearted coals. I checked the map while we still had light.

By my calculations we would reach the Well tomorrow. We might have made it tonight if we'd pushed like I'd been pushing myself when skating alone. But I didn't mind the slower pace. I didn't even mind if it meant Sven would catch up.

I couldn't bring myself to fear any longer.

I started laying out two sleeping places beside the fire.

"May we share a space?" Mutti asked before I got too far with clearing the snow. "It would be warmer."

Not as warm as my heart was in that moment. "Sure." We built up the fire, I laid out all my extra pieces of clothing for padding, and then we both tucked under the single blanket. Despite the snow, the winter air, and the setting sun, I was not cold.

Mutti pulled me close and wrapped her arms tight around me. I became a little girl again, breathing in her scent, resting in her warmth, letting myself be held. I remembered the many nights of childhood when Mutti held me like this. How I'd relaxed into her body and felt her relax in return. How we'd slept cocooned in the safety of each other's hearts.

There was no safer feeling.

The last thing I heard before I drifted into sleep was her warm, gentle breath in my ear and against my hair. "I love you, Myrthe."

We slept without waking. Without fear.

I woke cold.

No coals remained of our fire. I untangled myself from Mutti's arms, careful not to pull the blanket off her, but the silence of the morning—of her body—stilled my movements. I leaned toward her and brushed a strand of hair from her forehead. "Mutti," I whispered. "It's morning."

No movement.

My fingers on her brow felt nothing other than cold.

Mutti was gone.

CHAPTER 33

BASTIAAN

If I can't bring you to the Well, I'll bring the Well to you." Bastiaan held up a simple brown clay flask for Runt to see. "I used this during my pilgrimage. It seems right that it should carry Well water back to you."

"It's not the same!" Runt hadn't stopped pouting since Mother told him he couldn't make the journey. "I'm *fine!*" He struggled to lift himself into a sitting position but groaned.

"You may feel fine, but Mother said the wound was border-line infected when we arrived. If that's not monitored carefully, you'll . . . you could . . ."

"Die." Runt rolled his eyes. "People who feel as well as I do don't just die from little rashes."

"Runt . . ."

"How are you sure the Well will work like that? I thought I had to seek out the water for it to give me a Talent."

"A Talent has to do with the heart. Making the *heart* choice to drink the water is an act of seeking. It holds the same intentionality as an epic pilgrimage." At least, the idea made sense to Bastiaan.

He'd never heard of someone bringing Well water to another person who then received a Talent.

"Can't you wait until I'm better?"

"Sven and his group are already on their way to take the water for themselves. King Mattias is about to stopper the Well. Even if you and I leave today, we likely won't get there first, no matter how hard we ride. Which is another thing."

"Fine." Runt's voice was as flat as the cot he lay upon. "But a pilgrimage sounded so epic."

"We'll do it when you're better. Even if it's stoppered up." And every year and every month until Bastiaan felt like he'd made it up to Runt. In fact, he'd stop time and they could build a cabin next to the Well if Runt asked.

Except he couldn't stop time anymore.

His fist clenched. His Talent Mark burned.

The twitch of Runt's lip told Bastiaan he was pleased. "Don't die. Deal?"

Bastiaan clapped him on the shoulder. "I appreciate the confidence." He headed outside to where Mother stood at a clothesline, pulling Bastiaan's fresh travel blanket down to fold. It was stiff from the cold but dry. She hung laundry outdoors even in the bitter winter. He always wondered how it didn't freeze stiff.

"This isn't going to be like last time," she said, brusque as the incoming snow.

"Last time I still had my Talent."

"I'm talking about before you had a Talent." She folded his blanket without an edge ever brushing the ground and handed it to him. "You won't have Dehaan or his purse to get you through the Trials."

Bastiaan ran his gloved hand through his hair. "I know." His advantage was knowing what the Trials were, but he had never faced them. Not in the Awake.

And after two lifetimes his fear and dread of those Trials had only grown. He would, at last, have to face them: the tests that killed his father, that set a kingdom in uproar, and that would supposedly test his worth.

"You could die." She tore a sheet off the clothesline so hard it sent the wire bouncing into the air. A sock flew off its clothespin at the other end.

"I have to do this. For Runt."

She rounded on him. "Why not wait for this war to play out? Let the rebel band destroy the Trials and then purchase water from them."

"How do you know Sven will succeed?"

"Buy it from the king then!"

"I'm wanted by the king."

"Then give *me* the munten and I'll buy it." Her words were thick and her mouth twisted tight, not quite stopping the tremble in her chin.

Bastiaan set his folded blanket on the frosty ground and opened his arms. Mother stepped into them, stiffly at first like she knew he wasn't going to bend. She was right. But he felt her pain and fear as though they were his own—and maybe they were. Maybe it was a shared burden.

She'd lost a husband—to both the lust for power and the power of the Trials.

Now her only son was taking the same path.

"The Well water is not meant to be sold," he said. "It's a gift. I have to be part of this fight—to right my wrongs and to treat the Talent water with the honor and respect it is owed."

"You speak as though it's a person." She sniffed hard and stepped away, lashes sticking together from the tears. She wasn't ashamed of her crying. Somehow, her tears merely reminded Bastiaan of her strength.

"The Well water's alive. That much I know."

She snatched his blanket off the ground, then stomped back toward the windmill. "Let's get your vittles packed, then."

He followed, allowing her sassiness to bolster him. "Vittles?"

"Day-old bread and salted nuts that will likely stick in your teeth and drive you to madness."

"My favorite."

It took them less than a bell toll to pack, focusing mostly on food and warmth. Bastiaan was no stranger to surviving the cold. He'd used one of his early time snaps during a blizzard only to learn that time ensured the blizzard remained exactly as it was—blowing and blustering and blinding—until he returned to the Awake . . . three weeks later. He was thankful the sun and moon, at least, didn't stop their passing. Otherwise he'd never have kept track of time.

He ate as hearty a supper as his belly could hold.

"Ilse is gone," Mother said, as though such a statement could be delivered like an afterthought.

He looked up from his bowl. "When?" Ilse had been with them since their escape from the merchant. She and Mother had been deep friends since meeting.

"She left the same day you and Myrthe rode away from here."

"Why?"

"Said something about finding her daughter. She's been gone so long."

Bastiaan's stomach twisted. Ilse had been sick the past year. The idea of her traveling—alone—in conditions such as these . . . He prayed her pursuit of her daughter resulted in success. She'd been searching for years with little direction. What information had she come across in the past seven days that she didn't have before?

"I'll watch for her." It was all he could do.

He finished supper, then refilled his pack for travel: a hatchet with a leather sheath strapped over the blade, his skates should he need activity to get his muscles warm, and rabbit fur gloves. He also packed a drawstring bag of heetmoss, a little plant he'd discovered during his travels the last time he was in the Stillness. When crushed, the moss emitted heat that lasted a bell toll yet didn't quite burn the skin. Useless for starting fires but handy when fingers and toes started to succumb to frostbite.

Runt hardly looked at him. Even though Bastiaan was doing this for him, it didn't feel right. "Runt, if you don't want me to go, I'll stay."

It went against his every instinct to allow King Mattias to waltz to the Well and stopper it. Especially when Bastiaan suspected a much larger game was at play.

"I liked it better when you had a snap," Runt grouched. "You'd pause time and then a second later you'd reappear within a few feet from where you left, even if you'd been gone thirty-two years."

"A sour attitude isn't going to help you heal any faster," Mother said with a light swat on the boy's shoulder.

"Neither is a chipper one," Runt grumbled.

Mother handed Bastiaan the sack of food. "Best get going before any schloss militairen get here to arrest you."

"If they'd known I was here, they'd have arrived alread—"

A knock on the door lodged Bastiaan's final word in his throat. He glanced at the window. Night had fallen. They were expecting no one. Yet militairen didn't knock.

Mother stood firm by Runt's side, leaving Bastiaan to answer. If it was militairen, they would have Bastiaan whether he answered the door or hid on the top level. He set his pack beneath the spiral staircase as deep in the shadow as he could, then opened the door.

Snowflakes speckled the midnight hair of a figure who stepped into the light from the door.

Weather and woods, what was *she* doing here?

Bastiaan stepped aside with a sweep of his arm. "Queen Anouk . . . please, come in."

CHAPTER 34

Q ueen Anouk entered and Windmill Cottage swelled with pride. A female attendant entered after her. Bastiaan peered into the darkness. Two horses huddled against the wind.

"There's no one else." Queen Anouk stepped around him.

Runt perked up. "Hey, Queenie!"

She smiled. "Hello, Runt."

Well, weren't those two chummy. Trust Runt to be so casual after nothing more than a brief conversation with the queen in the schloss mere days ago.

"I'll stable your horses from the snow," Bastiaan choked out, then stumbled into the storm. No militairen? Not even one for her protection? How did she get here? Why did she come? What did she want?

This must have something to do with Myrthe. But Anouk was on the side of the king. She was his *wife*. If she knew where Bastiaan lived, then so did the king. Yet why hadn't the king sent his militairen? Unless Queen Anouk was the one he sent.

Bastiaan couldn't let her know he was about to leave for the Well.

He moved Mother's mare into a stall with Sterk, who snorted

his disapproval at being woken up. "Oh hush. We'll be out of here soon. Let her keep you warm until then, you big baby."

The queen's horses filed into the now-empty second stall, and he removed their bridles. Then he hurried back to the windmill.

Anouk sat at the window table, her hands now free of gloves and wrapped around a mug of herb tea. The attendant knelt at Runt's side. Upon Bastiaan's entrance, Runt bolted upright and the woman had to push him down with a barked reprimand.

"Bastiaan, this is a healer. With a *Talent*! She can get rid of the infection!" Runt's cheeks bulged with words unsaid. *I can go with you! I can go to the Well!*

Bastiaan raised his eyebrows but turned his questions to the young queen. "What have we done to deserve this honor?"

"You've done nothing . . . yet." Anouk stepped off the stool, though she was probably taller sitting on it than standing. "I heard about Runt's injury and feared for the boy."

"How?" And why would she come—in person—three days later with a healer? She'd been raised common, but compassion did not run *this* deep in those who lived in the schloss.

"Reports do not go to the king alone." The militairen were likely more inclined to serve her than their Murder King.

The healer stood from Runt's side. "His injuries should be fully healed upon the morrow's eve. The infection has been drawn out."

Runt let out a whoop.

The healer eyed him. "You'd do best to remain on your cot. Just because the wound is healing does not mean I've replenished your energy."

"His energy doesn't need replenishing," Bastiaan joked. The healer wasn't amused.

"Pushing himself too fast can lead to fevers and illness beyond a wound."

Runt clamped his hands over his mouth to muffle a snort.

Bastiaan tried to send him a firm glare, but the boy shook with glee all the more. "Understood. Thank you, Healer."

"Yes, thank you, Hilda." Queen Anouk gave a nod, and Hilda exited the windmill.

"Her horse!" Bastiaan exclaimed. "I removed its bridle—"

"She'll manage."

"In a storm like this?"

Queen Anouk did not deign to repeat herself. If Hilda could heal her own frostbite, illness, or wounds, she must be able to manage a journey alone through a blizzard. She'd be a handy one on his trip to the Well.

"I don't trust you, Bastiaan Duur." Queen Anouk crossed her arms. "My cousin, Myrthe, tried to help you. But you were commanded by the king to hunt her down and deliver her to the schloss."

Anouk *did* know more than she let on. The old worm of self-disgust knotted in his gut. "I don't plan to deliver her to the schloss. Ever."

Queen Anouk's eyes narrowed. Perhaps it was unwise to tell this to the king's wife. "A change of heart?" She sounded skeptical. Maybe even mocking.

"I call it more of an awakening." He pictured Myrthe's face— always switching between kind and indifferent. But even her cool indifference was not cruel. It seemed more of a defense mechanism. With her being the Wishtress, he didn't blame her. "I'll bring no harm to your cousin."

"I'm glad to hear it, though I'm unconvinced—something time might change." She folded her hands in front of her and seemed to summon her courage. "Would you be willing to take me to the Well of Talents?"

Of all the things he expected her to say, that wasn't one of them. "I'm common." In other words, *I have no right to the Well.* Was she trying to trap him with his words?

"You are Talented."

"I *was* Talented." His revelation didn't shake her. She knew about King Mattias's Bane.

"My point is you know the way. Myrthe trusts you. I need to get there. Soon."

Myrthe trusted him? He shook his head clear to take in the weight of her request. Everyone wanted to get to the Well. The race now had another contestant.

She held up a sagging bag that clinked from the motion. "I can offer payment."

Bastiaan didn't need munten. "Why now? Why didn't you go when you first became queen?"

"A visit to the Well was not offered to me, particularly during the uprising of those in protest." Another ripple effect from Sven's revolt.

"Wouldn't King Mattias miss you at the schloss if you disappeared for a week?"

"He, too, is traveling." Which explained why he hadn't sent militairen after Bastiaan yet. It also meant he had a head start to the Well . . . with an army.

There was no time to waste. "Your husband is going to the Well to stopper it up. To collect the water for himself, hold it at the schloss, and use or sell it at his will."

She didn't seem surprised. Bastiaan's respect for her grew. She knew how to keep knowledge private and to maintain calm when exposed.

"Why not wait for him to come home and ask for a sip of your own?" he asked. Either her quest was urgent, or she didn't trust Mattias to give her Well water when he returned.

"You're not giving me your answer."

"My answer is no. I'm not taking you to the Well." He didn't have time to wait on a queen or ensure her horse could maintain the necessary pace, even if she did try to bribe him with a healer for Runt.

The softness of her features turned all angles. "Myrthe was wrong, I see." She rose and gave a nod to Runt. "I'm glad you're well."

"Thanks for the help."

Bastiaan fetched her horse for her, tightening the cinch and putting the bridle back on. Queen Anouk stood beside the horse and waited. Possibly for him to change his mind.

"Do you need an escort back to the schloss?" he asked.

"I told you where I need an escort to." They had a brief stand-off. Then, with a sigh, she mounted and left.

Bastiaan watched her ride away, standing in the doorway for far longer than he could see her. It didn't feel right. Myrthe's very cousin, who had only ever shown him kindness. A fellow commoner, but with a crown.

"Why didn't you say yes?" Runt burst out the moment Bastiaan reentered the windmill. Already on his feet, the boy was stuffing clothes and matches into his pack. "She had *so* much gold. You could have bought all the Well water you wanted from the king when he comes back to the schloss!"

"The goal is to keep him from getting that Well water, Runt."

"And to get me a Talent."

"Of course."

Runt eyed his sharpening stone, then wrapped it in a cloth and packed it. "She sure is nice, though."

"That she is."

Mother hadn't said a word, but her posture said enough. He tried to keep preparing. To wait her out. She didn't soften. Every movement rigid and more vocal than words.

"Just say it," he said.

She faced him and folded her arms. "You demand that the king keep the waters free for all people—royal and common—yet you are equally as guilty of picking and choosing who receives it."

Her words were akin to a garden hoe to the head. She didn't unders—

"And don't you say I don't understand. I don't need to read all the books or texts to know hypocrisy when I see it."

Runt gave a low whistle, tucked his chin, and shuffled into a shadow.

"You're on a roll, Mother." First her reprimand about Myrthe and then this. "And as usual, you get your way."

Very well. If the queen wanted to freeze to death on a pilgrimage, so be it.

He threw on his coat and reached for the door handle as another knock sounded. Firm and fierce. Bastiaan's heart thundered in response. Who else lurked about the windmill at this time of night?

The knock repeated, a pounding this time. The militairen had finally come. He swung open the door.

Queen Anouk. Again. This time she didn't wait for an invitation. She swept into the windmill and faced him. "I will *not* give up. You are a seeker of information, so here's my offer. If you take me to the Well, you may ask me any question you desire and I swear to answer honestly."

That was quite the offer coming from a queen. "Only one?"

"One per day."

"And no question will be refused?"

"None."

The king's wife knew all manner of things he wanted to know. It was a gift only a fool would refuse.

But this was also Myrthe's cousin. And she'd helped Runt. Myrthe trusted her. The temptation to accept the payment pulled at him, but to do so would betray the type of man he desired to be. The man he was trying to be for Runt, for Mother, and maybe even for Myrthe.

"Keep your payment. We leave within the hour."

She opened her mouth once. Closed it. "Oh." She must have

been truly desperate to offer such a thing. One of his questions might have been to ask her why.

"I'll ask you countless questions on the ride. You'll likely tire of me on the first day." He smiled. "But you have the freedom to answer or decline."

"Thank you." She shrugged out of her cape. "Myrthe wasn't wrong about you."

That statement was payment enough. Did Queen Anouk know that Myrthe would likely be at the Well? With Sven? It would be an interesting reunion, that was certain.

Anouk and Runt went to the stables to gather the horses. Bastiaan moved to go after them, pulling the neck of his coat up over his chin, but Mother stopped him. "Come back to me, Bastiaan."

"You know that's not something I can promise," he said in a low voice.

She closed her eyes. "Try, at least."

"Of course." He embraced her and let his memories sweep him back to the years they'd spent together at the merchant's. How desperately he'd wanted to free her. And once he had, he abandoned her again and again into the Stillness. She'd endured a lot and complained very little.

"We'll see each other again."

"I know." This time she turned from him.

This was the farewell they'd grown used to. No standing on doorsteps waving a handkerchief. No lengthy exchanges or pleas for letters. A simple turn of the shoulder and walking different directions, so that one day when they looked back over their shoulders, one of them would be returning home.

Neither of them looked back.

CHAPTER 35

MYRTHE

I stared at my skates as though they'd leap from the snow and slice my throat open. I couldn't put them on. The sorrow of finding Mutti only to lose her within less than a day threatened to rob any joy remaining in this world. And yet, to allow myself to feel hopeless was to forget the joy and belonging of Mutti finding me.

I should have seen it coming. Should have been suspicious of Mutti's coughing or the fact that she'd looked as sick as she had when I saw her five years ago. She knew she was sick, and she came for me anyway. She knew she was dying, and she held me. She knew her breath was failing, and she used it to tell me she loved me . . . despite knowing me only in her heart and not in her memories.

I tried to stand beneath the heavy weight of sorrow. To allow myself grief meant allowing feeling into my heart—moving aside the guards flanking my emotional bridge and risking my life and my last wish for the sake of someone else.

Mutti would want me to keep going. Anouk would want me to break the curse.

So I could live.

Though the longer I told myself that, the more I wondered, why did I need to live? What exactly was there for me to live for?

I was only living for myself, to prove that Coralythe couldn't destroy me and that Oma was wrong about the Wishtress's purpose. But also for the hope of a cure. For answers from the Well. Throughout this entire curse my goal had been *life*. Break the curse, live my life.

I'd refused to consider failure. What if the curse couldn't be broken?

I shook my head. Focused on my goal. Reach the Well. Find answers. And then deal with Sven, the king, the Vier, and my curse afterward.

If there was an afterward.

I left behind the mound of rocks I'd spent half the day collecting to properly entomb Mutti. I covered her grave with prayers and the soft portions of my heart that remained.

With every step across winter plains and through shadowed forests, with every footprint left behind in the blanket of light beneath my feet, I risked being found. Followed. By Sven.

I reached the canal again, strapped on my skates, and left the pain, the memories, the light and darkness behind.

By noon tomorrow this would all be over . . . one way or another.

CHAPTER 36

BASTIAAN

We're like a tavern riddle," Runt said now that the sun had risen. "What do a Talented, a canal rat, and a queen have in common?"

"Prepare yourself," Bastiaan muttered to Queen Anouk. "This is day one."

They'd ridden from the windmill as quickly as the darkness and snow allowed, but a bouncing trot didn't leave room for conversation. Now that they'd left the road, they allowed the horses to set a slower pace for a breather.

"I give up," Queen Anouk replied to Runt. "What do they have in common?"

"Nothing! Only the canal rat is a commoner!" Runt cackled.

"That was definitely one of your worse ones, Runt," Bastiaan said. "I'm common too, remember?"

"You're a *Talented*."

"I was born common as well," Anouk said.

"But you're queen now, so it doesn't count!"

Bastiaan rolled his eyes. "Any joke that needs explaining is already a failure."

"How long did you say this journey would take?" Anouk whispered with a laugh.

"Three days, as long as the horses and our stamina hold." Mainly her stamina. Runt and Bastiaan were used to long, fast rides, pushing the limits of time in more ways than one. "Do you know if the king and his militairen were on foot or on horses?"

"Horses, of course."

It was a thin hope. "When did they leave the schloss?"

"A day and a half ago."

Bastiaan nearly kicked Sterk back into a canter. If they didn't beat the king to the Well, this journey was a waste. He had spent hours studying his memory of the council meeting and how King Mattias had said he would offer Banes to all his subjects. How could he do that? He couldn't bring every person in Winterune to submerge themselves in the secret pool of Nightwell water. And revealing the location of the Nightwell wouldn't achieve his goal either.

Something was missing. Bastiaan could see the individual leaves of the dilemma, but there was no trunk to ground these thoughts into a clear picture. It was infuriating.

Anouk nudged her horse nearer to his until they matched pace. "Don't let me slow you down. I want to reach the Well before my husband as much as you do. I'd rather not have to beg him for the water."

"Is that the reason you're trying to get there before him?" Pride didn't seem like a motivator for her.

"I've heard of a voice in the water. I wish to speak with it."

"There is a voice." But more than that. A poultice upon the wounded heart, a salve for the soul. Something about the Well water had felt continuously alive inside his body, inside his Talent Mark. Anouk sought the voice—had faith that it held answers or guidance or *something* to satisfy her purpose. And if Bastiaan knew anything about the Well of Talents, it was that the water honored that sort of seeking heart.

"Prepare yourself then. We'll water the horses at the river ahead." Bastiaan gestured to a copse of trees. "Then we'll ride so hard you'll be too sore to dismount."

Bastiaan was impressed by the young queen. She didn't complain when the cold hit. She didn't snub her nose when they bedded down on the lumpy ground for a mere three hours. She joined in chipping ice from the sides of the canal and melting it for the horses to drink. She removed her own tack, brushed her horse, and picked its hooves.

Whether she'd been raised caring for her own horse or simply had stamina, Bastiaan was proud to have her as his queen. Mattias did not deserve such a gentle yet resilient bride.

They pushed the horses as much as the beasts allowed. Since their pace left no room for conversation, Bastiaan spent much of the ride thinking. Too much thinking.

He was unused to the feeling of not having enough time. His destroyed Talent Mark itched and sometimes burned the more he thought about it . . . the more he wished he could stop time for all but them. Instead he had to function as the rest of the world. And he felt weak because of it. Less than. Like his identity had become nothing more than average.

There once was a time when he felt unique. Chosen by the Well to wield a powerful Talent. He'd spent years and years both in the Stillness and in the Awake gathering information, journaling his travels and discoveries so that someday the next generation would know everything they needed to about the Well.

He wanted to be the Talented who changed the course of history.

But he had not yet written about Mattias's Bane or its effect on his Talent. He was too ashamed. Defeated—deflated—by a mere touch from the king he was supposed to serve. Now he had to get himself, Runt, and the queen to the Well before it was too late.

Not only that, but before Sven and Myrthe arrived. If Mattias caught Myrthe there, he'd stop at nothing to claim the Wishtress for his own.

Bastiaan gave Sterk another nudge with his heels.

Time fought him. He held on to the slim hope that the water would restore his Talent. He always believed the Well of Talents was superior and more powerful than the Nightwell.

Mattias's Bane hinted otherwise.

If it could destroy Talents, there was nothing stronger.

"Did you ever find that canal rat you were searching for?" Runt asked the queen when they slowed their horses to a walk around midday the following afternoon. "Cairden?"

"Not yet." She patted her horse on the neck.

"You're still looking for him?"

She let out a long breath. "I'll continue looking until I find him."

Runt cringed. Bastiaan knew what the boy was thinking. *That crat kid is long dead.* There were no crats by the name of Cairden. Countless crats froze to death each year, especially young ones.

The kid must be her brother. Why else would she be so adamant about finding him?

"Are there canal rats beyond Fairhoven?" Anouk asked Runt. Bastiaan settled back in his saddle, curious to see how this conversation went.

"Probably. But they all learn pretty quickly to make their way to Fairhoven. There's far more opportunity here at the capital to beg, snitch coins, find other crats. Plus, free bread! Well, that used to be the case. Now with the canal frozen . . ."

Anouk sighed. "I miss those days in the markt. Have the other children—crats—been okay?"

"From what I can tell." Runt stuck his nose in the air to a comically stuffy level. "I've moved on to better things."

Bastiaan wanted to laugh, but Runt's "better things" comment stung him with guilt. Runt's idea of better things was Bastiaan, a friend who broke promises. Who abandoned him to torture in the schloss dungeon. Who relied on the boy to ground him after an overlong visit to the Stillness.

Bastiaan didn't deserve him.

"What about your family, Runt?" Anouk asked. "Don't you ever wonder about them?"

Bastiaan stiffened. The insensitive question was a stark contrast to her typical tactfulness.

"Who, Bastiaan and Diantha?" Runt asked.

"No, I mean"—she gave Bastiaan an apologetic shrug—"your parents."

"Haven't got any." Runt didn't seem bothered. Bastiaan had asked him about his birth parents years ago. Runt said he didn't want to talk about it, so Bastiaan had left it alone ever since. He'd assumed it was too sensitive, but Runt's current nonchalance proved otherwise.

"How did you become a canal rat?"

"My pa got the wrong woman pregnant. He didn't want to keep me because I wasn't supposed to be born. At least that's what the poorhouse woman told me. She saw my pa and said, 'I know what kinda man that is.' That's why she took care of me. Her own pa was the same kind of man."

"What happened to her?"

"Nin Jaalis cared for me until I was old enough to go to the canals to sharpen skates for coin. That's what she does. Almost all the crats have been in her home for a spell or two."

Anouk turned a bit green. "I'd like to meet this woman."

"You keep asking us for stuff. Even though Bastiaan didn't want the gold, I'll take it!"

"I'd be happy to pay you."

"After the Well, of course. But maybe I'll get a Talent that will let me travel really far! And I could take you with me, like Bastiaan sometimes takes me—"

"Or maybe you'll get a Talent that makes you croak like a frog when you talk too much!" Bastiaan tried to keep his tone playful to cover the interruption. While Bastiaan's Talent no longer worked, he still wanted to keep it private. Anouk might not know that Bastiaan was King Vämbat's murderer.

They crested a hill and nearly rode straight into a pile of firewood. Sterk dodged it expertly, then hopped over a doused fire. Bastiaan reined them all to a halt and took in the remnants of a camp.

A rather large camp.

Abandoned piles of wood, over two dozen burned campfires, hoofprints, and boot prints spoke more clearly than a notice board.

This camp had been set up by King Mattias's militairen. And judging from the direction of the tracks and the spray of wind-blown ashes from the fires, they'd vacated the spot over a day ago. The odds of overtaking them—or even catching them, for that matter—seemed bleak.

The benefit, though, was that he, Runt, and Anouk could now use the road and travel more openly without fear of being overrun from behind. A king on a mission rarely looked back.

"Let's keep going." They skirted the edge of the camp and followed the tracks at a distance.

They stopped three more times to feed and water the horses throughout the day. Every delay wriggled like an itch beneath Bastiaan's collar. But King Mattias was having to navigate the same setbacks. And he had even more horses to water.

Unless King Mattias had already reached the Well.

And stolen its water.

And captured Myrthe. Or killed her.

Bastiaan shook his head. He couldn't allow himself to think like that. *Focus on the Well. On the mission.* He'd get Runt to the Well. He'd find Myrthe. He'd make things right—and he'd fight the king in any way he could.

Bastiaan used to think he'd *feel* something if the Well was stoppered. But now that his Talent had been snuffed, he no longer trusted anything he'd previously thought about the Well. It was as though all his research and study had been for naught. Had he merely been gathering information for information's sake?

Had he missed the entire point?

"So what happened to my cousin?" Anouk piled kindling for a fire to melt more water for the horses. "I've been waiting for you to bring it up, but I'm not going to wait any longer."

Bastiaan fumbled the flint. "Myrthe?"

"Last I heard from her, you were going to take her to the Well. Yet we're making the pilgrimage and she's not with us."

"I left her with Sven." A spark caught and he gently breathed it to life amid the pile of sap and dried brush. "I regret it most bitterly."

"Surely she doesn't fault you for caring for Runt."

"I was cruel to her the last we spoke. I expected a wish to save Runt and then abandoned her when she wouldn't give one."

Anouk snapped small sticks in half and added them to the growing flame, nurturing it with a tender hand. "She'll forgive you."

He released a hollow laugh. "How can you know that?"

"Because she forgave me for the same thing."

"You asked her for a wish?" What did the queen want with a wish? Had Myrthe actually refused her?

"I asked for a wish before I asked for understanding."

He could relate to that. Dare he hope for Myrthe's forgiveness?

He eyed the young queen, more questions burning on his tongue. Though he'd refused her offer of knowledge as payment, he wasn't too timid to push the limits of her generosity. "Did she give you one?"

"No."

"Why not?"

Anouk tossed the last sticks in the fire, then brushed off her hands and stood. "That is not my question to answer."

"Can you at least tell me how she creates a wish?" He told himself he needed to add to the pages of research he'd assembled. But a deeper truth confessed he wanted to know *Myrthe*. Nothing more.

"She must weep." Anouk's forlorn voice almost disappeared beneath the growing crackle of flame. "Each tear she cries can be used to grant a wish."

Sorrow. Or, on rare occasions, joy. That was what it took to produce a wish. A torn and bleeding heart. Vulnerability. That explained the Talent Mark on her eyelash. It explained the many times he'd seen her steel herself against different words and interactions.

When Runt had lain bleeding in the field on the outskirts of Sven's camp, Myrthe had seemed so close to tears. She'd been about to create a wish.

Then Bastiaan had reassured her of Runt's survival, so she'd detached herself from the emotions. The more he learned about Myrthe, the more he knew there was a deliberate reason she'd kept that wish back. He wanted to know that reason. And he wanted to hear it from *her*. No more guesswork, no more asking her cousin.

"Prepare to mount up within a quarter bell."

Close to sunset they stopped. "We're a quarter day's walk away at most. Less on horseback. We'll rest for two hours."

Anouk's fingers trembled as she tried to undo the saddle cinch.

"Here, let me." Bastiaan moved to her side and she allowed him to remove the tack and spread the horse blanket on the ground for her—proof of her weariness. "Runt, can you manage the firewood?"

"Sure, Bastiaan," he said in a thin voice. Maybe they should rest longer.

Bastiaan would make that call once he'd assessed the scene at the Well. "I'm going to climb that hill and scout our situation."

The last time he'd been here was with King Vämbat. It was not a well-known location to anyone but Bastiaan. He'd found the hill and small rock cropping that rose above the plains and gave a clear view of the Well of Talents when he first visited the Well in the Stillness.

He would finally know how far behind King Mattias's men he was.

"Tell me what you see." Anouk's energy seemed to perk up. It must be tense deceiving the most powerful man in Winterune. A man with two Banes and a quest for control. A man she'd married.

Bastiaan set his pack against a stone and left them at a jog. Despite the physical exhaustion from a hard day's ride, moving his limbs felt good. It got his blood flowing, filled his lungs with icy air. He pushed through the crunch of old snow and ducked under the brittle evergreen branches. If King Mattias's army had already reached the Well, they'd be camped at the beginning of the Trials. There wasn't enough room at the actual Well for them all to fit through the ravine.

But maybe the army left a gap in their camp that he, Runt, and Anouk would be able to weave through to reach the Well first.

Bastiaan broke through the trees at the top of the hill and navigated to the edge of the rock cropping. The sun had nearly set but the alpenglow left a pink hue over the valley below. He stopped, chest heaving, and focused on the land between him and the mountain that housed the Well.

He peered at the base of the mountain—where the Trials began. Nothing more than a wall of mist marked the start of the first Trial.

No people. No army. King Mattias had not arrived. Neither had Sven.

How could that be? Had he passed them without knowing it?

To the right of the valley a long line of forest housed the still-frozen canals. That was likely where Sven and his followers were. He wouldn't travel in the open plains like King Mattias. Could Mattias have made it through the Trials already and to the Well?

For all Bastiaan could see, the valley and the Trials were as untouched as when he took in this view from the Stillness. Where *was* everyone?

He stepped farther out on the rock cropping to get a wider view—and spotted a dark mass of humans far to the northwest, like an ink drop on a lumpy, unfurled map.

King Mattias's army was not at the Well—they weren't even on the path *to* the Well.

Their camp lay far to the left, beyond the Well mountain completely.

And that's when Bastiaan understood. This quest of the king's had never been about the Well of Talents.

King Mattias had taken his army to the Nightwell.

CHAPTER 37

BASTIAAN

"This is our chance," Anouk said when Bastiaan gave a report. "The path to the Well of Talents is ours to take."

"King Mattias is planning something sinister at the Nightwell."

"What you call sinister some might call strategic." Her calm response coiled his muscles further. Could she not see the seriousness of this revelation? Would she really defend her husband in a situation like this?

"He said in his council meeting that he'd force Banes on all his people. I need to find out how he's planning to do that."

She lifted her chin. "You *need* to take me to the Well of Talents as promised."

Promised. Bastiaan glanced at Runt. The boy's face was artfully neutral as he listened to their exchange. Bastiaan had promised Runt a Talent. Then he'd gone and promised the queen a trip to the Well.

He'd delayed and delayed with Runt. They were so close, but . . .

. . . this could not be ignored.

"What Mattias is doing at the Nightwell could threaten the very existence of the Well of Talents. He bypassed it altogether. That alone is reason for concern. Get some rest here while you can. Runt, I'll show you the overlook so you can keep an eye on the army and Sven's group if they emerge. Anouk is now your charge."

Runt nodded, empowered with a mission. "I'll protect her, even if I have to use my Bane."

Bastiaan tried not to cringe. "You're a good lad. But don't use your Bane. Not for any reason—using it will give it more power over you."

Anouk pressed her lips into a tight slash of disapproval. "And what about you?"

"I'll enter King Mattias's camp, scout the situation. If I haven't returned by dawn, it's best you head back to the schloss."

"No way!" Runt exclaimed. "I'll come after you!"

"No, you'll protect your queen."

"You should know by now that Runt is more loyal to you than to his country. As is right with family." Family. The one thing Anouk seemed to care most about.

"I'd come after you, Bastiaan! Covered in blood. No one would be able to stop me or touch me. I'd free you!"

"No, Runt. Don't use your Bane." The boy was too young to carry the weight of murder. He'd already killed the dungeon master, and it nearly destroyed him—taking down a man who was ready to cut off his very fingers. If Runt had compassion and regret for such a death, he would not survive a battle of blood. Not internally, at least.

"Sven and his band of followers can't be far. Myrthe is with them. They're likely in the canals. They can direct you back to the schloss."

"If you don't return to us, I'll continue through the Trials on my own," Anouk said.

Stubborn queen of a woman! "The Trials will kill you if you attempt them alone."

"Then you'd best not get caught."

Bastiaan traveled in shadows. Beneath tree boughs or in the throat of the valley. He took Sterk only so far before he looped the reins over a branch, low enough that Sterk could get to the foliage beneath the snow and loose enough to tug free if Bastiaan whistled . . . or died.

He crept the rest of the way to the camp, taking a full bell to avoid alerting any scouts. He avoided the canal. It was as dangerous as walking on a road, but harder to leave once spotted. At least he had nightfall in his favor.

A distant *clang* met his ears. He stopped. Listened. Dim voices, a shout. He took a few steps closer, tugging his right glove off to free his time snap before remembering with a growl that it was dead. He had no emergency plan. No escape route. If only he were in a militair uniform.

The snow muffled his footsteps but illuminated his presence. He used the trees and noise and shadows as a shield until the clanging mixed with human grunts. Flickering torchlight met his eyes before the full scene could. There was too much light—both from the near-full moon and the torches. He couldn't move much closer without getting caught.

Something about the noise struck him as odd. These militairen were doing something . . . unusual. He opted for a different angle, traversing the scene and keeping his distance until the trees lent themselves to a better view.

There. An opening.

Ground torches formed long lines, curving like two parallel snakes deeper into the camp than the darkness allowed Bastiaan to see. The flames illuminated dozens of militairen . . . digging. They hefted mounds of dirt into wagons that were carried to a different place and poured to create berms. Bastiaan didn't envy their having to break through frozen earth.

At first they seemed to be working on a large hole—far too large for a latrine and too purposeful to be a sleeping shelter. Bastiaan studied the shadows, following the line of torches, and saw more militairen.

Not a single hole. It was a trench of some sort. Wide and deep.

He spread out the map of the land in his mind, locating himself on the edge of the camp and picturing this snake of a trench and where it might lead. Chills struck his body so fiercely he almost mistook them for a clump of snow falling on his neck.

They were digging a trench to the Nightwell.

No. More than that. *From* the Nightwell. But to where?

He followed the trail in his mind's eye. This wasn't just a ravine. It was a *canal*. They were connecting the trench to the Vier.

They were going to release the Nightwell water into the canals and infect all of Winterune.

CHAPTER 38

BASTIAAN

Bastiaan mounted Sterk and was on his way back toward the Well of Talents in what seemed like minutes. His mind thrashed theories back and forth like wind upon the weak boughs of a sapling.

A new canal would direct the water from the Nightwell straight into the water of the entire country. If it went far enough, it could even hit the Handel Sea and spread to the rest of the world.

Building a dam—building *ten* dams—wouldn't hinder it.

King Mattias was planning to force Banes on every one of his subjects. And they would accept it as a gift. Then he'd be able to command and control them.

There was no way to stop him.

No way except a far-fetched theory Bastiaan had concocted. It wasn't in any book by Well historians. It was based on his own knowledge that he once prized—a prideful knowledge that had played a part in his own ruin.

The Well of Talents was the only power equal to the Nightwell. Bastiaan used to view it as more powerful, but now he wasn't sure. His one hope was to get to the Well and . . . what? Talk to it? Ask it to remove Runt's Bane, give Anouk a Talent, restore Bastiaan's snap, and nullify the Nightwell?

Bastiaan didn't know if even *one* of those things would happen. They'd have to team up with Sven and make sure they secured plenty of Well water in order to offer the people of Fairhoven a cure.

He'd always understood that Banes and Talents linked to the heart of a person. That was why he was taking Runt to the Well— because Runt's heart was stronger than a Bane. Bastiaan was sure of it.

The glow of dawn began as he reached the opening of the ravine that led to the Well of Talents. The first Trial stretched as tall and wide and intimidating as Bastiaan remembered. The last time he'd seen it in the Awake was when he took his original pilgrimage to the Well. Rather, when he assisted Dehaan on *his* pilgrimage.

All other times had been in the Stillness when the Trials posed him no threat.

He averted his eyes and scanned for his comrades. Runt and Anouk weren't there. No one was.

He peered toward the overlook, but they weren't on the plains either. Could they have gotten lost? They wouldn't have entered the Trials alone yet, would they?

He waited another hour, but still no sign of them. They should have been here to meet him. He kicked Sterk into a gallop and headed toward the overlook.

It took him less than two bells to reach it, but all that remained was the now-dead fire. He let out a bird whistle that Runt would recognize. Perhaps Runt had taken Anouk to the canals and met up with Sven.

Had his instructions not been clear enough?

A warning tickled the hairs on the back of his neck. He spun. Movement in the shadows. His throwing discs were in hand before his next breath.

Runt emerged. "Bastiaan, it's me!"

"What are you *doing*?" Bastiaan hissed, stowing the discs.

"Searching for you." Tension coated Runt's answer.

Bastiaan gazed past him into the shadows. Something was wrong. "Where's Anouk?"

"They caught us, Bastiaan. Militairen. I think I let the fire burn too long into the darkness. They took Anouk back to camp—to King Mattias. I don't know what he'll do to her. I managed to get away, but they have my horse, which is why it took me so long to get to you—"

"Okay, okay. Calm down." *Weather and woods.* This was Bastiaan's fault. "When was this?"

Runt joined him by the snuffed fire, staring forlornly at the ashes. "A few hours back." He shoved his hands into his pockets. "I was told to give you this." He withdrew his fist.

Bastiaan stepped closer to get a better view under the weak morning sun. Runt's palm was smeared with blood. *His own* blood.

He thrust the bloody palm at Bastiaan's face.

Bastiaan reeled backward, narrowly missing a deadly splash of liquid. "Runt . . . what—"

Runt launched himself at Bastiaan with a bloody swipe. This time Bastiaan knocked his arm aside, but the boy scrabbled for purchase, reaching for Bastiaan again and again. One drop would be the end of him.

Bastiaan grabbed Runt's bony wrist and yanked it away. "For spring's sake, *stop*!"

"I have to do this!" Runt cried, tugging against Bastiaan's hold.

Bastiaan wrapped his legs and arms around the boy, pinning him to his body but holding the bloodied hand as far away from him as he could. They both heaved for breath, the shock of adrenaline still coursing through Bastiaan.

Runt had just tried to kill him. *Kill* him. "Explain."

Something wet landed on Bastiaan's wrist. He flinched away from it. Waited for pain. But then came Runt's sniffle. It had been a tear. "The king commanded me, Bastiaan."

"Just like that? A simple com—" *Oh.*

"I'm his subject! He's my king! You of all people believe Talents exist to serve the king and the people of the land."

"Runt . . . it's your Bane. King Mattias has the power to make you obey."

Runt stilled.

"Do you understand?"

The boy nodded.

"This isn't your fault. We're going to get you to the Well—like I promised—and get you a Talent." And pray with everything he had that the Talent would defeat the Bane inside Runt.

"When will you actually keep that promise?" Runt asked.

"Today. Now. This very moment." He could curse himself. If he'd taken Runt and Anouk to the Well first, none of this would've happened. "Can I let you go?"

Runt sniffed hard and nodded. "I'm sorry, Bastiaan. So sorry. I didn't want to."

"I know." Bastiaan eased his arms open until Runt fell out of them.

"But loyalty to my king has to come first." Runt spun, hand splayed, and leaped toward Bastiaan.

Despite his hopes, Bastiaan was ready. A knock of stone to temple sent Runt to the ground. Unconscious. He bent over the boy, fighting back a broken cry. He'd never struck Runt before in any way . . . not physically, at least. But he'd recently come to learn that his broken promises and obsession with Well knowledge had done its own damage—had driven Runt to receive a Bane that was being used against them both.

He tore strips from his undershirt and wrapped Runt's bloodied hands with the cloth. Then he gathered Runt in his arms. For a moment he cradled the boy . . . like a father would a son. Unconscious, Runt looked even more like the child he was. The responsibilities, life, and dreams Bastiaan had taken upon himself fell away and reminded him of the life Runt should have had—the life Bastiaan should have given him.

If Runt woke and still tried to kill Bastiaan, it would put them both in danger. He couldn't take him through the Trials like that. The Trials might kill them both.

He'd have to leave Runt behind. Again. He prayed the boy would understand.

He used Sterk's reins to tie Runt to a tree but left them loose enough that Runt could get free with a bit of work . . . in case Bastiaan didn't survive the Trials. Then he scratched a message on the face of a rock with one of the half-burned sticks from the fire.

Keeping my promise.

He mounted Sterk and directed the horse to the overlook. Concern for the queen niggled in the back of his mind, but he didn't let it take root. She'd taken this risk upon herself.

Down in the valley in front of the Trials he saw a small blob of shapes. Sven had made it. He was about to try to destroy the Trials, having no idea King Mattias and his army were on the other side of the mountain preparing to flood the canals.

Bastiaan headed for the Well. This time nothing—not Mattias, not Sven, not the Trials, and certainly not himself—would stop him from getting Runt water from the Well of Talents.

CHAPTER 39

𝕸YRTHE

The Trials.

I could see them from the tree line. The path to the Well of Talents led into a narrow valley between two treacherous cliffs. The rocks resembled sliced Night Forest cake—black, smooth, not a handhold to be seen. Impossible to scale.

A curtain of white mist blocked the entrance. At first I mistook it for snowfall, though the sky was clear, but something about it looked too unnatural. That was how I knew it was the first Trial.

But more intimidating to me than the Trials was the group of people between them and me. Sven and his woodsfolk. They'd beaten me here. The map truly had been secure in his mind as much as in his pocket.

What was more, they'd beaten King Mattias and his militairen.

Had Mutti not found me—had Mutti not died—I would have made it long before Sven.

I'd spent the last day thinking about her. Her sacrifice. She'd used the last of her energy and life to find me. To be with me. She'd known she was dying and had gone into it with *joy*. Calm.

I'd been so focused on saving my own life, I never considered maybe this curse *was* going to be my end. And maybe something was worth dying for in order to use my last wish.

The concept shook me. I couldn't manage to tuck it away or silence it.

I tried to focus on the Trials again. Sven. My original goal. I'd studied the map. A tiny thread of a canal led around the mountain to the back. Could it possibly lead to the Well a different way than through the Trials? I couldn't risk losing the time to find out.

Sven was going to empty the Well—steal the water for himself to use for bargaining with Mattias. I needed to get to it before he gained control.

Which meant I needed to face Sven.

When I first stole that map, I thought it was to break out on my own. To finally be free, reach the Well, write my Wishtress story. Instead, maybe it was so I could be found. Not by myself but by my mother. To learn that I could be—had been—loved deeply for exactly who I was despite my mistakes, my regrets, my guilt, and even my future.

That was real freedom.

It empowered me to go through with whatever came next.

I removed my skates, replaced my boots, and walked along the tree line, keeping out of sight as long as possible. Eventually I crossed the exposed plain toward the Trials . . . and the woodsfolk. I felt their anger before I saw their gazes turn to me. Their fingers point. Their mouths whisper. Luuk and Archer looked ready to nock their bows and fire at my heart. The woodsfolk welcomed my approach as one would a leper. I was distinctly aware of my limp and the chaos in which I had left them.

The almost-lie of the wish in the vial.

What had Sven told them about me after I fled? What tale had he spun to remain the hero and paint me the villain? He stood ten yards from the Trial, planting himself between them and their fear. A stepping-stone from old ways to new freedom.

I walked to the wall of mist. I couldn't turn back. There was nothing to turn back to. I had chosen this path and I must face it.

The closer I got, the broader it seemed, and soon the murmur of speculating onlookers dimmed until I no longer heard them. The mist hung unmoving and undisturbed yet seemed to be breathing. I caught the faintest of inhales and the shudder of an exhale minutes later.

A sleeping dragon.

"You enter by walking through it." Sven waited for me to come to him. How very like him. But he didn't seem angry. That was almost more nerve-wracking. "But since you've changed your mind, we won't need to do that, right?"

"Changed my mind?" I asked.

"You're here. You rejoined us. You can give me the wish right now and I'll wish the Trials away."

Give him the wish. He still thought I was his tool to be used for glory. It was time for this to end. For the truth to come out at last.

"It was cruel of you to give me a fake. Make me fight my own people for it." His voice turned to cold, sharpened steel. "Threaten me with it."

"I did what I had to do."

"Then you can do the same right now. Give me a wish. A *real* wish."

"I can't make wishes anymore." I bit my lip. This wasn't like when I'd told Mutti—which had been easy and natural. However, unlike when I told him I was the Wishtress, this time I felt freedom. A desperate sort but freedom all the same.

He gave a half laugh of disbelief. "Another lie? This is where it happened." He gestured to our surroundings. "My vision. This is where you give me the wish."

I frowned. I didn't see any trees like he'd described. "What . . . what happened in the vision after I gave it to you?" Did he see me give other wishes? Cured?

"I destroy the Trials. I lead everyone to the Well. We *win*."

"But, Sven, I can't make wishes anymore." He wasn't hearing me. I wasn't sure he'd ever truly heard me.

A long pause. "That's not what you're supposed to say." The statement held an undertone of warning.

To keep talking would be to intentionally skate into the middle of a thawing lake. But there was no going back now. Sometimes when faced with thin ice, skaters needed a burst of speed to pass over it before it could break beneath them.

"I was cursed the day after I told you about my Talent. When I froze the Vier, it killed a woman's children. She had a Bane, so she cursed me in return. The next time I make a wish, I'll . . . I'll die."

Sven closed his eyes as though drawing up the last vestiges of patience from within. "Stop, Myrthe."

"I *want* to help—"

"Just *stop*."

I did, but where I used to quail and cave into myself, I now felt anger replace that weakness. Defense, though I had no ground to defend myself.

"You never intended to help me." Thunder rolled over his face, his eyes turning dark and teeth flashing like lightning.

"I'm going to the Well to *reverse* the curse. Then I can help everyone."

"And how will you get there?" He grabbed my shoulders and shook me. "We're at the Trials with no way to destroy them. Your wish was our only plan! What was *your* plan?" He sneered. "Did you think you could get through the Trials on your own?"

"You saw me giving you a wish. Right here in this spot. It must be after I return from the Well. That's proof of our success, right?"

283

"That vision never happened!" he burst out. "I told you that because I thought you were nervous about giving me a wish!"

Lies upon lies. My inner ice wasn't thick enough for this. I was still weakhearted from burying Mutti. "You got past the Trials last time, Sven."

"I didn't!" His fingers dug into my shoulder blades. "Every last one of my companions died trying to get through these Trials."

I struggled to find words. What did he mean he didn't get through the Trials? "But you had a wish. I *gave* you one—"

"I'd already used it!" The confession spilled out of him like a splash of venom. He released me abruptly. I suspected he hadn't intended to tell me his secret. "That's how I got my ability to see the future. I wished for it."

I stumbled backward. "You didn't use the wish to get to the Well?"

"Seeing the future would tell me if we succeeded either way. I thought it would give us the upper hand." And it would give him a power—a fake Talent—even if they failed. "But the wish gave me *partial* foresight. It's unpredictable."

"You weren't specific enough when you used it."

"You didn't prepare me! You could have told me how to use it effectively!"

So it was my fault he'd used the wish for personal gain? "All these people here believe you have a Talent. They believe you made it to the Well and came back to fight for them. You need to tell them the truth. King Mattias could be here within the hour."

"I'm not lying to them. They know about my Talent—"

"It's not a Talent." His entire fame, entire rebellion, had been built on this story he told of completing the pilgrimage. Being granted a Talent. Returning after losing all of his companions . . . when he hadn't even made it to the Well. He didn't even know what the Trials were.

Sven clamped a hand over my mouth, but my echo still bounced between the rocks. His eyes flicked toward the gathered people. He turned back to me, and I hardly recognized him beneath his twisted snarl.

"You disgust me." He released me and wiped his hands on his coat, ridding himself of the very act of touching me.

I snorted. "What a mood change you've had since declaring your love a few nights ago."

"I never loved you, Myrthe. Not even at the beginning. Anouk was far superior to you—even without a Talent. I'd hoped that pursuing you would make her jealous. You've only ever been a means to an end."

Though I'd suspected this, it didn't make it hurt any less to hear it from his lips—lips that kissed me many a time after declaring sweet promises.

I wanted him gone. Or more: silenced. Instead of crumbling from his words, I wanted to hurt him back. "At least I know what I am—my flaws and weaknesses. Your followers lap up your words like a dish of honey but don't realize you're all manure beneath the surface."

Something akin to regret crossed over his expression. He stepped right up to me and looked into my face. For a moment I thought maybe he would apologize. "You got yourself cursed. My followers have to destroy the Trials on their own."

"Don't you mean *you* have to destroy them? Or are you too much of a coward? Like last time." He would make *them* do his dirty work and then take the glory.

"You think *you'll* survive them?" He laughed—a dead, angry sound. "Well, someone's got to go first. It might as well be you. Prove yourself useful for once."

He shoved me backward into the first Trial.

CHAPTER 40

BASTIAAN

The scout who stopped Bastiaan was the same one he'd encountered in the forest with Myrthe. The same one whose arrowhead he'd severed from its shaft with his disc. Luuk.

"Are you really going to try to stop me?" Bastiaan growled.

Luuk stepped aside. "It's not like you can put us in a worse situation than we're already in."

What did that mean? Did they learn what King Mattias was doing?

Bastiaan scanned the camp, passing over the unfamiliar eyes or dark heads. When his gaze moved over Sven twice, he realized Myrthe was nowhere in sight.

Sven stood before the people giving another one of his speeches. That man and his words . . . and his face. People followed him for it. Bastiaan was still waiting to see the actions line up. The Trials would likely bring them out, and his future-telling Talent would only take him so far.

At least Sven had made it through the Trials once before. That gave him an edge they desperately needed.

And it was more than Bastiaan had ever done.

He trotted Sterk into camp and dismounted, then strode toward Sven, angling himself through the spaces of the crowd until he was close enough to catch Sven's words.

". . . lied to us! But we don't need a wish to defeat these Trials. Plenty of people have done it before. *I've* done it before. We'll gather together and draw lots to see who will battle the Trials. Once through them, we'll drink from the Well of Talents and use our Talents to destroy the Trials once and for all!"

He said nothing about taking the water for himself. Did his followers even know about that part of the plan? Or were they too drunk on the promise of a Talent?

Kees and Hedy stood on either side of Sven like personal bodyguards. The effect was impressive.

"If you're afraid," Sven went on, "there's no judgment. But if you're willing to fight for your rights, for the freedom of Talents, and for the freedom of Winterune, your name will never be forgotten! We'll draw lots in one bell."

He turned to speak with Kees and the muttering began. Bastiaan wound his way through the crowd until he reached Sven, but several others were already waiting to speak with him. Hedy and Kees ran interference, taking questions and answering what they could.

Bastiaan shoved his way to the front despite protests.

A firm hand to his chest blocked his advance. Hedy. "You'll have to wait your turn."

He firmly removed her hand and continued toward Sven. She made a grab for his coat, but he'd already garnered Sven's attention.

"I've seen Mattias's army," Bastiaan said. "We need to talk."

That stopped Hedy. It also kept Sven's focus on him. He waved away those who stood in line, and they begrudgingly gave him privacy.

"How long until they're here?" Sven asked.

"They're not coming here," Bastiaan said. "At least not yet." Hedy snorted, but Sven folded his arms and waited for more. "They're at the Nightwell, not even a two-bell march from here."

Sven showed very little reaction. Even Hedy and Kees didn't gape at the revelation of the Nightwell's location, but Hedy did pale. She had a Bane, after all, so she must have visited the Nightwell before.

"That's good news for us," Sven said. "They'll leave us alone for a bit."

"Don't be daft, man! They're digging a new canal from the Nightwell to connect it to the Vier. All of Fairhoven and the sur-rounding towns will be infected."

"Why would King Mattias *give* people power?"

"Because he can control those with Banes. Don't you get it?" Runt was proof.

Hedy turned panicked eyes to Sven.

"What do you suggest?" Sven sounded irritated—like this was Bastiaan's fault. He wasn't completely wrong. "It's not like we have a wish we can use to stop him."

Myrthe. Bastiaan wanted to ask where she was, but he needed to finish the conversation at hand.

"The only way to fight Banes is with Talents." Bastiaan hoped that was true.

"*If* the Well even gives people Talents," Hedy snapped. "It's a selfish pool, that."

Bastiaan swallowed. Maybe she didn't understand. "You've tried getting rid of your Bane with water from the Well of Talents?"

"I tried the Well of Talents first! I did everything right. After almost a year of searching for it, Kees and I found the Well. We both drank. *He* received a Talent and I did not. I wasn't about to go home empty-handed. We'd heard the Nightwell was nearby and found it within a day. So I got myself a Bane."

Her lips twisted. "We encountered a pilgrim on our trip home.

Wanting to help him, we shared our story, and the moment he learned I had a Bane, he ran me through with a blade. Asked no questions. Didn't care about our story, or *why* I'd sought a Bane. I would have died had Sven not found Kees and me the next day. Unlike the pilgrim, Sven had compassion. The Well of Talents is fickle. Selfish."

Bastiaan turned to Kees. "Do you agree?" Kees had a Talent, after all.

Kees merely shrugged. "Hedy's been through a lot. I don't have a Bane, so I don't understand her pain or her struggle."

"I don't need a Talent." Yet Hedy so clearly feared her Bane being used at the hands of the king. "The Well of Talents was stingy, yet the Nightwell welcomed us with open arms."

The Well of Talents asked for her patience. Bastiaan suspected if she'd waited long enough and humbled her heart, a Talent would have awoken.

She had to be wrong. The Well of Talents *would* stop the Nightwell. Somehow.

Otherwise, they were doomed.

"We need to get to the Well."

"We will in time," Sven said.

"There *is* no time!" Bastiaan couldn't waste breath on these imbeciles. Let them dig their own graves. *He* needed to get to the Well. At the very least he could tell Myrthe his findings and let her try to convince Sven to be less of an idiot. "Where's Myrthe?"

Bastiaan scanned the people again, stopping on each light blonde head but not finding her. A chill entered his chest and he snapped his attention back to Sven. This time the demand came out unrelenting. "Where is Myrthe?"

Sven's nose wrinkled against an imagined stench. "Gone."

"What do you mean, gone?" The way Sven said *gone* implied more than her absence. He grabbed Sven by the coat and barely held back a growl. "What happened?"

Sven shoved him away. "She entered the Trial. Probably seeking glory for herself."

"You let her go in *alone*?" The Trials claimed lives within *seconds* sometimes. "How long ago?"

Sven shrugged. "Quarter of a bell. Maybe more."

The man's flippancy scalded the blood in Bastiaan's veins, and his fingers curled to deliver a blow. But there was no time. Bastiaan whistled for Sterk. A minute later the horse was at his side. He mounted and Sterk lunged forward toward the Trials.

"With your dead Talent and her curse, you're perfect for each other!" Sven hollered from a place of fractured pride. He knew more about what happened to Myrthe. Maybe even had *done* something to her. Bastiaan hoped he could get to her in time.

Screams broke the crisp morning air as Bastiaan thundered away.

"Militairen are coming!" someone shouted. "The king's militairen are coming!"

"Gather your weapons!" Sven hollered. "Hedy! Get somewhere safe!"

As the people panicked like bees, Bastiaan didn't tear his eyes away from the Trial. Let the militairen come. Let the people fight. Let the Nightwell be unleashed.

In that moment he didn't care.

Myrthe was in the Trial. Alone. Possibly dead. He reined Sterk parallel to the mist. A magic veil of death. The one thing he feared most . . . the thing that had claimed the lives of father, friend, and foe.

He would not let it take her. At the very least, he refused to let Myrthe die alone.

Bastiaan launched himself from the saddle straight through the white mist.

CHAPTER 41

MYRTHE

The frostbite was instant.

I sucked in a gasp, still reeling from Sven's words. His shove. He'd pushed me *into* the Trial. To . . . die. That was the extent of his bitterness—as unrelenting as the cold battering my underclothed body.

Howling wind stole my hearing and my very thoughts. Sven's name—and the fury, betrayal, and hurt that came with it—disappeared from my mind as quickly as the red from my cheeks. I stood in thigh-deep snow—crusted on top and light as feather dust beneath. The wind kicked it up, pummeling every inch of exposed skin with needles. I clamped my lips shut do I didn't choke on it.

Hoarfrost branches. White blizzard. The familiar shock of cold accosting a previously warm body.

The first Trial was Winter. How did one defeat a *season*?

I tried to take a step. The ice crust atop the snow cut into my thigh like razor tips. Dots of blood seeped through my pants and froze in droplets atop the fabric.

What little warmth had filled my body turned prickly and thin, drawn out of me like an insect being emptied by a spider.

A hopeless surrender took hold. Why fight? This type of cold would take my breath, pulse, and will within minutes. Why *not* allow myself to die? Here, in this magical storm designed to kill, I tallied my reasons for living the same way I used to tally loaves of bread for sale at markt.

And came up wanting. Unsatisfied. Longing for something . . . more.

Who was there to live for? Oma saw me as nothing but a tool. Sven had loved my Talent, not my person. Anouk and I were on separate paths. Mutti was dead. And Bastiaan . . .

Bastiaan was gone. Angry with me for not saving Runt. Despite that, our brief encounters had formed one of those rare acquaintances that built into a flame of understanding and shared hurts. It could have become something if he'd stayed with me . . . and if I'd had a working heart.

There was no one to keep breathing for. Except myself. And the mystery of what I *could* have been as the Wishtress. If I wasn't broken, I could have thawed the canal. I could have helped Anouk. I could have healed Mutti.

Chances missed.

I couldn't seem to recall the conviction I once had for breaking my curse.

To allow Winter to be my end seemed fitting. Justice for how I'd killed Coralythe's sons. So why did I want to keep breathing? Why did my lungs still inhale and exhale? Why did my mind shy away from the idea of forever darkness?

I pictured Mutti skating on the canal after me. Pushing herself to her limits—to her very death—in order to find me. To embrace me. To tell me she loved me.

She didn't give up. She ran the race to the end, beyond her

own pain and incomplete memories. She didn't approach death as an enemy in battle. She had treated it like the end of a long road, a well-skated race, a full-lived life.

I would not give up. I was her daughter, and the least I could do was learn from her sacrifice and example. If I was to die today, it might not be unwelcome, but it wouldn't be without a fight.

As though sensing my determination, Winter attacked. This was more than a storm; it was as though I'd stepped into Winter's very soul and the season had become a raging, wild thing.

Wind was its voice; frostbite its clawed hands; ice its mirror-like vision.

The thinness of my inhale told me the temperature lurked colder than any winter in Fairhoven I'd lived through. This cold guillotined warmth. Bitter and angry.

Like me.

Frostbite swept its talons across my cheekbones. I shoved it away but my hands passed through air. It renewed its attack double-fold, but I had always been part winter. Since I was born on the winter solstice, my blood ran colder than others'. My tolerance for chilled bones ran deeper and lasted longer.

You can shred me with your teeth, bite away my skin, but I will not yield to you!

The wind battered, tearing my hood from my head and screaming in my ears like a furious woman. I screamed right back, bent at the middle, and forced a step forward, breaking through the razor-ice and leaving a path of smeared blood.

Another gust. Another step. If the wind was pushing against me, that meant my path forward must be into the gale.

Winter screamed louder and in its multitoned wail I felt its anger. Fury. Pain.

I dragged myself forward. Again. Again. Then I fell. The ground beneath gave way and I tumbled down a slope and cracked my head on ice. Through the sluggish churn of my groaning thoughts, I caught Winter's laughter. It was winning.

I lay on a frozen canal. A place I'd once called home more than Oma's gable house. The wind gave a mocking *poof*, and my body slid along the ice like a soap bar on porcelain. No matter my will, my feeble form slipped and slid. Helpless.

Winter shrieked. *Get away, you foul thing. Leave me be!*

The plea felt familiar, like how I felt about my curse, my broken choices. My mistakes. About my heart's insistence on beating when my worth and desire to live were trampled beneath the rhythmic feet of my traitorous pulse.

In that moment, as Winter screamed and frostbite's rabid teeth dug into me, I felt a kinship with the cold loneliness. I was battling Winter, yes, but I also *understood* it.

"We're alone, you and I! We have no one but ourselves!"

Winter's wind took a breath—like the breath I'd taken when I felt *seen* by Bastiaan for the first time. A tentative relief.

"Even *we* can't comfort each other! That's our true curse. You, trapped here as a Trial. Me, trapped by the curse to live a half life. We pity each other, and we're both helpless. You wish to destroy me. I wish to destroy you. And yet I also wish to destroy myself."

Winter wailed again. Seen. Known. In this moment I would have cried if I could. But my eyes ached from the cold and nothing within me could maintain warmth enough to be set loose— certainly not a tear.

Winter attacked harder than ever. Slam. *Slam.* It didn't like being seen. That only angered it more.

I flattened myself against the surface of the icy canal, my frost-bitten cheek sticking to the pane of glass, then tearing free again. The wind fought for purchase, ripping at the folds in my clothes, sending sand-like snow into my eyes. Icicles shot through the air, landing near me like stray arrows.

One would find its target soon.

Blinded and covered with blood like cold tar, I managed to reach my skates tied to the strap of my pack. I kicked off my boots and they went flying down the ice, tumbling into the white gusts of the blizzard. I couldn't bend my toes. Could hardly bend my knees up enough to pull on the skates.

But I'd shoved my feet into the pliable leather and yanked the laces enough to do it without feeling or seeing what I was doing. By the time I got the laces in a messy double knot, the skin on my fingertips had turned stark white. Next up would be black, and that led to amputation. I'd seen it plenty of times. Been near it myself at least twice.

I shoved to my feet. On my blades. And I faced the wind.

I no longer faced Winter but my own heart. Cold. Raging. Closed off and bitter. If I continued hardening myself against empathy, against feeling and caring and loving, I would become like this Trial. A vicious, unrelenting being with no warmth left for life.

It was like I battled my future self—what I would become if I continued down my current path.

But I'd seen new life. Examples of beauty that I wanted to experience and replicate. I wanted to be like Mutti. I wanted to be like Anouk. I wanted to understand the Well in the awed way Bastiaan did.

That was my new path.

And I was taking it.

I bowed my head and dug my skates in. The ice gasped beneath my blades, surprised by my resilience. Oh, this was only the beginning. With each shove forward my glide grew more established. I crept forward. Flew forward. Up the canal and against the wind that screamed profanities to get me to turn around. Icicles landed in the ice before me. I dodged them. Weaving like I used to around stones when practicing for races.

I fastened a new cloak around my shoulders: a cloak of memories. Racing along the canals. Skating with Anouk. Mutti teaching me to tie my laces. Pappje carving my skate guards. The freedom that came every winter once markt ended and I traveled Fairhoven without Oma on my heels. Mutti holding me through her final night.

This Winter Trial thought it could beat me down, but the actual season of winter had always made me feel alive.

As I picked up speed and surrendered my skin to the bite of rime, a neglected emotion peeked its head up through the snowdrifts around my heart.

Joy.

As sudden as a hiccup but subtle as a blink. Yet it was there. Unbidden and beautiful. I threw my arms wide and laughed. *Laughed.* In the face of Winter. In the face of my curse. In the face of death.

The bark of my laughter shattered the Trial's will. Icicles fell to pieces. Wind was snuffed like a candle flame. The storm fell to the ground like spilled flour, leaving a giant cloud of snow dust.

I skidded to a stop, sending a spray of ice into the air. My chest heaved. The silence pressed upon my ears louder than Winter's shriek. Through the settling snow mist I saw a silhouette. A person. Standing. Stunned.

Bastiaan.

CHAPTER 42

ℳYRTHE

I stood, arms raised in the air from my wild laugh.

Bastiaan stared. I couldn't read him. All I knew was that I felt exposed. Seen to my very core. Vulnerable. I curled my arms in a twisted tangle against my chest, scrambling to reassemble my internal armor.

Bastiaan strode across the frozen canal, his tread purposeful and unwavering despite the slick ice. Before I could lock my thundering heart away, he was upon me. In front of me. Gathering me in his arms and pressing me tight against his chest as though he could tuck me into himself.

Surprised, I allowed myself the momentary comfort and safety.

"Myrthe, you . . ." He swallowed and I felt him shake his head. "You're alive." Two words, hardly a breath of noise in my ears.

He was here. With me. Around me. How? "Why?"

"What?"

"Why are you here?" How was he in the Trial? Holding me? Last I knew he was with Runt at Windmill Cottage. Gone. "Did Sven shove you in too?"

"I couldn't abandon you." He yanked off his coat and wrapped it around me. It smelled like him. Felt like his embrace. He had entered the Trial . . . willingly? For *me*?

"No. *No*." I couldn't protect myself from this. Why would he endanger himself like that? There must be another reason. I pressed my hands against his chest, desperate for space. "You came for a wish, didn't you?"

He frowned, warm hands still on my shoulders. "No."

"Admit it!" My accusation manifested itself as a stone atop my rickety wall. I needed to keep building. Separate myself from his invitation to be *safe*. To feel. "That's why you came after me. That's the only thing I'm good for." That was the only thing that made sense.

He tugged the cloth of his overlarge coat tighter around my shoulders. "Myrthe, I'm here to beg forgiveness."

"For what?" I croaked.

"For seeing you as the Wishtress instead of Myrthe. You're a human, not a resource. A person. A girl who makes my heart beat fast and whom that same heart misused. Please . . . forgive me?"

Remorse marked his face like the stain of frostbite. I wanted to forgive him. Wanted to *believe* him. But I couldn't risk trust. Couldn't risk emotions. Yet if I couldn't have emotions, was I even fully alive?

Maybe he really *did* regret wanting wishes from me. I could think of one way to test his genuineness.

"I'm cursed." The confession tumbled out. "Coralythe cursed me to die by my next wish." *Tell him why. Tell him why. Tell him why.* I couldn't. Not Bastiaan. Not when he was looking at me with such gentleness.

I didn't want to be the one to end this.

I didn't want to see him react like Sven.

"I'm so sorry it took until now for you to feel comfortable telling me." No judgment in his voice. No cheap pity. Just compassion.

I shivered and he stepped back. "You're so cold." He dug in his pack and pulled out a small pouch, then stuffed fistfuls of some plant into the palms of my hands. He shoved his own gloves over my stiff white fingers. Instant warmth wrapped around them.

"Heetmoss," he muttered. "I got it from Verstad."

A place I'd only ever seen scrawled on Sven's map. And Bastiaan was using this incredible plant to warm me. I couldn't thank him. Words weren't enough. But I could give him the truth. Finally.

"I can't give you a wish. I can't give you what you want."

His right hand lifted, ever so gently, and touched the edge of my eye. Tender. Too tender. "I want nothing more than *you*. Alive. Safe."

He had hardly blinked at the confession of my dead Talent, at the revelation of my curse. Even after I told him, he didn't see me as broken. He saw me as Myrthe. Just Myrthe.

I was enough for him.

It felt like Mutti's love again—the long-desired warmth and peace that came with it. But this was different because it was *Bastiaan*. He was not family. There was no obligation to extend care or acceptance.

This was his *choice*.

He chose me.

No stones remained on my wall. I was laid bare. I shut my eyes tight.

"Stop!" He didn't know what he was proclaiming. He didn't know I was a murderer. "My wall . . . It's not strong enough . . . for this." What was I saying?

He took my face in his hands. Waited until I dared to open my eyes again. "Let me be your wall," he whispered

Could I risk this sort of trust? Should I? "I'm going to the Well. To ask it to break my curse." He had followed me into the Trials, but I couldn't expect him to continue with me.

He allowed an inch of space to enter between us, if only to meet my gaze. "You're not going alone."

"I'm not asking you to come with me."

"There's more going on outside these Trials. King Mattias is at the Nightwell trying to send the water into the canals. Runt has been compromised with a Bane. Militairen are attacking Sven's camp."

"What?" Had I been in the Trial that long?

"Right now, the Well of Talents is the only hope any of us have to combat what's coming. I'm pretty sure King Mattias's entire army now has Banes. Which means he can control them with a single word."

Nightwell water going into the canals? My beloved canals. The people of Fairhoven would be so desperate for water again, they would lap at it like parched dogs. I pictured a Winterune filled with Coralythes. *Winter's breath.* This would be the end of all things good. "Can the Well of Talents stop that?"

"I have faith it can fight it."

This pilgrimage was beyond me—so much more than my own curse or Wishtress Talent. "Then let's go."

"How sweet." The cold sneer split the thin air like an axe would a twig. Sven stepped into view, the wall of mist a few feet behind him. Hedy and Kees flanked him.

The fallen stones of my inner wall trembled, trying to rebuild. But I'd let Bastiaan in and there was no way to refortify so quickly.

Kees took in my recovering state. "She's been in the Trial all this time. She came back to defeat the Trial for us."

"You didn't tell him?" Bastiaan asked Sven. "What, you didn't want your loyal bodyguards to learn you forced your *love* into a Trial?"

Kees turned to Sven for an explanation. Sven didn't acknowledge him.

"I knew." If Hedy meant to validate Sven's loyalty, it didn't work. Kees now looked betrayed and confused.

I wanted to say something, but I wasn't sure what. My voice

stuck in my throat. How did Sven know I'd defeated the Winter Trial?

"Where's everyone else?"

"Captured. By Mattias and his militairen with their Banes."

"Yet you're here," Bastiaan pointed out.

"My foresight gave us barely enough time to conceal ourselves."

Bastiaan snorted. "You mean abandon everyone else."

Sven ignored Bastiaan's jabs—though his ears turned pink. "Kees saw the Trial mist go still and told us that meant it'd been defeated. We entered in order to save everyone." He addressed me for the first time. "And you'll do the same thing in the next Trial."

Only then did I realize a second mist awaited on the other side of the frozen canal. This mist was a budding green color. It must represent Spring. What sort of threats could Spring bring? I'd always hated the shifting of the seasons to the warm months because that meant working for Oma at markt, not being able to escape onto the canals, and being trapped by my own physical weakness.

"I'm not doing this for you, Sven."

"I don't care who you're doing it for. Get us to the Well." His eyes darkened. "It was the original plan after all, right? You pave the way?"

"It was *your* original plan, reliant on me giving you a wish I don't have."

"Oh, but you do have one." His hand twitched and Hedy nocked an arrow. Aimed at my chest. "Even if it's *only* one."

"You want me to die?"

Bastiaan stepped in front of me so the arrow now had him in its sights.

"That's not how this is, Myrthe!" Sven's fury burst out, a contrast to the calm he'd shown moments before. "Your final wish could save all these people! My people who are now being marched back to the king to be tortured and killed. Or worse, *controlled*. You, of all people, should know how wretched that feels. Except you did it willingly. *They* won't have a choice."

I flinched.

"A wish from you could bring Talents to all of Winterune. It could dethrone Mattias! It could put a stop to all this evil."

"That's a long way of saying yes, you want her to die," Bastiaan ground out.

"If threatening *her* life won't bring forth the tear, maybe threatening *his* will," Hedy whispered to Sven.

I tried to push past Bastiaan, but my skates found little purchase. "Stop this." I could handle a threat against myself. But not him. Not because I didn't believe Bastiaan could defend himself. But because I had little doubt Hedy would follow through on the threat.

"If you so much as twitch, Bastiaan, I'll release this arrow and I guarantee it'll hit one of you."

"Sven, this is absurd! Do you even hear yourself? See yourself?" How had I ever kissed this boy? Or thought I *loved* him, even for a brief time?

He wasn't the same person. That's how. Perhaps this darkness had been tucked deep inside him all along and the lust for power had brought it to the surface.

"I've become someone who's willing to put the lives and well-being of others above taking the easy road."

"Oh, so letting me *live* is the easy road?" I asked, surprised to hear my voice come out so calm. He would shoot me—rather, he would allow Hedy to shoot me. Or Bastiaan. All to claim my last wish.

Bastiaan took my hand in his, dropping his gloves to the ground. My own hand trembled. His didn't. His steadiness calmed me.

"If you kill Myrthe now, you'll have to use her wish to get you through the next three Trials. But if you wait for us to defeat the other Trials, you can use it to save your people."

Sven seemed to consider this. Hedy had far less patience. "Well?" she hissed, sounding like she *wanted* to shoot. Wanted to see Bastiaan fall to the ground with an arrow in his temple or me collapse in tears and die by my own curse. Who *was* this woman?

If I continued to harden my heart, would I become like Hedy? I'd rather die.

"Does she even know *how* to cry anymore?" Sven muttered. "She's become a monster." Then a wicked gleam flickered in his eye and he addressed Bastiaan. "Do you know why Myrthe is cursed?"

I went cold. Colder than I'd been when I battled Winter. "Stop."

"She didn't tell you, did she?" There was no need for Sven to share this—no reason other than malice.

"Sven, don't—"

"She's a *murderer*." Sick delight coated his words.

Bastiaan waited . . . as though more was coming. Or maybe he hadn't heard Sven correctly.

"She murdered children," Sven continued.

I closed my eyes, exposed in the worst way—before my enemies and the man who, minutes before, had asked to be the safe wall around my heart.

Bastiaan's hand in mine didn't waver. "We'll enter the second Trial for you, Sven. You don't have to threaten us."

"Did you even hear what I said?"

"I heard." No change in Bastiaan's voice. He was likely speaking through a filter of stone like I had been doing since waking with my curse. I knew how to maintain indifference despite pain, disgust, fear, hurt. It seemed Bastiaan did too.

"And you're still holding her hand?"

"Yes." If anything, Bastiaan's grip tightened. His fingers squeezed and then twitched, like he was snapping them. "Do we have an agreement?"

"*You* can defeat the second Trial. I think we'll keep Myrthe as a bargaining chip—as a reason for you to do your job and not abandon us."

"He'll need her," Kees said quietly.

"I'm beginning to think you never made it to the Well, Sven," Bastiaan said. "Or have you forgotten that the way out is the way we came in?" Bastiaan's fingers snapped again, then something in him seemed to settle. Resignation. Was he trying to use his dead Talent?

Kees frowned. "How *did* you defeat the Trials alone, Sven?"

"Of course I haven't forgotten." A layer of panic hardened Sven's words.

He looked to me . . . waiting for me to spill *his* secret. I liked that he feared me in this moment. I liked it so much that I allowed a cool smile to grace my lips.

"These Trials will reset by sunrise." Bastiaan sounded impatient. I marveled at how Bastiaan had become the one dealing out threats.

That was why Sven hated him too.

"Go then."

We needed no further permission. I skated in reverse, not ready to take my eyes off Hedy's arrow tip. Bastiaan turned his back on them and walked toward the Spring mist, tugging me after him.

"Don't forget who you're with!" Sven called after us. "Look the wrong way and she might stab you in the back. If she can murder children, there's no telling what she's capable of!"

I could hardly breathe. My hand felt ashamed to be in Bastiaan's. He probably thought Sven was bluffing.

What would he say when he learned Sven's words were true?

The first time, Sven pushed me unwillingly into the Trial. But this time, on the heels of his shredding words, I sprinted—skates and all—into it.

CHAPTER 43

BASTIAAN

His Talent had fooled him.

Rather, he'd allowed himself too much hope. He'd thought it was coming back, fighting the Bane, but when he tried to stop time against Sven . . . nothing had happened.

"Bastiaan, where are you?" Myrthe's voice came from far off. Though they'd crossed the mist together, somehow it had separated them. His hand felt cold without hers.

"I'm here," Bastiaan called loud enough for her to hear, but he made no sudden movements. He stood in a forest of tall, smooth trees and a thin undergrowth of vines and grass. No dead sticks to snap or dried twigs to break to alert him to anyone—or any*thing*—approaching.

He'd been in this Trial several times but never to fight it. The first time it had already been defeated, and all the subsequent times he'd entered it in the Stillness. It had always struck him as the most beautiful, but that was because it had not been his hunter.

The off-kilter patter of Myrthe's feet announced her approach mere seconds before she was at his side, stuffing her gloves into her pockets. Her skates hung from her pack, wooden guards strapped over the blades. She was barefoot.

Her breath echoed with every exhale. The forest was too quiet. Unnatural. No beasts or birds or wind. Neither of them spoke, but her eyes darted from tree to tree. She didn't seem afraid, just wary. Observant.

How was she unafraid? His own pulse seemed to be filling the silence with its pounding.

"It's not like Winter," she whispered. "There's no voice here."

No voice? He didn't ask for clarification, just followed her lead. She'd defeated Winter all on her own. He'd arrived to see her silhouetted and fierce through the surrendering snow.

"What dangers can spring bring?" She shifted her weight from one foot to the other, brushing off the soles of her feet.

"Floods. Mudslides. Deadly insects. Strong winds if the temperature changes too quickly . . ." He could think of a thousand other threats. The leaves rustled as though his very mention summoned the wind.

Myrthe yelped and leaped on Bastiaan's back. He barely kept his balance but had his throwing discs in hand within seconds. Tense and ready for battle. "What? What is it?"

"The ivy!" Her legs clamped tight around his waist and one hand gripped his shoulder. Her other hand held a skate aloft, blade at the ready.

The forest floor moved. What he had mistaken for the rustle of leaves was actually the crawling and growing of vines underfoot. Vines with red-tipped star leaves. "That's fire oak!"

"Aptly named," she griped. "I should have left my skates on."

Her feet, locked around his midsection, bloomed with a red-and-pink rash atop the black spots of frostbite. How long had she stood on the fire oak? "Can you get them on?"

She twisted her limbs to reach her burned feet, all the while muttering, "My skates'll be ruined after this."

The fire oak crawled toward them like stray fingers. Faster and faster, growing longer and thicker. Bastiaan backpedaled, but there was no place to backpedal *to* other than through the mist and into the arrow tip of idiot Sven. His mind spun. His throwing discs were useless against the vines and he wasn't about to waste them.

"We could climb the trees." Myrthe yanked the laces tight on her first skate.

"So can they."

Something pricked his neck. He swatted at it. A bug carcass smeared on the palm on his hand. Myrthe jerked and nearly dropped her second skate. "Bees!"

"Wasps." Silent black wasps. What Bastiaan had first thought were tree shadows were actually clumps of wasps. Crawling on the ground, hovering beneath boughs. Coming for them.

She got her second skate on and jumped to the ground, ducking a diving wasp. "What do we do?" she shrieked.

He offered the same suggestion he gave anyone facing wasps during a regular nonenchanted spring. "Run!"

They took off through the forest, dodging the fire oak and wasps. Myrthe's running in skates was clunky and her limp put her at more of a jogging speed, though she expelled breath and energy as if she were sprinting.

"Turn left!" At least he knew which way to go. "To the third Trial!" He hoped they could bolt through the sunset-orange hue of mist that was a hundred yards off.

Wasps converged like a cloud about his body. He dropped and tumbled, losing his sleeping roll from the top of his pack. The fire oak leaped upon him with viscious tentacles, burning everywhere it touched exposed skin.

He wrenched it off his body and sprang back to his feet, but the small tickling legs of wasps crawled beneath his clothing. A shuddering panic built in his chest as he swatted the creatures. Attacking him from the outside was one thing; getting inside his *clothes* was a nightmare.

All went dark. Cloth pressed on him from above, and he dropped to his knees. Myrthe had flung his sleeping blanket over them both. He tucked the edges down around them, smashed a wasp in his armpit area, and they hunkered down beneath the cloth shield.

Within seconds their hot breaths mingled and grew stuffy.

"This is romantic," he joked, hardly caring whether it was appropriate.

"It's certainly not how I pictured my first foray beneath a blanket with a man," she replied.

He barked a laugh. Tiny vine fingers tugged at the blanket and squirmed over top of them. Bastiaan pictured the fire oak creating a dome of burning tendrils that they'd have to claw through. Then what sounded like large raindrops pelted the blanket. The wasps.

"We can't stay like this forever."

"I needed a moment to think." Her body pressed against his at odd angles and her breath tickled the back of his neck.

"The vines and wasps can't get through this thick cloth." He didn't mention they'd somehow gotten *inside* his clothes.

"Do you have an extra blanket in your pack?"

"No, but I have my cloak."

"That'll work on me." She rummaged blindly in his pack and tugged the roll of material free. "We'll wrap ourselves as best we can and make a bolt for it."

The plan sounded feeble at best, but the vines and wasps were creating an intimidating pressure from above, and they needed to move. She'd beat Winter. He had to hope Myrthe's line of thinking would work a second time. Why had he never asked the hired Trial expert how he defeated them?

"Let's go!" Myrthe flung the blanket off herself, threw his cloak about her shoulders, and took off, her movements half hobble, half skate glide. If Bastiaan hadn't seen the vine-covered ground with his own eyes, he would have thought Myrthe was skating over ice. She'd removed her skate guards and every step sliced through the vine arms, sending them curling away in pain.

And leaving a brief path for him.

He didn't waste the opening. Blanket over his head like an oma's scarf, he rushed through the forest after her toward the clearing between the woods and the third Trial wall.

Myrthe shrieked but kept plowing forward. The vines tried wrapping around the angles of her skate blade, tripping her, but she kept her balance.

Something moved near the base of the Trial wall. Bastiaan couldn't quite tell what the brown lumps were, so he risked pushing the blanket off his face a bit more. Bear cubs. Two of them. Sitting innocently and stripping the bushes of their berries.

The sight seemed so odd compared to the attack of the fire oak and wasps. So calm and almost . . . cute.

Then he remembered. "Myrthe! Wait!"

She was almost to the wall when the mama bear burst out of another patch of berries and lumbered toward her. Myrthe spotted the bear at the last moment and dove out of the way of a deadly paw strike. Bastiaan threw one of his discs, and it struck the bear in the shoulder. She didn't even flinch.

Myrthe rolled onto her back and threw up her skate blades as the bear snapped with her wide-open maw. Blood spurted. Bastiaan's heart stopped.

He threw the second disc. Struck the bear between the eyes. But the enchantment on this creature must be thick. She didn't stop her attack. Her cubs abandoned their bush and ran to where Myrthe lay to get their own bites in.

He had seconds to act and no plan.

The bear raised herself on her hind legs, tensed, and then dropped her body weight onto her front paws to crush Myrthe's skull.

CHAPTER 44

MYRTHE

I went deaf.

The silence struck like when Oma boxed my ears. Did the bear attack and I was still in shock? Or had Bastiaan shot the bear? That must be it.

I braced for the blow of a falling carcass, trembling from the strain on my muscles. The silence stretched on. Something was . . . off. I squinted my eyes open.

The bear towered over me. Jaw wide. Drool shining beneath the mocking spring sunlight. I slammed my eyes shut again, yet silence reigned. I peeked one eye open and dared to keep it that way. The bear seemed almost frozen. Not a hair moved. The drool didn't drip. Its angry eyes didn't shift when I scrambled out from beneath its shadow. The cubs stood like statues, half batting at me with bared teeth.

Only then did I notice Bastiaan beside me, stretched out on the ground as though skidding to a halt after a wild dive. One hand extended to where I'd been lying. I hadn't even registered his touch. Or presence.

But now he propped himself up on an elbow and stared at his right hand in wonder. "It's back."

Thousands of black wasps hovered above my head in midflight. No diving. No wing flaps. How did they stay aloft? My brain registered what Bastiaan said. "What's back?"

"My Talent." He pressed his closed fist to his forehead and mouthed something that looked like, *Thank you.*

His Talent did this? "You can . . . control animals?"

"I don't deserve this second chance." He seemed to be talking to himself.

I rose, as tense as if it were the start of a schaatsing race. I circled the bear. It could very well be a stuffed trophy kill in the entryway of the schloss. Incredible. In a moment of recklessness, I poked the bear's shoulder. The fur gave way to my touch but sprang back once I removed my finger. No reaction from the beast. But it wasn't just the bear . . . or the wasps. The vines no longer moved.

"What did you do?"

"I stopped time."

Time. *Time?* That type of Talent was . . . godlike.

"I thought the king destroyed your Talent."

"I thought so too. It seems King Mattias's Bane has limitations."

"How long has it been since he touched you?"

"Seven days."

I looked back at the still bear, a statue of fury and wrath. "What opportune timing."

Bastiaan gained his feet and took a breath. "I tried using it when Sven threatened us." He flexed his gloveless hand.

"Is that how you enact your Talent? By snapping your fingers?" He nodded. "And what about me? Can I affect it at all?"

"You're in the stopped time—the Stillness—until I start it up again. Trapped, essentially."

I didn't feel trapped. I felt free. "But what if you die?" Why was my mind always going there? Thinking of death and the end and broken Talents?

"I . . . I don't know. I think time would start back up for you." He turned his hand over and over, delight and wonder spreading across his face.

I had so many questions but spent a moment absorbing Bastiaan's joy at his restored Talent. No wonder he'd traveled so much and learned so much while researching the Talents—he had unlimited hours!

"How often can you stop time?"

"Once per month. My snap resets each full moon."

"Tonight's a full moon."

"So it is."

"You'll have another snap by nightfall then?"

"I hope so." Was he afraid the king's Bane might still be tied to his Talent? "That doesn't explain why it's working right now. Maybe it's because I'm getting closer to the Well."

I tried to be happy for him. Bastiaan had regained his heart's desire. Now it was my turn.

"We should keep going then. Get to the Well before . . ."

Before Sven caught up. Before the Trials reset. Before we ran out of time.

Except there was no time. My brain strained to understand it.

"How long does this last?"

Bastiaan laughed and jumped to his feet. "As long as we want! A day. A month. Years!"

"*Years?*" I balked. "Have you tested it that long?"

A cloud blocked the sun of his mood. "Yes. To my great regret."

I waited for more. The silence waited for more. Bastiaan's jaw worked, twisting his lips to the side before he finally nodded toward the Trial mist. "Shall we continue?"

Disappointment settled in my gut. Bastiaan had chosen not to

313

open up to me. I wanted to respect his right to his own secrets, but he now knew all of mine—my Wishtress Talent, my curse, and the fact that I'd murdered two boys.

Hollow illness churned inside me. Was that why Bastiaan wasn't sharing his own story? Because he knew who I was? *What* I was?

I pulled off my skates, trying to distract myself from the emptiness spreading in my chest. I wanted to know about him—wanted him to open up and share. I thought we'd reached that depth, but maybe he was no longer comfortable with me.

"What Sven said about me . . ." *Winter's breath,* this shouldn't be that hard.

He paused in his movement toward the third Trial. "You don't have to defend yourself. Sven is a rat."

Bastiaan must think Sven was lying. That made it worse. "What he said about me is . . . It's true."

"It doesn't matter," he responded immediately. Had he heard me correctly? He swept one hand through the mist. It was passable, so he held out his other hand toward me.

I didn't take it. "How can you say it doesn't matter?" Barefoot on the corpses of time-stopped fire oak, I felt as though the vines now burned my insides. "It doesn't matter that I've *killed* someone?"

"Myrthe, your past matters. It's the ink of your story. But it doesn't write your future."

"And that's enough for you? You can . . . accept that about me?" I couldn't keep back the skepticism.

He sighed. "Yes. Because it's possible to make a mistake and not be seen only as that mistake." I had a feeling he wasn't talking about me anymore.

Wasn't this what I wanted? To be seen beyond my mistake? So why did it feel wrong? "I don't think you understand. I used a wish and it *killed* two *boys.*" He continued assessing the mist to the next Trial. I grabbed his shoulder. "Stop and *listen*! I'm a murderer!"

314

He spun on me. "No, you're not! You regret it! You wish you could undo it, don't you?"

"Of course I do!"

"That's where the difference is. Sven is the grandson of a murderer. His grandfather never regretted it, and Sven regards those actions with pride. Look what it's made him into."

A monster, willing to murder for his own cause, like his grandfather.

"We all have murder in our pasts—whether by action or by heart. But all of us have the chance of life in our futures. You can't use your mistake to define who you are. That will destroy who you could be."

It would. It had been . . . slowly. Was it possible to release oneself of guilt?

"You're already paying the price with your curse. Coralythe should be punished."

"She was their mother," I whispered.

"She serves the king now. *She* gave Runt his Bane. She's the reason I'm trying to get to the Well. Like you, I wish to undo my actions. And more."

Did I dare? "What mistakes are you trying to unwrite from your past?"

"Oh, Myrthe, if you knew . . ." He held out his hand. "Let me instead take in this moment of being with you in safety."

I took his hand, savoring the warmth and trust in his touch but also sensing—again—his reluctance to open up. "Alright."

He stepped into the orange mist, and for a moment, he was in the third Trial and I was still in the second. I looked back, briefly, to bid farewell to the Spring Trial, hopefully forever . . .

. . . and could have sworn I saw the mother bear blink.

CHAPTER 45

BASTIAAN

A shock of static jolted Bastiaan's muscles as he pushed through into the next Trial. A leaf skittered across his boot. Then a beetle.

Bastiaan stumbled to a halt. Silence pressed against his ears again. The beetle froze. What had just happened?

Myrthe bumped into his back as she emerged. "Is time still stopped?"

So it hadn't been his imagination. "You saw it too?"

She nodded. "The mama bear. She moved. I'm sure of it."

"I meant the beetle. The bear is worse." He lifted his Talent Mark to eye level. The silver ring and purple smoke flickered like a thunderstorm in his skin, almost as though the two were battling. "This has never happened before." Time flickering on and off?

"Not even when you stopped time for years?" She was trying again—trying to steer the conversation back to him and his story.

When he'd used his snap in the Spring Trial, a burst of assurance and calm filled him. Now that it flickered, he realized how much he relied on his Talent to bring ease to his mind.

He didn't like that reliance.

Or was it that he didn't like the lack of control taking place with his Talent? "Let's keep moving."

As they stepped forward as one, leaves crunched beneath their feet. Though the Stillness stopped life, it didn't stop the wind or its motion through branches or weather. The weather repeated itself every day. Even after almost two lifetimes in the Stillness, Bastiaan still hadn't mastered all the rules behind his Talent.

"Is this Trial autumn?" Myrthe asked. "What happened to summer? We skipped a season."

"The Trials are in a different order every time," he said distractedly. Myrthe was gracious enough not to push him about his years in the Stillness. Why couldn't he tell her? She'd revealed her mistakes and regrets to him. She'd even caused the death of two boys.

It was his turn.

"So what happens in the Autumn Trial?"

"I've never known." He ducked beneath an intricate spiderweb stretching between two trees. No spider hung in the middle.

She hurried past the web. "But you've been to the Well so many times!"

"The first time I traveled to the Well, I was a servant going along solely to provide for my master, a boy a few years my senior. Dehaan hired two men who had completed a pilgrimage to defeat the Trials for us. They were paid handsomely." Bastiaan released a resigned smile. "Kind of defeats the purpose of the Trials, don't you think?"

"You don't support the Trials anyway."

"True. Once the Trials were conquered by these men, we walked right through them before they reset, similar to how Sven entered Winter. Every time I've visited the Well since then has been in the Stillness."

"So when you came after me—into the Winter Trial—you didn't know what you were about to face." Her expression twisted against an unseen pain. "You could have died!"

Did she think she was responsible for his choice? "As could you. I wasn't willing to let that happen." Somehow she had entered the category of Runt and Mother. Myrthe had become a person to protect.

"So all this time you could have brought countless people to the Well using your Talent. Have you ever done that?"

"My time snap only stops the Trials for those with Talents. Anyone without a Talent would still have to defeat them." Or die in the attempt—like Father.

"Tell me about when you got your Talent."

He used to love returning to this memory. Something inside him would swell with joy—with purpose. But now it hurt.

"I never actually drank of the water."

Despite all the time—stopped and active—that had passed since then, the memory sat in his mind like yesterday.

"Dehaan drank and prayed and then drank some more. After almost two days of this, he demanded that I pray with him. *For* him. So I knelt by the Well and spoke to the water in my mind. I told it I'd really like to get home to take care of my mother, so could it please give Dehaan a Talent so we could leave? Then I felt it: a searing on my right hand. A voice in my blood. A Talent blooming inside me filled with mystery and purpose. It was the most amazing feeling of . . ." He wasn't sure he could finish.

"Of what?"

He slowed. Sighed. "Of hope."

"Did Dehaan ever get a Talent?"

"Not while I served him. He was furious that I did. Me, a commoner. He tried to beat it out of me a couple times. My mother helped me learn how to use it. We discovered I could stop time and anyone I touched while time was stopped would enter the Stillness with me. The main difference was they aged in the Stillness and I didn't. I gathered Mother and the other women who'd been indentured to the merchant for measly pay, and we all left. Those are the women who work the fields at Windmill Cottage."

Despite his misuse of his Talent, that act at least was some good he could be proud of.

"My mother was one of those women," Myrthe said softly.

Bastiaan stopped walking. Her *mother* had lived at Windmill Cottage? Oh. "Ilse."

"You knew?"

He shook his head. "I'm only now connecting the pieces. Ilse has been searching for her daughter for years. One time in the Stillness I returned to her old home to look for clues but found nothing except two graves—one marking her own name and the other her husband's."

Ilse had left Windmill Cottage because she saw Myrthe. "She must have recognized you when I brought you to the cottage."

"I feared the women had seen the king's reward when they spotted me. I never even saw her."

"Where is she now?" He suspected the answer by the somber tones in Myrthe's voice.

"She found me. Followed me. I think she pushed herself beyond what her body could handle. She . . . she died." Myrthe pressed a hand to her forehead, and Bastiaan remembered with a jolt the risk she took by sharing these emotions. "We were together for a day. It was . . . so perfect." Her voice broke.

Bastiaan wanted to know more—to hear more of her heart—but he also wanted her to be safe. He'd asked her to let him be her wall; he must protect her in this moment. He took her hand.

"Let's keep walking. I can see it's fresh in your mind."

He wanted to kiss her temple. The desire took him aback.

"Thank you," she whispered.

He squeezed her hand. He was glad she saw the encounter with Ilse as beautiful. More than that, he was thankful the women were

319

reunited, even if only for a brief time. He knew what life his own mother gave him with her care and love. To grow up without that was almost unthinkable.

The spiderwebs grew thicker, yet still no spiders hung in the middle. The sun barely glowed and the shadows of the forest seemed like tar instead of absent light.

He'd always hated walking through this Trial even when it was time-stopped. The imagination did strange things when facing the unknown. He wanted to get through it as quickly as possible, but a building tension pushed against his will—his pride—and he knew this was the time.

He hadn't finished telling Myrthe *his* story. And he could no longer leave it unsaid.

He guided them into a patch of forest that still gathered a weak beam of light, despite the temptation to remain in the shadows where he wouldn't have to see her reaction, then he stopped and faced her.

"Do you want to know what I was doing when I entered the Stillness for thirty-two years?"

She didn't nod. Didn't answer. Just stared at him and let him decide whether or not to tell her.

"I was with King Vämbat. I brought him into the Stillness with me, befriended him. Spent half a lifetime with him . . . and then I killed him."

CHAPTER 46

MYRTHE

Bastiaan murdered the king. *Bastiaan* murdered the king. The way he said it sounded intentional. Almost void of regret.

Unease rolled in my belly. I was such a hypocrite! How could I recoil at Bastiaan's past when his and mine were one and the same? Both murderers. Both desperately hoping the other wouldn't see us as anything less.

But *were* we the same? He *meant* to murder. Mine was unintentional. What man could snuff the life from another and go on living with himself?

"Why?" *Why did you kill him? Why did you bring him into the Stillness? Why did you tell me?* I let him choose which way to take the question.

But I wanted all the answers.

"I thought if I could get him alone I could convince him to open the Well of Talents to the commonfolk. To get rid of the Trials and make the Well accessible to all. I thought we'd be in the Stillness a week. Maybe a month. But he refused to give in."

"Why wouldn't he lie and say yes so you would start time again?"

"That wasn't his way." This statement hinted at affection for the king. A relationship. Something beyond the cold ownership of his assassination. "We had a lot of discussions. Endless discussions where we refused to agree on anything. He seemed amused by my determination—almost like it was a game to him. We entered a stalemate. He wouldn't change his mind and I wouldn't restart time. Each of us waiting for the other to cave. So to pass the time he started teaching me."

"About his reasons?"

"About everything. The kingdom, politics, neighboring kingdoms, fighting techniques. I didn't know why he would do that. It made me more skilled. More powerful and knowledgeable. I think he was trying to gain loyalty—befriend me to the point that I would give in. Everything I learned—disc throwing and archery, the layout of the schloss—was from him. He even taught me about relationships and leading the people. I started to see a goodness in him I didn't know existed before. Maybe it was new to him too."

It was like hearing an aged man tell his life story . . . except it was coming from Bastiaan's lips. His youth was a mask over a wrinkled soul.

"We entered a rhythm and an impasse for so long that it became an afterthought. We traveled the world, Myrthe. He wanted to see other kingdoms—to learn about them. We visited the Well of Talents countless times, researched it together, and studied the Nightwell. I think he enjoyed being able to do all these things that being the king of Winterune didn't allow him to do."

Winter's breath. Bastiaan had lived half a lifetime with one other person. No wonder he "needed practice" with conversation when we'd first met.

"One morning I woke up and he was gone. I searched from sunrise to sunset. At first I thought he was testing me to see if I'd start time to find him. On the second day I found him at a nearby village's old library. I don't know what he'd been reading—probably something new for us to discover. But his oil lamp must have spilled because the library was burned to the ground. He lay out in the road, burned beyond recognition."

His voice cracked. "I was certain he was dead."

"Oh, Bastiaan . . . you couldn't have known that would happen."

"But I could have freed him sooner." He shook his head and closed his eyes. "So much sooner."

I placed a hand on his arm, suspecting where this story was going. "You got him back to his family, though, didn't you?"

"Back to the schloss, yes. I laid him in his bed, knowing servants would find him the moment I snapped my fingers. The odds of his recovery were slim to none, even if they brought in a Talented healer."

The tale was a heavy one, and yet the longer Bastiaan spoke, the lighter he seemed. As though poison were being drawn out of his body.

"I returned to Windmill Cottage . . . and I started time again. He died three days later."

"I'm so sorry."

He met my gaze, his own face twisted with uncertainty. "You don't blame me?"

"No. And even if I did . . . I'm not your judge. Your guilt—your actions—answer to the Well that gave you your Talent. And clearly the Well is still allowing your Talent to work—to defeat Mattias's Bane, even."

Bastiaan flipped his hand over back and forth. "Is it working, though? That leaf—"

A roar crashed through the silence and sounds burst to life like animals themselves—dark night sounds. Growls. Rhythmic buzzing and the chirping of unseen biters. Bastiaan paled and his hand gripped mine like a vise. He opened his mouth once. Twice.

He saw it as his Talent failing him. Unpredictable. Volatile.

But to me, it was merely time starting back up again. Time I was used to living in. I could do this. We could do this.

I was the first to run—well, *my* version of running, at least—pulling him after me.

The roar returned, right on our heels. The mama bear.

"Why is she in the Autumn Trial?"

Bastiaan finally found his voice, though I hardly caught the croak. "We never defeated Spring. She passed right through the mist wall."

That was when the buzzing hit my ears, mixed with the Autumn night sounds. The black wasps. *Winter's breath*. We were about to fight two Trials at the same time.

I burst through a spider's web and hit something bulbous and slimy. I screamed and knocked it from my face, but not before the hairy legs tangled in my hair and scratched my neck. I writhed, batting at the overlarge arachnid. "Get it off!"

Bastiaan finally managed to wrench the spider off me. The bear roared. "Go! Go!"

We sprinted and were hit by a wall of silence as though submerged underwater. Bastiaan stumbled to a halt and I ran into him. "Don't stop!" I pleaded.

"It's working again."

I pushed at his back. "I don't care! We have to get out of here!" Didn't he realize if time could stop so unpredictably, it could start back up again like before? "Bastiaan, go!"

We went as fast as my limp would allow, despite the darkness now having thickened like tar. Bastiaan acted as my shield, knocking aside the spiderweb strands and their black-and-red occupants that seemed to have burst from the branches at the first instant of moving time.

I ran like a stiff marionette, certain time would resume any second and the spiders would converge on my body, sucking my blood until I lay limp and pale.

A wall of yellow-and-green specks glowed through the trees. I yanked Bastiaan to a halt. "No, no," he assured me. "It's the next Trial."

My breaths came in heaves. "Are you sure it's not something that's going to melt the skin off our bones?"

"Time is stopped. We're okay." He tucked my hand into his arm. "I've been through it before. Trust me."

Trust him. Trust him. Trust him. "Okay."

"Ready?" His panic had all but disappeared. I marveled at the confidence his Talent brought. Was that something I could've had if I'd been allowed to be the Wishtress on my own?

"Ready." We walked through the mist to the fourth Trial together.

Summer.

The heat hit me first, sticking in my lungs like a flour dumpling. This wasn't like the Fairhoven summer sun. It was heavy and wet and smothering. I tried to suck in a breath, but my lungs seemed weighted.

We walked tentatively, still recovering from the Autumn Trial. The ground went soft beneath my bare feet. I leaped back onto the hard ground along the mist wall. Sand. Burning red sand.

I stuffed my fresh wonder down into the pocket of my mind for later. Sand? Stifling heat? This was the stuff of legends and storybooks. Faraway lands! Not Fairhoven.

Little specks of insects dotted the granules, and I spied a stinger or two.

"Don't step on the scorpions." Bastiaan uncovered one of the nasty creatures with the toe of his boot. "They're stuck in time but their tails can still sting."

Black wasps. Mammoth spiders. Sand scorpions. The Talented who created these Trials had cruel imaginations.

The longer I stared at the strange new creature half buried in sand, the larger it seemed. And then . . . its tail twitched. It shook sand from its body and, despite the fact that it was an insect, it angled its spiny face upward and *looked* at me.

"Bastiaan . . ."

I glanced up to find his jaw set in grim determination. "Myrthe . . . I'm sorry. My Talent is failing us."

"It's not. You're not!" I took his face in my hands. We had mere seconds. But this was important enough to risk them. "We can do this, Bastiaan. You and me. We were made to do this. Together."

He leaned his forehead against mine, then nodded.

For a moment we were one. United in thought and heart and pulse. I felt the most human in this brief breath.

Then the roar sounded again. Behind us. We separated and faced the desert. As though incited by our gaze, a dune exploded, pelting our faces with scorpions and burning sand. I covered my face, but Bastiaan cried out. I squinted against the onslaught of sand.

The dune had become a great hand and wrapped around Bastiaan's midsection. He fought against it, but the hand yanked him down. Into the sand.

He disappeared, swallowed by the grains.

"Bastiaan!" I dove for him. I dug, but with every scoop I shoved to the side, sand poured into the hole to fill it. "Bastiaan!"

The scorpions regained their footing and converged to where I knelt. I continued digging.

Then, with a roar that only enchanted nature could make, the sand roiled again and a dark form went shooting through the air. Bastiaan landed, his body skidding through the sand until it stopped at the base of the mist entrance.

He didn't move.

I stumbled to him and gently grabbed his shoulder. "Bastiaan?"

He groaned and pushed himself up to standing, shaking off a layer of sand. He moved stiffly and blinked against the sun. His eyes looked glassy, unfocused, and they skimmed right over me.

"Are you okay?" He'd been under the sand for what seemed like several minutes. At least he was *alive*.

He didn't respond. He seemed confused.

"We need to get to safety." I took his hand. "Follow me." I could lead him for now, as long as we *moved*.

The bear's roar from the other side of the mist captivated his attention. Bastiaan frowned at the mist, flicking his gaze up and down as though seeing it for the first time. Had he hit his head during his crash to earth? I tried to tug him forward, but he lifted a hand to brush his fingers along the granules of Summer dust.

"Bastiaan!" I yelled, though we were inches apart. "We need to *go*."

Finally he turned toward the desert once more. But before we took a single step, a colossal bear paw ruptured the mist, claws extended like knives.

With one swipe the mama bear sliced Bastiaan's throat.

CHAPTER 47

MYRTHE

B lood splashed my face.

Bastiaan's hand slid out of my grip. He crumpled to the sand. Before I knew what I was doing, my skate blades were in my hands. I chopped at the bear paw, sending the blades into the mist again and again like a hatchet. Feeling them connect with bone, flesh, fur.

A roar of pain.

I struck again. Again. With no plans of stopping.

An anvil of fur hit me from the left and I went flying. A great *flump* shook the ground. I pushed myself up, black spots swimming in my blurred vision.

The bear lay dead. Half inside the Summer Trial and half inside the Autumn Trial. Its face slashed to ribbons.

I scrambled to Bastiaan's side.

He had a hand clamped over his throat, but blood trickled through every crack between his fingers. The slice went beyond his throat and into his shoulder. His eyes were open. Seeing. Panicked.

Perhaps it was my weeks of building walls against my emotions.

Or maybe it was the shock of the moment. But I stared hard into his eyes and said in a calm, firm voice, "This is not your end."

A scorpion crawled onto his arm. I crushed it with my fist and threw the carcass far from me, my hands flying almost as fast as my mind. I tore off the sleeve of my shirt and wrapped it around Bastiaan's neck. Then I packed sand over the section already bleeding through and wound my other sleeve around that. If nothing else, it might help the wound clot better.

I only needed long enough to get to the Well.

The Well would heal him. And if it didn't, the Well would free me of my curse and I could use a wish. It always seemed to be the answer that came to mind, and I believed there was a reason for that. The Well was hope.

And hope *never* failed.

Bastiaan wasn't coughing, so I had to hope blood wasn't pouring into his lungs. I knew so little about healing. If only I had a wish *now*!

I looped his arm over my shoulder and heaved. He twitched and I knocked another scorpion off his hand. My weak knee buckled.

"Help me!" I grunted, trying to get him upright.

He managed to get his feet under him, and I angled him on my back like a turtle shell. Hunched over, I plodded through the sand. He tried to move his legs, to take off some of the weight, but his movements were sluggish and sleepy. His head drooped onto my shoulder, soaking blood through what was left of my coat and shirt.

Heat bit my foot and I hissed, but it wasn't a sting. It was the burn of hot ground. Sun-baked sand. *Forward. Forward.*

The scorpions converged. Skittering over the sand on their pincer feet, smelling blood and destruction. I had never encountered a scorpion before, but these ones seemed *fast*. Faster than any insect had a right to be.

Forward. Forward.

The bottoms of my feet blistered and screamed. The sharp daggers in my bones pierced my nerves, but not my will, with every movement. My thighs burned from the strain; my knees trembled from the weight. My lungs heaved against the draw for sticky air. Every movement shot pain into my hips and groin.

Then the stings came like lightning bolts to the tops of my feet, my calves, crawling up my pant legs. Again and again.

I released a guttural roar as though to frighten the creatures away.

Bastiaan moved—either trying to help or trying to swat away the little beasts. That small, unexpected movement sent my knees buckling.

His weight almost crushed me, but the scorpions stopped.

Time had frozen once more.

Thank the Well.

Sweat poured down my face, sticking my hair to my temples. I tried to stand but my knees wouldn't support me. Bastiaan's eyes were closed. My heart leaped into my throat and I shook him. Then slapped him.

"Bastiaan!" His eyelids fluttered and I exhaled. "Stay. Alive."

I couldn't get him on my back again, so I grabbed his wrists and pulled. My hands—sweaty as they were—slid right off. I needed to get us out of here before the Trials awoke again.

I unbuckled his belt and tied it to each wrist like shackles, then looped it around my body and marched forward with every fatigued muscle that remained. He scooted along on the sand, inch by inch. My feet struggled to find purchase, but I didn't stop. *Refused* to stop.

This was the last Trial. Once we conquered this . . .

Ahead rose a massive dune. With every agonizing step, my skin turned a darker shade of red, burning with every minute that passed. Halfway up the dune, my skin started to bubble. My stomach lurched and I focused forward.

Bastiaan grew heavier. I gripped his coat and heaved. One step gained. Heave. A half step. Heave. A quarter step.

The blisters burst, exposing raw wounds to the scorching heat. Burns on burns. I growled and forced another step. When I crested the sand dune, I nearly cried. On the other side, at its base, rose the wall of dust marking the end of the Trial. We were almost there.

I hauled Bastiaan on top of the dune, every movement stretching my tight, burned skin. Buzzing tickled my ears.

Time started again.

A haunting scuttle followed. I threw a glance over my shoulder. Behind us, the scorpions formed a red-black current along the sand, winding toward me and gaining speed. They did not falter. They knew their prey, and they would not stop until they devoured us.

There would be no surviving this attack.

I shoved Bastiaan over the dune crest. His limp body tumbled down the slope at a wild speed. I skidded after him, groaning at the relief of the cool sand his body unearthed. The scuttling increased. The scorpions crested the top of the dune and tumbled down our side like crunchy balls of fire and venom, leaving sand trails in their wake. How were they so fast?

Bastiaan rolled to a stop feet from the Trial wall. The exit. I didn't slow but crashed right into him, sending us both toppling toward the mist.

It wasn't enough.

We were inches away. *Mere inches.* I had no way of knowing if crossing the mist would stop the onslaught of Trial creatures, but I shoved Bastiaan's body anyway. Pushed. Howled curses against the Trial. I was so close, the mist a mere handbreadth away. Bastiaan felt as heavy as a slab of stone.

The scorpions reached the base of the dune. Was it my imagination or could I hear them breathing? Panting? Salivating?

They'd be on me in seconds. My survival instinct built in panic, urging me to abandon Bastiaan and bolt through the mist. *Go to the Well. Come back for him.* The temptation tasted sour on my tongue and yet addictive.

"No!" I bellowed against the sky. "I will either die *with* him or *for* him! You can't have one without the other!" I gave another shove. The scorpions leaped upon my macerated feet, teeth and tails striking my nerves like serrated knife blades.

I brushed them away from Bastiaan and gave another push, but it hardly got the toe of his boot through the mist.

My strength was gone.

I threw my body over his, wrapped myself around him as a shield, and waited for the scorpions to devour us with stingers and fangs and whatever mad weapons the enchanted Trial had given them.

The attack stopped.

Had time frozen again? I peeked my eyes open. The scorpions were gone. More than that, the *heat* was gone. This was something more than Bastiaan's Talent. Sounds pricked the air. Time was definitely still moving.

Bastiaan lay as one dead. Urgency writhed in my chest. Whatever this moment of grace, I needed to take advantage of it. We needed *out*.

Now.

I forced myself to rise. To grip his tattered clothing and give one last effort. I prayed the Well was right on the other side of the mist. Bastiaan slid against the sand, hardly an inch. The ground pulsed beneath his body, awakened by the movement. Like a sleeping ocean yawning.

Hungry.

Sand rose around Bastiaan like a coffin and consumed him, pulling him into the earth as though it were as soft as dough.

"No!" I gripped his wrist, but his very skin dissolved beneath my fingers.

"*Bastiaan!*" The scream ripped through me and I dug and dug and dug, hardly able to see what I was doing through the bursts of sand and dust. Desperate swallows clogged my throat.

I unearthed nothing. Sand upon sand upon sand. The Trial would *not* take him from me. If this was the time to use my final wish, I was ready. "Give him back! *Bastiaan!*"

A voice on the wind. Behind me. Distant yet . . . familiar.

I stopped digging and looked around, disoriented. There—atop the sand dune. Bastiaan was running toward me.

Whole. Healed. Perfect.

How? A sob burst from me and I stumbled toward him. He ran down the dune, spraying sand in his wake.

We met at the base and I slammed into his arms, clinging to him tighter than I'd ever held on to anything. I gulped for air.

"Shh." His gentle tone made it worse. Hysterics owned my emotions. I buried my face in his sand-covered coat, heaving from the deepest part of my chest while also fighting the inevitable tears.

They welled within me, but they felt *right*. I could die now and give him a wish and be content. I had everything I wanted or needed—him. Alive. Holding me.

Bastiaan stepped back and held my shoulders firmly. "Myrthe. Stop." Tenderness was still there, but I could hear him fighting for a different emotion. Logic. Lightheartedness. "I'm fine. We're okay. Look at me."

I couldn't open my eyes. This could be my end. And it would be beautiful.

He gave me a forceful shake. "Don't you *dare* cry, Myrthe." His voice broke—a cymbal clash of panic and emotion. "Don't you dare leave me."

I sucked in a breath. Squeezed my eyes even tighter. Let the darkness calm me. It felt impossible, but I fisted down the emotions, groping for the ice-cold wall of protection around my heart. It wasn't there anymore.

Instead, the emotions settled under the control of something else. *Peace.* Rather than locking away my feelings and tears, I tucked them into a warm, safe haven. Kissed their foreheads and bid them sleep.

"That's my girl." Bastiaan moved my wild hair from my eyes.

"What . . . what happened?" My hands moved of their own accord up and down his arms, over his forehead, down his chest. "The sand devoured you. How are you . . . here? Healed?"

"Whoever—*what*ever—you were with wasn't me." He peered at the sky, regular and warm like a typical summer's day. "It was a trick of the Trial. I wrestled in the belly of the sand for what seemed like hours. It finally released me, not because I won, but because *it* ended the fight. I think because of you."

"I dragged you here. To the other side. That . . . that wasn't you?"

He shook his head.

"But your Talent. It kept flickering on and off when I moved you."

"It happened while I fought with the sand. Every time I was about to claw my way free, time would start up again, then the sand would drag me back under."

Clues pieced themselves together. False Bastiaan's glassy eyes once he'd emerged from the sand. His confusion over the Trial dust. It wasn't him.

"A test," I murmured. That's what these Trials were, right? "Summer was testing me." That's why they were created—to test the pilgrim. To make sure the person was worthy of a Talent. Why would the Trial present a dying, wounded, false Bastiaan?

"Whatever it was, you passed. That's two Trials you've defeated on your own," Bastiaan mused.

"And I killed the bear."

He choked a laugh, then stared at me in amazement. "You *what?*"

"With my skate blade." I could still feel the impact of my strikes rattle my bones. It wasn't a pleasant memory, but Bastiaan's appreciative whistle helped me move past it. After all, it was a creature of the Trials. For all I knew it would regenerate when the Trials did.

"Then dragged what you thought was me across this scorching piece of desert." He shook his head. "You should have left me."

Click. "That was the test." It was so clear now. "The Trial wanted to see if I'd leave you behind." If I'd save myself. That explained Kees's earlier comment asking Sven how he defeated the Trials alone. Sven didn't. And Kees knew what the Summer Trial demanded.

Part of me had been tempted to leave Bastiaan behind. I could have spared myself so much pain—the wounds and wreckage that were now my feet. I sat on the sand and stretched my legs out in front of me. Would I ever skate again?

Bastiaan frowned as he took in the state of my feet. "Why didn't you abandon me?"

"How could I?" I tried to tuck my feet out of view. "You've brought me life. Can I repay you with death?" Did I really admit that to him? He would think me an imbecile. But I'd been willing to die mere minutes ago if it meant saving him.

He took my face in his hands. I lifted my eyes to his, holding my breath against his next words. "We two have broken pasts. Broken stories and broken Talents. And yet . . . for some reason there's a promise of wholeness when we're together."

We were inches apart, yet the space felt too far. His words—his *meaning*—rang in my ears. Relief and freedom came with acknowledging and accepting our brokenness. It was okay to be broken as long as we didn't build a home in it. It was okay to admit it. And to unite with a goal of healing.

"In all the years I've lived, I've never met anyone like you," he whispered. "And I think I'm going to kiss you."

"I'd like that," I whispered back.

He smiled, and that was the last thing I saw before his mouth was on mine. Gentle. Tentative. And beautifully uninterrupted.

I could have stayed in the deadly Trial desert like that for eternity. Built a cottage. Abandoned my skates and love for winter. In that moment it could be home—with Bastiaan—and it would be enough.

But the moment air separated us once again, purpose and memory swept back into focus.

"The Well," I said. "My curse. The canal. Runt. Your Talent. King Mattias. Sven." Listing the reasons for our quest brought back the reality—the severity—of what we were trying to accomplish. Somehow during this journey, my purpose for reaching the Well had become about more than just me.

He nodded grimly. "If my Talent weren't broken, I'd keep us here forever."

"I know." I grinned. "If *my* Talent weren't trying to kill me . . . I'd let you."

He laughed. I was glad he did because my curse didn't feel so daunting in that moment. Had I not been cursed, I never would have been found by Bastiaan and taken to Windmill Cottage.

We stood. I wobbled and sucked in a breath as the pressure of my weight hit my feet.

"Let me carry you."

"No. I want to arrive at the Well on my own two feet." If I could still call them that. "Is it . . . Is it far?"

He shook his head. "Just on the other side of the mist." Hand in hand, we stepped through the wall of dust into a shock of cold. Wind met my peeling cheeks and soft sounds brushed against my ears. Snow was falling.

Bastiaan released a strangled sound of surprise that made me giggle. The thin air rushed into my lungs and cleared my head so I could finally straighten and take in our new surroundings.

We were in the true season of early winter again. If time were still stopped, would the wind blow? Would snow fall?

If not, I wasn't sure I'd want to be in the Stillness.

"Why do you love winter so much?" Bastiaan tucked his hands under his arms and hunched over. He'd been watching me beneath the snowfall.

"In winter I was free. Spring and summer—the times of markt with Oma selling my wishes—were when I was enslaved." My explanation sounded dramatic, even to my own ears. But I knew Bastiaan would hear my heart.

Smooth cliff walls rose on each side of us, creating a narrow ravine. The path up the center was smooth and glassy, like a frozen riverbed. Illuminated by moonlight.

"Shouldn't the moon be higher in the sky by now?"

"We were in the Stillness. When time stops, so does the pulse of life." He said it so casually. How many times had he entered the Stillness? "The sun and moon continue their course, but they reset once time resumes."

"It's a full moon, Bastiaan." I looked at his hand, hoping for something other than the purple and silver strands fighting each other.

"I know." His Talent Mark appeared the same. "It renews at the peak of moonrise." He didn't sound hopeful. But I was certain his Talent would regenerate as he said it always did. I didn't know why it struggled during the Trials, but the fact that it wrestled against Mattias's Bane was a good sign.

"The Well will have answers." I could hardly breathe. I was *here*. On the other side of the Trials. I'd made it.

"It's around the curve."

For the first time since waking after Coralythe's attack, I strode forward without gazing back. The Well was ahead and nothing—no one—could stop me from reaching it. From seeing what would happen when I finally peered into its glassy depths and drank of its water. Perhaps nothing would happen.

Then again, what if everything happened?

I didn't wait for Bastiaan and he called out no warnings. My bare feet, stinging from poison vines and burned from sand, flew across the now-icy dirt. The pain didn't slow me because this was the end of it—internal and external. Up, up, up along the path I ascended, noting how smooth it was.

The ravine opened into a wide circle like a courtyard and in the center rose a mound. A ring of stones encircled the top like a crown. The stones were dusty and simple. There was no sign posted or fanfare. Was that the Well? Such a grand thing couldn't be so mundane, could it?

I swallowed hard. Now that I was here, my feet didn't seem to want to move. To approach the Well was to finally have either an answer or silence from the water that had strong-armed my life. Every Wishtress had stood here.

They never wrote about what they'd found at the Well, but it was enough for them to record the journey. Now it was my turn.

After all I'd been through—selected to be the Wishtress, forced to surrender my wishes to my guardian's greed—the Well had better not dare be silent.

I advanced with fierce purpose. My heart pounded with each step. When I reached the stones, I planted my palms on the cold rock and leaned over to peer into the heart of the Well—to dive in if needed.

There was no flicker of cold water. No reflection to meet me.

The Well was bone dry.

CHAPTER 48

BASTIAAN

For the twelfth time, Bastiaan took in the Well of Talents. It was just as plain, just as unassuming as it had been the first time he'd approached it. Only this time, instead of his rough, selfish boy-master Dehaan demanding a Talent from the water, Myrthe stood at its edge. Tentative, hopeful, curious.

It was a stunning contrast, and he determined to tuck the moment away in his memory.

She was meeting the Well for the first time. Could she hear its voice? Was it explaining her Wishtress Talent the way it had explained his Time Talent? Did her Talent Mark tingle with the magic?

His hands itched for his journal, his tongue biting back the questions. If the Well gave her answers, he was about to unlock a whole new understanding of Talents, the Wishtress, curses, Banes, and the Well—if she chose to share. He wouldn't pressure her. It had been such a long time since the thrill of new knowledge had been before him.

Myrthe leaned over the stones. He kept his distance, held his breath. Gave her space.

"It's dry."

Was she speaking to him? "What?"

"It's dried up." Her voice sounded as hollow and empty as she claimed the Well to be. Of all the things he'd expected her to say, that was not one of them.

"Impossible." He ascended the mound—ran to the Well—and leaned over the ring of stones. The wide mouth led to a parched throat of dirt. At the bottom . . . dust.

He shook his head. "But . . . this isn't possible."

"Wells run dry." Myrthe grew stiffer by the moment. "This one ran its course."

She didn't understand. "I said that's impossible." Why was he growing angry? It wasn't her fault. "This isn't just a well, it's a *spring*. Springs don't dry up. Not this one. This one's *alive*." It wasn't mere water.

She didn't answer.

The Well—now a depressing pit—sat there. Silent. Drab. Dead. "I've studied the Well my entire life! *Two* lifetimes, even. This can't happen—"

"Then explain it!" Myrthe spun on him. "If you know everything about it, explain why there *is. No. Water.*"

He couldn't. Nowhere in his extensive study had he read a single word about the Well running dry.

"The Well has existed since the beginning. It's supposed to be timeless." He shook his head as if he could brush away the confusion. "The water used to flow down this mountain and into the rivers and canals. Even when men contained it in this Well, they couldn't stop it."

"It seems there's an end to everything . . . and everyone." Her voice rang with defeat.

Bastiaan spared her a glance. Her glassy eyes wouldn't lift from the gaping maw of dry dirt before her. A shadow caught his eye in the center of the pit. Had that earth been dark before?

"Myrthe." The dark spot grew. "Myrthe! I think it's still damp!" He hurled himself over the edge.

Myrthe cried out but the drop wasn't far. He kept his feet upon impact and pressed a finger into the dirt. Even as he stared at the wet circle, it shrank before his eyes, receding back into the ground. He dug earth away in great scoops, chasing the liquid. A drop—a mere drop for Runt was all he needed!

He unearthed a thimbleful of liquid, but before he could scoop it into his hand it sank back into the earth. Despair swelled and the water was gone.

"No!" He scraped at the dirt, now drier than ground wheat. "It was here! For a moment it was here." What made it return? What made the Well heave what seemed a final liquid breath?

Above, Myrthe practically blended in with the stones with how statuesque she stood. He could almost see her schooling her features, ignoring the disappointment, and hardening her will. Her emotions receded from her face, draining away almost like . . .

Almost like the Well water.

"Myrthe," he gasped. "Were you . . . ?" This was going to sound insensitive. "Were you about to cry?"

"I'm fine." Her voice was cold. Hard. Empty.

"I think maybe your tears are connected to the Well."

She finally looked at him, and it was impossible to miss the skepticism on her face. "What does *that* mean?"

"Just now, the water dampened the earth as you . . . as tears formed in your eyes."

"It was a moment of weakness."

She didn't get it. She thought he was talking about her emotions, but it was so much more than that. Could it be . . . ?

He forged onward. "You pushed back your tears and the water receded. Maybe the Well is dry because you and it are connected."

"You think this is *my* fault?" She spun away. "So I should cry to fill up the Well for us?"

No. It wasn't blame; it was new understanding. He took a deep breath, trying to acknowledge how fragile she was in this moment. He'd been there—dreams shattered, desperation having no escape. If *only* she could see the hope this revelation brought.

"Myrthe—"

"Be quiet," she snapped. She was angry. Hurt.

Hear my heart. "I'm sorry—"

His rope sailed into the well, nearly smacking him in the face. The other end was lodged in the stones above. "Get up here."

He hauled himself out of the Well in five lengths. As he gained his feet he heard the voices. He couldn't make out the words but didn't need to because a shaggy blond head came into view around the bend.

Sven. Hedy. Kees.

All three had bows drawn, arrows nocked, and aimed to kill.

CHAPTER 49

𝒪MYRTHE

S ven stood in the opening of the ravine with Hedy and Kees at his
back. Their skin peeled away from their foreheads, burned to
a crisp from merely *walking* through the Summer Trial. I imagined
how I must look after all my time spent beneath the forge-like sun.

Their arrowtips caught the moonlight, aimed mainly at
Bastiaan. I stepped in front of him.

Sven actually laughed. I'd never heard a sound so ugly before.
"How cute." He gestured to Bastiaan. "You'd actually let her take
the hit for you?"

Bastiaan emerged from behind me, throwing discs in hand.
"That's the thing. I don't stop her or 'let' her do things."

"How quickly you've figured out the intricacies of love." He
sneered. "By all means, hide behind her again if that makes you
feel like the hero." Sven lowered his bow. Kees followed suit. Hedy
did not.

Sven approached and bypassed me entirely, going straight for
the Well. "Did the water fix you, then?"

I braced myself for what he was about to discover. I wanted to
make a run for it, but Hedy blocked the exit by bow and arrow. I

couldn't expect Bastiaan to kill again. Nor did I want to partake in snuffing another life. Even if it *was* Hedy's.

Sven peered over the edge of the Well. He maintained that position for one breath. Two breaths. I could almost physically feel his rage building.

He turned a murderous gaze to me. "What. Did. You. Do?"

I didn't have the energy to be surprised by his blame. "The Well was dry when I arrived." I wasn't about to tell him about the moisture we saw or Bastiaan's theory. It had already disappeared, as though imagined.

"It's dry?" Hedy croaked.

Kees had yet to move since lowering his bow. He appeared lost in tortured memories, hardly caring about the Well or me or anything else. Haunted by the Trials. They'd had to defeat most of Spring and all of Autumn to get here. That was the second time for Kees.

"You stopped it up, didn't you?" Sven accused. "To stop me from getting a true Talent."

Everything truly was about him. "How would I do that?"

He gripped my collar. "Undo it."

"Get your hands off her," Bastiaan growled, lifting his throwing discs.

"Undo it!" Sven's spittle sprayed my face.

I tried to shove him back, but he didn't budge. "I can't, you fool!"

"You're *choosing* not to!"

"Choosing not to *die*."

"You are so selfish!" He threw me from him and I crashed into the ring of stones, barely keeping myself from toppling over.

Bastiaan released a disc and it caught Sven in the shoulder. Sven hissed and blood splashed his sleeve.

"That's a warning." Bastiaan had another disc at the ready.

"Don't touch her again. There's nothing here for any of us. Myrthe and I are leaving." He held out a hand for me.

Sven straightened the same way he used to before a schaat race. Resolved. Determined. Unshakable. "Hedy."

She released an arrow.

It stuck in the caulk of the well rocks behind Bastiaan with a *twang*. I exhaled. She missed.

Then Bastiaan swayed.

Blood spread from his middle. He stared down, confused. The arrow had gone clean through him. In his stomach. Out his back. Leaving behind a shock of silence.

Bastiaan dropped to one knee with a grunt. A scream ripped out of my body of its own accord. I launched myself over him in case Hedy sent a second arrow.

It didn't come. Hedy and Sven seemed to be waiting. Waiting for my screams to stop. Waiting for Bastiaan to die.

Or waiting for a wish.

The same helpless panic that gripped me in the Summer Trial rose again. This couldn't be happening. Not again.

Bastiaan trembled under my touch, fumbling for my hand. His was slick with blood.

"No," I whispered. *"No."*

It was so much worse than the Summer Trial. This was *real* Bastiaan. *My* Bastiaan. Not a false, enchanted one. No glassy eyes, no confusion. He saw me—all of me. And he felt every thrum of approaching death.

"I . . ." Bastiaan licked his lips, already turning pale, whether from fear or blood loss, I wasn't sure. "Myrthe. I'm so sorry."

Sorry for *what*? "No!"

As though immune to the dying man at their feet, Hedy and Sven turned back to the Well. "It's hopeless then." Hedy looked ill—more from the dried well than her actions of murder. "We've lost."

345

Sven nodded toward Bastiaan. "We may not be able to use the Well water to our advantage, but we have one last bargaining chip."

I angled myself in front of Bastiaan, still holding his hand in a desperate grip. "You can't have him. Do you really believe Mattias cares about avenging his father *now*? Imprisoning Bastiaan?"

"He has my people! The ones you abandoned! Because you wouldn't share your wishes, we were *stranded* in the valley when Mattias's men came."

"There was no other way. I'm sorry, Sven." This time I allowed myself to feel. To remember. To regret every selfish choice I'd made. To will my last tear to fall.

Because I was going to save Bastiaan.

This was it. The time to use my last wish and bid farewell to this life. I'd been holding on to life so tightly. Determined to live, in defiance of my curse. But now, with Bastiaan at my feet bleeding out because he had helped me, I realized that my story was not about what was worth living for. It was about something—some*one*—worth dying for.

I would save him.

For us. For hope. *Joy*, even, that my Talent could finally be used for something that moved me. Used for someone else.

Wasn't that what Bastiaan was always saying? Talents were to serve others.

Then he would save everyone else. Like when he plucked me from the hedgerow and took me to Windmill Cottage to heal. Because that was the type of heart he had.

It was almost moonrise. He could use his time snap and get free of Sven. Get to Mattias. He had all manner of knowledge and plans that would help the people of Fairhoven—stop the Banes from being let loose.

Knowing I was about to die made my words bold. "You can't save lives by sacrificing another, Sven. Your own people are held

346

by Mattias because you lied about your Talent. You claimed to have one when you didn't. They trusted you." My voice cracked. Kees looked to Sven, confused.

"Myrthe." Bastiaan's hand wrapped around my wrist.

I sniffed hard but maintained my focus. I had to say this. "I finally understand my Talent. It's for others. You used a wish for your own false Talent, which you *still* used for your own gain. The Well sees the heart. And even though mine is stone . . . yours is dead."

My anger at Sven fell away like a dropped cloak, and all that remained was sorrow—for him and the life he'd led and was going to continue leading. Because the fire in his eyes showed me he wasn't considering my words. Not as something to change him. Only something to fuel his hatred.

"Oh, Sven." The tears were close. "I'm sorry my wish turned you into what you are."

I turned my full attention to the man in my arms. The man I loved. Did Bastiaan know I loved him? It was so different from when I thought I loved Sven. With Sven I viewed love as a choice—if I *chose* to love him with action, the heart would follow and then he'd free me from Oma.

That wasn't love.

With Bastiaan it was still a choice, but it was a choice of head *and* heart. A mutual one. I moved hair off his forehead, my touch gentler than the breath of a snowflake.

"Myrthe," Bastiaan croaked. "Don't."

I looked into his tortured eyes. "I have to." It had been so long since I'd allowed my emotions to work as designed that my tears felt distant and buried.

"On the contrary, Myrthe. *Do*." Sven pulled a small glass bottle from his pocket—the same one that had formerly held the wish I gave him so long ago.

He had Bastiaan shot so he could claim my final wish.

I blinked once and steel threatened to dam my tears. I couldn't give the wish to Sven.

"That's my girl." Bastiaan sounded so weak. I scanned his body, but all I saw was blood. Everywhere. I didn't need to be a healer to know his wound was fatal.

"This is taking too long," Hedy snapped. "We have one chance, Sven. What if you miss the tear? What if she wastes it on *him*? We should turn *her* in to the king—a trade for our people."

A hand gripped my hair and yanked me back.

"No!" I twisted away from Sven, individual strands snapping from my skull. Sven's grip tightened and he kicked the back of my knees so I fell to the ground.

"Let's go," he said to the others.

"What about Bastiaan?" Hedy asked. "The king *does* want him dead. Two bargaining chips are better than one."

Sven peered around me as though assessing how difficult it would be to carry Bastiaan. "Cut off the finger with the Talent Mark. Then throw him into the Well. I don't want to risk him surviving and coming after us."

"He's not surviving *that* wound," Hedy snorted, withdrawing her dagger.

"With his history I wouldn't put it past him."

"No!" I screamed. "You can't do this! *Sven!*" I writhed against his hold. He leaned away from me as though dodging a mosquito. I fought harder, desperate to get free. To tackle Hedy. Knock her to the ground. Throw myself over Bastiaan. *Something.*

Hedy pressed her knee onto Bastiaan's midsection. He cried out, trying to push her away, but already he was so very weak. Hedy yanked his arm straight, searching his fingers for the Talent Mark.

"Stop! You have to stop!" I elbowed Sven in the face. He growled and yanked my head back so hard my neck popped.

"Here it is." Hedy splayed Bastiaan's right hand on the ground. Then she stabbed right through the bone. I screamed. Bastiaan bucked against the pain, an animal sound ripping through him.

Hedy tucked his severed finger in her pocket and got up. "Done."

"Bastiaan!" I cried, gulping in a breath. "I'm so sorry!" This was my doing. The tears were coming. Finally. How could Hedy and Sven *do* this to another human?

Sven released me and I ran to Bastiaan. Pulled him close and tucked his head to my chest.

"Don't . . . ," Bastiaan pleaded. "Don't cry."

"I love you," I whispered.

He turned his head. "It'll be the death of you." He kissed the soft spot of my neck. "And I can't let that happen."

I saw the sweep of his arm. Stone to skull. All went black.

CHAPTER 50

BASTIAAN

Bastiaan landed with a *crack* in the belly of the Well. Hedy's hands weren't gentle. He didn't need to see the sharp bone pressing against his skin from the inside to know his arm had broken from the fall.

The pain was nothing compared to his arrow wound.

Yet he directed his focus not to his pain, but to the dirt beneath him. It felt damp against his cheek but grew dry with every breath. He relaxed as much as his perishing body would allow him.

Dry dirt meant Myrthe was safe from her tears.

Someone hauled up his rope, ensuring he couldn't escape. He closed his eyes against the sounds of Sven and Hedy collecting Myrthe's unconscious body to take her to the king as leverage. She would be crushed when she woke, but he couldn't let her die for him.

He would never get to share his theory about the Well. The connection between the Wishtress and the water. The Well had chosen Myrthe to bring its Talents to the people . . . through her tears. Her emotion, her heart. Yet she'd been used by others. Been a slave to those who'd sold her Talent for their own gain.

He had to trust that somehow, someday, Myrthe would learn

the truth about her Talent—and the beauty it was designed to spread. The Well would not abandon her—had never abandoned her. No matter how convinced she was that it had.

"You sure you want to leave him alive?" Hedy asked. Bastiaan started—he'd almost forgotten they were still up there.

"He won't be for long," Kees's low voice responded.

Sven peered into the Well and something like triumph crossed his face. "Shoot him, then."

"Leave it be," Kees said wearily. "It's not worth the risk. He could still be armed."

"He's dying," she snarled. "Fish in a barrel."

"Shark in a puddle, more like it." Though Kees was on the wrong side, Bastiaan disliked him least. "I don't want you living with his blood on your hands, Hedy."

"I don't mind."

Boots sliding on dirt. Bastiaan readied himself. At least it'd be quick. But the sounds grew more and more distant. Then . . . gone. And Myrthe with them. The swollen rage inside his chest could refill the Well within seconds if it could be released. Instead he closed his eyes and took deep breaths.

The moon hung like a coin against a splash of black ink. Even *if* he had his time snap back, it wouldn't free him from the Well. It wouldn't heal him. His Talent had its limitations and the Well had a reason for that.

He ought to have used his Talent better. For others—the thing he always told people but seemed to do terribly on his own. How could one know the right thing to do yet always fail at doing that very thing?

He stared up at the stars. Felt them moving as time ticked by. He was glad to be dying in the Awake and not the Stillness. It felt natural. Right. The more he accepted his end, the less pain he felt—almost like it didn't matter anymore.

The Well must have been dry since Myrthe's curse. Since before Mattias was king—which made so much sense. Mattias must have made the pilgrimage to the Well and found it dry. That was why he turned to the Nightwell—to Coralythe—for power.

The moon passed out of view, tucking itself behind the cliffs. Moonrise had arrived, but he felt no change in his Talent Mark— *Oh.*

Pain burst across his hand at the very memory of Hedy's brutality. His Talent Mark was gone. He lay bare. Empty yet at peace.

The Well was in Myrthe.

And the Well protected its own. *Take care of her.*

Bastiaan exhaled and closed his eyes, lying like a bull's-eye in the center of a target. Trapped in the very place that first gave him freedom. Yet about to be fully free for the first time.

CHAPTER 51

MYRTHE

*B*astiaan! *Bastiaan! Bastiaan!*

My mind shouted his name in an endless echo as I returned to consciousness. My ribs burned, pressed against someone's shoulder with my hands tied behind me. My teeth ground against a gag in my mouth as I remembered what had happened.

The Well was dry. Bastiaan left for dead. I'd been *useless*. I had, however, given Sven a bloody nose. That was something at least.

The world spun in grey skies and brittle winter earth. I squirmed against the arm holding me and was promptly deposited on the ground. Knives stabbed through my heels and shins. My knees buckled, but Hedy yanked me up by my hair.

"Finally. Sven, she's awake." To me she said, "Stand up and be quiet."

A pointless command since I was gagged. I struggled to my feet. Still bare—no boots or skates to protect them. They didn't cooperate, and I teetered against the mixture of numbness and pain. They didn't even resemble feet. Riddled with black frostbite and peeling flaps of ripped skin. Blood smeared every inch and welts rose like poison bubbles. I didn't know what was fire oak burn, sand scorch, or scorpion sting. My feet were nothing more than stubs of flesh.

I didn't look at them again.

How much time had passed? Bastiaan. *Bastiaan.* The moon had moved. Several bell tolls. Staring at the sky sent my head throbbing and vision spinning. I focused on the ground again, taking deep breaths against a swell of nausea.

Bastiaan had knocked me out. To *save* me. To stop me from saving *him*.

He could be dead because of his rash actions! I tried to catch Hedy's eye as she dug through her pack. *Is Bastiaan still alive?* I'd beg if I had to. But Hedy wouldn't engage. Neither would Sven. Kees wasn't with us. When had he left? And to where?

Cold fear gripped my core. Did Hedy finish the job after I'd gone unconscious? So much blood . . . Bastiaan didn't have long. My pulse pounded in my throat and memories replayed. The arrow going through his body. His plea for me to save my wish.

He'd sounded so . . . *helpless.*

Bastiaan, who could do anything. Escape the king, defeat bowmen, learn everything about Talents, save his mother, raise a canal rat . . . He couldn't stop Hedy's arrow.

I'd allowed him into my heart—the first voice to speak to my soul since my curse. I wanted to be with him—*needed* to be with him. As long as he'd have me. Even if he wouldn't, I had to give him life.

Because that was love. Beyond infatuation. It was *action*. It was an action of the heart, of the mind. Of forgiveness and grace and seeing one another. He'd given that to me, and I was determined to live long enough to give it back to him.

Kees emerged from the trees leading two horses. "They were still there. Mattias's men left 'em."

"Small favors." Hedy popped her neck and took the reins of one of the horses.

I caught Kees's gaze, desperate for an answer. *Is Bastiaan alive? Did you leave him alive?* He dropped his eyes to the ground. Ashamed?

If they left him breathing, he'd hold on as long as he could. Courage was Bastiaan's way.

"We're almost to the *kleinschloss*," Sven said. "Mattias received our message of parley. He'll see us, but he'll likely be surrounded by militairen. Our new goal is to get Hedy close enough to him."

Kleinschloss. Mattias was in a small palace? I'd pictured him out in the forest with his soldiers—like Sven and his crew. How foolish of me to think he'd been on an equal playing field.

When had the kleinschloss been built? And for what reason? Had it been built for the king to visit the Nightwell or the Well of Talents? Or maybe both. I would ask Bastiaan—

My thoughts screeched to a painful halt. I couldn't ask him. Might never ask him.

No. I will. I would ask him once I healed him. Except I'd be dead. *Winter's breath.*

"I've seen the future," Sven continued. "None of us will be killed."

Hedy pounded her chest with her fist. She ate his words like honey off a comb. For the first time I really appreciated—with disgust—Sven's level of manipulation and control.

"We have something the king wants," Sven said. Hedy gave a dark, low laugh. "If he wants the Wishtress, he'll have to give our people back."

I'd gone from being their savior to their sacrifice in half a day. I didn't blame them for their anger, but anger should never be allowed to result in revenge. That was how Talents got cursed, how towns got destroyed, how morals died, how blood spilled.

But even a wish couldn't undo human nature.

"Let's go." Hedy's eyes burned like campfire coals.

Kees untied the reins of the two horses. "Let's double up. Don't want her slowing us down on foot." He jerked his chin toward me. Though he tried sounding gruff, I caught the compassion in his tone.

Then to my surprise Kees, Hedy, and Sven stripped themselves of weapons and left them on the forest ground. They'd likely be searched upon arriving at the kleinschloss, but to walk into Mattias's domain with no weapons struck me as foolish.

Had Sven really seen the future about their attack? Or did this have something to do with Hedy's Bane? Sven had mentioned getting her close enough to the king. Close enough to kill him? She must be powerful.

But she could also be controlled if Mattias knew she had a Bane. Could he sense that sort of thing? How far away could he be and still control her?

Sven mounted a horse, then gestured to me. "Get her up."

Kees shot me an apologetic look, and I felt a bit more human beneath his gaze. He hoisted me onto the horse behind Sven. If I didn't have the gag, I'd bite his shoulder until I drew blood.

Not long into the ride, he twisted and tugged the gag down and shoved his canteen at me. "Drink."

Maybe I wouldn't bite him . . . yet. "What did you do with Bastiaan?"

"You really want those to be the first words out of your mouth to me?"

"Answer me."

"You have five seconds." He shoved the opening of the canteen against my lips and tipped it up. Icy water poured down my face, my neck, but hardly a swallow went down my throat.

I gulped the liquid until Sven wrenched the canteen away. I glowered at him, dripping and cold. "How does it feel to trade in a person for your own gain?"

"By strengthening myself, I can better serve my followers. For a people to be strong, their leader needs to be strong."

"For a people to be strong, the people themselves need to *choose* to be strong. We are not sheep!"

"Says the girl who was a wish cow her whole life."

My mouth went dry and my lungs couldn't seem to find air. "You claim to oppose the king, yet now you want to give him the last wish in existence?"

"We both know you won't give it to him."

He was right. I wanted to give it to Bastiaan. Why was I talking? I needed to get that tear out.

Sven shoved the gag back in my mouth. I wrenched away, but he shoved it back in and tied it in place. At my furious glare he said, "You're so much more attractive with this on."

I growled behind the cloth, calling him all manner of names. Even with the gag I was pretty sure he caught a few of the insults.

With every minute that passed, Bastiaan could be taking his last breath. I tried to focus on that—resurface the memory of the arrow going through his body, him folding to the ground. I let the sickness surge inside me, willed the emotions to come.

But I was too angry, too guarded, and the tear wouldn't come. Frustration made me want to scream. If I couldn't speak the wish, would it even work? I could waste it—die for nothing.

Maybe I could toss myself from the horse and rub my face against the ground to remove the gag. By the time they got to me, I would've had plenty of time to speak a wish.

I just needed to cry.

Sven eyed me and I startled. Had he been watching me that whole time? He shook his head. "Hedy!"

Kees nudged their horse until the four of us were side by side. Instinctively I leaned away from Hedy, but she looked to Sven for instruction.

"We can't risk her using her wish," he said.

Winter's breath! Had my thoughts been that loud?

Hedy nodded. "I'll have one use left after this. Are you sure?" Her Bane. She was about to use her Bane on me.

"I'm sure."

That was all the push Hedy needed. She yanked my gag free so hard it left a burn on my cheek. "I've been wanting to do this for a long time."

This was my chance. "Kees! Is Bastiaan alive? Did you—?"

"Shh." Hedy pressed a finger to my lips as one would shush a child. Her pupils pulsed purple and a pressure hit my throat, like someone was pressing their fingers against it. Then a pulling sensation released with a snap.

I gasped but no sound came out.

What? My mouth moved to form the word. Breath exhaled to deliver the question. But again. Silence.

Hedy's Bane had stolen my voice.

CHAPTER 52

MYRTHE

I couldn't use my wish even if I wanted to. What was worse was that this helplessness got me the closest to crying. But I had to shove it back. Again. And again. And again.

We reached the edge of the woods and halted. "On foot from here." Sven dismounted and yanked me down. My pathetic feet couldn't handle the impact, and I crumpled.

"You two ready?" Sven asked.

Kees nodded, standing stiff as a weathered oak. He never answered my question about Bastiaan, but I gathered it was because he didn't know if Bastiaan was still alive. And that frightened me the most.

Sven stepped close to Hedy and said in a gentle voice, "You'll be fine. I won't let anything happen to you."

I snorted. Rather, I would have if my body were capable of making vocal noises. Perhaps it was best Hedy and Sven didn't hear me. That didn't stop me from rolling my eyes at his false tenderness.

He needed Hedy to silence Mattias. She was just another tool.

Sven pulled something wrapped in cloth from his pocket and

handed it to Hedy. She took it but whispered, "What if this doesn't work?"

"It will." Then, more to himself than to her, "It has to. From what I understand, you have to hear the king's command for it to compel you. Silence him and he'll never speak again unless you undo it."

What did Sven mean by her undoing it? Was the muteness permanent otherwise?

She unwrapped the item, and I barely made out a little lump of clay. Hedy tore off two pieces and stuffed them tight into her ears. Would that keep her from having to follow Mattias's orders?

Hedy gave a firm nod, and we continued on foot. I limped as best I could, but every step now sent spikes of pain up through my legs and even into my back.

I breathed a sigh when a dozen militairen intercepted us at arrowpoint not two minutes later. "Ah, the 'rebel leader,'" one militair scoffed.

Sven didn't flinch. "King Mattias is expecting me."

"But are *you* expecting *him*?" The militair laughed. Then they searched us.

If they found it odd that Sven and company had no weapons, they didn't say so. "Matches, canteen, a few bowstring bracelets with no bow, and . . . someone's finger." After getting over his disgust, the militairen inspected Sven and the others. "You really thought you'd get the best of the king?"

Their loyalty toward Mattias seemed to have shifted. I suppose that was to be expected when he gifted them with power—or what seemed like power but was really a ploy.

Kees stuffed his matches back into his pocket and adjusted the bowstring around his wrist. Sven rolled Bastiaan's finger back up in a piece of cloth and put it in his pocket. I swallowed bile.

"Let's go." A militair poked Sven in the back with his arrow. I gritted my teeth and continued the walk. Step after step. Soon this would be over. I'd be dead. Bastiaan would be saved. My feet—this pain—wouldn't matter.

Despite being called the kleinschloss, the little palace was larger than all of Fairhoven's markt. The main difference was how militarized it was. Weapons and shovels lined the walls of barracks filled with militairen on rotation.

The kleinschloss rested on the top of a hill, and as we entered the keep, my eye caught a line of torches snaking across the plains from the little palace toward where I assumed the Nightwell rested. A giant, empty canal lay like a deflated snake awaiting its morning meal.

Very little movement interrupted the flicker of torches. From what I could tell the canal was finished. All it needed now was the water from the Nightwell. And then it would spread all the way to Fairhoven.

We walked a dark path lit by the moon and what light shone through the kleinschloss's windows. Untamed foliage choked the pathway—no gardeners out this way. It was a wild schloss meant for wild hearts seeking either Talent or Bane. Service or Self.

The longer I spent away from the markt—away from Oma— the more I realized how many lies had twisted their knotted laces around my understanding of my purpose. The Well made me the Wishtress for a reason. There must be something in me that would wield that Talent rightly.

The militair leader stopped at the edge of a fountain. "Here we are."

Sven glanced back at the kleinschloss. "Where's the king?"

"Waiting for you."

An arrow tip poked me in the back. Judging by Kees's and Hedy's outcries, they were prodded too.

"What is this?" Sven demanded.

A figure loomed from the darkness, wrapped in shadows and Bane mist. Her dark hair tumbled to her waist, and when her dark eyes met mine, I nearly choked. Coralythe.

She jerked her chin at me. "That one."

Hands grabbed my arms and hauled me toward the fountain. I tried to shout, but no words emerged from my broken voice. My useless feet posed no resistance.

"Stop!" Sven hollered. "That's the Wishtress! She's who the king wants!" If he thought this proclamation would slow the militairen's efforts, he was wrong. It seemed to incense them.

A third militair joined the two pulling me toward the water.

"Of course she is," the leader said. "And after a little dip in the Nightwell water, she'll be loyal to him until death. Giving him any wish he needs."

They lifted me from the ground and with one swing threw me into the depths.

The water closed around me like a blanket of midnight. I tried swimming for the surface, but the surface seemed to have disappeared.

As the world went silent, the water found its voice.

You finally made it.

I stilled. Unlike when I was in regular water, my filled lungs did nothing to provide buoyancy. I sank deeper as though the fountain had no bottom. But my lungs didn't burn for air. Instead, they rested. Waiting.

Myrthe.

It knew my name. It knew *me*. And it sounded kind. Understanding.

I didn't trust it. *Let me go.*

You're not my captive. No one wants you free more than I do.

Free. I had spent most of my life listening to other people tell me what they wanted for me. Oma wanted to "train" me. Sven wanted to "protect" me. Both wanted to control me. *You don't know what I want.*

I know all my children. Hedy was silenced her entire life, so now she has the power to finally be heard. Mattias's father was murdered by a Talented, so I gave him the ability to remove Talents from those who would misuse them.

People have only ever wanted to use you, Myrthe. Oma. Sven. Even Anouk.

The longer I spent in the water, the more it seeped into my skin. My bones. Cold, then warm, then pulsing like blood in my veins. *I don't want your power.*

A warning bell rang in my mind and my limbs remembered how to move. I clawed for the surface, despite how comfortable it was to rest in this conversation. *I don't want a Bane!*

I don't force it on you.

The water around me lightened to a soft purple. Was that because I was near the surface? I kicked harder, but something dangerously sweet pressed against me—like an embrace with a knife blade against my throat.

It's a gift.

Burning filled my veins. A door opened in my mind, letting in a flood of new knowledge about myself. About this new power crossing my threshold: a power to direct a person's limbs like a puppeteer.

Scenarios spun through my head as though a forbidden desire deep within me had been awoken—approved. Me being able to stop Coralythe midcurse. My power to force Oma to walk away from the markt. The ability to make Hedy bend over backward until her spine snapped—

My head broke the surface and I gasped.

No matter its promises and no matter my protests . . . the Nightwell had forced a Bane on me anyway.

I sat in the fountain, heavy against the stone base. No more than three feet of water lapped at my shoulders and back. How had I been swimming? Kicking? *Sinking* in such shallow water?

My shivers had nothing to do with the winter air meeting my wet skin.

Sven, Hedy, and Kees stood surrounded by militairen. Watching me. Wary. Why didn't *they* get thrown into the Nightwell water? Wouldn't Mattias want to control them too?

I eased myself into a crouch, supporting as much of my weight as I could on the fountain edge. The militairen waited for me to climb out of my own accord. I could use the Bane—force one of them to pick me up. Carry me to my next destination.

For that matter I could force all of the militairen to surrender their weapons. Or better yet, guard me against Sven and Mattias.

As swiftly as the thought entered my mind, an understanding of my Bane surfaced. I could control only one person at a time. Coralythe was already gone, so my gaze landed on the militairen. There were half a dozen of them.

If I turned their leader against them, perhaps I could escape.

Wait. How had this so easily become a consideration? Using my Bane was not an option.

364

Then again, neither was using my Talent. Because of my curse. Not until I had my voice back. Then I could save Bastiaan.

My eyes slid to Hedy. I knew what I needed to do.

"Hurry up," a militair said. I made sure to splash him as I clambered over the edge.

This game Mattias and Sven were playing would be the death of Bastiaan. I could use my Bane. Just once.

Bastiaan wouldn't approve. But he'd never had a Bane. He didn't realize the doors it opened. Or the way it would free me in this moment. Would he really argue if I used it to save him?

We entered the kleinschloss and my eyes relaxed against the wave of light, no longer straining for clarity. The militairen thrust me into a high-ceilinged meeting room of sorts.

In the corner sat a woman with her head bowed. Stringy hair concealed her face. Chains were roughly nailed into the stone wall, keeping her wrists elevated. More shackles constrained her ankles, but she didn't look like one to put up such a fight. Militairen stood on each side of her. She peered up at the noise of our entrance. Dark hair fell to the side, revealing tanned skin. A new mark on her cheek seemed like a bruise.

Anouk.

I would have shouted had my voice worked. What was my cousin doing here? *How?*

Anouk nodded briefly toward the king. Mattias stood in discussion with several men over a table of unfurled parchments weighted down with stones. *Mattias* did this to her? There was only one reason he'd display his own wife in such a shameful and violent way: He wanted everyone to know that *no* one was above his wrath . . . or his control.

Mattias continued his conversation, making it clear that Sven was little more than a gnat in his agenda.

This was my chance while the king was distracted.

Sven glowered and stepped up to my side, then gripped my arm as though he still had control over this situation. Hedy cowered in Sven's shadow. She'd lost her fire. Lost her strength—all to the scythe of fear. She feared the king's control over her—feared what he'd use her to do.

What she wasn't prepared for was *my* control.

My Bane swelled at my calling. It tasted of forbidden relief. I wanted to use it but also didn't want it near me. But I could handle the discomfort. For Bastiaan. This was a small price to pay. If he disapproved of my choice, well . . . at least he'd be alive to disapprove.

The Bane nodded its agreement, interacting with my mind far more than my Talent ever had. So I gave it its first command. *Give me control over Hedy's body.*

Hedy's head snapped my direction. Eyes wide. She knew. She *felt* something.

Good.

I salted my smile with malice. Then with a few pointed thoughts, I puppeteered Hedy's body ever so slowly in my direction. Foot over foot. Scoot by scoot. The control came naturally, like I'd had this Bane my entire life.

I felt Hedy's futile resistance, which made the control all the sweeter.

If I'd had this Bane a few hours ago at the Well, I could have stopped her from shooting Bastiaan. Stopped her from cutting off his finger.

Hedy whimpered. Her fingers stretched backward away from her palms. Cracking and straining. Her pinkie finger snapped. Hedy cried out and I startled, releasing her.

Hedy cradled her hand to her chest. Regret clawed at my throat. This was wrong.

But Hedy deserved it. She had no right to functioning

appendages when all she did was use them to cause pain. I had to finish what I'd started. I resumed control and Hedy slid to my side, jaw clenched.

Please work.

Hedy lifted her right hand—the one with the Bane mist—and touched that same finger to my mouth.

My voice returned with a punch to the throat.

Free. I was *free*. Free to speak. Free to cry a wish and use it for Bastiaan. I let Hedy go, and she darted back to Sven, tucking her hand with the broken pinkie into the other hand. Now . . . to cry—

"Very good." King Mattias clapped. Slow but proud.

I surfaced from the intoxication of my power to a silent room, eyes on me. Purple smoke tendrils floated around me and sank back into my skin. My Bane had been visible that whole time? Did his ability to control Banes show him that?

"At last we meet."

Sven must have thought the king was talking to him, because he thrust me forward despite being a captive himself. "The Wishtress for my people."

He pressed something cold and metal against my eye. Where had he gotten a weapon? I flinched away and got a brief glimpse of the tool before he pressed it against my eye once more.

"A spoon." King Mattias sounded amused. "How quaint."

A door to the right opened and Coralythe strode in, accompanied by a militair.

She glanced at me and a grim shadow passed over her face, which flickered with myriad emotions like sunlight through wind-tickled leaves. But there was a fragility in her expression. Maybe even . . . fear? So different from her demeanor at the Nightwell fountain.

What did she have to fear from me?

"Well done, Coralythe." Mattias gave a nod of approval, but she tangled her hands in the layers of her dress the same way she had when in the tent asking Oma for a wish. Unsure. Nervous.

Oh. *Oh.* Coralythe hadn't told the king about my curse—that my wishes were limited. To one last use. He must not know that was Coralythe's fault.

It wouldn't take much for him to piece it together.

"I'll carve her eyes out before you have a chance to touch her," Sven growled. "Then you'll never have a wish. My people first."

I no longer knew Sven well enough to know if he'd follow through on the threat. But I'd crack his skull open with my own if he dared press that spoon any harder. I was going to die as soon as I had the chance anyway. But would the loss of both eyes rid me completely of my Talent? When Bastiaan lost his finger, had he lost his Talent?

"I don't need to touch her." Mattias looked at me. "Make me a wish."

Sven pressed the spoon into my eye. "My people first!"

But it was too late. Mattias had spoken to my Bane, and despite the spoon cupping my eye, my body willed itself to obey. I sought my Talent, pulled up old memories, tried to find the last wish hiding inside my emotions, but . . .

It wasn't there anymore.

My Talent might as well have been invisible inside me. A writhing bewilderment swirled inside my spirit—the desire to obey my king and the inability to do so.

Where was my last wish? Had the Bane taken it from me?

I'd used the Bane once. Now I was done with it. But if I was truly done with it, Mattias's command wouldn't have affected me.

Bastiaan had been right: Banes and Talents couldn't coexist inside a person. One needed to rule. The other needed to fade. And I'd given authority to the Bane.

How did I take it back?

"I . . . I can't."

A flicker of annoyance crossed Mattias's face. "Come here."

This command was altogether different. I felt the yank of loyalty. Servitude. A desire to obey. But also a confusing resistance in the back of my mind. Was this how Hedy felt as I made her prance to my side and touch me? Helpless? Furious? Determined to resist and remain her own person?

I took a step forward, but Sven yanked me back, digging the spoon into my eye socket. I cried out. He really *would* carve out my eye!

"I'm warning you, Mattias . . . my people. Where are they?"

"Make me a wish." Mattias tried again, unmoved by Sven's threat.

"I can't." What form of *can't* did he not understand?

Mattias rounded on Coralythe. "How can she refuse me?"

Her mouth trembled as she struggled for words. But her voice remained steady and collected. "It's likely because she's the Wishtress. Her power is unmatched among the Talented. She does not work under the same . . . rules."

It was that sort of mindset that put me under Oma's thumb. The idea that I was greater than the rest, the only difference being that I was born with a Talent whereas others made the pilgrimage.

"You told me this would work," Mattias growled.

"I . . . I thought it would."

So Mattias's plan had been to capture the Wishtress, force me into a Bane, and then command a wish whenever he wanted. He turned back to me. "Why won't you serve your king?"

"If I give you a wish . . . I'll die."

He ground his teeth. "Elaborate."

Coralythe sucked in a sharp breath and pursed her lips against the pressure. Her wide eyes found mine and we held each other's gaze. A spider thread of temptation urged me to tell King Mattias about my curse. About what Coralythe had done.

But I finally saw the difference between us.

She had lost her sons, and she fought the grief by cursing me, joining the king, and bringing Banes to Fairhoven. I lost Mutti and I had a choice in how I grieved. Whether I sought revenge or a different path.

Revenge sounded nice.

But it wasn't lasting. Coralythe appeared no happier than when I first met her. Revenge was bitter and only birthed more revenge. I was tired of hurting myself. Mutti and Bastiaan had showed me another way.

"It's the Bane. My Talent is gone now." My voice broke. *Gone.* It sounded so final. I refused to believe it was so. "I can't use both, just the one."

"Mattias . . ." Sven growled. He dug the spoon into my eye and I screamed. My vision went black, and my Bane flashed in my mind. I used it to wrench Sven's arm away from my face so hard the spoon went flying from his hand.

Mattias watched me for several long seconds, perhaps to incense Sven more. He must have concluded he'd collect a wish from me a different way, because he finally rolled his eyes over to Sven. "Desperation doesn't look good on you, Sven."

He had the upper hand and everyone knew it. Sven was a fool to have walked right into Mattias's hearth. The flames of danger grew.

Mattias gave a lazy wave and the side door opened. A group of militairen filed in, dressed in sharp uniforms with even sharper swords. Once they stood in a line at attention, I recognized the three closest to me. Woodsfolk. Luuk. Archer. Runt!

I gasped. "What have you done?"

"I offered them freedom."

The woodsfolk now saw Sven as the enemy because they'd all been given Banes.

Mattias turned to the group. "Go to your former leader."

As one the group stepped away from the militairen. They marched across the room to Sven, determination on each face. As though commanded by an invisible generaal, they drew their swords. They circled Sven, Kees, Hedy, and me, tips pointed toward our vulnerable and exposed bodies.

Sven looked his former woodsfolk over with resignation. Sadness even.

"I have you to thank, really," Mattias went on. "A woman from your group received a Bane of fire. She is thawing the Vier as we speak."

A few militairen cheered. Even I breathed a relieved sigh knowing Fairhoven would have water again. The Handel Sea would be passable again. Though I disliked that the undoing of my wish came from a Bane power.

Mattias accepted the hurrahs with a nod, then jutted his chin toward the woodsfolk. "Your man Luuk finally received the other Bane I needed."

Luuk leaned forward from the circle of swords and spit on the wide head of the spoon lying on the ground. The utensil disintegrated into metallic dust.

"That works on humans too. Though the results are a little harder to clean up. All I have to do is . . . command him."

Luuk stepped from the circle and stood at Mattias's side. Two militairen flanked him, guarding him as they would the king.

Why was his Bane so valuable? The Vier was already thawing.

"Get him to the Nightwell," Mattias commanded in a low tone that still echoed as though shouted. "It's time."

"The dam," Hedy breathed, though how she pieced all this together when unable to hear baffled me.

Luuk needed only to spit on the dam and it would disintegrate, freeing the Nightwell into the now-functioning canals to spread to all the people of Fairhoven. Possibly even beyond. People would be so desperate for water that they'd lap it up. Swim, drink, boat, wash—and they'd all get Banes.

Then Mattias would have control of them, all with a single word from his mouth to their ears.

Coralythe, the militairen, and Luuk exited the room. "Wishtress. To me." Mattias pointed to his side, and I obeyed without hesitation.

Enough of this. I would not let him command me any longer.

I summoned my Bane.

Before I could enact my plan, Mattias gave one final command to the woodsfolk who still surrounded Sven, Hedy, and Kees. "Kill them."

"No!" I wrapped my Bane around Hedy and sent her sprinting to the king. Hedy screamed, a wild contrast to the determined sprint of her body. Mattias opened his mouth, but I sent Hedy into a dive, hand outstretched. She clamped her hand over the king's mouth. Shock slapped his face. When she released him, he gaped like a beached trout. Silenced by her Bane.

He drew his sword in a flash of fury and sliced it across her chest. She fell to the ground with a ragged gasp and curled into a ball.

"No!" Sven and I cried at the same time.

The woodsfolk converged on Sven and Kees, lifting their swords as one.

King Mattias raised his own sword above Hedy. "Stop!" I sent my Bane to Mattias but found it wouldn't obey. It wouldn't stop his arm from descending. He was my king.

"Kees!" Sven hollered.

Kees slapped his hands together above his head in a single deafening clap. Every sword, dagger, and arrow vanished from the hand of its wielder. Hands still moved to strike, the people not yet aware of their weaponless state.

That was Kees's Talent.

Sven barreled through the masses to get to Hedy. He yanked her to her feet. "Get up!"

She clutched a hand over her chest where blood bloomed, but it didn't seem deep enough to cripple her. Kees slung her free arm over his shoulder.

The woodsfolk recovered from their shock, but they didn't need weapons to complete Mattias's command. Purple mist oozed from their skin as Bane after Bane came into play. Someone struck Kees in the chest, leaving behind a scorched fist imprint. Tiny flames stuck to Kees's clothes and he hurried to stamp them out.

Another militair picked up a stick, cracked it in half over his knee, and then lifted two shining blades—transformed in his very hands. He went after Sven.

Sven wore his rebellion like an armor that no weapon could penetrate. He punched and rolled and kicked his own woodsfolk in the face if it meant interrupting the use of their Bane. This . . . this was his finale.

Sven whirled and grabbed me by the back of the coat. He hauled me toward the exit. "Give me your wish. *Now!*"

I gave him my Bane instead. Threw his hands off me. Sent him to the ground in a fetal position. Finally I was the one in a position of power. "Never. Touch. Me. Again."

The desire to crush him rose within me. To break every bone until each was turned to dust. I could do it with a single mental command. He'd cost me Bastiaan. My freedom. My very *Talent.*

He'd deserve it.

But so would I. The thought came unbidden. Unwelcome. True. I'd taken lives. Created countless wishes for Oma to sell to greedy merchants. I'd used Sven for my own gain.

It took everything within me to leave him lying there. At least he wasn't in danger of being stabbed. He had Kees to thank for that.

A gust of purple wind swirled around me, tightening around my chest and squeezing. A woodsman stood mere feet away, focused on me with a hand outstretched.

The squeeze increased, bending my ribs inward. I curled over my midsection, grimacing against the sharp pain. My ribs would snap any moment. Puncture lungs. Crack my chest cavity like an eggshell.

King Mattias bowled the woodsman over. He screamed in the man's face, neck veins popping, but no sound came out.

The woodsman got the picture and dropped his hand in horror.

King Mattias headed my way, but I wasn't going to wait to become someone else's captive. I couldn't risk him touching me—I remembered what happened to Bastiaan's Talent when the king touched him.

My Talent was silent, but I wasn't ready to fully bury it with Mattias's Bane touch.

I bolted for the corner door after Coralythe and Luuk, sparing one last glance over my shoulder. The moment I rounded the doorframe, Sven looked up from the militair he was strangling with his bowstring. He met my eyes.

I could see his thoughts as clearly as if they were written in the air above him.

You did this.

He blamed me for the death descending upon him. He was one who would always strap blame onto the backs of others. I turned my back on him and the guilt that came with him.

I burst out of the kleinschloss, the opposite side from where we first entered. The movement was disjointed and labored, my ragged feet functioning on nothing more than a memory of what feet were supposed to do. The numbness would last only so long.

But adrenaline banished any threat of pain.

I didn't know where to go. How to get away. Voices screamed

from behind. Shouting commands. Amid the fray I thought I heard King Mattias, and that frightened me the most. If he'd regained his voice from Hedy, a single command from him could undo my very will.

I crossed a frozen garden of snow-dusted plant skeletons and ducked behind a statue to catch my breath. I opened my eyes again and realized how light the sky had grown. The cusp of sunrise. That much time had passed?

I could see beyond the kleinschloss now. Down into the valley where the freshly dug canal wound its serpentine trail. Tools and torches and workers had all been moved. The mouth of the canal rose up the bank of a hill to meet the enormous lake that was the Nightwell. A colossal dam held the waters at bay.

Two figures stumbled up the hill on the left. Coralythe and Luuk, mere moments away from reaching it.

"No," I breathed.

Luuk reached the top first. Coralythe delivered the final command with a single nod. Luuk spat upon the stone of the dam, not a moment's thought for the repercussions that would come from his actions.

The dam turned to dust finer than the most delicate snowfall. Nightwell water tumbled free like a viper upon the sleeping prey of Winterune.

CHAPTER 53

ꝳMYRTHEꝰ

Nightwell water overflowed the freshly dug canal, disobey-
ing any attempt at control or direction. It flooded the plains.
Rising. Rising. Rising until it splashed the stones of the kleinschloss.
It swirled around my ankles, and I clutched the stone statue as it
rose to my knees. Thighs. Waist. A fierce current tugged at me.

As swiftly as it came, the current moved away as though realizing there was no food to be found here. Bursts of purple mist
rose from the foam lining the edges of the flood. Already, the water
flowed beyond my sight, into forest and glade and river.

Mattias never even needed a new canal. The Nightwell swept
over everything into canal after canal after canal. There was no
stopping it.

I dropped to my knees.

Banes would be forced upon people. I knew how that felt.
Intoxicating but also imprisoning. The Bane made me *think* I was
in control . . . while it controlled me. I'd given in so quickly. So
easily.

Used it again and again almost without thought.

Now I couldn't even sense my Wishtress Talent in the back of my mind. My curse was likely gone as well since it was connected to the magic of my Talent. And yet . . . I wanted it back.

I wanted that last wish.

The only way I could think to retrieve it would be to deny the Bane—to give my Talent the complete authority over my mind and will. And if I was going to give my Talent authority, I needed to believe it was worth it. Not just for Bastiaan but for myself. I'd resented my Talent since it appeared, but Bastiaan saw it as beautiful. As having a purpose.

It was time I saw it that way too.

He saw *all* Talents that way. Again and again I'd seen how right he was. About Banes. About Talents. He had made mistakes, yes, but he'd never wavered in his care for people. His desire to see all people have access to Talents.

He believed in that dream so much he was *dying* for it.

Behind me, someone splashed across the courtyard. Sven. Blood dripping down the side of his head. Face twisted in fury.

I ducked back behind the stone but not before his gaze snapped to mine. The splashing increased. "Myrthe!" His bellow sounded murderous.

Fleeing was futile. My feet and weak limbs wouldn't do much good.

This was it. This was my end. *Please*, I begged my Talent. *Return to me.*

Sven rounded the statue. He grabbed my hair and slammed me against the stone. "Give me the wish."

It would take me less than a second to send his body careening backward. I could make him bash his own skull on the stone. Force him to release me, to turn himself over to Mattias's men.

But to do so would allow the Bane authority over me. Again. Somehow I knew that the one way to defeat the Bane was to *starve* it.

But this moment is desperate!

Every moment thus far had been desperate. If I told myself I'd use my Bane only in desperate moments, there'd be no end. Someday I'd have to put my trust in something beyond my own power. That was the power of the Well of Talents. It chose me to be its Wishtress. It must have had a reason—and if I could trust its plan for me before my own birth, I could trust its power and purpose for me. Even now.

Sven pinned me. I let him scream in my face. But I closed my eyes and breathed deeply, entering a refuge in my mind far from his frantic demands.

My Bane cried out, indignant.

I served you well! We're only just beginning!

Oh, Bane . . . for you to exist my Talent needs to die. And that's not an exchange I'm willing to make.

"Give me my wish," Sven growled in my ear. He wrapped his bowstring around my neck and tightened it, taking my air.

I used to turn to sad memories—pain and sorrow and anger—to draw up a wish for Oma. This time I followed a different path in my mind: to the happy memories. The moments that brought joy with a distant tug of sorrow over the fact that they'd already been lived.

Schaat racing with Anouk. Giving button rolls to canal rats. Mutti holding me tight and showing me there were things worth dying for. Bastiaan running down the sand dune to me. Alive.

The tear needed little prodding. It came willingly, like a soldier called to a final fight.

The swell of pain and finality of breath cocooned me and I didn't fight it. This wish was mine and mine alone. I knew it intimately, and it hummed its excitement to be given a purpose.

378

"I wish . . ." My whisper was tender, a soft gust of final air.

A hand clamped over my mouth and a glass bottle pressed to my cheek.

Sven.

But he was too late. Though the wish left my skin, it had already declared its loyalty.

I didn't need to speak the words. It was part of me. And as Bastiaan's face swam before my fading mind's eye, I completed the wish.

For him.

For those he loved.

For everyone.

I wish for the Well of Talents to be released and to flow to all people.

It wasn't the wish I thought I'd make. I didn't save myself. I didn't save Bastiaan. But the wish was still for him. Maybe not for his healing, but for his dreams.

With my final exhale I succumbed to death. I'd completed Bastiaan's one pursuit. He'd be proud. I knew that much. So I bid him farewell. Maybe—just maybe—he felt the same peace in death as I felt just now. I held on to hope, knowing I'd see him in mere moments . . .

. . . on the other side.

CHAPTER 54

BASTIAAN

If only the earth would devour him.

Bastiaan had never felt such prolonged agony, of both body and soul. It lapped at what remained of his senses. Needles of helpless pain stitched him into the floor of the Well. Death lurked in the shadows, laughing at his suffering. Creeping close, then feinting back in an elusive dance.

Let me fade. Let me die. He longed for the black nothingness of unconsciousness. Death, even.

His body felt hollow and breathing became labored. Every time he thought it was the end, his will seemed to defy him and hold on a little longer. But he could *feel* it—the finality. His body couldn't recover from this. Even if help came. Even with Mother's healing hands or Hilda the healer's appearance.

The minutes ticked. The hours stalled. His own blood soaked his whole side, no longer warm.

Was this how King Vämbat felt after crawling from the inferno? Alone? Ready to die? No longer afraid of his story's ending? He hadn't seemed angry when Bastiaan found him and wept over his brokenness. He had never placed blame on Bastiaan during those last days.

Death left no room for regret. It was time to acknowledge his story. His choice. His mistakes. Bastiaan had not lived the story he'd once envisioned for himself. But he'd lived as best he could. And wasn't that all the Well had asked of him when it gave him his Talent?

Use this Talent. For me.
Use it for others.

Those were its final words before his Talent Mark burned his finger. He'd vowed to obey. Now, as he thought through the flow of his life story, he realized how often he'd used his Talent for himself. To save himself. To educate himself. To learn more . . . so *eventually* he could do what the Well asked.

He'd missed so many chances to use his Talent for better purposes.

A tear trickled from the corner of his eye. *I'm sorry.*

It dropped to the earth and made a small, almost inaudible splash.

I'm here.

Bastiaan stilled. It had been *so long* since he'd heard the voice of the Well. To be honest, it'd been a long time since he'd sought it out. *What can I do?*

He turned to face the heavens, though the movement withdrew a groan from his shattered body. The sky had lightened. Sunrise? Icy wetness met the dry patches of his skin as he rolled. He shivered. Had he bled that much? Water slicked the side of his face.

Bastiaan dropped his hand to the ground. *Splash*. Almost an inch of water! The Well of Talents was refilling.

That meant . . .

Myrthe was using her wish.

"No!" He struggled to sit up and failed. *She'll die!*

The water swelled and rushed over his body. He barely managed to lift his head above it with a gasp.

"Myr—!" Water caught him in his mouth. His lungs heaved and he tried to cough, but his dying body didn't allow him to.

He convulsed, which sent its own jolts of pain through him.

The water rose higher, lifting him from the floor of the Well. It seemed to be taking deep breaths, as if preparing for a mighty shout.

Bastiaan got his head above the surface and managed a cough. He blacked out. A moment later he was above water again. It was higher. His feet couldn't touch the ground.

Myrthe was dying.

Dying.

Dying.

"No!" He lifted his hand—the one that should have held a Talent Mark. It was crusted with blood and bits of hanging skin turned black. His finger gone.

But the Talent Mark had never been the *source* of his Talent. Just the evidence of it. Moonrise had come and gone over his fading body. His Talent should have renewed.

He pressed his thumb and ring finger together. Snapped. The movement was weak, but his heart and intention were the strongest they'd ever been.

The Well of Talents slowed its swirling. He felt the change of time in his blood.

It had worked.

He'd stopped time. And hopefully stopped Myrthe's path to death.

Relief was short-lived because what could he do? He couldn't even *cough*. He'd paused Myrthe's lungs, the flow of her blood, the beat of her pulse . . . but once death finally came for him, time would start back up.

Myrthe would die anyway.

As though to remind him of his weakness, his legs stopped kicking. He had no core strength. He slipped beneath the surface. No buoyancy filled his lungs.

There'd be no resurfacing.

He allowed the silence to press against him. Fill him. Erase him. He'd failed.

Except . . . *Water? You said . . . you said . . . Are you really here?*

The silence after his question almost ended Bastiaan. But then. Small. Still. Gentle as the day it first whispered in his mind:

I am.

Relief filled his body like an inhale. Somehow, his fears washed away into the depths. Crushed like withered weeds.

Please . . . save her. Take away her curse. You put her Talent in her even when separated by leagues and leagues. I know you can save her. Take me instead.

I don't trade life for life.

Bastiaan opened his mouth to argue and water filled it.

Just as I am here with you . . . I am there with Myrthe.

How? How could the water be with her when it was *here* in this Well?

A stream of bubbles rose around Bastiaan. Was the water . . .

laughing? What felt like enormous hands wrapped around his body and lifted him to the surface.

I'm in you, Bastiaan. I'm in her.

Their Talents. They were not just gifts—not just power—they were water. Bastiaan had always thought that since he never drank of the water and Myrthe never visited the Well, Talents must be disconnected from the water itself. But it seemed so obvious now.

The Talent water existed both in the Well and in its Talented.

Bastiaan rested his arms on the edge of the Well, half submerged. Though time was stopped, the water itself still moved and acted like water. No one could stop the maker of stopped time.

The wind reminded him of life. This time, he spoke to the Well with his voice, weak as it was. "So . . . is this my end then?"

Why ask me?

The water now seemed warm. Soothing.

Why was he asking? His wound was fatal. He had balanced on the brink of death for hours now. He knew this was his end, and yet he asked the Well as though . . . as though it could change that.

Did he want it changed? Did he want to live? *I don't deserve a second chance.*

None deserve even a first chance. That's grace.

Like when Bastiaan received his Talent—a gift. Grace. Dehaan hadn't allowed him to drink the water or even approach the edge of the Well. Bastiaan used to think he was given a Talent because he was a better man than Dehaan. But now he realized his merit had nothing to do with it.

I see the heart of man, woman, child. I see futures and pasts and untold stories.

The Well had seen him. Seen his future—seen how he might use his time Talent. It had seen his story of failure with King Vāmbat. It had even known his magic would result in the king's death, and yet it still gave him the Talent.

That truth settled into his body, giving both hope and despair. *You must be so disappointed.* He didn't want to hear the Well affirm his assumption. How could it be anything *but* disappointed in how he'd used his Talent? *What now?*

It's your time, Bastiaan.

Oh no. Not yet. He deserved it, but . . . Myrthe. *I'm not ready.* His Talent. He wanted to try again. He wanted to save her. *Please.*

It's your time.

"No!" His shout echoed over the water and skidded among the morning shadows. He clung to the rock, but his will pleaded with him. He'd been fighting the Well for his own will since receiving his Talent. Would he truly fight it until death? Did he have no faith in it?

He'd fought on behalf of the Well his entire life. But with *his* agenda. "I wanted to get you to all people."

You brought Myrthe to me. She has finished your task.

"So she is to die too?"

The Well did not answer. It surrounded him with its warm arms of comfort. Bastiaan held on to the rock a little longer but finally released his grip and slid back into the depths. *I trust you.*

The Well made him what he was—all the good parts. It gave him life. A Talent that rescued both his and Myrthe's mothers and other women from destructive servitude to the merchant. It had established Windmill Cottage as a home for Runt and those fleeing dark lives. It had given him a lifetime with a new father—King Vämbat. The Well was all things good. Wasn't that what Bastiaan had been telling people his entire life?

He exhaled his last breath. *I surrender.*

The water closed over his head and pushed him down. Deep. But it wasn't dark. It was light and life and rest. There was no fear. There was no pain.

And Bastiaan was no more.

CHAPTER 55

BASTIAAN

I t was raining light. Droplets splashing the crown of his head, sliding down his nose. Tickling the creases of his face.

Bastiaan awoke, but his eyes hadn't been closed. It was like his mind gasped in air and a film of darkness receded from his vision. He blinked against the flicker and shimmer of water around him. The rain grew heavy, then light. Fell downward, upward, hovered in front of his face.

He stood on the surface of the Well water. It rippled beneath him in gentle pulses, light springing from below. He was completely naked. The hole in his abdomen had closed, though it was still extremely sore. His maimed hand no longer bled. All traces of bloodstains had been washed clear.

A new Talent Mark painted his other hand.

He wasn't dead. Somehow his soul knew this, though the scene around him did not fit with the world and reality he had known his whole life.

Where . . . What am I?

You are new.

Something deep in his core understood and marveled. The Well had said it was his time. He had thought death. End of life. But it was giving him a choice:

Cling to his old life: his old heart.

Or surrender it.

He'd surrendered fully to the Well, and in turn, it renewed him. He had died to his old life. Taken on a new mantle with his Talent. To use it as it was meant to be used. To enter into the oncoming battle between Bane and Talent. He'd studied Talents and Banes his whole life. Today—the day the wells were being released to flood the lands—he had a new purpose.

He strode across the surface of the Well of Talents and climbed over the edge onto dry ground. His pack lay against the edge of the ring of stones. Inside he found a set of clothing and dressed himself.

His hand hovered over his weapons. The stacks of discs he'd forged and sharpened himself and then spent years perfecting his throwing accuracy. He couldn't bear to arm himself.

Although he was striding in among enemies, he would kill no one. Not one person more. Not Hedy. Not Mattias. Not Coralythe. Not Sven. Nor did he even want to threaten them. They would call him a fool for even thinking like this.

He didn't care.

He had to trust that the Well of Talents had given him all he needed.

Time remained stopped—no flickering on and off. He now knew the flicker had been caused by the battle in his own heart. Mattias had silenced his Talent for a time, but when it started returning to him, Bastiaan treated it as an idol, not a gift. Once he surrendered to the true purpose of Talents, the Well cleansed him of Mattias's Bane attack.

He'd never felt this new—not even when he first received his Talent.

Now clothed, he dipped his canteen into the water and filled it. He took a long draught. It was perfectly cold and quenching. Then he slung his pack over his back. The Well water ebbed and flowed, light still swirling in its midst.

"I'll see you soon." He turned toward the open valley, then paused before he rounded the corner. "And . . . thank you."

He wasn't leaving the Well. He was merely leaving the ring of stones he'd once foolishly believed could contain the water. The Well was in him.

He set his eyes forward.

It was time to save Myrthe.

CHAPTER 56

BASTIAAN

Bastiaan shoved through the knee-deep water. His course to the kleinschloss had been a zigzag like that of a drunken snake as he made his way around and through the paused Nightwell waters. Unlike the Well of Talents, the Nightwell *had* been paused . . . or at least slowed. It still lapped at his ankles and nearby stumps and boulders. Rising ever so slowly. Straining against stopped time.

He could feel its anger at being forced to halt its roiling attack on the canals. It seethed as he waded through it. Awake. Hungry. Watching him.

The Well of Talents had dominion over the Nightwell, but both wells were beyond Bastiaan's own Talent. Their water was rising, coming no matter how long he left time stopped.

He needed to move quickly. He wasn't willing to risk getting a Bane by submerging himself in the water.

Where was Myrthe? Was she underwater somewhere? Drowning? Urgency pulsed in his chest. He would not restart time until he'd found her. Until he'd fixed this.

The kleinschloss made the only sense for where Sven took her. He said he'd turn her in to King Mattias. Bastiaan had spent many months using the kleinschloss as an abode during his times in the Stillness. Ahead it rose like an island of deadwood and spires from a swamp of dark water.

He found the road beneath the water by memory. The water rose to his waist, but never any higher. Every step forward was a step up toward air and light.

He approached the gate. Two militairen stood guard, their frozen faces turned toward the paused rush of the Nightwell. Despite their servitude to their king, fear clearly gripped their core.

Bastiaan strode through the front gate. It didn't take long to realize the kleinschloss was in a panic. Doors hung open. Small groups of militairen cowered on raised balconies against the rush of rising water.

If Sven brought Myrthe here, they would have been presented to King Mattias. Even if Sven thought he had the upper hand, King Mattias liked the power of authority. He enjoyed standing above others, sitting on a throne, being called king. His Bane was evidence of the desires of his heart: Power. Control.

Bastiaan arrived at the door to the main hall. It was shut and the water reached his waist. No matter how he heaved, he couldn't get it open. He found and ascended the servants' stairs until he was toward the back of the main hall where King Mattias would have entered. The door here was a little more elevated than the main entrance and hung open.

Bastiaan entered and stopped short.

Purple mist floated in the room like a fire smoking of magic had been left to burn. His lungs constricted at the sight of the Bane's dominance.

The haze wasn't so thick that he couldn't see silhouettes and forms through the madness. He ducked under a snake of purple smoke that rose from the fingers of a militair whose face twisted in fury. Bastiaan followed the man's gaze to his target.

Hedy.

Hedy had a thin purple cord around the neck of one of her own woodsfolk, dressed in a militair uniform. It wasn't hard to see what Mattias had done—he'd given all of Sven's followers a Bane and then commanded them against Sven, Kees, and Hedy.

Now Hedy was choking one to death to save her own life.

And another of the woodsfolk was trying to save his fellow . . . and kill Hedy. Whatever this man's Bane, it was doing a number on her. Hedy's veins bulged from her temples, about to burst. Blotches of broken blood already marred the inside of her neck.

Across the room a woodsman wielded two daggers—the only clear weapons in the battle. Purple smoke rose from the blades, indicating they were crafted from Bane power. Bastiaan plucked one from his fist and carefully sawed through the bowstring Hedy had wrapped around the other woodsman's neck. He nicked the skin once or twice, but since he had no skin-to-skin contact, the man remained in stopped time.

It was slow going, weaving through the room and ducking out-stretched hands or unconscious bodies. Aside from the daggers, there were no weapons. No swords being thrust or arrows being shot. No matter where Bastiaan looked, he could find no weapon except the wielded Banes and Hedy's bowstring.

Touching a single person would bring them into the Stillness with him. And he didn't want to welcome war or death into this frozen time. The only way to get them back out of the Stillness would be to restart time for everyone.

Myrthe was his focus. Only Myrthe.

Then he saw a small form in a militair uniform that pooled around his ankles and wrists. A freckled face of determination and brokenness.

Runt.

Blood smeared the palm of his hand, which he splayed outward into the fray . . . ready to snuff a life with a mere touch. Even in the Stillness Bastiaan detected the inner turmoil straining Runt's muscles. Despite a command from the king, Runt didn't want to take life.

Bastiaan stood beside him for a long moment. His hand raised halfway to touch the tips of Runt's fingers. But he restrained himself. He wanted Runt at his side—not as an assistant but to gather the boy to himself. To speak reassurance to him. To present him with the canteen of water from the Well of Talents. But with Runt under the command of King Mattias, he couldn't risk it. It was too precarious—for himself and for Myrthe.

"Your time will come, my friend." He dropped his hand and turned away from Runt. "It's nearer than ever before." As Bastiaan walked away he couldn't help but feel like he was breaking another promise to Runt. Every time he walked away from the boy, he vowed to himself it would be the last time. Yet it kept happening again and again.

The next time Runt saw him in the Awake would be with water from the Well in front of him. And if Bastiaan's theories about his own Talent were correct, the water could silence Runt's Bane.

That choice would be up to Runt.

Bastiaan searched the kleinschloss for another hour looking for Myrthe, but he didn't find her. Most people seemed to be gathered in the courtroom . . . in battle. But he'd also yet to find Mattias or Sven. Where those two were, Myrthe would not be far.

Bastiaan exited the kleinschloss into a flooded garden of statues and drowning shrubbery. A few scattered militairen were outdoors, caught midflee or perhaps on an errand for the king. The glow of sunrise lit their skin in a gentle contrast to the madness implied from their expressions.

Then he saw a shock of sun-colored hair from behind a statue, a man kneeling over a pale form half submerged.

Sven.

He knelt next to Myrthe—no, *on* her. Pinning her in the water with a small glass vial in his hand. Staring at her with unveiled victory and greed.

A wish. *Myrthe's* wish. He'd caught it. Stolen it. Was drowning her for it.

Bastiaan roared like a stabbed bull, the sound echoing eerily in the Stillness. He gripped the broken bust of the royal statue to keep himself from charging Sven. He would pummel him. He could do it easily—bury Sven in the water as a beaten mess before he even fully awakened in the Stillness.

Instead Bastiaan shoved through the water to Myrthe.

Her face alone remained above water, roughly propped against the marble plinth. To keep her wish accessible. Blood ran down her icy hair and pooled around her ear.

A rope burn from a bowstring wound in two rings around her throat.

Bastiaan's anger burned. But the longer he gazed at Myrthe, the more his fury crumbled away into a desperate sorrow. Her wish had already been spent. She was likely dead.

He would not give up. He did not abandon a task, not even when it seemed hopeless.

Was this how she'd felt in the Summer Trial? When she believed the bear had dealt his death blow? And yet she dragged him across the scorching sand anyway. She never left him. She'd been willing to die with him.

He lifted his face away from the scene, careful not to disturb the water so much that it lapped into her mouth, though it was still rising. He had perhaps an hour before it reached her mouth, poured down her throat. If he adjusted her body, she'd enter the Stillness and die.

The only way to save Myrthe was to reverse time. No snap or wish could do that.

There was one person who might be able to pull it off.

Coralythe.

Before he searched for her, he turned back to Sven. On impulse, with the tips of his fingers, he worked the little bottle free of Sven's fingers. He corked the wish and stuck it in his pocket.

Coralythe stood atop the hill at the edge of the dam, a fearsome statue of rebellion. Her purple-and-black clothes were paused in a windswept blast from the release of the Nightwell. The sunrise darkened her countenance as it sent light from behind her.

She was the target, Bastiaan an arrow. He flew across the terrain toward her as though shot from a bow. Purpose fueled his muscles, numbed the dull pain still throbbing in his abdomen. Then the slick earth beneath his feet sloped downward, deeper into the water, and he skidded to a halt, almost losing his footing altogether.

He fell backward and caught himself with his arm, water splashing his neck. He cried out. Stilled. And gingerly pushed himself back to his feet.

That was close. This was no mere water; it was *Nightwell* water.

He'd be at war within himself—Talent versus Bane. And though he fully believed his Talent would win, he did not welcome an unnecessary battle. He didn't want to end up with blood that could poison or the ability to curse someone. He couldn't afford to be tempted.

Because he was weak. And Banes harvested a person's weakness.

He stood at the kleinschloss edge, a sea of Nightwell between Coralythe and him on the raised hill by the destroyed dam. He glanced around as though a canoe or raft would present itself for his use. Even the flotsam was too large to move or too small to be of any use. There was no other option.

He'd have to swim.

The very thought sent a tightening around his chest, squeezing his lungs. His limbs trembled as he threw off his jacket and boots. Next came his belt and pack. He hung them all over the wing of an angel statue, shedding what weight he could until he was in nothing more than trousers and an undershirt. The chill of winter raised his skin in dots like seedlings ready to break through spring earth.

He entered the water. It rose to meet him as though sensing his vulnerability. He kept his feet on the earth beneath until he was on his toes. He tried to remember what King Vämbat had told him about swimming.

Keep the lungs full to provide buoyancy. Keep the limbs moving. Legs were more effective than arms. If he got tired, float on his back—that part always scared him. Every time he tried to do it, he sank. And if his head went under . . .

"Stop thinking," he growled and pushed himself forward into what felt like an abyss beneath his feet.

He kicked furiously, but his legs did very little to propel him forward or even upward. He forced himself to relax, though shivers wracked his body.

The water turned warm. Hot even—not to burning, but like a drawn bath after a long winter day on the canals. Something he'd experienced only once. His shivers and lungs calmed. His limbs worked for him. With him. Like the water was helping him. Boosting him.

The comfort made him want to stay. Only his head and neck remained cold. It would feel so nice to dip them into the warmth for a moment. Maybe even clear his mind.

But he hadn't lived 107 years to give in to the first little temptation the Nightwell had to offer. "You'll have to do better than that!"

Icy cold swept back in, removing any semblance of warmth. His limbs turned sluggish. Numb. He kept kicking, but a headache rose from where the water pounded against the back of his skull like a garden pick. He was hardly halfway across the expanse of sea. With this frigidity he'd never make it.

He wanted to tuck his limbs close to his body, find what little warmth he could from his core. The water rose to his ears. Or was he sinking? He tilted his head upward and flailed his limbs. It sent him downward.

"No!" He fought the liquid and gained an inch, sucking in as deep a breath as he could manage to create that buoyancy King Vämbat had talked about. Warm water met his feet, trying to lure him under.

Water splashed his face. He gasped and a wave surged down his throat. He choked. Sputtered. Managed a painful cough and tried to spit out what he could.

He would *not* fail.

Even if he couldn't breathe. Even if he grew so numb his entire body emerged frostbitten. This was not his end. *You cannot have me.*

A furious whisper came from below.

You cannot beat me.

And then the water turned to tar.

Bastiaan fought the weight. This was like another Trial. Except the consequences of this one were everlasting. No amount of kicking, inhaling, or fighting accomplished anything. Buoyancy had no place against a sea of poisoned honey.

Bubbles popped around him, releasing a dark laugh with each pop. *Help me!* he called frantically to the Well of Talents coursing through his veins. The Well resided within him. It could do . . . something!

The tar passed his ears. Stuck to his hair. He tilted up his chin, taking a final breath.

Then the Nightwell sucked him under.

CHAPTER 57

BASTIAAN

The Bane latched onto his mind like a parasite, piercing his will and clawing into his body and mind.

Not once did Bastiaan invite it. Not once did it resume its gentle, luring tone. This was a battle.

The Nightwell spit him out of the water, and he landed hard on the opposite bank at Coralythe's feet. But he was no longer the same man who had entered the water on the bank of the kleinschloss.

Now he was a man with the ability to suck time from a person's life.

One year. Ten years. A single touch paired with a single thought would subtract as many days, months, or years of life as his heart desired.

The Bane spoke to him, whispered its uses in his ear. A thick circlet of purple wound around his arm above his elbow. He stared at it, aghast that the Nightwell had *won*.

It was a perfect balance of control and innocence. Possibilities darted through his mind as he pieced together the implications. He could take away forty years of King Mattias's life, limiting his reign but not actually being responsible for his death.

The Bane enticed him . . . which disgusted him. Was he so weak?

He rose from the ground, trembling and dripping the poisonous water, and faced Coralythe. Though a Bane had been forced upon him, he'd made it to the other side. The Nightwell was so bloated on its own victory that it hadn't considered its victim might put up a fight with a weapon that had invented the word *victory*.

"I am a Talented. I will not set aside that gift or calling for the temptation of anything less." The Bane inside him tried to laugh, but there was little heart in the sound. Perhaps it sensed his determination.

If he gave in—even one time—it would be like a drug. Calling him back for more. Compelling him. The best way to mute a voice was never to give it attention in the first place.

He strode to Coralythe, stood before her long enough to gather his thoughts. Then he touched her.

Her clothes fell from the frozen breeze and flapped against her body. She blinked several times, then frowned, her gaze passing over the paused Nightwell water. When she saw Bastiaan, understanding smoothed her brow into a blank slate.

"Ah. He lives." She glanced at his maimed right hand. "Even without your finger, I see your Talent still works. You are truly unstoppable, Bastiaan Duur."

"I'm here for one thing."

She smirked. "You think you're so beyond those of us with Banes." She gestured to the purple ring around his arm. "You have a Bane now, Bastiaan. You're like us. Now you get to suffer with power too."

"I've already suffered with power, and it didn't have to be a Bane for me to use it wrongly. We are all alike, Coralythe. Everyone has a choice." This wouldn't be a quick conversation, so he sprawled out on the damp, icy earth. Showing her he wasn't intimidated. Nor was he a threat.

The Nightwell water still rose. He tried not to imagine it passing over Myrthe's pale, open lips and filling her lungs as she slept in stopped time.

"My Bane is no different from any other weapon and the choice that comes with it. I can choose to nock and shoot an arrow at a man's heart. I can choose to spike an enemy's glass with poison. I can choose to suck away your life with a single touch."

She paled.

"But that's just it. The Bane will always be subject to my choice. Nothing can overpower my will unless I *let* it."

"The king can." She put more space between them, then seemed to realize what she was doing and stepped forward again, throwing her shoulders back. "He can control you now." She offered the retort with confidence, but her body spoke of uneasiness. King Mattias could control her, too, and she didn't like that. Not one bit.

"Mattias can control me only if I give the Bane sovereignty over my life. That, too, is a choice. You still don't see it? You chose to destroy Myrthe's Talent because of your own pain—"

"She murdered my sons!"

"An accident." He pushed himself forward and leveled her with a gaze that still bore the same intensity as if he were standing eye to eye with her. "Tragic. Terrible. Devastating. I do not minimize that."

"You can't possibly *understand* it," she seethed.

"We've all lost people dear to us, but not everyone chooses to take revenge or destroy lives in response to grief. Any additional pain you're suffering is brought on by yourself. You are hindering *yourself* from healing."

Her chest heaved with deep breaths, with arguments caught in her throat, with fury and rage. Hatred.

He shook his head. "You hate Talented so much that you'd force Banes on the world?"

"It's a gift."

"A gift to be controlled by the king? To be given Banes and denied Talents? Denied the opportunity to choose which one you give power over your life?"

"You don't understand." Had Coralythe ever even considered drinking from the Well of Talents?

Instead of anger he felt sadness. "You could have so much more *life*, Coralythe."

"What do you want?" she spit out.

He rose, posing his request in as humble yet firm a way as possible. "I want you to remove Myrthe's curse."

She scoffed. "*Reward* her? Let her go about using her wishes for her own gain?"

"You and I both know she's learned that lesson. You forced her to harden her heart—to become an even colder and less compassionate person than she was before the accident with your sons."

"Don't try to unearth compassion in *me* for my children's murderer."

"I don't expect compassion. Nor do I expect forgiveness. But I do ask you to make a choice. Think about the trajectory of your life and which way you want it to go."

"Everything is going the way I want it to."

"Everything?" He raised an eyebrow.

She didn't respond, nor did she bend. He wouldn't let her leave the Stillness until she did. No one could restart time except him. Coralythe was trapped and she knew it. But she didn't know the clock was against him as the Nightwell continued inching its way higher and farther with each minute.

He pulled the corked vial from his pocket. "Would you consider an exchange?"

She peered at the droplet inside the glass. "What is that?"

"Myrthe's last wish."

401

"She's dead then," she breathed.

Bastiaan stumbled back as if an arrow had struck his chest. It took him a moment to recover his voice. "I'm hoping not."

Coralythe cackled. "She's dead!" She actually *danced* for a moment. "You couldn't have that wish in your hands if she were alive! I know my curses. I know how they work."

"Then remove it from her corpse." He held the bottle between them with two fingers. "Let me bury her free of the curse. And you can have this."

She eyed it, then must have concluded she had nothing to lose. "Mattias will be most pleased." She took the wish from him, turned the bottle over in her hands.

She tucked it into a fold in her dress. "It's not as easy as you're saying . . . removing a curse."

"Whatever it takes, do it."

"Curses cannot be destroyed. They can only be created or transferred." She lifted her eyes to his, and the twisted, delighted confidence returned to them. "I'm not about to waste a fresh curse just to make your poor bleeding heart feel better."

That left one option: transfer Myrthe's curse. To him. He tried to think back to the last time he wept a tear. It would be far easier for him to manage such a curse than Myrthe because neither crying nor emotions affected his Talent.

"Very well. Transfer it to me."

"It won't be the same, Bastiaan. The curse will be unique to you, as it was to Myrthe."

He swallowed hard. "Okay."

She smiled. "I like seeing you nervous." Then she closed her eyes and lifted her hands. Bastiaan kept his eyes open. He would face this curse head-on. Where Myrthe was the Wishtress—chosen by the Well to bring its water and Talents to the people—Coralythe was the opposite. Child of the Nightwell spreading curses and Banes, welcome and unwelcome.

No matter her power, Bastiaan had to believe the Well of Talents was stronger than the curse of the Nightwell.

A spire of smoke rose from across the flooded valley. Lifting from where Myrthe's body lay. Bastiaan held his breath as it flew over the water toward them. Toward him. He settled his weight into his legs and steadied himself for the impact.

The curse slammed into him. Though his body did not move, his subconscious stumbled back. Then fought tooth and nail. He forced it to relent and let the curse take effect. It wound through him, and Coralythe's voice rose over a rushing wind in his ears.

He couldn't make out her words until the wind stilled. Only then did he catch the details of the curse.

". . . for eternity. The next time you stop time, you will never be able to start it again."

CHAPTER 58

BASTIAAN

He left Coralythe on her self-made Bane island. Paddled a dead log from the dam site across the Nightwell water, though it didn't matter so much now if he went under. He already had a Bane. And now a curse.

He'd never be able to enter the Stillness again. Unless he wanted to be trapped there forever.

He was tempted to despair over having received healing and renewal from the Well of Talents only to give it back up again. But this was not the end. Not even a curse could unseat the power of the Well. He hoped.

He'd freed Myrthe. That was what mattered.

Once back at the kleinschloss he loped across the flooded courtyard. He needed Mother or Hilda. A healing touch. All the book knowledge he'd gained from years in the Stillness had not prepared him to care for the ones he loved—King Vämbat. Runt. Myrthe.

But Mother was days away at Windmill Cottage, and the Nightwell was not sleeping. The water roiled and pushed against his Talent, trying to move toward the canals and Fairhoven. It was gaining ground, and he felt the strain against his Talent.

It was all up to him. He didn't have the endless time he'd grown so used to with past visits to the Stillness.

He found Myrthe at the base of the statue just as he'd left her. Water lapped at her lower lip, trickling drop by drop into the crook of her open mouth.

She looked even paler than before. Was that because the curse was gone? Or because her life was flickering? Fading? Snuffed?

Please, he begged the Well. *Don't take her yet.*

Ever so carefully, he slid his arms beneath her body. She melted into the movement, her form softening as she entered the Stillness. He pulled her free of Sven and out of the icy water, ready to sprint to the warm interior of the kleinschloss.

But she was too heavy in his arms. Too cold. Too . . . still. He stumbled to a raised patch of dry grass and knelt there. Holding her. Ear pressed to her chest. He detected no heartbeat. He put his cheek to her mouth, waiting for a weak puff of warm air.

Nothing.

"Myrthe," he whispered, desperate for his voice to be the one thing that brought her around. "Wake up. I'm here."

His arms trembled, but he held her tight. The only warmth came from the burn in his eyes. He kissed her face. Gently. Tenderly.

Like a goodbye.

"You weren't supposed to die in my arms," he whispered. "You weren't supposed to die at all."

Crusted blood held strands of her hair against her cheek and temple. He couldn't bring himself to wash her with Nightwell water, so he pulled out his canteen. He'd gathered this water from the Well of Talents to give to Runt but spared a few drops into his cupped hand, then dabbed it on the small gash along her brow line. It mingled with the blood, sliding down her face in a light pink line like the sunrise.

The tinted water met the tear trail of her final wish and

converged, making a single drop. Wish water, Well water, and blood united as a liquid three-cord strand. As the droplet slid down her face, it changed course, curving around her chin and back up again. Weaving past creases and freckles and a stray eyelash until the new drop shone like a freshly made wish. It slowed its course and slipped back up toward her eye, where it latched onto her eyelashes.

The whole splay of them turned white, like her Talent Mark.

Bastiaan's hands shook, but he dared not move for fear of interrupting whatever magic was taking place.

He stared at the new fan of ice-white eyelashes. What did this mean? What was the Well—

The eyelashes lifted. One set ice, the other black.

No confusion. No surprise. Myrthe didn't even blink—just held his gaze as though she'd expected to wake to him holding her the whole time. A smile. A breath. And finally, a voice.

"I love you, Bastiaan."

He dropped his forehead to hers, and a single broken sob cut through the gentle silence. "And I, you, Myrthe. Beyond time or wishes or Talents or Banes."

She was alive. *Alive!* Breathing. Blinking. *Smiling.*

And his.

CHAPTER 59

MYRTHE

I was new. There was no other way to put it. When I gave up my final tear, I'd prepared to exit this world and enter whatever eternity looked like. Instead I'd entered someplace wholly separate. Somewhere only the Well of Talents existed—deep within myself and yet separate from me.

It had met me in darkness. It had met me in light.

I chose you to show the people that I choose everyone. Men tried to lock me in a Well, but walls do not control me.

The Well had chosen me. But it took my seventeen years of life to choose it in return. All this time I'd believed my wishes were commodities to be sold or traded or used for personal gain. But they were Well water to bring to the people.

"What happened?" Bastiaan asked.

"I surrendered." He didn't seem all that surprised by my response. I had died to my own desires and given up my breath for others. For the will of the Well. "And you— How are you alive? Healed?" I didn't want to admit I hadn't used my wish to save him, but he seemed to know.

"The Well made me new." He moved my hair from my face, unsticking the strands from the blood. He frowned, then lifted my hair farther. "You have a Bane?"

I grimaced. "It was forced on me, but . . . I let it rule me. For a time."

"Yet you overcame it. You gave it up for your Talent. I'm so proud of you, Myrthe."

I shook my head. "You shouldn't be. It was only in the last moments that I resisted. I should have been stronger."

He lifted his shirtsleeve. A purple ring wound around his arm, pulsing with smoke. Waiting to be used—to be given dominance.

"It's the struggle of this world: to have to choose between Bane and Talent, except the fight will be that much harder since few of us have Talents and Banes are being forced on all." He looked over at the sea of Nightwell and his muscles tensed. "The Nightwell is gaining strength."

"You feel it?"

"Pushing against my Talent. Yes." He planted a hand on the ground to keep himself upright. There was more to his weakness than the battle between Nightwell and Talent.

"Bastiaan, what happened?" I saw movement by the dam. Coralythe. Pacing like an agitated thundercloud along the edge. Her face turned toward us and she paused, seeming to swell with rage and fury. Then she resumed her pacing.

"Why is Coralythe in the Stillness?" I turned to Bastiaan. "What did you do?"

He took a deep breath, straightening. The grim set of his jaw set my hair on end. "I took on your curse."

"What?" I shoved myself upright. "Why?"

"Transferring it was the only way to remove it. You would have died, Myrthe."

"So what?" My voice turned shrill. "I was ready! And perhaps the Well would have defeated it on its own."

"Perhaps." He sighed. "But I do not ask forgiveness."

"What did she do to you?"

"The next time I enter the Stillness, I won't be able to exit. I—and whoever I bring into it with me—will be trapped in stopped time and my snap won't work."

"Oh, Bastiaan."

"It's a sacrifice I was willing to make." He steadied himself, as though to withstand a pang of sorrow. Loss. Pain. But then he lifted his eyes to mine. "Truly, Myrthe. I feel no loss. Not when I've gained you."

I had to believe him. Had to accept that he'd made his choices just as I'd made mine. And in truth, I was thankful to have more life to live with him.

Bastiaan cried out and bent over, clutching his stomach. A splash of Nightwell water tumbled farther into the valley. "The longer we stay in the Stillness, the more pain I feel."

"Then it's time to start time again."

"With what hope? How can we save people?"

I smiled. "Are you ready to see what my final wish was?"

He groaned and tried to stand. "I gave it to Coralythe. Sven had it . . . in a bottle." His breathing turned labored.

"Sven was too late." I laid a hand on Bastiaan's cheek. "Trust me, Bastiaan. Trust the Well."

His veins bulged. He didn't have much fight left, but I saw when he surrendered. He straightened, lifted his free hand, and snapped his fingers.

Sound slammed into our ears as the rush of the Nightwell pouring into the canals and the valley resumed, like liquid thunder.

Purple smoke and mist billowed up from the waters. I stood tall and faced the mountain where the Well of Talents resided.

"Look there." I pointed. Bastiaan followed my gaze.

Then the Well of Talents exploded.

CHAPTER 60

ℳYRTHE

The water from the Well sprang into the air like a geyser. Higher than the mountain, disappearing into the clouds and filling the sky with a spray of white rain. The wind caught it and gusted it toward the kleinschloss. The water grew and grew, tumbling over the tops of the mountain, drowning the Trials, gushing over hill and plain and rock and tree. It did not follow the downward slope of the hills.

No, the Well of Talents galloped across the plains *toward* the Nightwell water. And the Nightwell swerved in its course, trying to dodge the oncoming warrior.

The waters collided in a wall of wrestling. I squinted against the spray but refused to close my eyes.

This is happening because of you. You were faithful to me.

People burst out of the kleinschloss—the battle interrupted by the melee outside. Militairen and woodsfolk alike stumbled to a halt to watch in awe.

The impact of Talent against Bane sent the two bodies of water into the air like another geyser, but their drops did not fall back to the earth. Instead they rose into the sky like a writhing mess of warring snakes. It grew and grew, sucking up the water—both Nightwell and Well of Talents. Both drawing from every drop of power they possessed.

I clung to Bastiaan who, in turn, clung to a marble garden bust as the mighty wind pulled against us, trying to toss us into the battle taking place.

But we'd already fought. We'd already won. And we knew who the victor would be.

The waters lifted into the air until the ground beneath was bone dry—no moisture left on leaf or twig. Rubble from the burst dam tumbled down the hill and settled in piles. Coralythe cowered behind Luuk. People out in the garden gazed toward the sky. Waiting. Waiting to drown once the waters crashed back to earth. Waiting to die when one or the other came out victorious and poured its wrath upon the unfaithful.

The world stilled like a held breath.

Then the sky beast burst like a star shot with an arrow. Green mist detonated outward. It covered the sky like an enchanted wall of morning fog. And then it descended. Slowly but swift enough that none could escape it.

Screams rent the air and people fled. But there was nowhere to go. I was not afraid. I released Bastiaan and stood, face toward the sky. It was unclear which well the mist came from. But I did not fear the Nightwell, and I did not believe the Well of Talents could be defeated.

The mist met the earth, and bursts of purple and silver-white popped around us as Talent and Bane alighted upon every person.

No change came over me. I already had both. But around me I saw the crackle of Talent Marks finding their homes on the skin of surprised militairen.

412

A great wind blew the hair away from my face and struck me so hard, my clothes were nearly dry by the time it passed. I spun to see the mist sweeping over the land, back toward Fairhoven.

There was no more water. No more Well.

The Well of Talents hadn't entered the fray to defeat the Nightwell; it entered the fray to finally give people the ability to choose between Talent and Bane.

No one would be a slave to their Bane or to their king unless they chose to be.

Everyone watched the departure of the mist as one. It was a slow movement, pushed by the wind, but no man or animal or Talent or Bane could stop it now. It traveled away from the kleinschloss, stretching until there was no end.

Traveling to all the lands.

I did that . . . with my final wish. I made it possible—the Well of Talents and me joining together as we should have from the beginning. I could have made that same wish years ago from the comfort of my home—brought Talents to Fairhoven. To the world.

But there was no use lamenting passed time. Only learning from it. Growing from it.

Now my Wishtress Talent was gone. I could feel it. The Well still resided in me, but my tears were just tears. The Wishtress was gone until men inevitably tried to take control of the Well again.

When that happened, a new Wishtress would rise up. And this time, I'd make sure she was prepared. It was time a Wishtress shared her full story in that journal from Oma.

"Bastiaan!" A small form skipped through the confusion toward Bastiaan and me. Covered in blood but face shining. "I have a Talent!"

Runt's voice was the lone sound over the courtyard. Still-stunned militairen watched him move unhindered and delighted to Bastiaan's side. He gasped for breath but spewed words faster than he could inhale them.

"This big cloud showed up in the middle of the battle and knocked everybody down, and I heard a voice in my head and it was the Well of Talents talking to me! To *me*! And it gave me a Talent and all I had to do was choose it instead of my Bane!"

All he had to do. I loved how easy he made it sound. In truth it *was* a simple concept. For Runt it had taken very little to abandon control of the Bane. I prayed the choice was the same for many, many others.

"Look what I can do! The Well explained the whole thing!" He drew a line in the mud between Bastiaan and him. "Throw something at me."

Bastiaan tossed a pebble Runt's way. It struck an invisible wall, directly where the line rested, as though it were a closed door of glass. Runt cackled. Bastiaan stared at the air in awe. He reached out a hand and his fingers crumpled against the invisible barrier.

"Now try!" Runt rubbed his foot over the line. Bastiaan's hand passed through the air. The barrier was gone. "I can protect people! I can make invisible shields! Just by drawing lines! I can use dirt *or* blood!" Runt danced a jig. "If what the Well told me is true, the shield can stay up for *hours*!"

"Amazing," Bastiaan breathed.

Runt turned somber. "I'm sorry I tried to kill you."

I snapped my gaze to Runt. "You *what*?"

"The militairen found me and Anouk and took us to the king. All he had to do was tell me what to do and I couldn't help but do it! It was almost like I *wanted* to do it, but I didn't like it." He shook his head, his eyes shining. "I . . . sorry."

"I never should have left you and Anouk in the first place," Bastiaan said. "No. More than that. I should have taken you to the Well of Talents years ago."

A few militairen rose from the ground, the shine of their new Talent Marks fading. Their trance of shock ebbing away. Some turned to face Bastiaan and me. Were they still loyal to King Mattias, or had they decided to give the Well sovereignty over their wills?

"We should go," Bastiaan muttered.

We'd been protected in a bubble of chaos and stopped time and surrendered death with the Well. Now time had resumed. The chaos had settled. A new world existed, but I was still seen as the Wishtress, Bastiaan was still the accused assassin of King Vämbat, and Runt was a sympathizer. There was no reason to expect lenience, not even after what we'd done to stop the Nightwell.

Especially after what we'd done to stop the Nightwell. We'd ruined Mattias's entire plan. We'd given the world Talents alongside the Banes. King Mattias couldn't control people unless they let him.

"I need to get Anouk." The last I'd seen of my cousin involved shackles and a disturbing display of King Mattias's power. But I couldn't ask Bastiaan to endanger himself any longer. "I'll meet you—"

"I'll help you." He ran a hand down his face. "It's my fault she's even here."

Runt planted his fists on his hips. "And *I* will protect us all!"

A few yards away, Sven lifted himself off the ground, dripping and bleeding. Not two yards from him lay Hedy. Her skin was mottled and bruised as though her very veins were tied in knots inside her body. For all I knew they could have been.

She must have run out of the kleinschloss during the Battle of the Waters.

Sven crawled over to her and took her hand. Pressed a finger to her neck. She didn't move. Didn't awaken. Even her Bane Mark had turned black.

She was dead.

He moaned and gripped her to his chest. A Talent Mark lined his temple, but it appeared dull and sleepy. On the opposite temple purple mist wove among his ratted hair. Strong and active. Angry.

His eyes found mine and burned through me with fury.

I didn't stick around long enough to learn what his Bane was. Bastiaan, Runt, and I sprinted toward the entrance to the kleinschloss.

"Myrthe!" Sven gave chase. "Get over here and *fix this!*"

I stumbled over the threshold. Runt paused at the door and swept his finger through the dust at its base. Then he folded his arms and waited.

Sven barreled into his invisible barrier. He fell back with a burst of blood on his forehead and a smashed nose. That was the second time for him. The first had been from my headbutt at the Well.

Runt smirked. "Stay down, little bird. There are more glass panes to come."

We continued into the hall. Runt's barrier would keep Sven out for only so long. There were other entrances. Other doors. Sven wanted a wish. To escape. To undo.

I wasn't the Wishtress anymore. And I knew long before Sven became a power-hungry maniac that regular Myrthe wasn't enough for him. I doubted anyone ever would be.

The noise from the meeting room reached me first. Shouting. Screaming. Bastiaan slowed and we eased into view. The woodsfolk and militairen fought among themselves with both their powers and their voices. It appeared that half had chosen their Talents and the other half were still subject to their Banes. The Talented were trying to get the Baned to stop long enough to see reason.

No one listened to each other.

Anouk still sat chained in the corner, head hanging even lower than before. How long had she been in that position? Hours? A day?

My eyes burned with furious tears. Everyone had just *left* her like that! I sucked back the emotions before I remembered I didn't have to anymore. I could let the tears fall and they'd be nothing more than tears. Empathy. Sorrow or joy.

I rushed into the fray.

"Myrthe!" Bastiaan leaped after me.

I pushed through the bodies, ducked outstretched arms, and knocked over one person wielding a Bane against a Talented. When I reached Anouk's side, I yanked at the chains in the wall, but they held firm.

Anouk lifted her head and I dropped to my knees. "I'm here. I'm here, Anouk."

"Where's a blasted sword?" Bastiaan cursed from somewhere behind me.

"Some Talented guy clapped his hands and got rid of all the weapons," Runt shouted. "I'll be right back!"

"No, wait!" Bastiaan hollered.

"Kees was the Talented," I explained.

"Myrthe . . ." My name was a rasp out of Anouk's throat. "You're crying."

I pulled at the chains again to no avail. "I'm no longer the Wishtress. I served my purpose. I'm free of my curse." For the first time the joy at my freedom dampened. "I'm so sorry. I'm so sorry I can't help you find Cairden."

Anouk shook her head. "I have a new way to find him."

"You do?"

"It will take time, but . . . my Talent."

I finally noticed the Talent Mark. It was the largest one I'd seen—a thin circlet of white silver around Anouk's brow, blinking from behind her greasy hair strands. Like a secret crown. "What is it?"

"I can see people's stories." Anouk coughed and her voice grew stronger. "Through touch, I can see someone's whole life. I haven't used the Talent yet, but . . . the Well explained it to me. In my mind. I know I'll find him. This is the key."

I laughed. "Of course it is." I wasn't surprised one bit that the Well would give Anouk a Talent to help her find her missing son.

Or that she'd choose her Talent over a Bane. Anouk had the purest heart of anyone I knew. If anyone could protect and enter into other people's stories with kindness, understanding, and grace, it was Anouk.

"Here!" Runt burst back into the room holding a cupped leaf. "Move, Myrthe."

I stumbled aside. Bastiaan reached our side moments later, but Runt was already pouring the viscous liquid onto the shackles encircling Anouk's wrists.

"What is th—?" Bastiaan asked.

The chain disintegrated and the remaining links clanged to the floor. Runt poured the rest on the shackles at her ankles. "It's Luuk's spit!"

"Runt!" I exclaimed as the final shackle turned to dust. "You could have . . . That could have disintegrated *Anouk*!"

"I was pretty careful." He threw the leaf into a corner.

"But how did you carry it in a leaf without the leaf turning to dust?"

"Luuk held the leaf. If he spits on something he's touching, it won't fall apart."

I didn't ask how he convinced Luuk to give him his deadly Bane saliva, especially with Luuk still serving his Bane over his Talent.

Bastiaan helped Anouk to a standing position. "Time to go."

"Look out!" Runt dropped to the ground and swept his muddied hand over the marble, forming a line in front of us. Arrows directed at our heads pinged off the invisible shield.

King Mattias marched into the room with a line of militairen armed with fresh bows and arrows. A smear of blood painted one half of his face. A small cluster of militairen held a fuming Sven.

Runt nicked his finger on a rough piece of chain and used the blood to make a shield from wall to wall, curving around us and securing us in a cocoon of safety.

But also in a trap. There was no door out.

Mattias walked through the room, touching Talented as he passed. Their Talents went silent under the destruction of his Bane, as Bastiaan's once had. As their powers quieted, militairen sent arrows into their chests.

"No!" I screamed.

Talented dropped, their blood painting the marble floor. Some ran. Few made it out alive.

Those with Banes abandoned the now-won battle and turned toward their king, awaiting his new orders. But he gave none.

It seemed they could be compelled to obey him only if he voiced his commands to their face.

A new man stepped forward. He faced the Baned.

"I am Baron Hartmut, the acting spokesperson for the king until he regains his voice."

King Mattias's eye twitched at Hartmut's words. His power to control them was gone. Even though Hartmut was the king's voice, he had no sway over those with Banes.

Hedy's attack on the king held fast, even though she'd died. "Why didn't her Bane wear off?" I asked Bastiaan quietly.

"It affected him physically. It's the same as if she cut him or stabbed him—her death wouldn't undo that."

King Mattias scribbled something on a scroll and passed it to Hartmut. Hartmut read it, nodded, then addressed the militairen. "Watch the Wishtress and her group on rotation. They'll have to remove the shield eventually or they'll starve to death. Once they do, take them into custody."

"What of their Talents and Banes, sir?" a militair asked.

"Shackle the boy's hands." He eyed Bastiaan's maimed hand. "We don't have to worry about the time stopper anymore. Coralythe cursed him. And it seems the Wishtress used her last wish." His gaze found the Talent Mark circlet around Anouk's brow. "The queen has a Talent of the mind—not one that will directly affect you unless she touches you."

This man was as knowledgeable as Bastiaan about the Talents. He understood the markings and what their location implied. Why would he serve King Mattias, who hated Talents?

"I'm not your enemy, Hartmut." Anouk rose from her place in the corner. "I'm still the queen and I care for my people. No matter what my husband has put me through, I'm loyal to the throne and to Winterune."

Mattias's eyes bulged, and if he could have spoken, I had no doubt vitriol and accusations would have come out.

Anouk placed a hand on Runt's hand. "Please, let me out—*agh!*" She dropped to her knees, releasing Runt.

"Anouk!" I knelt by my cousin. Had she touched Runt's blood? Did it still poison those it came in contact with?

Hartmut took two steps our way. "Do not touch the queen!"

Anouk breathed fiercely, then rose. "I'm fine." Tension sent her fingers into tight fists.

She must be wounded somewhere I couldn't see. "Are you—?"

"Stop." The command alone was clipped. A single, manageable word between sharp inhales of pain. "I'm fine. Just . . . weak from the chains."

Anouk looked to Runt. Intense. Confused.

He eyed her with wide, nervous eyes, as though waiting for her to turn wild or lash out.

She managed a smile, even though she seemed on the verge of tears. "Runt, if you would." Her gentle voice was a stark contrast to the prior stiffness.

"Of course, Queenie." Runt wiped a small portion of his shield line away. "But . . . you're still on our side, right?"

"I'm no one's enemy." She said something similar when we met in our small haven so long ago. That we were on opposite sides but not enemies. Did Anouk still believe that?

As stiff as the courtyard statues, Anouk exited our safe haven, then settled at her husband's side, standing proud and royal. I didn't know how she managed to remain calm, gentle, and fierce as the bride of the man who brought her such pain.

But I didn't blame her for stepping out of our company. By aligning herself with Mattias, she'd given us an ally back on the side of power. She would look out for us as best she could. It might not be much, but I far preferred that over Anouk being in a prison cell.

"Hartmut, hear me." Sven attempted to straighten beneath the strain of his captors.

Hartmut's eyebrows shot up at the interruption, and he faced Sven.

"You are the voice for the people now. You have a Talent—like I do. You don't need to bow to the king's whims anymore."

"Even now—captured as you are—you're against the king?"

I didn't know if Sven was desperate or truly ignorant, but the note of challenge in Hartmut's voice didn't deter him from giving a blunt answer.

"King Vämbat was a scoundrel, and I see no reason why the Murder Prince would be anything less. The only thing Mattias has done for us is rid us of his father!"

"Hmm."

Fuming, Mattias fumbled with a piece of parchment, scribbling, but Hartmut didn't wait for whatever Mattias was about to write. He turned to a militair. "Kill him."

The militair didn't even turn to his king for permission. He drew his sword and plunged it through Sven's belly.

I screamed and pounded the invisible wall separating us. Despite what Sven had done to me, I didn't want to see him killed. At the very least he deserved a trial.

King Mattias looked as shocked as I felt. More from the fact that the command had come from Hartmut than from actual remorse over a snuffed life.

"I can see the future," Sven choked, sinking to the cold, still-wet floor. "I can . . . help you."

"With all the Talents and Banes currently spreading across the land, you're expendable." Hartmut turned to Mattias. He didn't apologize. Didn't ask for forgiveness. Only gave the king a shrug.

Sven shuddered, then stilled.

Dead.

I trembled and Bastiaan's reassuring hands gripped my shoulders. His strength transferred to me and I kept my feet. Bit my tongue.

King Mattias left with Anouk. Militairen dragged Sven's body out of the room.

Hartmut waited.

He was not wrong. We had nowhere to go and no defense. So when Runt finally removed the shield line, we went quietly with the militairen. Bastiaan had no intention of fighting back—he still considered himself guilty for King Vämbat's death.

I wasn't sure what my charge would be: denying the king a wish, perhaps? Murder of Coralythe's sons? Freezing the Vier and taking countless lives and livelihoods?

Runt looked so small in chains, but he allowed a militair to shove chain-mail gloves on his hands and then shackles around his wrists.

"Nothing I haven't escaped from twice already."

The militair tightened the shackles an extra notch. Runt actually laughed.

Where did that boy get such confidence? Likely the multitude of secrets and stealth he clothed himself with.

Hartmut handled me himself. After securing me in chains he

touched my exposed wrist, using his gift of identifying Talents on me.

"Fascinating." He peered at my white eyelashes. "I've seen a Talent silenced by Bane power. But I've never seen one . . . run out."

"If you use your Talent for the Well, maybe someday you'll understand."

"Seems to me that just leads to chains."

"But also peace." I smiled. "I'd happily live a lifetime in chains if it meant peace in my heart."

He grinned. "Well, will you look at that? You didn't even need a tear to make that wish come true."

CHAPTER 61

BASTIAAN

Bastiaan's cell smelled of corpse. It likely hadn't been cleaned for as long as the schloss had been built. This was not how he imagined his return to Fairhoven: he in one cell, Myrthe in another, Runt in a third. At least they were adjacent. Small favor.

They'd been in their cells a mere day. Myrthe could no longer walk on her own. Bastiaan had screamed at the militairen for locking her up. "She needs a healer! Tell the queen!"

"We're not telling anyone anything," the militairen responded.

That was the last he'd seen of them. No food. No healer. No news.

"I can hear you fretting again." Myrthe rested her head against the back of the cell with her eyes closed.

"How can you stay so *calm*?" Especially while in pain. "Are you sure you don't have a new Talent?"

She smiled. "I'm used to not having an escape hatch. You, however, no longer have your time snap, so you're a bit more antsy."

"It wouldn't get me out of this cell anyway," he muttered, unwilling to admit that she was right. It had served him his entire life—having a Talent in his back pocket to use for emergencies. For

424

escape. But he could no longer use it. Not ever, because that would be the end of his life Awake.

He kept his hand splayed, nervous that he'd somehow use the snap without realizing it. If he trapped himself in the Stillness, how would he die? Since he didn't age, it would have to be an accident . . . or self-inflicted. That wasn't an option he was willing to consider. He didn't give himself life; therefore, he refused to put himself in a place of authority in which to take it.

Voices entered the stairwell. Bastiaan pushed himself to his feet and stood inches from his cell door, arms folded and ready to meet whatever was coming. Ready to demand help for Myrthe—despite her eerie calm.

Two militairen stepped into view. One had a set of keys. Bane smoke rose from both hands. Half the strength of Banes came from their mystery. The militair didn't say what his Bane was.

Bastiaan wasn't planning to resist. *He* deserved to be in this cell. He deserved to face justice for his actions.

The militair with the keys stopped before his cell. "The regent has requested an audience."

"Is this my trial?" Bastiaan asked, then registered the rest of the sentence. "Regent? What happened to the king?"

"Winterune currently has no king. Mattias was deemed unfit to rule due to his . . . impediment." The militair smirked.

Mattias's inability to speak. The council had used that as their opening to dethrone him. Since he couldn't use his militairen against them, he was as powerful as a limp fish at markt. His militairen had never been loyal to him anyway, except by Bane command.

The militair fitted the key into the lock and opened the door. Bastiaan stepped out. The second militair took up post beside him, weapons still sheathed but hand on his hilt. Then the one with the key ring moved to Runt's cell.

"You too, boy."

"What does the king—the regent—want with Runt?"

The militair gave no answer but swung open Runt's door. Runt sat in the corner playing a cross and rings game with himself in the dirt, his restricting Talent gloves discarded to the side.

"Come on, boy."

"Hold your hedgehogs, I'm about to win." Runt drew some swirls in the dirt.

"Get out here!" the militair shouted.

"Why don't you come get me?" He still didn't look up.

"Runt . . . ," Bastiaan warned, though he was pretty sure his own amusement crept into the warning. Runt was always one to test wills and see where the wiggle room or loopholes were.

The militair marched into the cell. A foot away from Runt, he ran into an invisible barrier with a cry.

"Get out of there," Bastiaan's militair barked. "He still has a Talent!"

"Put your gloves on," Runt's militair growled, nursing a swollen lip.

Runt stood. "Oh. Oops. Sorry about that, mate." He slipped on his gloves and wiped the line in the dirt clear. "Shoulda warned you."

"The king will silence that Talent of yours!"

Runt made a mock pouting face. "What king? Didn't you say you ditched him for a regent?"

Before the militair could grab him, Runt sauntered out of the cell and stood beside Bastiaan like an obedient angel. The militairen left the cell doors open and yanked Bastiaan and Runt toward the stairs.

"What about Myrthe?" Bastiaan asked.

The militair's hand tightened around his arm. "Her presence isn't requested."

Bastiaan glanced over his shoulder at her. She shrugged. "It's fine." But it wasn't fine. Would he see her again? Would she be okay?

"She needs food and medical care."

"That's not your concern."

He yanked free. Runt leaped free of his own militair, planted himself at Bastiaan's side, and swept a line between them and the militairen. "We're not coming with you until you take care of Myrthe."

The militair pounded a fist against the invisible barrier, then planted it stiffly at his side. He'd likely hurt his knuckles. "Undo your wall."

"Nope." Runt cocked his head to one side. "So what'll it be? An angry regent or a healer for Myrthe?"

"It's not like it's going to cause harm," the second militair muttered, then without permission from his friend he disappeared up the stairs. It didn't take long for him to return with Hilda. When she saw Bastiaan and Runt, she raised an eyebrow. Neither of them gave her a greeting. They didn't want to expose her for helping Runt.

Runt brushed away his barrier, offered her an elaborate bow, and swept his arm toward Myrthe's cell. The militair unlocked it and let her in. "We'll be back for you in an hour."

"It won't take me *that* long," Hilda squawked.

"Then best get comfortable. You can thank these two for that." The militairen pulled Bastiaan after them and left Myrthe and the healer in the cell. Myrthe managed to mouth *Thank you* before Bastiaan rounded the corner and left her sight.

The minute they were separated he shifted his focus forward. Upward. Into the throne room where he was about to encounter . . . something. The regent wanted him. This could be his trial. Or perhaps he wouldn't even be given a trial.

It didn't take them long to enter the room in which he first met King Mattias. This time the throne sat empty, but a smaller, less elaborate throne rested off to the side of the platform upon which Baron Hartmut sat. Bastiaan should have guessed.

The rest of the council sat along either side of him, as though ensuring everyone knew that even though Hartmut was the regent, they were the deciding power. Mattias was nowhere to be seen.

Anouk stood off to the side, her queen throne behind her but unoccupied. Winterune law did not allow a queen to take the king's place. She was a supporter and nothing else.

Bastiaan and Runt were deposited in the middle of the room.

A young girl with choppy black hair walked across the space with nervous, jerky movements, glancing up at Hartmut with every other step. Hartmut nodded. The girl stopped next to Bastiaan.

"This is Verena. Her Talent is to detect falsehood. Lying. Which means everything you say shall be tested."

With every Talented Bastiaan encountered, he swelled. People were choosing Talents over Banes. Not everyone, but at least there was resistance—enough that the schloss had to enlist the help of the Talented. Perhaps Talents could still win.

"I have no lies to tell." He didn't expect them to believe him, but it was worth declaring all the same. He was not an enemy of Winterune or the throne—whether it had a king on it or not.

"Your first visit to the council was quite a different story."

"I was quite a different man then." Bastiaan didn't resist Verena when she placed her palm on his shoulder. A Talent Mark was briefly visible beneath her thumb before it pressed against his shirt. Apparently the Talent still worked even if the touch wasn't skin to skin.

"We are going to ask you a series of questions. It would be in your best interest not to resist them." Hartmut waited for a nod from Bastiaan, then gestured to Runt. "Who is this boy to you?"

That wasn't a question he thought he'd be asked. "Runt? He's my most trusted friend."

"Friend? This *boy*?"

Runt stiffened.

"Yes," Bastiaan said. "Or if you're unfamiliar with friendship . . . He's my comrade. Ally. Companion."

"How did you two meet?"

"I encountered him in a canal when he was four years of age and hired him to sharpen my skates. I liked the boy and offered him room and board."

"In exchange for what?"

Bastiaan frowned. Could Hartmut and the council not understand compassion? Desire for life? "In exchange for him not freezing to death."

"I mean, how did he pay off such a debt?"

"It wasn't a debt. It was a gift."

Hartmut gripped the arms of his regent chair and seemed to resist an outburst. He glanced at Verena, who shrugged. "And what has his role been with you?"

"He often traveled with me into the Stillness—"

"For how long?" Hartmut interrupted.

"Three or four years, off and on."

The council muttered among themselves and shuffled papers. "In the Stillness?"

"Yes."

"Did you know anything of his backstory—before you found him in the canals?"

"I did not." Bastiaan tried to piece together their curiosity about Runt.

At a nod from Hartmut, Verena left Bastiaan's side, then put her hand on Runt's shoulder. Runt jerked away, but following a look from Bastiaan, he allowed Verena to touch him.

"What is your name, boy?"

"Runt."

"Who were you before you met Bastiaan?"

"I was a canal rat. Do you know what that is, sir?"

Hartmut didn't deign to respond, but the implication was clear. A wealthy council member with a Talent taking over the throne likely hadn't spent much time among the commonfolk.

Was Hartmut trying to implicate Runt in King Vämbat's death? That could be the only reason for these questions. If they kept drilling him, they'd back Runt into a verbal corner and he'd share whatever fate they placed on Bastiaan.

"Enough of these questions. Runt had nothing to do with my interactions with King Vämbat."

Anouk stepped forward. The council went silent. Watching her. Wary. She was the queen—they couldn't control or silence her, but Bastiaan could see from their tension that they wanted her to remain in the shadows.

She stopped a few yards away. Cautious, as though afraid to get too close to them. Or maybe afraid she'd scare Bastiaan and Runt. The council members wrinkled their noses as if in disgust.

Anouk had eyes only for Runt. "Runt . . . when we were in the kleinschloss, I grabbed your hand. In that moment my Talent sparked. It showed me your story."

Runt listened, attentive and polite. Curious, even. Meanwhile Bastiaan's mind whirled, trying to hear what Anouk had not yet said.

"I have reason to believe that . . . that you are my son. Mattias is your father. Runt . . . you're the heir to the throne."

CHAPTER 62

BASTIAAN

For the first time since Bastiaan met him, Runt had no witty comeback. He stared at Anouk. She waited, pale and a knot of nerves. Bastiaan hardly breathed . . . until Runt inched a few steps closer to him, pressing against his side the way a son would a father.

Was he afraid?

Bastiaan placed his arm around the boy, and that seemed to return his voice to him.

"I'm not your son." Runt sounded defiant. Angry, even. "You said Cairden's six years old. I'm ten! He's probably dead!"

Anouk gazed at Bastiaan, waited for him to offer the explanation that he—like a fool—had never considered.

"You're ten only because you entered the Stillness with me for several years. Had you remained in regular time with everyone else . . . you'd be six."

Runt peered up at him. "You actually think I'm her son?"

"I don't know." Bastiaan met Anouk's gaze. "But I trust her."

Whatever fear or uncertainty had been stiffening Runt's limbs passed. He shifted his weight and folded his arms, and his voice came out strong. "Fine. So I'm king then?"

Anouk smiled. One council member laughed, but it wasn't enough to cover Hartmut's whisper. "That was easy enough."

Runt. Heir to the throne. *Royalty.* All this time Bastiaan had been fixed on changing Vämbat's mind, advising Mattias in matters of rule and the Well, and neglecting the relationship he had with a certain canal rat who deserved every bit as much care and guidance as a future king.

"You're not king yet," Hartmut said. "You're the heir. You will not take the throne until you are of royal age. Fifteen. Until that time . . . we will train you."

"*Bastiaan* will train me." Already Runt spoke in commands and not requests. Young king indeed.

Hartmut took a deep breath through his nose. "Bastiaan is a matter we'll discuss among ourselves. For now we'll give you a room. You're free of your cell."

"Bastiaan too!" Runt demanded.

Bastiaan squeezed his shoulder. "It's okay, Runt. These things require procedure and discussion." In a lower voice he muttered, "I need to look out for Myrthe. You, my cunning little crat, need to gather information."

Runt brightened with the charge. To him, this could be approached as another adventure. Yes, Bastiaan wanted information, but more than that, he wanted Runt to enter what would undoubtedly be a new life with a forward mindset of learning. Not of resistance.

It all seemed so easy as militairen led Runt out, free of chains. No roughhousing. Bastiaan didn't expect them to be loyal, but that wouldn't take long.

Anouk moved to follow Runt, but a militair stepped in her way. She had a few words with him, but he gestured to the council and shook his head. With pursed lips Anouk remained in the throne room.

The council wouldn't let anyone get into Runt's head. That's why they'd accepted him as the heir so swiftly: He was young. He was *moldable*. Their missing peg. They would have to find a king eventually—the laws of Winterune demanded it. They'd not be allowed to run the country on their own, no matter how much they desired it.

They accepted Anouk's history, rejoiced at Mattias's poor decisions in the past that resulted in an illegitimate heir . . . made legitimate by his hasty marriage.

The council planned to carve Runt into their puppet.

As much as Bastiaan wanted to hope Runt was stronger than that, he knew the power of time and strong voices. Eventually, the council would mold him into the king they wanted—the king they could finally control.

"Now for your testimony, Bastiaan Duur." Hartmut waved to Anouk and nodded to Verena. Both descended the platform to stand at Bastiaan's side.

"I'm sorry," Anouk whispered.

"I have nothing to hide," he said.

She lifted her hand until it was mere inches from his skin. Verena stepped forward and, to Bastiaan's surprise, placed a hand on Anouk instead of on Bastiaan. Then Anouk touched him. He felt no change, but the tension that shocked her body made him reach out to steady her. It took mere seconds.

She released him, gasping for breath.

"What did you see?" Hartmut demanded.

"I need a moment." Had she just seen his entire life story? All 107 years of it? Or had she selected bits and pieces that involved King Vämbat?

A chorus of pulse beats passed before she finally straightened.

"Well?" Hartmut asked.

"He's innocent." She sounded surprised. Bastiaan frowned and looked to Verena, who merely nodded to the council. Anouk was telling the truth?

"It is not your job to draw conclusions or make judgments. It is your job to tell us what happened."

"Of course." She inclined her head in a bow of submission. "Bastiaan took King Vämbat into the Stillness to change his mind about letting commonfolk visit the Well. Neither would bend in their opinions. Years passed until King Vämbat had an accident. He was trapped in a burning library and managed to crawl out. Bastiaan found him, returned him to the schloss, and resumed time in hopes that a healer would be able to save him. As we know, the king then died."

"He would not have burned to death if he hadn't been trapped in time," Hartmut argued.

"But it was wholly separate from Bastiaan." Anouk stepped aside, leaving him exposed once again on the throne room floor.

"This does not excuse him from kidnapping the king!" someone else said. "Just because the king died from an accident inside the prison of this man's Talent doesn't make the captor innocent."

They deliberated for several long minutes, then Hartmut finally took a vote. "Those in favor of acquittal?" Three hands went up—all from the older council members. "Those who find him guilty?"

More hands raised, Hartmut's included. No hesitancy. One after the other until they outnumbered the first set of voters.

Hartmut faced him, mouth grim.

"Bastiaan Duur, you are hereby sentenced to death by Bane, to be carried out by Luuk at sunrise."

CHAPTER 63

CORALYTHE

Coralythe paced the chamber. Runt would be arriving any minute, and she'd yet to decide how ill to allow herself to feel. He was bound to hate her—to misunderstand. Or perhaps he wouldn't. She didn't know. Oh, this was a mess.

Yet it had the potential to be so *perfect*.

She stopped in the middle of the room, hands clasped behind her back. No, in front of her. Loose at her sides. Curse it all.

A key fitted into the lock, and at the last moment, she darted into a shadow along the side of the room. A militair entered with Runt. The militair looked around the room with a frown, then spotted Coralythe. He didn't say anything, just released Runt and left. Insolent worm. The militairen had never shown her any respect, not even as she stood at Mattias's side. Not even after she made it possible for them all to receive Banes. Ungrateful, they were.

But she hadn't done any of this for them.

The lock clicked behind him.

Runt surveyed the room, then strode to the dresser and peeked in the drawers. He rifled through the folded clothes and then worked at prying something off the inner side of the drawer.

Coralythe had planned to reveal herself by this point, but curiosity won out. At last his hand emerged with a bent piece of metal—a chunk of the drawer's metal paneling.

He spent a moment bending it to his will. A ticktock later, he had a workable key that wiggled neatly in the chamber's main door. He unlocked it, peeked out into the hall, then closed the door again and relocked it.

Brilliant child. My, she was fond of him.

"Quite impressive." She stepped from the shadows.

He spun on his heel, the makeshift key disappearing from his hand as though it never existed in the first place. Defensive. On guard. But then recognition widened his gaze and the tension left him.

"Coralythe!" He rushed two steps toward her, then stopped. Frowned. "What are you doing here?" He glanced around, as though piecing together that she was here of her own free will—maybe even on an assignment.

He'd seen her at the kleinschloss—at Mattias's side—but they'd never been able to speak. She never got to explain herself.

"You lied to me in that dungeon," he said.

"You freed me." She needed to tread carefully, tell as few lies as possible. "Thanks to you, I *did* escape, but . . . I returned. The king apologized for his treatment of me."

"He's not king anymore."

"So I've heard." She directed the conversation to more comfortable waters. "How do you feel about your new role as heir?"

He'd yet to fully relax in her presence. Even now, he surveyed her with a suspicious squint. "You gave me a Bane. You made *everyone* have Banes."

Not true. People now had to *choose* a Bane over a Talent. The wisest would do so. Only the fools would settle for Talents.

"I gave you the power to escape." It hadn't been her assignment from the king—to gift Runt a Bane had been a personal decision. She'd wanted to help him. Wanted to save him. Wanted to *teach* him how such a power could be freeing.

"I did what I had to so you could live—so *I* could live. Maybe I did not make the best choices, but it was all I could do in the moment."

He nodded and she praised the Nightwell for this small victory. Runt, at least, seemed to understand that adults could make mistakes—could betray trust—and still have good intentions.

"I didn't like my Bane," he said. "It almost killed Bastiaan."

"It will take practi—"

"I have a Talent now. My Bane is dead!" The joy on his face was a fierce contrast to the rush of anger that gripped her.

She searched for the Talent Mark and cringed when she found it dotting his fingertips. Curse Bastiaan Duur! No matter. Over time she could get Runt to choose his Bane again. But she needed to be careful—especially in this moment. If Runt found out she was working for the council, he'd never let her train him as the next king. His cooperation was everything. It was the only way the council would let her stay on. Stay alive.

"Don't give your Talent power. Talents are selfish. Don't let it draw you in—your Bane is something you can control and use when needed." *Stop.* She needed to stop before her irritation got the best of her. "The Well of Talents never should have been released. It has brought confusion to the people."

"Well, I like my Talent—and the voice of the Well—a lot more." He frowned. "Didn't you get a Talent when the mist hit?" He peered around her. "Where's your Talent Mark? What was it? Did you try it out?"

She stiffened. "I don't want it. I've properly silenced it. Something you need to work at as well."

A soft knock sounded on the chamber door. Who was daring

to interrupt? This was her time with Runt, and she hadn't even begun to discuss his future.

The knock repeated, this time with a voice. "Runt?" Soft. Gentle.

"That's Anouk!" He rushed to the door.

"Don't—" Coralythe reached for him with no real intention of physically restraining him.

He fitted his makeshift key into the lock and swung the door open. "Queenie!"

Anouk appeared pleasantly startled. "It was unlocked?"

"By me!" He swept an arm. "Come join the party."

Anouk stepped inside and he locked the door after her, not missing a detail. "Thank you for letting me in—" Anouk saw Coralythe and her eyes hardened. "What are *you* doing here, Coralythe?"

"I'm here to train the heir to the throne."

"You have no right to that role."

"Actually, I do. If not for me, the council was going to slit his throat in that dungeon cell."

Anouk paled, gripping Runt's arm as though she could protect him more than Coralythe could. What did Anouk have? Some weak Talent that read people's histories. Coralythe could actually *do* things—stop people. Kill threats. Protect Runt.

"What do you mean?" Anouk demanded.

"The council never wanted an heir. They'd rather have the throne. But I made sure to point out that Runt is young. He needs training." She would go on, but she didn't want Runt to catch her implications.

Unfortunately, Anouk didn't seem to have the same desire to protect Runt from unpleasant knowledge. "You mean they want to control him. What did you do? Tell them you'd raise him up in their ways? To be an obedient puppet?"

"I told them what they needed to hear in order to keep Runt

alive. I will teach him everything I know. I will care for him like a son."

Anouk fumbled for the edge of the dresser and gripped its corner until her knuckles turned white. So. Weak. Then she turned to Runt and her voice came out impressively calm. "Do you know what Coralythe has done?"

Chills swept over Coralythe's arms. "Stop."

"She's the one who released the Nightwell," Runt said. "I know."

"And she's been on King Mattias's team since the beginning of his reign," Anouk finished.

"Get out." Coralythe advanced on Anouk, but Runt stepped between them and drew a line of blood on the carpet. Coralythe hit an unseen barrier. Her hand flew to her forehead.

Runt held his ragged key aloft—the tool with which he must have pricked his finger. "Leave her alone."

"I'm not going to harm her, Runt. She shouldn't even be *in* here. This is supposed to be a time for me to answer your questions, for us to talk about your future. Get to know each other."

"She belongs here." He pressed against Anouk's side. "She's my mother."

Anouk bit her lip and hesitantly put an arm around Runt's shoulders. He wasn't cowering behind her. He was at her side as if he were a grown man protecting his family. Could his loyalty be claimed so quickly? With a single announcement of his heritage?

"She's a child! She doesn't know how to be a mother!" Why would he suddenly be so loyal to Anouk after what he and Coralythe went through together in the dungeon? "The council won't let Anouk stay. Not with you. Maybe not even in the schloss. If you want to be king—if you want to help the people you love—then you'll let me come alongside you until you're of ruling age."

Runt glanced between Anouk and Coralythe. Was he trying

439

to decide who to choose? She couldn't make him pick one or the other—she didn't have enough leverage for that.

"I'll ask the council to allow Anouk to stay in the schloss. They trust me. But she has no power right now, Runt. I do. You and I can work together to help her. Help you. Help everyone."

"Help Bastiaan? Help Myrthe?"

"Of course." He didn't need to know she was the one who cursed Myrthe in the first place.

"Bastiaan's been sentenced to death," Anouk said softly. "The council voted. It's happening at sunrise."

"What?" Runt squawked. He snapped his gaze to Coralythe. "Can you stop that? Stop them?"

"I can try." She wouldn't. Bastiaan was the biggest wrench in all her plans—he had Runt's deepest loyalty. Once he was dead Runt would be broken. And she'd step in as the caulk.

His eyes narrowed. "You're lying." He backed toward the door.

"Runt." Coralythe reached her hand out in a pleading gesture, but it encountered the invisible barrier and her fingers curled into a fist.

"I . . . I need some time." What an adult thing to say. He fit the makeshift key into the lock and turned it. "I need to think."

He fled the room, yanking Anouk with him.

"Runt!" Coralythe tried to squeeze past his barrier, but it was too long. Curse it all! The council would murder her for this.

CHAPTER 64

MYRTHE

You'll never skate again." That's what Hilda the healer said after binding my feet with herbs and poultice. "But you should be able to walk . . . with time. And likely a cane."

What Hilda didn't understand was that if I could walk—even minimally—I could skate. I *would* skate. Perhaps not race and not for long distances, but I refused to allow my passions to perish in this prison cell.

Hilda had used her Talent, but it had limitations. She was able to restore the torn skin and remove the scorpion wounds and sunburns. But frostbite had already claimed several toes, and the muscles in my feet had been so lacerated and wrecked that it was difficult for the healer to return them to something that resembled or felt like a foot. She could do nothing about my pox weakness because it had been part of my body for so long.

Bastiaan and Runt had been gone a long time. I hated not knowing what was happening. I expected my own hearing would take place soon, and I wasn't sure what it would look like. I was no longer a threat—or advantage—to the crown. I'd loosed the Well of Talents. It all came down to whether the regent and his council saw that as a criminal act.

It would be so easy to let myself spiral into despair.

But even with my Wishtress Talent gone, I felt the presence of the Well of Talents inside me. I couldn't forget my encounter with the Well at the kleinschloss. It had chosen me as the Wishtress— for a great purpose despite my limitations, selfishness, misuse, and mistakes.

It knew my story from the beginning. And it knew my end. That brought a comfort that nothing was without purpose. Even my time in this cell.

Scuffles on the stairs preceded the appearance of Bastiaan and a militair. Bastiaan walked tall with his chin high, but he appeared . . . resigned. What had happened to Runt?

When he saw my bandaged feet, a sigh seemed to calm his muscles. The militair placed him back in his cell and left. Bastiaan stood for a moment and surveyed the small space. Then grimaced. Something was wrong. Very wrong. And he was trying to be strong. Accepting.

"What happened?"

He dragged a hand down his face. "A lot."

"You don't have to mince words. Start with whatever is weighing on you most. Right now." I tried not to push him too hard, but I needed answers. Information. "Where's Runt?"

"He's heir to the throne. Runt is Anouk's *son*."

"What?" Runt was the canal rat she'd been searching for all this time—Cairden? "Isn't he too old?"

"He entered the Stillness with me. I'm the only one who doesn't physically age in the Stillness, so during the few years he joined me he still aged. That's also why King Vämbat returned an old, weak king and I looked . . . the same. It's why, if I ever use a snap again,

I'll be stuck there for eternity. Anyone who came with me would outlive me, and I'd have to watch them die."

"The Well of Talents is greater than Coralythe's curse." I reached through the bars and touched his knee. "Bastiaan, do you believe that?"

"It doesn't matter if I do. I'll never risk it." He released a gust of air. "At least Runt is free and alive. Though the council will try to twist him to their will and thinking."

"He has Anouk."

"That's all he'll have." Bastiaan thunked his head on the back wall of his cell and gave a wry laugh. "I used to dream about mentoring the young king, Mattias. I'd share all the wisdom King Vämbat passed on to me. I'd teach him all the knowledge I'd gathered over the years. I used to see myself as the man who saved the kingdom." He sighed. "I was so arrogant."

"You thought it was your calling, though. You were being obedient."

"I wish I could accept that excuse. But I know my heart. There was arrogance and pride. Now I finally see that proper guidance comes from an example of humility and service. Not from power and pride in knowledge. I'll never get to teach that to Runt."

"He's learned more from you than you think." Like I had. All anyone had to do was *watch* Bastiaan's heart bleed into everything he did and they'd become a better person.

A distant yell came from the stairwell, followed by a body thudding against stone. "Bastiaan!"

He jumped to his feet and was at the door of his cell in seconds. "Runt?"

A squeal and another yell from Runt pulled me to my own cell door, though I didn't stand. Not yet. I slid across the muck of my cell floor until I sat as near the stairwell as I could.

An echoing clamor tumbled through the air until not Runt but

Anouk stumbled into view. Runt crashed into her from behind with a muffled "Oomph!" He pushed away from her, leaving a bloody handprint on her dress.

"Runt, what's going on?" Bastiaan gripped the bars. "You shouldn't be here. Your position is precarious enough as it is."

Runt didn't appear to be listening—or maybe he didn't care. He smeared his hand along the bottom stair, creating a barrier with his Talent. Then he brushed his hands against his pants. "That should do it."

Both he and Anouk were panting. She was pale but seemed exhilarated. Runt grinned as though playing a mischievous prank. He faced Bastiaan and me.

"Hello, my little lawbreakers! It's time for the crat to save the adults."

Every word from Runt's mouth endeared him to me further. Where Anouk was soft and gentle, Runt was snarky and impish. But he was so clearly her son.

"What are you doing?" Bastiaan growled.

"I'm doing what kings do—taking control and doing what I want."

"You're not king for another five years."

"And until then, they're making Coralythe my new teacher—and she lied to me! She's been working with Mattias this whole time. The whole time we were in the dungeon. And now she's working for Hartmut!"

Bastiaan grimaced. "I'm so sorry." A distant noise came from far out of view.

Bastiaan's gaze darted toward the stairwell, but Runt waved off any potential concern.

"There are so many barriers up there and I just knocked out a militair. We've got time."

"Listen, Runt." Bastiaan took a long breath and closed his eyes for a moment. "You need to go back."

"To Coralythe?"

"Yes, even to Coralythe. If you rebel and run, the council will decide you're not worth keeping around for five years. They'll kill you, Runt. And you . . . You're this kingdom's only hope. Besides, you have Anouk."

"They won't let me see him," Anouk said softly. "The reason I'm with Runt right now is because he snuck me here. The council is sending me to the kleinschloss with a small assortment of attendants and militairen."

"They can't do that!" My burst of fury dashed away any chill that clung to my skin. "You are his *mother*. You're the queen!" She'd only just found him! How could they dismiss a mother's role in her son's life so easily?

"I have no power. The council is in control . . . as is the law." Each word seemed forced out of Anouk's mouth. She had finally found her son and would not be allowed to see him or get to know him. Did the council have any idea what she'd gone through to find Runt? "At least he's safe and has a future."

Runt snorted. "You're all talking as though this is our only option."

"It is," Bastiaan said firmly. "You and Anouk need to return to your chambers now, before you endanger *both* your lives."

"They're going to execute you tomorrow!" Runt hollered. "Did you know that?" Tears filled his wide eyes.

I gasped. Execute? Bastiaan already had his trial? They'd found him *guilty*? I spun to him, awaiting his answer. His lack of surprise told me everything. He'd known and didn't say anything to me. Probably trying to protect me or something else ridiculously noble.

Bastiaan squared his shoulders. "It's justice."

"No, it's not!" Runt yelled.

"I know your story, Bastiaan," I said. "Vämbat's death was an accident. The Well renewed you. You surrendered to it at the kleinschloss. Don't you think that if you were guilty and deserving of death for your actions, the Well would have taken that into account?"

"The Well is very forgiving."

"So you're placing the word of the council over the word of the Well?" After everything we'd learned about the Well?

"What would you have me do, Myrthe?" He rounded on me, the bars the only barrier between us. I wanted to gather him into my arms. Hold him close. Breathe him in and comfort him.

"I would have you hope," I whispered.

"What can hope do in such a short time? Sunrise is mere hours away."

"So let's keep it that way." Runt held up a janky piece of metal that slightly resembled a key.

Bastiaan stared at it. "What are you implying, Runt?"

"Use your snap, Bastiaan." It was the most serious I had ever heard Runt. Almost sounded like an order—a kingly one at that.

"I'm cursed," Bastiaan said woodenly. "I'll be trapped in the Stillness."

"We'll find a solution."

"We?" Bastiaan asked.

Runt pointed at himself, me, and Anouk. "The three of us. Well, *four* including you. And Diantha if we bring her in later."

Bastiaan was already shaking his head. "That's even worse. You'd be trapped in there with me! You know I can't return someone to the Awake without a snap."

I stopped him with a touch on his boot. "The Stillness is not your end. It won't be *our* end. You saw how your Talent fought when

Mattias silenced it. It's stronger than Banes. Than curses. You were just telling me how you believed your calling was to train up the next king of Winterune."

Runt jabbed his two thumbs into his own chest. "That'd be me."

"What if I die in the Stillness?" he said quietly. "What would happen to you?"

"You said time would resume," I said, determined to meet every fear of his with my own peace and confidence.

"It's but a theory." His arguments grew weaker and weaker. I could feel him bending. Giving in. Maybe even daring to hope.

"Take us into the Stillness," Anouk urged. "Help me teach Runt."

"Time to use those journals of yours!" Runt said.

"You spent thirty-two years in the Stillness with a king you loved," I said. "It's time to pass on the knowledge he gave you. The knowledge you wanted to give to Mattias."

Bastiaan seemed so unsure, and I didn't blame him. Faith and hope were a risk of the heart, which was what made them so powerful when someone allowed them to defeat fear.

"It's ridiculous that we're having to convince you to *survive*." Runt folded his arms in front of his chest and said no more.

Bastiaan closed his eyes and gave a small laugh. "You three . . . I don't deserve you."

That was enough of a yes for me. Runt whooped.

"This way!" a militair shouted from above. Boots on stone steps.

Runt thrust the key into Bastiaan's cell door and worked it with his tongue between his teeth until the lock popped open. He had to bend mine a few new ways to get it open, but it didn't take much longer.

Bastiaan hauled me to my feet. It was so good to be held by him, even in a situation as dire as this.

The four of us stood in a small circle.

"Let's do this." Runt shoved the key into his pocket and held his hands out.

Hesitant, shaking, Bastiaan took one. I gripped Bastiaan's wrist with one hand and Anouk's trembling fingers in the other.

"Five years," Runt said. "Well, four and a half. Then we'll come back. I'll be of age. I'll be king, and the laws of Winterune will stand. Not even the council can stop the rightful king from claiming the throne!"

They'd thought it all out. Mother and son. Queen and crown prince. Already they were a force to be reckoned with.

"What if we can't come back?" Bastiaan whispered.

I pressed my forehead against his. "Have faith, Bastiaan. The answers are there. We'll find them. Together." I didn't fear. After all I'd been through with the Well and with Bastiaan, I was free to be strong. To have confidence even when facing the unknown. I wished that confidence to flow into Bastiaan, to ease his worries and let him feel my love for him, my admiration of his courage to dare to survive.

"Are you sure?"

I lifted my lips to his. Felt him smile. He pulled me tight against him. Militairen yelled. Runt laughed.

And Bastiaan snapped his fingers.

$\mathcal{A}$CKNOWLEDGMENTS

To every reader who just turned the last page and either hates me, loves me, or vascillates between the two . . . thank you for giving this book a chance. I've had the idea for over seven years and wondered if it would ever end up in a reader's hands. And here we are.

The final story turned out so different than the original concept. It surprised me and thrilled me and captured my heart for adventure, motherhood, mistakes, healing, and heart-journeys. The year I drafted the majority of this book, I spent over eight months unable to walk normally. Whether on crutches or in bed or in pain . . . I'd never felt so helpless, and yet I had to push through anyway: live life and raise children and write books. I learned how strong I could be . . . particularly when I accepted my weakness and let Jesus step in. I learned respect for so many others who deal with constant chronic pain. It was something I wanted to write into Myrthe's story, because it had become part of my story. If that's ever been part of your story . . . this one's for you.

Now to the rest of the acknowledgments where I'm bound to forget very important people:

Jesus. I wasn't sure why You gave me this story. I went into it wondering what You'd teach me. Now that it's done, I look back and see the greatest year of growth I've ever lived through. Thank You for inviting me to write with You, for inviting me to surrender my ink. It's more and more mind-blowing and rewarding with every book. You are so faithful.

To my incredible husband for all the sacrifices he made to allow me to meet my deadlines and write when I needed to. I couldn't do this without you and I wouldn't want to. You're my greatest support. Multiply Bastiaan's awesomeness by a hundred and he still falls short of you. YAM.

To my three sweet babies. This is the first book I've written as a mom. Between the drafting of *Romanov* and *Wishtress*, I became a mama of three and writing has taken on a whole new meaning. I can't wait to share these stories with you someday and tell you how I wrote them while you snuggled me. I hope you will see my love for you through Anouk and Mutti.

To my besties: Sara Ella, this would be such a different book without you. You gave me some of my best plot twists and talked me off the Ledge of Despair more than once when I got stuck. I can't imagine ever writing a book without our daily talks and the many prayers you give for me. Ashley Townsend, my first ever reader (as always!), your love for and cheerleading behind my every story is something I value and appreciate far more than I can ever express to you. You're the type of person I invite to live in my basement every chance I get. (Yes, it sounds creepy . . . . BUT JUST DO IT, OKAY?) Sisters forever.

To my agent, Steve Laube, as always for being my Gandalf as we traverse the publishing realm. To my amazing Thomas Nelson team for all your hard work and endless time poured into making this book the best it can be. A special thank-you to Becky Monds for all the brilliant edits and ability to see so much that I couldn't in those early drafts. Thank you, also, for tolerating my ridiculously long word count.

To Mommy (my Anouk and Mutti), for being a shining example of a mother who loves so deeply that you would still chase after your children even if you had no memory of us. This book is just a shadow of what I wish I could say. I suppose it all comes down to: I love you. And to Daddy for supporting me in all the small ways and all the big ways and all the ways that make me cry (in a good way).

To my beta readers, Megan, Libby, Lacey, Natalie, and Aaron, for giving me my first "reader feedback" and bringing me to tears over how much you connected with the story or with Myrthe or Bastiaan or Anouk or Runt.

To the Realmie Roomies (Tricia, Katie, and Ashley) for being the first to hear the pitch for this story way back when and loving it. To my Ninjas for being, well, my ninjas and always sending me Oreos (both real-life and virtual). You amaze me and encourage me in so many ways I could never recount them. Hidden ninja in chapter 36!

I know I'm forgetting people, but since I'm writing these acknowledgments thirty-nine weeks pregnant with major baby brain, I hope you'll forgive me!

Discussion Questions

1. If you could have one of Myrthe's raw wishes, what would you ask for and what might the consequences be?
2. Which Talent would you want if you visited the Well?
3. Myrthe spends a lot of time thinking about what is worth living for and what might be worth dying for. What is something that gives you reason to live?
4. Grief is a theme in the story. Compare and contrast the way Myrthe deals with her grief versus the way Coralythe deals with hers. Who do you relate to more?
5. If you could stop time like Bastiaan, what moment would you stop and why?
6. Bastiaan repeatedly broke his promises to Runt. Do you think he was justified, or should he have kept those promises?
7. Which character do you relate to most? Why?
8. Often we see in the story that even the best intentions can have dire consequences. Think of a time you meant something for good but it didn't turn out the way you planned. How did you handle the situation?
9. By the end of the story, characters have a choice to give a Talent or a Bane power over their lives. How do you think this relates to choices you can make in your own life?

ABOUT THE AUTHOR

Photo by Sara Ella Photography

Nadine Brandes once spent four days as a sea cook in the name of book research. She is the three-time Carol Award–winning author of *Fawkes*, *Romanov*, and the Out of Time series. Her inner fangirl perks up at the mention of soul-talk, Quidditch, bookstagram, and Oreos. When she's not busy writing novels about bold living, she's adventuring through Middle Earth or taste-testing a new chai. Nadine, her Auror husband, and their Halfling children are building a Tiny House on wheels. Current mission: paint the world in shalom.

NadineBrandes.com
Instagram: @NadineBrandes
YouTube: @NadineBrandes
Twitter: @NadineBrandes
Facebook: @NadineBrandesAuthor